FRACTURED LEGACY

ALEX J. FISCHER

For my Family and Friends

1

"It's nice seeing everyone's prompt." Bernard said with a grin. "As you can see," he said, pointing at the land, "we've found our first property."

"Is this it?" Molly asked, running a hand through her dyed purple hair. She looked over Bernard's and Roger's shoulders at the multi-story home. Molly took her glasses off and wiped them clean. "It looks like something out on the Oregon Trail." She donned the glasses and turned her head. Her green eyes wandered to the right toward the bright red barn sitting a few hundred feet behind the home. "Are we ranching?"

"Aren't you a ray of sunshine?" Roger asked. He chuckled. "It'll take some getting used to, sure. This is what we could afford and comes with over ten acres of land for future expansion. It also has a place we can assemble our weapons before sale."

"You're talking about the barn, aren't you?" Jackie didn't look enthused.

"A barn's a fine place for a start-up operation," Chris

said. "It's cheap, effective, and spacious." He elbowed Jackie in the side. "What's the matter? Afraid of a little cold?"

"Do you know how fucking cold it gets in Tennessee?"

"I like it," Kyle said.

Jackie turned to Kyle with disbelief in her eyes. "You do?"

"Sure." He inspected the barn and his eyes glazed over. "It reminds me of home. I grew up on a farm, you know."

"That's neat and all," Molly said, chewing gum as she spoke. "Do we have internet access here? How many megabits upload and download are we talking about?"

"Easy," Bernard said. "The company's coming by later today to install the cable or whatever it is ISP's do. We got the best package for our tech extraordinaire." He winked at Molly, who rolled her eyes at the attempt at placation.

"How many bedrooms and bathrooms are there?" Jackie asked, placing her hands on her hips. "Please tell me it's at least four. The six of us won't have a fun time with only three bedrooms. Tell me it's three or more bathrooms, or I'm walking. I won't smell this old man's shit in the morning."

"I doubt yours smells like fresh lilac either, sweet thing," Chris said.

"There are three bathrooms." Roger pointed at the home's upper floor. "There are two upstairs and one downstairs. We're not cruel and unusual here after all," he said with a smirk. "Now, let's move this tour on over to the business area." He and Bernard turned and walked toward the barn on the property.

"It's a barn," Molly said. She trudged after the group. "What more is there to know?"

"You'd be surprised," Bernard said. "We changed it a little before everybody got here to suit our purposes. It's also worth noting, I doubt you've seen a barn like this."

"I don't know," Kyle said. They were within fifty feet of the looming building. "I've been in a lot of them. There's not a lot of difference."

"You want to bet?" Chris asked. "Fifty dollars says they're right."

"You're on," Kyle said.

Bernard and Roger reached the structure, and each grabbed a handle on the giant gate/door.

"Check this out," Bernard said. They opened the creaky doors and let everyone get inside.

Inside the barn there was no hay, farming tools, or anything normally found inside one. Instead, there were over a dozen tables stuffed inside without touching the sides.

"Tables?" Kyle asked. "That's it?"

"Not quite," Bernard said. "Rog, the honor is yours." He extended his hand toward his friend in an exaggerated sign of formality.

"This way." Roger showed them around the tables toward the back of the barn. He got to a knee and gripped a handle on the ground. "Check this out." He lifted it with a squeal of the hatch. "What about that?"

Kyle kneeled, looking into the opening. "What in blazes? I've never seen a barn with a cellar before."

"You owe me fifty bucks," Chris said. "Is that where we're going to store the product before we sell it?"

"Remember, it's a starter location, but yes," Bernard said. "We'd rather not leave crates filled with automatic weapons out on the tables or in here." He spun around with his arms at his sides. "It's temporary, but this is home. All it took was convincing the guy to sell. He claimed smugglers had used the space for moonshine."

"Whoever built it also connected it to some tunnels for

ease of privacy. We could use that if we got inventive enough," Roger said. "Yesteryear's moonshiners are today's arms dealers."

"We're not selling drugs, are we?" Kyle asked.

"Not currently," Bernard said.

"I didn't think the Syndicate endorsed drug sales," Jackie said. "Are you planning on it in the future?"

Roger took a step forward and spoke. "Officially, the Syndicate doesn't have a rule about drugs. My grandfather frowned at them, but my mother's rules are ambiguous."

"Drugs are a dirty business," Chris said. He shook his head. "It's also a lot of heat."

"Arms dealing's clean and cool though, right?" Bernard asked. "We're criminals, boys and girls. Let's not get caught up on arbitrary honor codes and morals. Besides, we've not even decided yet. Don't get your panties in a bunch. It's an option."

"Shit yeah," Molly said. "May I plant some weed in the backyard over there? I guarantee I will grow the best bud you've ever smoked. It looked like the perfect soil. I can get the pH balance right, and we can make tons of cash."

"Along with you being high all day," Jackie said. "That's the assumption I'm making."

"I work better high," Molly said. "It's a well-known fact the FBI has had trouble in recent years finding hackers. Do you know why?"

"I'm sure it's a stupid answer you're concocting on the spot." Jackie was obviously tired of this conversation. "Go ahead."

"They have a no weed policy, and none of us even tries to join them because of it."

"Sure," Jackie said, full of sarcasm. "I believe that."

"We need to focus here, ladies and gentlemen," Roger

said loud enough to grab their attention. "This property is all we have. We don't have the personnel we need to automate this."

Bernard closed the cellar door with a loud thud. "Not to mention, we haven't secured a fresh supply of weapons. We need to work out deals. Mrs. Morris won't want to supply us with her stock again after our last interaction."

"There's also the matter of deciding who will vet our new recruits." Roger looked between Kyle and Chris. "Any volunteers for that duty?"

"It should be me," Chris said. "No offense to young Mr. Evans intended. I have more experience, and I'm a better teacher."

"I can do the job, Mr. Morris," Kyle said. He jabbed his right thumb into his chest. "This place reminds me of home. Look at all those trees and hills. Nobody'd think twice if a person disappeared there. I would hate for Mr. Bristol to hurt his back digging all those graves of the cowards who buckle."

"Oh, really?" Chris asked.

"Calm down, grandpa," Molly said. "It's a shit job anyway. You know what happens if they chicken out and refuse the kill."

"Which is precisely why I'm volunteering for it," Chris said. "As the kid here eloquently stated, I'm getting old, boys. Training the next generation is a wonderful goal for an old killer like me. Let the young bucks fight it out for the prestigious positions. Nothing says I can't advise too. I only trust myself or Jackie for this."

"For a second there, I thought he was nice," Kyle said.

"You're a little naïve, aren't you?" Molly asked. She approached him and flicked his nose.

"About that," Roger said. "After deliberation, we've

already decided everyone's duties. Mr. Bristol will indeed be our recruiter and trainer."

"Mr. Evans will be muscle for now, but your future here is bright. You'll also oversee finding a suitable location for our firing range, basic as it will be. We need a place to practice, and you're the country boy."

"What about me?" Jackie asked.

"You're part of the team we send out to get things done, along with Kyle and us," Bernard said. "You're our tactician in the field, making the plans should worst come to pass."

"Until we have more hands, we're expecting everyone to do their part," Roger said. "That includes assembling and packing merchandise."

"Now when you say everybody," Molly said, "you didn't mean me, right?"

Roger turned to the shorter purple-haired female. "You heard my words, Ms. Turner. I know you have the training. Besides, it's only in the short term. We'll have you stuck behind a desk in front of a monitor before you know it."

"Yes, sir. Can I go set up my PC then? Let me get settled before we get to assembling, at least. We can't have our cyber security go to shit."

"Fine," Bernard said. "I'll help carry it in, then." His gaze lingered on Molly a little too long.

Jackie noticed. "Hey, I need help with my things. It's imperative we get the security set up first. I need your help. Rog, help the girl, would you?"

"Sure thing."

"Whoever the hell's carrying it," Molly said, moving toward the vehicle she rode in.

Roger jogged to catch up and looked over his shoulder. "We'll be back in a minute."

Bernard watched the young pair walk off before he looked over at Jackie. "Alright, what was so important?"

"Let's go get the plans I drew up." Jackie grabbed Bernard's arm and led him to his car. "Retrieve it from the trunk, would you? A powerful man like you won't have problems, boss."

"You're lucky I respect you," Bernard said once they were far enough away from Kyle and Chris that they wouldn't hear.

"Don't get bent out of shape," Jackie said. She popped the trunk and waited for Bernard to heft out an enormous pair of suitcases. "You'll have your chances with her. Let him have his first. Be a considerate leader and the grunts will respect you more."

"Don't be ridiculous," Bernard said. "Lifting a PC is easier."

Jackie walked with Bernard toward the house. "Is that what it is, huh?"

That evening...

"I set up the first meeting with one of your mother's contacts here," Chris said. "I figured I may as well, since I have no personnel to prepare yet." He and the rest of the group sat around the dining room table with a pizza box between them.

"Which one was that?" Roger asked.

"You two will meet with Percy Hudson in a couple of hours. Percy's a local arms dealer. He usually only deals with individual clients, but he's willing to sell to us. His normal clientele are local gangbangers in the area. The guy's getting old and wants someone else to do the footwork of selling."

"Where's the meeting place?" Bernard asked with a mouthful of pizza.

"It's a half hour drive from here in Nashville," Chris said. "He owns one of the smaller comedy clubs on the main street. You're to meet him in the back of it at ten pm."

"A comedy club? Are you serious?" Molly asked.

"It's a decent cover for someone in that business," Jackie said. "Laundering money is something we'll have to set up ourselves soon. Any ideas on that?"

"We've got a few ideas, but I know you won't like them," Roger said.

"Such as?"

"We can start a business of our own, legitimately," Bernard said. "Mrs. Morris already gave us the name of a banker. Mr. Keller should have ideas. I'll meet with him privately and ask his opinion on what type to use. He'd know the local scene and what would be believable to the populace. We can't make an unpopular shop type and then launder hundreds of thousands into a business nobody uses, can we?"

"That meeting is tomorrow morning," Chris said. "You need to grab me some recruits. I do not enjoy being your secretary right now."

"You're great at it, it appears," Molly said with a snicker. "Better than I could ever be."

"Shouldn't you be doing this?" Chris asked. "You're the one who can investigate people's contact information on your computer. Why am I doing this?"

"That's a good point," Bernard said.

"Oh, don't tell me," Molly said. "I don't know if you've noticed, but I don't have that skill set. I'm not a people person."

Chris nodded. "Good point."

"Excuse me?"

"You were the one who admitted it." Bernard cleared his plate and took it over to the nearby sink. He rinsed it off and placed it in the nearby dishwasher before standing up. "Let's get ready. We can't be late."

"Is it already that time?" Roger looked at the watch on his wrist. "Evans, Jackie, you're coming with us. Molly, I want you to aid Chris here by finding the rest of our contacts while we're gone. With your help, he'll finish in half the time, so we'll spend more time assembling weapons and making cash."

"With her help, I can contact some names I couldn't find," Chris said. "That'll get us pairs of hands to order around at least."

"Make it happen," Bernard said. "Now let's get changed. We'll put our best foot forward for Mr. Hudson if he's going to be a business partner from now on."

Later at Hudson's comedy club...

"That's quite a crowd for one of the smaller clubs." Roger's eyes were wide as they approached the property. A huge line of humanity waited in front of it, desperate to get inside. They parked in a nearby parking lot and walked. The club's parking lot was obviously full already.

"It's Nashville," Jackie said. "They love their nightlife here. It doesn't surprise me."

"You can hear the music out here," Kyle said. He could hear country music outside on the main street. The grandiose signs towered above them, bathing them in their artificial light in the cool night air. Indistinct conversation between the guests grew louder as they approached the club.

"We're heading this way," Bernard said. They approached the club's side entrance. A large man stood beside the door, and he didn't wear a pleasant expression. He had his arms crossed and was scowling.

"Who are you?" the man asked. "No entry permitted back here. Enter in the front if you want inside."

"We're not club goers," Bernard said. "We have a meeting with Mr. Hudson."

"Oh, do you?" the bouncer asked. "Do you know how many idiots try that line?"

"Tell your boss that the Morris representatives are outside right now," Roger said.

"Or what?"

Jackie and Kyle stepped forward. She wore a smirk. "You want to find out, big guy? We have a meeting, and your sasquatch looking ass isn't going to stop us."

"Let me check, because I don't want to hurt such a pretty lady." The bouncer reached down to his belt line and pulled out a radio-looking device. "I got some uninvited guests at the side entrance. They claim their name's Morris and they have a meeting."

A male voice tinged with a southern accent answered. "It's about time. I was wondering if they would wait until closing. Send them in right away."

"Right away." The bouncer clipped it back to his belt and glared at the group. "Fine. It looks like your story checks out." He stepped to the side, allowing them access to the door. "Don't try anything in there. Security will shoot first and ask questions later."

"They sound like our kind of people," Bernard said. He led the group and opened the door.

"Good luck," the bouncer called after them before slamming the door behind them.

"What an asshole," Jackie mumbled once they were inside. Loud, muffled country music and the smell of cigarette smoke met their senses as they found themselves in a corridor decorated with various country music and comedy memorabilia ranging from autographed framed posters to photographs.

"He's security. It's their job to be assholes," Bernard said.

An older gentleman stepped out of a nearby door. He wore a stylish and formal suit, complete with a tie and dress shoes. This complimented his thin white mustache and clean-shaven chin. "Ah," he said, "there you are. Step into my office. Your security can wait just outside." He disappeared back inside the room he'd just exited.

"You heard him," Roger whispered. "Stay right outside."

"Got it," Kyle said.

Roger and Bernard followed Percy into the office and closed the door behind them.

"Please, sirs, take a seat." Percy was already behind a large desk and leaned back in his chair with a squeak. "I must admit, I didn't expect the representatives of the Morris Syndicate to be so..." he trailed off.

"Handsome?" Bernard asked, flashing a smile.

"Young." Percy chuckled. "Which one of you is Roger?"

"That's me, Mr. Hudson," Roger said. "It's a pleasure to meet you. We look forward to working together."

"You should know the only reason we're having this meeting is because your mother helped me out five years ago. Normally, I do not discuss this business with anyone else. Now, what do you boys need?"

"We need a steady supplier of weaponry," Bernard said.

"What types do you want?" Percy asked. "I have handguns, rifles, some modifications, and even some shotguns."

"All the above." Bernard reached into his jacket and

pulled out an envelope. "I've written the fine details in this." He placed the envelope on the desk and pushed it over to Percy. "That's how much we'll need per shipment, by my calculations."

Percy picked it up and opened it. He read it and looked at the pair. "This is doable. Just know it'll cost a pretty penny."

"We're not buying pre-assembled," Bernard said. "We just need the parts."

"That drives the price down a bit. Yes, that will work," Percy said. "Will you gentlemen write the email address we can contact you at? It's to set up delivery. I run this business old school. No phone calls, and encrypted messaging from both sides."

"It's a sensible precaution," Roger said. "I'm glad safety is paramount. Far too many fools in this trade overlook it. You are not that man."

"Flattery gets you nowhere," Percy said. "Unless you're my ex-wife, that is. Am I right?"

"Undoubtedly," Bernard said, playing along. "We're just showing respect. Honey attracts more than vinegar. No sense in upsetting a valuable partner. Pleasantries are cheap and mean the world."

"You're a couple of sweet talkers. You remind me of myself twenty years ago. Give my regards to your dear mother." Percy leaned back with a squeak.

"She'll hear of your eagerness to help us," Roger said.

"Supplying you with merchandise is where my role ends. You pay on time, and we won't have a problem. I'll tell you the same as my other clients. I take money, not excuses."

"Message received," Bernard said.

"Then I have business to attend to." Percy pushed his seat backwards and stood up. "I'll contact you ASAP. If you'll excuse me." Percy walked to the door and opened it before passing through.

"Enjoy yourself tonight, sir." Bernard waved goodbye after they exited the room.

"I always do." Percy walked past numerous paintings in the narrow corridor away from the group.

"He was happy." Jackie grabbed Bernard by the tie and yanked. "You took my advice from earlier."

"Maybe."

"Let's get home already. This place is a security nightmare. Besides, I hate country music."

2

———

Chris pulled out his phone. He looked at the single-story home outside and dialed the number on the paper taped to his dashboard.

"Yeah?" an unfamiliar male voice asked.

"I'm here. Hurry outside." Chris's words were short but chosen with care.

"How many more are we picking up?" the passenger in the car's rear asked. He was clean shaven, dressed in clean if casual clothes, and wore sunglasses.

"We initiate in pairs, Mr. Lionel."

"Call me Lyle."

The door to the house opened. His target stumbled out with a grunt. He wore a wife beater, stained with God knows what, along with torn sweat pants. His unkept facial hair stood in stark contrast to Lyle's visage.

"Stellar candidate there," Lyle said. "I smell the booze on him from here."

Chris looked over his shoulder. "Focus on yourself." He honked the horn. "Come on. I don't have all morning."

The back door opened, and he climbed in. "Sorry about that. I overslept."

"Not interested in your life story," Chris said. "I hope you're ready to work. You'll need suits if you're going to fit in. Those clothes are unacceptable, especially yours, Wallace King."

"I'm honored you remember my name," Wallace said. He looked down, trying to avoid the morning sunlight outside. "Shouldn't you have tinted windows?"

"That draws attention from cops," Chris said. "Be quiet. Oh Lord, Lyle's right. I can smell the alcohol."

"Rough night," was all Wallace said.

"Your indiscretions are not my business, nor do I care," Chris said. "You both know why you're here. We're not going to summer camp. You're here to prove loyalty to your new family. Odds are one of you will fail, and I'll kill you. Did that sober you up?"

"Point taken."

Chris turned the wheel. "Before we get you to build defenses around our compound, we're stopping someplace first. Call it the first test."

"Involving what?" Lyle asked.

"You two know the local scene. You'll tell me who the big players are in the guns game here. I want names, locations, and their reputation."

"Wanting to eliminate the competition?" Lyle leaned forward between the seats. "Or is this more diplomatic in nature?"

"That's above your paygrade," Chris said. "Answer me."

Wallace answered first. "You're looking for Mr. Powell. He's a mean son of a bitch too. He supplies anyone who can't get a firearm legally because of their past. I hear tale he sells to local gangs and anyone else with cash."

"You buy weapons from him." Chris stopped at a traffic light. "What about you Mr. Lionel?"

Lyle cleared his throat. "I know a few drug dealers, but weapons aren't my thing. The big cheese around is Mr. Bailey. Nobody knows his first name or even if it's his real name."

"Where are we going anyway?" Wallace asked. "You never mentioned."

"We're here," Chris said. He stopped the car outside of a local gym. "Do either of you recognize this place?"

"It's where wannabe boxers train," Wallace said. "Nobody worth a damn has made it big that trained here. It's a wonder anybody still takes the trainers seriously."

"I'm surprised to hear you say that." Chris unlocked the car's doors. "We're heading inside."

"Come on," Wallace said. "The owner and I don't get along."

"Sounds like an intelligent individual I want to meet," Chris said with a click of his tongue. He threw open the driver's door. "Get out! It's a test of your skills and determination. We don't tolerate quitters and losers. Prove your worth and stop bitching."

Both prospective gangsters hurried out of the car. They followed Chris inside to the smell of sweat, deodorant, and body odor. A boxing ring sat in the middle of the floor space. Various workout machines lined the room's walls, most of them already in use by various patrons. Two men in protective helmets and gloves danced around the other inside the ring, occasionally jabbing at their opponent.

A hunched over geriatric trainer stood outside of the ring, leaned on the ring mat, and yelled at the two. "Stick and move, you fools! Keep your hands up and keep your head moving, or it'll get knocked off." He adjusted the black beanie covering his balding head before launching another order. "Fight like you mean it, you bastards."

Chris led the two recruits toward the ring. "Mr. Fitch, it's nice to see you again."

The trainer turned to the group. "Mr. Bristol, I'll be with you in a moment. I'm working on a couple of bums." He checked the stopwatch in his hands. He pushed a button and called out. "Time!"

The two fighters met in the middle of the ring and touched gloves before moving toward Mr. Fitch. They leaned on the ropes above their trainer in preparation for their evaluation.

Mr. Fitch was red in the face from his yelling. He pointed toward the empty line of treadmills across the facility. "Go hit the treadmill. Your cardio is embarrassing if you're out of breath with that. Do the stretches I told you to before you leave. It wouldn't do for one of you to pull something like an idiot."

"Yes, sir," both men said before exiting the ring.

"Are you here about what we talked about yesterday? Are these them?" He looked at Wallace and Lyle behind Chris. "They don't look like much."

"Looks can be deceiving. Gentlemen, get ready in the locker room. Is the gear I purchased waiting for them?"

Mr. Fitch reached into his pocket and tossed two keys to the men. "It is."

"What are you waiting for?" Chris asked the two. "Get moving, slackers."

Chris and Mr. Fitch watched them disappear into a nearby door.

"Reginald, I appreciate your help."

"What else is new?" Reginald asked. "Call me Mr. Fitch. We're not friends. I knew you before you ruined your life

and left your family, but I had to experience the consequences, not you. It devastated your mother."

"You never forgave me for joining the army."

"Neither did your family, as I recall. What brought you
back home?" Reginald asked. "You come crawling back
because you need a job?"

"I'm on one."

"The blood of others paid for that fancy suit, I'm assuming." Reginald tugged at the expensive tie completing the
suit Chris wore. "Don't involve me with you. I'm only
agreeing because I need the business. If fresh blood shows
up, it's good for business."

Wallace and Lyle returned. They were wearing a t-shirt
and boxing shorts, along with different shoes.

"Grab a helmet and gloves from the storage." Reginald
pointed toward the equipment rack nearby.

"I won't tell you how to do your job," Chris said. "I'm
here to see their potential and their ability to follow
instructions."

"Lord help me." He raised his voice, looking at the pair.
"What's taking so long? Hurry!"

Both rushed back, holding the equipment.

"Finally," Chris said. "I want to see you two spar."

"They can't spar without warming up, you fool," Reginald said sharply. "They'll injure themselves."

"In the field you won't have the luxury of warming up.
Do it. Wear helmets and gloves and get in the ring. Give it
your all."

"The field." Reginald's tone was mocking. "Listen to you.
You're a civilian gramps, like me. Start acting like it." He
helped the two potential recruits secure their gloves and
helmets.

"That's where you're wrong. Let me borrow that." Chris

snatched the stopwatch from Reginald. He watched his recruits climb inside and go to opposing corners. "Go on my signal."

"One looks like he's about to fall already." Reginald noticed Wallace's swaying. "Are you drunk, boy?"

"Just hungover."

"That's much better." The sarcasm was clear in Reginald's voice. "This won't be much of a test between a drunkard and this guy."

"Go." Chris hit the stopwatch and watched the spectacle unfold.

Lyle shot out of the corner. He raised his hands up and danced around the swaying Wallace. He tried a jab but instinctively leaned back when a hook fanned his face.

Wallace burped deeply. "Almost," he said.

"The drunk one's as bad as you were," Reginald said.

Wallace stumbled forward before delivering a wicked uppercut to Lyle's defending glove below his chin.

Lyle used his right to deliver a gut punch and hopped away from the immediate response.

Wallace's swings were powerful but slow. He used his opponent's cautious nature to back Lyle into a corner.

"Get out of the corner." Reginald gripped the bottom rope as he called out.

Lyle ducked under a head level hook and slithered out of the corner.

"That one might have talent," Chris said. He rubbed his chin and looked at the timer. "You have one minute left. Make it count."

Both met in the center of the ring with renewed vigor. Punches flew, blows landed, and neither gave ground. Their heads swayed, bobbed, and weaved.

Lyle abandoned the direct fight after an especially hard

hit he suffered to his gut. He danced around Wallace, trying to go back to hit and run.

"Twenty seconds," Chris said.

That lit a fire under Wallace. A burst of speed enabled him to push Lyle into the corner and pummel him mercilessly. Blow after blow landed on Lyle's abdomen until the final uppercut which snapped Lyle's head back.

"Time!"

Wallace backed off, leaving the still standing Lyle in the corner.

"I expected one of you to fall, if I'm honest," Chris said. "What do you think, Reggie?"

"The drunk one has power, while the other has real boxing talent." Reggie beckoned the two recruits over to the ropes. "Chubby, were you a bouncer before this?"

"Not quite," Wallace said. "I was in sales."

"What about you?" Reginald asked Lyle. "You have speed and some talent."

"I was in a different branch of sales."

"You brought a couple of salesmen, huh?" Reginald laughed at Chris. "Did you get what you needed today?"

"Me?" Chris asked. "Yeah, I saw what they're capable of. Do you think you can whip them into shape?"

"No doubt. It's just a matter of them listening."

Chris kept his voice firm. "You two will follow every command Reginald here gives you. I don't care if you're exhausted. Treat him as you would me. If you quit, I'll know and pay you a visit later. Is that understood, boys? I'll be back to pick you up later. Don't let me down."

"You're leaving?"

"I've other business, old man. Don't worry, I'm giving you two of the most dedicated men you'll ever find. I'll be visiting on the regular with new recruits for you to whip into shape."

"So long as you pay for their training, I don't give a damn."

Chris pulled out a fistful of cash and handed it to Reginald. "That should cover it."

Reginald whistled, counting the money. "Pleasure doing business with you."

"Remember what I said," Chris said, walking away from the ring. He tossed the stopwatch back to Reginald before he reached the door. "Work hard."

He exited the gym and emerged outside in the sunbaked parking lot. He climbed into his car, pulled out his phone, and dialed a number.

"Status report?" Molly asked.

"I have our first two recruits and they show promise. How's the other recruiting effort coming along?"

"Jackie's out checking with the other names as we speak. No word yet. I'm betting it'll be successful. Wait, that's her. Be right back." He heard a click and buckled his seat belt while he waited. "That went better than I thought."

The line came back, and Molly spoke immediately. "That was her. She was successful."

"I should also mention I learned of a couple of big names in the area. Both sound like treats."

"Understood. What's next for you today?"

"I didn't know you cared," Chris said. He looked over his shoulder at the busy street. "Worried about the old man?"

"Worried about my ass and what I'm going to tell the bosses."

"You're supposed to go along with me."

"I didn't get that memo. Now answer me. Bernard's right here, and he looks antsy."

"Why didn't you say so earlier? Inform him we need to secure some targets for our initiates soon. Mr. Lionel and Mr. Wallace show promise, but I'm remaining cautious until they're fully committed. I'm on my way to the next two names now."

"I'll relay it. Good luck out there."

Meanwhile, back at the base...

"He said he's on his way to the next pair of recruits now." Molly took off the headset. "He also said we need targets for our initiates soon. They must be promising if he's thinking that far ahead."

"Targets already?" Bernard asked. "I hate to bury bodies this soon after arriving, but we need proof of their loyalty. Any ideas?"

"You're asking me?" Molly asked. She turned back to the monitor. "Why not the big bosses he mentioned?"

"Not without knowing their loyalty. We'll think about it for now. What about you? How are you settling in?"

"It's not the metropolis I'm used to. Nashville's large, but we're out in the sticks. We're lucky to have as fast an internet as we do. I appreciate your springing for their best package."

"I trust helping Chris hasn't proven difficult."

"As if. It's a cakewalk job. It's just cyber stalking and relaying information to and from the old fogey. What about you, boss? Speaking of which, may I ask a question?"

"Consider it always fine," Bernard said. He pulled out a seat and sat beside Molly. "I find it's better to respect your men and women, not treat them like automatons. Permission to speak freely granted."

"You love this boss shit, huh? Permission to speak? You get that from an old sci-fi show?"

"I'll admit I enjoy command, but I recognize I have a lot to learn."

"Which one of you outranks the other?" Molly asked.

"You go right for the jugular, huh?" Bernard rubbed his hands together at the awkward question. "Technically speaking, Roger outranks me."

"Noted."

"That's it? No questions about how we got this command or our past?"

"I joined the Syndicate a year ago and heard all the rumors. I don't believe any of it. It's never a good idea to believe the grapevine. It always distorts the story. Is it true you guys were there when the war with the Russians started?"

"That one's true." Bernard stared at the monitor as he spoke. "It was Roger's first job, and I acted like a big shot. Artyom, Oleg's second in command, ignored me and was all over Roger. He took us back to our car and slaughtered the rest of Mrs. Morris's men in front of us and his little sister. That single event set in motion their downfall. They pissed us off."

"I'm sure that was the determining factor in the war." Molly snickered. "Sure."

"Hey." Bernard said. "We found Mikhail, burned their restaurant down, raided their weapons storehouse, and set in motion the events that led to their Ghost of Moscow being killed by Kyle." He went quiet. "Damn him."

"Sorry to remind you of your mother's unfortunate passing." Molly's voice softened. "I heard you saw it happen."

"Yes. I'll never forget that day, nor will I forget my suspicions about why it happened."

"Suspicions?"

"Never mind that." Bernard waved off the question. "Our

recruiting is in full swing. Now we'll make our first buy and then find some clients."

"What about the local bosses? I doubt they'll enjoy having new competition around." Molly navigated the mouse to the internet browser and opened it. She opened a window showing Nashville's map. "It may not be a metropolis, but I'd bet they're every bit as brutal as the Russians and city gangs. Country boys are not to be under-estimated."

"Quite so," Bernard said. "Only a fool underestimates his opponents based on preconceptions. There's nothing saying we must eliminate them unless they press the issue. If they do, we'll fire back and end it before they know what happened."

"Big words," Molly said. "It's rarely that easy."

"You have something to say, Ms. Turner?"

"I don't think a war is prudent when we're setting up, with all due respect."

"We rarely get to pick wars. I'm with you. Peace is prefer-able, but we will not back down and sully the Syndicate's reputation either. We will earn their respect by showing we're dangerous and hammer the point home." He pointed at the screen. "What is that?"

Molly couldn't hide her giggle at the obvious question.

"Is something funny?" Bernard was serious.

"Sorry, boss," Molly said. "That's the standard encryp-tion program. I thought you'd know that already. It's true you're hopeless with machines, huh?"

"How do you know that?"

"Crystal."

"You're friends with her?"

"Ever since I joined," Molly said. "She spoke a lot of you and Mr. Morris. It's all she talked about. It surprised me when they offered this position, if I'm honest. I thought my verbal jabs and attitude would disqualify me from working with the boss's kids, but I tried anyway."

"You really think you're better than Lee?" Bernard asked.

Molly blew a bubble and popped it, still chewing her gum as she spoke. "I know I'm better than that fat tub of crap. He's been resting on his laurels for over a decade now. He's skilled, sure. It doesn't matter when you're coasting though. I suspect that's why he recommended me – to get me away from Mrs. Morris and him. He was afraid they might compare us."

"You're certainly confident. I'll give you that. Temper that attitude. Arrogance is not helpful." Bernard climbed out of the chair. "I have things to do. Anything else before I go?"

"Can you send in Mr. Morris?"

"Sure, why?"

"It's private."

"Private, huh? I didn't know you two hit it off so fast."

"Not that, you brute," Molly blushed. "It's about Crystal. She's sent me messages, and they concern him."

"I'll send him in and take his place with Evans. I think they're building the firing range as we speak."

"They know how to wire that? That seems dangerous and unnecessary."

Bernard made for the door. "Don't worry about it. You focus on your job. We've taken precautions."

"Whatever you say, boss. As long as they don't start a forest fire from their wiring, I don't care." Molly spun the chair back to the monitor again. She hammered away at the keyboard. Her finger flew across the keys and got so absorbed in her work, she jumped when she heard a knock. "Come in," she called out without turning around.

"I heard you wanted to see me," Roger said, opening the

door. He smelled of sweat, and his t-shirt attested to that fact, judging by the sweat stains. He wiped his brow clear of perspiration as he came closer.

"Yes, it's about Crystal." Molly used her left hand to gesture to the now empty seat. "I knew you'd want to hear this in private, given how we left Ohio."

"Mom won't forgive that one soon." Roger chuckled and took the seat. "I imagine Crystal's been lonely since. I've been talking to her every night."

"Quite so," Molly said. "She's sent me some files that she instructed me to open only with you in the room. I don't know what they are, but I wanted to honor her request."

"Right. Let's put this on speaker."

"Who uses speakers anymore?" Molly asked. She took out one of the ear buds from her ear and handed it to Roger. "Here."

He stuck it in his ear and leaned toward her since the cord wasn't very long. They were nearly touching cheeks at the close contact. He couldn't stop his heart from racing from being near the cute young woman but kept his composure. "Remind me to get you a pair of wireless headsets."

"What's the matter? Don't enjoy getting this close?" Molly asked.

"It's not like that."

"You've never dealt with women much before, have you?"

"Is it that obvious?"

"You and Bernard," Molly said. "Hurry. Bernard wouldn't be happy if he knew I wasn't working."

"Simmer down and hit play. I've got your back if he returns."

The video popped up. It showed Crystal in her bedroom. Dark circles had formed under her eyes, and her blonde hair was disheveled. "Hey, Bub. I hope you two idiots are alright. Mom's beyond pissed at you and Bernard. I told Molly to play this for a different reason."

Molly paused the video. "I've been meaning to ask something."

"Always feel free to speak freely," Roger said.

"Your mom's aware we weren't involved with that, yeah?"

"Yes."

"Good."

The video resumed. "I can't do this anymore." Crystal shook her head. "You know they have Lee home schooling me now. Do you believe that? I couldn't. The guy's an asshole. Mom and Dad treat me like I'll run away too and keep me on the property. I'm barely allowed to run the trail behind the house without personal security tailing me like I'm a convict in the prison yard. It's like they're gripping tighter after you departed. I can't stand it, which brings me to my point." Crystal looked over her shoulder before she spoke again to the camera. "I've concocted a plan for getting out."

Roger hit the space bar, pausing the video. His other hand rubbed his forehead. "Oh no. Don't tell me she's serious."

"Crazy hypothetical question coming. Would you be angry if I already agreed to help?"

"You earn points for wanting to aid my sister. You lose points for going behind my back." He resumed the video.

"The scheme's in the second file," Crystal said, smirking at the camera. "You'll be proud of it."

"Something tells me you're wrong," Roger grumbled as the video ended. "Anything you want to tell me?"

"I may have moved some money around for her."

"Who's cash specifically?"

"Hers, don't worry," Molly said. "I'm not stupid. Stealing from members is a one-way ticket to a dirt nap. She needed help accessing it, so I may have moved it from one account to another of hers. I didn't take a dime. Her money was tied up. I simply facilitated the transfer to her regular checking account that she could access."

"You moved the cash Mom left for her college out of that account?" Roger's eyes were wide. "You don't think they'll tell her?"

"No. She went to the bank herself. That's why she got grounded. Your mom was suspicious about why she went there, and she didn't want to cause a scene by visiting it herself and asking."

"Why does she need money?"

"Beats me." Molly shrugged. "She never told me. She simply said to play these files with you here. I followed orders from Crystal Morris herself. No honest grunt would blame me for following orders."

"My mother might, but I'm not handing over our tech specialist."

"Nice to have the boss's support. Now let's hurry." She clicked the second file, and another video came up. It looked like Crystal was holding her phone as she walked through a forest. She had a light sweat as she walked, and the camera shook.

"Here's how it's going to happen," she said, glancing over her shoulder. "I'm going to schedule a ride to the nearest car dealership. I'll buy a vehicle immediately with the cash Molly moved, and then I'm riding."

Roger sniffed for effect. "You smell that?"

Molly paused the video. "What?"

"The shit storm is coming soon. Mother will flip her lid

if she up and leaves. Is there any way I can contact her besides email? She never responds promptly."

"You don't know your own sister's phone number?"

"Mom confiscated her phone routinely when we were growing up. I can try the last one. Hold on." He pulled out his own cell and dialed. "Pick up. Come on."

Someone answered his begging. "Hey, who is this?"

"Your brother. I just watched something interesting with Ms. Turner. Tell me you weren't serious. All that will accomplish is her sending Father to return you."

"Not when he's still laid up," Crystal said, sounding smug.

"If not him, then another. Don't play dumb. Is that an engine?"

"You're too late. I'm already free."

"At least until Mom sends her best to fetch you. I'm already on her shit list. You want her to disown me completely?"

"You won't allow her to send me back, will you?"

Roger sighed. "No. Against my better judgement, I won't. Just know there will be a reckoning. She'll send someone to drag you back kicking and screaming. You two have certainly made my life complicated today. Drive safe. You know where we are?"

"Molly told me this morning. I'll be there tonight."

"Jackie and Chris will pitch a fit. Alright, talk to you soon. Love you, bye." Roger hung up and glared at Molly.

"Don't blame me." She refused to meet his gaze.

"I should call Mom now and get ahead of it," Roger said. "Any advice?"

"You're asking me? She's your mom."

"I was never adept at deescalating conflicts; I was more

the stubborn jackass type. She's worked herself into a frenzy over this turn of events. Mark my words."

"Who's worked themselves into a frenzy?" Bernard entered the room.

Roger glanced at Molly. "We're expecting a guest tonight. Didn't you hear?"

"What?"

"My sister ran away from home," Roger said. "She bought a car using her college savings and sneaked away this morning."

Bernard burst into laughter for a good minute. "You're serious?" he asked when he noticed Roger was not laughing along. "You're serious."

"Mom is pissed. I guarantee she's noticed by now. I think calling would be best. The longer we wait, the angrier she'll be."

"That's your domain. Kyle's almost finished the range out back in the woods."

"Fantastic. If you'll excuse me, I have a pissed off mama bear to placate before she comes roaring down here and rips me apart." He left the room in a hurry, pushing past his friend. "What am I going to say?" he asked himself under his breath. He rushed to his room, lost in his own world.

Roger slammed and locked the door. He walked over to the dresser with a large mirror on it he and Bernard shared. He stared at his reflection and the phone in his hand. "Rip the band-aid off."

He raised the phone and hit speed dial to a number he never imagined he'd call again anytime soon. He dreaded the voice that answered.

"You orchestrated this?" Rachel's irate voice asked.

"I just found out," Roger said.

"I'd love to believe that. Unfortunately, I can't. Lee's done some digging. Seems someone very good hacked into your sister's account and moved a lot of money. Money that seems to have gone to a local dealership. What a coincidence, wouldn't you say?"

"If you wouldn't believe me, why did you ask? Besides, why would I leave, and then orchestrate this amateur hour crap? I'd have been smarter than this. She's a techie, not a criminal."

"For all your faults, you are smarter than that. You swear you didn't know?"

"On Father's life," Roger said. "I swear I didn't know, Mom."

"Mom?"

"You are still my mother," Roger said, his voice softer. "Even if not by blood. Sorry for how I acted last week."

"Damn it," Rachel said. "How can I stay mad at that? I know you're trying to get out of this, and I still choose to believe my boy."

"Mom, I feel bad about how we left. I'm not asking for forgiveness, but let me talk to Crystal. Maybe I can convince her to finish out the year up home. Alright?"

"If she doesn't?"

"She's stubborn, Mom. I won't force her away. She feels abandoned with my leaving. That'd make things worse."

"Be convincing," Rachel said. She hung up.

Roger pressed the end button. "Why me?"

3

The waitress led Bernard through the busy restaurant, passing dozens of patrons who were already eating. He had informed her he was there to meet someone when he arrived. She led him through the restaurant to a booth where a man was sitting with his menu open.

"I'll be back soon to take your orders." She left the pair alone.

Bernard sat opposite his appointment and adjusted his dress suit.

"Mr. Morris," the rich man said. He adjusted his tie before he reached across the table to shake his hand. "It's a pleasure."

"Likewise, Mr. Keller." Bernard returned the gesture of respect. "I'm surprised you wanted to meet in a public place like this." He picked up the menu sitting on the table between them and looked at it.

"There's a reason we're in this booth, and please, call me Robert. No one should bother us back here so long as we're observant. This place also has the best food in Nashville. I wanted to welcome you properly."

"I appreciate it."

The waitress, true to her word, returned promptly. "Are we ready to order?"

Both men gave her their orders.

"Your cousin gave me the summary of what you need," Robert said. "I've a perfect idea that will keep your names out of it."

"We're aiming to make millions here," Bernard said.

"That's the beauty. It'll be revolutionary." Robert pushed the folder on the table toward Bernard. "Look."

Bernard opened the manilla folder. "You're serious?"

"It's a booming business. It's no longer illegal. That ended in 2030."

"A dispensary? Don't you need tons of licenses and shit to operate legally under the radar?"

"That's the beautiful part," Robert said. "You wouldn't have any connections on paper. You'd be an investor. Assuming you hired me as the accountant, your worries would disappear."

"Pardon my skepticism, but this sounds like a fairy tale - too good to be true."

"I understand your reticence. Let me ease your fear by explaining the details. We have plenty of time, so what are your concerns?"

Bernard raised an eyebrow. "You're telling me we can own a dispensary without having to go through the hoops? That's where I'm falling behind."

"What if I told you I knew someone who desperately desires to open a dispensary? She already went through said hoops, grabbed the necessary licenses, and just needs investors to afford the final bribe? According to her, a Mr. Bailey has made life difficult."

"I've heard that name."

"I'm not surprised at your quick adjustment," Robert said. "He's a prominent businessman around here in various illicit circles. Now, I've already discussed this proposition with our potential business partner. She's willing to split the revenue with you two, fifty-fifty. I know that sounds hefty, but she's the one doing all the work and management."

"You'd be the one doing the books then?"

"That'd be my job. I'd make sure you get what you need."

"You vouch for this partner?" Bernard asked. "She's trustworthy?"

"Fresh out of college. She's driven, honest, and a hard worker. You won't find a better manager for your business venture. She's got a perfect location picked out. We're just waiting for the initial investment to make it a reality."

"How much?"

"Twenty-five thousand. We have the storefront purchased already. Someone local bribed an official to jam up the process. This greases the axle. With that, they'll never bother us again."

Bernard whistled. "That's a chunk of cash."

"Well spent, I assure you. I thought Mrs. Morris furnished you with some before you left."

"We can afford it, no doubt. You give your word this is the best idea? I don't know the local scene."

"Cannabis is mainstream. Most do it, and Nashville is barren. It'd skyrocket to instant success. No matter the quantity you need to clean, you'd be free and clear. I'd bet my livelihood on it. You need to jump on this. Others are trying to set up a dispensary as we speak, but they're having the same problems. You can break this stalemate and make a pretty profit."

"You're sure you're a banker and not a car salesman?" Bernard asked with a chuckle.

Robert shared in the laughter with a jolly laugh. "To clarify, she majored in horticulture. Cannabis has exploded in popularity with the widespread availability. Sure, anyone can plant some in their backyard and have a supply of middle grade stuff. She makes potent stuff, and people around here know it. She used to have a seedy past, shall we say. I've seen her plants myself. There are trichomes covering it, and the effects are the most potent I've experienced. Demand is there. Trust me."

"I've always wanted to be a legitimate business owner. Alright." Bernard reached into his coat's front pocket and pulled out a paper. He pushed it toward Robert. "Come here tonight. We'll have the money ready for you."

Robert picked it up. "Ah, you're out in the country. Good thinking."

"We thought so. This better pan out. I don't appreciate getting taken for a ride, Mr. Keller."

"There're no guarantees in business, but this is the closest you'll get, Mr. Morris."

"Right."

The waitress interrupted the pair with two plates in her hands. She placed one in front of each man. "Here you are. Enjoy." She left as quickly as she arrived, swamped with work.

"Hell, you may not even need additional sources of income from whatever you do. I don't want to know, but this income may dwarf it."

"I doubt that, sincerely."

"Never underestimate a man wanting to intoxicate himself," Robert said. "They keep coming back forever, so long as they have cash. That's the kicker. They'll search for that illusive high again and again. That's why drug dealers usually make more than arms."

"You pulled that out of your ass." Bernard looked at the band on the stage playing. "Guns sell for more than flowers."

"Maybe, but how many are repeat customers? You hope they come back, but because of the nature, they might not survive."

"This girl sounds promising."

"Her being a girl isn't a problem, is it?"

"Nonsense. So long as she's skilled and motivated, I'm fine with it. I hire based on merit, Mr. Keller, not because of what's between her legs."

"I'm glad to hear it. She'll be ecstatic when she hears we will make her dream a reality. It wouldn't surprise me if she wants to tag along tonight. Is that alright? She's old-fashioned and will want to thank her benefactors personally."

"It'd be no problem. We're always ready to meet those we work with."

"We'll be there tonight then..."

Meanwhile...

Chris sat in his car on the phone. "Are you sure this is the right location?"

"One hundred percent," Molly said. "I've checked the website, and it lists them as employees. Why do we want arcade employees again?"

"I ran with their fathers in high school. They'd appreciate their kids getting this opportunity."

"You're sure about that?"

"I already talked to them. They gave their blessing."

"On your head be it," Molly said. "You're going to be the one training these guys."

"Heading inside then." Chris hung up, got out of the car, and headed inside.

"I knew I'd find you bums here." Chris let the doors behind him close. Electronic noises and sound effects played in the background. Some flashing lights accompanied them, illuminating the black carpet full of colorful art.

"Look who it is," a gruff man with a beard said. "If it isn't Chris Bristol. Our dads thought you'd maybe died in the army or something, old man."

"No such luck." Chris watched them come over to shake his hand. He exchanged pleasantries with every man before backing up. "What are you all doing here? Your fathers know you work here?"

"Seriously? We always loved video games, and this place is the only arcade."

"Bums, one and all." Chris's insults didn't offend them. Their smiles showed that. "Anybody looking for a well-paying job? You can't tell me you're satisfied making change for quarters for a living."

"Hey!" a teenage male behind a nearby counter said. He had a tag on his chest reading 'Manager'. "Get back to work already. We don't pay you to socialize."

"A teenage boss? Yikes," Chris said. "Come on, boys. I'll walk with you, so the man doesn't yell at you."

"Dad said you always were an ass." The group moved from the front of the building into the heart of it.

"It must be slim pickings here. Your fathers always wanted to join an official outfit."

"Is that what you did?"

"I'm recruiting for one, as a matter of fact." Chris had an air of confidence as he spoke. The group passed behind rows of arcade machines, most of them occupied by teenagers and kids. "You were my first choice. I know you're trustworthy. Your fathers have taught you discretion, I trust. I know you want the job. Think about the glamorous life you envisioned when you were teens. Don't you want boatloads of cash, respect, and women aching to accompany you every evening?"

"I don't know," the shorter one said. "There're two outfits in town, and neither likes competition. It's bad for your health to compete with them. They're like a cartel here, only worse."

"We just won a war with the Russian Mafia, boys. A couple of hick town groups do not scare us," Chris said. "Besides, don't you want hundreds of thousands of dollars a year, compared to whatever this pays? You could build your own arcades with that money. Hell, you could have whatever you wanted."

"It's minimum wage, you jackass."

"My point exactly," Chris said. "Nothing in this life comes free. I'm simply asking for you to apply yourselves and live the life you always wanted. I already talked to your dads. They were ecstatic. This is the big time, gentlemen. I know the bosses personally, and they want to pay some young men to learn and apply themselves. You'll have to prove yourself to join, but once you're in, you're set for life. You'd learn from me, and I'll whip you into shape."

"Like the army? I'm not cut out for that."

Chris found a quiet corner of the arcade, only one unoccupied cabinet was there. "I won't lie. It'll be hard work, but it's worth it if you're strong enough. Trust me."

"Every time we heard 'trust me' growing up, shit went down. Remember our prank at the end of high school?"

"I still can't believe they called the cops on us."

"See this suit?" Chris tugged on the expensive coat. "It costs two thousand dollars. I have a dozen more hanging in my closet. Does that sweeten the deal? You could take care of your parents with that cash. Your folks wouldn't have to worry about your financial future."

"Where and when do you want us?"

"Go to this address tomorrow morning." Chris pulled out a paper and handed it to the group. "I'll greet you personally and you might even get to meet the boss. If you do, be respectful and don't argue. We're starting up here, and you're getting in on the ground floor. You won't regret it, boys."

4

"The range is ready," Kyle said. He saw everyone sitting in the living room. None of them returned his greeting. "Hello?"

"We heard you," Molly said. "Did you not hear?"

"No. I was busy. Buying hay, moving it, and setting up the targets took all day. At least I know the area by heart now."

"We're expecting my sister anytime," Roger said. He kicked back in his chair.

"Oh."

"Yeah," Jackie said.

Chris looked out the window. "You'd better buck up. She's here. We should give a warm welcome. She's exhausted from that drive, no doubt. At least let her sleep a night. It'd be cruel to send her off."

"I'd drive her myself if it came to it," Jackie said. "I don't want problems with Mrs. Morris. No offense, boss, but she outranks you."

"Here she comes." Chris peeked out the drapes and sat back down.

Roger jumped to answer the door. He opened it after the knock. "Look who it is."

She barely let him get the sentence out before giving him a hug and forcing her way inside. "You couldn't pick a place easier to find?"

"That's kind of the point." Bernard leaned against the nearby room's archway. "You've caused a stir back home today. Your mother's irate, and it's directed at him." He pointed at Roger. "She thought it was his idea."

"Seriously? How? He's down here."

"Same way your friend did." Roger looked at Molly.

"Regardless, I'm here now. Where am I staying?"

"About that," Bernard said. "You're sleeping on the couch here since we can't spare any rooms. We're already packed. We weren't expecting any further guests to sleep here."

"Fair enough. It's my fault showing up unannounced."

"May as well make you feel welcome while you're here," Chris said. "I hope your brother was right about what kind of pizza you enjoy. They're almost done."

"Homemade pizza? Seriously?" Crystal asked.

"No pizza joint would deliver out here. Trust me, I looked," Molly said.

"Roger," Jackie said. "Remember what I said earlier?"

"Later."

"It better be later and not never," Jackie said. Her phone interrupted any further talk. "That's the pizzas. It'll be a few minutes before we're ready." She disappeared into the nearby tiled kitchen.

"How's business going?" Crystal asked.

"Almost completely ready," Bernard said. "What about recruiting, old man?"

"I have seven prospective recruits I'm working on. Five are friends' kids and two are from your aunt's recommendation. I need tests to give them to prove loyalty, and we don't have any targets."

"We'll have some soon enough if I'm right," Bernard said. "If Chris is right, we have two big organizations here already. One deals in weapons, and the other in drugs. We're fixing to piss off both at this rate. To hell with them though."

"Not quite," Chris said. "We need bodies before a war kicks off. Or we'll have to go guerilla tactics. That's an option."

"Not to mention we need buyers still," Kyle said from a nearby chair. "It's worthless having merchandise with no one to buy."

"I have a solution to that," Jackie called out from the kitchen. "It's temporary, but it'll work. Get in here. It's ready."

The group got out of their seats and moved to the kitchen. Everyone sat around the gargantuan table and waited for Jackie to finish the preparation.

"What's the idea, hot and dangerous?" Chris asked. "You know someone here?"

"You don't remember?" Jackie asked. "We can sell online." She put on the oven gloves before opening the oven. She pulled each pizza out one at a time before placing them on a wooden stand sitting on the countertop.

"How does that even work?" Kyle asked. "You just package it and send it after you receive payment?" He eyed the tantalizing pizzas as Jackie grabbed the pizza cutter.

"Essentially." Jackie pressed the circular cutting device against the delicious smelling food and cut slices. "I know the protocols for shipping. It's a precise art and easy to fuck up. You need a mask, gloves, hairnets, and a production area, which we have. I need Molly's help to set up the account and payment details, then we'll be set."

"Is that safe?" Roger asked. He was already fetching plates and handing them out as he asked the question.

"In theory," Molly said, accepting her plate. "People have been doing it since the internet was invented - some from the beginning. If you're careful, it's safe. If you're sloppy, not so much. The bonus is you can diversify and sell on multiple sites, increasing your revenue and orders. It becomes a full-time job, and you can sell drugs the same way."

"You're still on about having that grow out back?" Kyle asked.

"Supplementary income is never dumb."

"Speaking of income," Bernard said, "that reminds me. I secured our money laundering business today. We'll be legitimate business owners soon."

"Doing what exactly?" Chris asked. "Tell me it's not a restaurant. Those don't launder enough cash unless it's a huge franchise chain."

"The guy Mrs. Morris directed us to said we should invest in Nashville's first cannabis dispensary. He said we'd make a killing, and he has someone with all the licenses and experience to run it ready and waiting. They need an investor and we'd be the owners of the company. It's all legitimate."

"Lord help me," Jackie said. "I suppose she can't complain if her man suggested it. I remember when it was illegal, and the black market was the only supply. It's weird how the times change."

Chris grabbed another pizza cutter and worked on the other two pizzas. "If we can sell online, then that takes care of the buyer situation - assuming we can master the packaging and shipping."

"It's busy work." Jackie finished her meal. "You drive dozens of miles and ship them from different mailboxes. It's easy, just a pain. The packaging is crucial. Fingerprints and hair specifically. We cannot leave DNA behind. Law enforcement sometimes orders, and you want nothing leading back. We have hair nets and you boys are going to learn how to use them. I won't risk arrest because you're too embarrassed."

"It's a risk of the medium," Molly said. "Can't make money without risks. I'd handle the digital orders, print out the invoices, addresses, and then it's up to production. It'd be like running a business from home, only lucrative and dangerous."

"How fast do we get paid per sale?" Kyle asked. "Is it mail?"

"It's crypto currency, which would be more busy work withdrawing it, but anonymous. Depending on the site, either immediately after they place the order or when the order arrives. They use tracking to confirm. We'd need to hold that for proof. They're not big on their clients getting ripped off. We get banned, and our income drops. No ripping off customers if we want steady business."

"Goes without saying," Roger said. "Sounds like a good plan to me. At least until we drum up local interest organically."

"I see you're focused on business as usual," Crystal said. "No different from home in that respect."

Chris grabbed Jackie's plate with a smirk and was met with narrowed eyes. "We need to find targets to guarantee loyalty with our recruits soon. Doesn't have to be murder, but something to hold them loyal. Any ideas?"

"Focus on training first," Bernard said. "We'll have targets soon enough. Be ready for a few jobs soon."

"Acknowledged."

"What about me?" Kyle asked. "The range is finished. Am I learning how to pack the merchandise?"

"Damned right you are," Jackie said. "Molly, get the accounts ready tonight before bed." She finished cutting all the pizzas completely.

"Already taken care of, actually."

"You did that without orders?"

"Call it planning for an eventuality." Molly reached for another piece. "I didn't list any merchandise yet, but we're verified. You're welcome for that. Normally it takes days on these sites. Aren't I great? I got it pushed through since I knew the guy that owns the website."

"You know the guy?" Bernard asked.

"The owner of the darknet site, yeah," Molly said, as if it were normal. "We go way back. He's a good dude. Just stay on your toes around him. He's as cutthroat as they come."

"Speaking of cutthroat," Bernard looked at his watch, "Mr. Keller should arrive soon to finalize the business. I'll get the money ready. Rog, we should greet them personally. Making a good first impression is important to our manager." He got up along with Roger. "We'll be back soon. Leave pizza for us, you bloody animals."

"I'm on it already." Crystal placed a couple of pieces on empty plates for her brother and Bernard's return.

The pair left and went upstairs. They entered their room and slammed the door.

"How much was the investment?" Roger asked.

"Twenty-five thousand."

"You're serious?"

"We'll earn that back with the first round of sales on the darknet." Bernard grabbed the briefcase by his bed and plopped it on the bed. He opened it to reveal stacks of cash stuffed inside. He took the wads out and counted the cash as they spoke. "It's to push through the paperwork for her."

"You think it's the work of Bailey?" Roger asked.

"Probably. He doesn't want competition. He bribed the right people, so we pay more and we're set."

"That's a prime way to start a war."

"Stepping on toes is a requirement for our job." Once he was satisfied, he closed the suitcase. "He's not our boss. Within a week, the shop will be open."

"You invited them here?"

"It's no different from hosting business VIPs at the house. Your mom did. Here, it's a young entrepreneur and banker. He'll cook the books, and she'll run the business. Then once we sell some guns, we can explain the money away."

"Seems a lot for a bribe, if you ask me." Roger crossed his arms. "It better be worth it."

"Trust me, brother," Bernard said. "We're on the path to success. Just stick with me. Soon, the whole Nashville underground will know our names and fear us."

An hour later...

Bernard and Roger moved to the door, briefcase in tow. Roger opened the door to reveal Reginald and a young woman on their porch.

"Hello," Roger said. "Mr. Keller, was it?"

"That's right, Mr. Morris." He looked to his side. "This is Abigail Gomez, your future manager and partner in our business venture."

Roger stepped to the side and welcomed them in. "I'm Roger Morris." He motioned toward Bernard. "This is

Bernard Morris. Please, get out of the cold. Come and let's complete this inside."

"Our thoughts exactly," Robert said. The pair entered the home, and the boys led them to the living room. It was empty now, except for the group of four.

Everyone took a seat. Bernard placed the briefcase he was holding onto the coffee table in front of the pair. He unlocked it and popped it open. "This should push the paperwork through."

"I'd say," Robert eyed the money.

"I expect this to grease the gears, not find its way into your pocket," Roger said, eying Robert.

"Of course," Robert said.

"Thank you both for this," Abigail said.

"You're doing us the favor." Bernard turned his gaze to the young woman. "We've always wanted to co-own a business. Mr. Keller tells us there are no dispensaries in Nashville?"

"Correct," Abigail said. "They're legal as of five years ago, but a local dealer knows how to pull strings and keep the competition suppressed. He's convinced that if there're dispensaries, he'll lose business, and he's right."

"It's a free country as he's about to learn," Bernard said.

"You're not scared of incurring his wrath by opening a dispensary anyway?" Roger asked.

"Scared? No." Abigail shook her head. "More like determined," she said. "I've tied up every penny I have into this. He pisses me off, trying to dictate what I'm allowed to do. I'll admit, my defiance of his will is a bonus. My brother's the one who inspired me to open the dispensary, but that's a delightful bonus."

"Brother?"

"Yeah," Abigail looked away.

"No need to explain if it's a touchy subject. My apologies," Roger said. "It's an honor to meet you."

"Nonsense, the honor is mine. You are helping me accomplish a lifelong dream. This feud's dragged on for over a year now. He had deeper pockets to throw money at the situation until now. I owe you two for this."

"Nonsense." Bernard waved off her vow. "We hate bullies like him. I assume Mr. Keller has informed you of what we want?"

"You want a partnership and to hire him. I'm fine with it."

"In addition, we'll provide protection from Mr. Bailey and his goons if he gets upset," Bernard said. "Because he will," he said.

"I'm counting on it."

"The money's all here," Robert said, closing the briefcase. "I'll deliver this to the right people tomorrow morning, bright and early. Within a week, we'll be up and running."

"You two should come see it when we're open," Abigail said. "The spot I've purchased isn't downtown, but trust me when I say that we'll get plenty of business. We'll serve the finest cannabis this state's ever known. I already have a laundry list of clients just waiting for opening day to pay hundreds for ounces of our best."

"We'd love to see the place," Bernard said.

"May I ask a question? I mean no offense with it," she said.

"Don't worry about it. Speak freely, Ms. Gomez."

"How old are you two?"

Bernard and Roger looked at her. "Eighteen," Bernard answered. "We're looking to make our name in the wide world. We've decided you're the best way to do that."

"So long as you buy nothing it's legal for you to enter,"

Abigail said. "It's odd, wouldn't you say? You can own a dispensary, but not partake until you're twenty-one. It's ass backwards." She caught her slip and covered her mouth. "Sorry."

"Don't worry," Roger said with a chuckle. "We're not sticklers for manners. We're known to curse too, believe it or not."

Jackie's voice wafted down from the second floor. "Damn it! How many times have I told you to put your shit in the laundry basket, girl?"

"Sorry about that." Bernard scratched his reddening cheek. "Our housemates are an unruly lot. Ignore them the best you can."

"Bite me!" Molly fired back.

"Are they your girlfriends?" Abigail asked.

"Huh? No. They're family – kind of," Bernard said.

"Kind of?"

"A story for later," Roger said quickly. "Excuse their lack of manners. We arranged for this room to be empty, but we can't control their outbursts. You know how family is."

"Only too well," Abigail said. "My brother is the same way, along with his friends. Well, whenever he's home anyway."

"I have a question," Roger said, shifting his position. "Do you mind?"

"Not at all."

"I assume you grow the product yourself. Robert said you were skilled at horticulture. He said you were the best he'd seen. I'm not familiar with the business model, sorry to say."

"It's fine. I expected you'd have questions. Yes, I grow my produce. I own a plot of land outside the city limits with a greenhouse built on it. I currently grow over twenty different strains, ranging from pure indica to hybrids, all the way to pure sativa. The pH balance of the soil is imperative in getting results."

"Half of that flew over my head, but I appreciate that you're knowledgeable. Would you be open to us donating supply if we had it? One of our cousins wishes to grow her own stash here. We'd love to learn and contribute to the shop. If you don't have time though, it's perfectly alright."

"I don't mind," she said. "We can always use more. Even if it's mediocre, we can use it to make edibles. The top shelf flower is the one everyone wants, but no one cares if the cannabis was amateur grown or not in edibles, since the magic's in the butter making. Any grade will work. Still, I'd love to teach you how to grow better. It's a fascinating process."

"Really?" Bernard asked.

"Of course," Abigail said. "Teaching another my passion would never be a burden. I can't guarantee how much time I'll have until after the business is open, but I'm happy to share."

"Thank you," Bernard said. "She'll be happy to hear that."

"Plus, if it helps with the bottom line, we'll all be ecstatic," Robert said. "It's a win-win. Is there anything else before we leave you, gentlemen?"

"Know you're always welcome here," Bernard said. "We'd love to have you over for dinner and build a friendship. Nothing says we can't be friends and partners."

"I'd like that," Abigail said. "I haven't had time to hang anymore. It's been all business for the past year. Time to relax sounds nice. I'll be careful not to abuse that privilege though. We'll make tons of money. You watch."

"I know," Roger said. "You're a driven young woman. That passion burns bright, I can tell from here."

"Maybe I'll tell you another time," she said. "We should get out of your hair. We've taken enough of your valuable time. You have a perfect plot of land for growing."

"That was her thoughts exactly," Bernard said.

Molly descended the nearby stairs in the adjoining room and glanced in. "Oh, are you the weed lady?"

"Molly," Bernard said. "Be respectful. She's our partner in our newest business venture. Show her respect."

"You can call me the weed lady if you like," Abigail said. "I don't mind. It's a healing plant. I don't mind being associated with it. Are you the cousin that wanted to grow your own outside?"

"Cousin? Yeah, I am." Molly entered the room and leaned against the couch Abigail was sitting on. "Sorry about earlier." She pointed over her shoulder. "My roommate is on edge. What else is new?" She reached out a hand. "I'm Molly Turner."

"It's a pleasure, Molly." Abigail took her hand and shook it. "I look forward to teaching you all how to better grow our favorite plant together."

"For real?"

"She said yes," Bernard said. "You're sure it's not an inconvenience?"

"Nonsense," Abigail said. "I'd be thrilled."

"We should get out of your hair tonight." Robert ambled over to the women and donned his coat.

Bernard and Roger shook hands with both Robert and Abigail one final time. They showed them to the door along with Molly and said their farewells before closing it.

"She was nice," Molly said. "I can't believe you two asked if she'd help teach us."

"We did it for you," Bernard said. "You're welcome."

"Thanks. You are sure I'm the reason? She was hot."

"Are you calling us liars?"

Molly's smug smile accompanied her instant response. "I'm calling you teenage boys."

"Don't tell me you're jealous?" Jackie's voice was nearer now.

They turned to see her standing on the stairs with a smug grin. "I'm sure they'll still chase after you, don't worry. At least one will anyway."

"As if." Molly rolled her eyes and pushed past Jackie and headed upstairs.

Jackie waited until she was gone and whispered to the group. "She's jealous."

5

"Mr. Powell, we've received word."

Clyde Powell stood overlooking his operation. He wore a formal suit and scratched his chin while he observed his workers. Men and women bustled below, working efficiently. They stacked crates on both sides of the warehouse. Workers below loaded each crate up nearly to the top before placing a removable tray inside each one containing a few rows of tea, to disguise the shipment from prying eyes. The workers labeled each side of the crate as Powell Incorporated Tea. He didn't bother looking at the man talking at his side. "Word of what, exactly?"

"Senile Hudson is back in the game."

"Don't be ridiculous. I ended that fool's career in arms trading decades back. He only sells to friends and family now."

"Precisely, sir," the man said. "Word on the street is he's friends with the Morris Syndicate now. He's selling guns to them wholesale. We found their address. Shall we send a welcome party?"

"No kill squad yet. Keep a close watch on the property. If one of them leaves, I want to know where they go. If Hudson's selling to them, they have blackmail material on him too. We can't act in haste, lest we give away our hand."

"You don't think he's more scared of them than us, do you?"

"The Russian mafia just suffered a humiliating defeat at their hands," Clyde said. He gripped the smooth metal handrail hard. "Now they're expanding their territory and business. It's a gutsy, high risk/high reward move. I'd respect it if it weren't in our backyards. Who's their local leader?"

"Two eighteen-year-old men. A Mr. Roger Morris and Mr. Bernard Morris."

"The boss's kids." Clyde pushed off the rails. "Why them? Does she not value our city enough for genuine talent? She doesn't think we're a threat? Is that it? Whatever the reason, we will not tolerate this incursion. Am I understood?"

"Sir, there's more."

"What else? Hurry, I'm losing my patience."

"Mr. Bailey sent a message. He wishes to speak to you."

"What else could go wrong?" Clyde turned and entered the nearby door. His office was lavish compared to the warehouse floor he overlooked earlier. It contained a work desk, a laptop, framed movie posters on the wall, and a coffee machine on a nearby table. An extravagant seat awaited his return, along with his massive desk. He sat behind the desk and grabbed the landline nearby. He dialed a familiar number and waited while staring at a family photo placed on the desk.

An elderly voice greeted him. "Mr. Powell?"

"Yes. Mr. Bailey? I heard you wished to talk?"

"Are you aware of the Morris envoy sent here?" Mr. Bailey asked.

"It's come to my attention, yes. The old man Hudson is selling them inventory. This is not acceptable. What about your business? Why concern yourself?"

"They're helping Abigail Gomez to open the dispensary that she's been on a crusade to open for the past year. I'd paid off the proper person, but I've been told they paid more. A banker associated with Mrs. Morris paid him off. Twenty-five thousand to push through the final paperwork and receive approval."

"It seems we share a mutual problem," Clyde said. "Shall we coordinate in pushing them out? They're weak from their recent war with the Russians. Now's the time to strike. It's their children leading, not Rachel Morris herself. They know nothing of the world in which they willingly stepped into. We should show them how business works."

"They need to learn how professionals conduct their businesses," Mr. Bailey said. "I agree. We'll be in touch. Happy hunting, Mr. Powell."

"Happy hunting, Mr. Bailey." Clyde hung up. "Problems are never in short supply." He saw his employee standing outside the window facing the warehouse's interior. He beckoned him inside. "We have an ally in our fight."

"It's official then? We're going to war with the Morris Syndicate?"

"This branch of it, yes," Clyde said. "She doesn't have enough resources to send more bodies and weapons. She's licking her wounds up north. The boys are without protection. They won't live long enough to learn their mistake."

"What's our move?"

"I want you to pay a visit to Mr. Hudson next week. Not now. We're waiting on Mr. Bailey. We're going to coordinate our strikes for a rapid-fire effect. They'll get a two-pronged war. I'm betting they'll fold and run home to mama."

"She could send reinforcements, sir. We can't fight the whole Syndicate if push comes to shove."

"What do you know?" Clyde snarled. "With our combined might, Mr. Bailey and I will crush them."

6

A WEEK LATER...

Abigail stood in the tiled bathroom in the back of the dispensary. She had on pajamas and hung her head into the sink. Her hands kneaded the shampoo into her hair and rinsed it out using the running water. She stopped in her tracks when she heard glass shattering nearby. She didn't delay in leaving the bathroom and grabbed a baseball bat beside the door leading to the storefront. Shaking, she opened it and called out. "Whoever's there, leave now. I'm not afraid to use this."

No one answered her except for the screeches of the wind outside, now infiltrating the store. She saw the cause when she stepped inside.

The front window was shattered by the brick now laying inside. It had a paper tied to it, complete with writing. She looked down at her house shoes wearing feet and stepped forward. The crunch of glass underneath accompanied every step. "I'm not joking!" Fear tinged her voice. "This isn't funny."

Abigail gripped the handle of the baseball bat until her knuckles turned white. She bit her lip and walked through the whole storefront, which was only one room. She inspected every aisle and cabinet until she was sure she was alone.

Rubbing her shoulders, she felt the chill of the night air blowing inside. "This will be a bitch to clean." She stopped and picked the brick up before untying the knot. She pulled the paper free, unfolded it, and read aloud.

The note's writing was messy, but legible. "Close the dispensary. You've been warned. Further defiance will result in forfeiture of your life and your family's. It'd be a shame if something happened to your terminal brother. Do not make us involve him. He's going through enough without his sister adding troubles."

Tears welled up as she tossed the brick through the shattered window out into the street. An unfamiliar car roared to life and burned rubber. Smoke came along with the squealing of tires before it faded into the night. "Shit." She ran back behind the glass counter and entered her home area in the back. She locked the door behind her for safety's sake. "They said to call if there're problems. This qualifies." She grabbed her phone sitting on a nearby table and dialed.

Bernard's groggy voice answered. "Who is this?"

"Abigail Gomez."

His voice audibly perked up. "Ms. Gomez, my apologies. What's wrong? You sound out of breath."

"Someone threw a brick through the shop's window along with a note. You said you'd protect the store."

"Okay, keep calm. We'll be there soon and have that window fixed by tomorrow morning. What time is the grand opening?"

"Noon."

"We will finish it before then. Try to relax. We're bringing security in case they come back. Is that alright?"

"Please do, Mr. Morris."

"You can call me Bernard. Now take a deep breath and exhale slowly."

She did as he said and inhaled before slowly exhaling. "I think I know who did this."

"I suspect I do as well. We'll talk more when we arrive. After I get the security set up, you can head home and sleep."

"I sleep in the back, but that's appreciated. Just hurry, please."

"See you soon. Watch your feet. You don't want glass in your feet."

"Noted. Bye."

The call ended. She felt a chill run up her spine and looked over her shoulder. She made sure she had locked the door leading to the storefront and tried to calm down. "What did he mean by security?" She sat down on the only seat available, the lone couch in front of a mounted thirty-two-inch flatscreen on the wall. A small table sat beside the sofa and a digital clock on it read eleven p.m.

"Damn you, Bailey. I hope Reggie was right about these boys. Bailey won't stop here. I guess I'm staying awake..."

Next morning...

Abigail stepped out into the store front area to see the window already replaced.

Kyle stopped in his tracks, holding a broom, when he saw Abigail enter the main room. "Hello, ma'am. I'm Kyle Evans, Mr. Morris sent me. Please watch your step. I'm double checking for additional glass. We can't have beloved customers stepping on any."

"Thank you, Mr. Evans. You've been a tremendous help."

Outside she saw a large van, presumably the window repair vehicle judging by the artwork and text. Bernard and Roger were talking to the repairmen. Roger slipped their leader some cash and shook hands. Bernard looked over and saw her. He waved as she unlocked the door. She popped it open and ushered them inside. "That was early."

Kyle slipped past the pair, heading outside to finish cleaning.

"We got them to expedite the repair with our signature charm," Bernard said, patting his pants pocket, signaling they'd bribed the business. "Now, Ms. Gomez, we'll take care of this. Don't let Bailey and his thugs scare you off, alright? The ugly side of business is our specialty."

"Are you sure? He's dangerous."

"We're capable," Bernard said. "He wouldn't be the first big shot we've tangled with. He won't be the last. Focus on getting the place ready for opening." He inspected the glass cases containing jars of green lumps of buds. "Lucky for us, they didn't hit the cases."

"What do we do?" she asked. "Your men can't stay here forever. What if next time they come inside?"

"We're going to meet Mr. Bailey and sort this out like men. Don't worry your pretty little head," Bernard said.

"I don't think that's a good idea. He's notorious in the underworld around here for no mercy. You can't deal on a street corner without his authorization. I'm lucky it was just a brick."

"We can handle ourselves," Roger said. He pulled his suit coat back to reveal the firearm in its holster. "You know where he's holed up? Info's scarce. I assume he went to great lengths to hide it."

"No address, but I have a number you could use. He called me and gave me terms on opening months ago. It was ridiculous. He wanted eighty percent of the profits and for me to buy my weed from him. I'd have gone bankrupt if I had accepted, which he wanted."

"We know the type," Bernard said. "On the positive side, Evans got the glass shards cleaned I see."

"He's a Godsend," Abigail said. "He's hardworking, strong, and doesn't complain. If he wasn't your employee already, I'd try to hire him myself."

"Sounds like him," Roger said. "He's famous in our circle. That's why we sent him."

"Famous? For what?"

"For what he's accomplished," Bernard said. "We can't tell you specifics, but you're safe with him here. They won't attack during the day, so we'll take him for business today. He'll be back tonight and every night until we solve this. Alright? Can we install an alarm system here soon? You have any ideas?"

"If you can pay for it, yeah."

"Schedule it," Bernard said. "We'll pay. I don't know if it'd dissuade Powell's men, but it'd give you warning and call the police automatically."

"It was a cost I thought I could cut," Abigail said. She scratched her reddening cheek. "Stupid looking back, huh?"

"Stupid? No." Bernard rubbed his chin. "You were saving cash to achieve your dream. Nothing wrong with a woman who knows how to manage money."

"I neglected to set up a security system despite knowing I would be targeted. You're not angry?"

"Angry with you? No. We're not quick to anger. Especially when it's a woman chasing her dream and striving for it with as much passion as you," Bernard said with a wink. "Forgive me, I shouldn't have said that. I didn't mean to make you uncomfortable. We'll fix this. You have our word."

"Besides, Molly'd never forgive us if we didn't." Roger leaned against the brick interior of the building. "She likes you, and we'd never hear the end of it." He chuckled. "She's looking forward to our gardening sessions."

"Never mind him," Bernard said. "This Mr. Bailey will answer to us for this brazen attack. You're under our protection, and we take these matters seriously."

"That makes me feel better, but I'm still nervous."

"I don't blame you," Roger said. "A brick through a window with that creepy ass note would rattle anybody."

"It takes a brave person to stand up in the face of aggression. Never forget that. I don't know your reasons, but hold them close to your heart and never forget them."

Kyle passed by the window and looked to see his bosses inside. He opened it and greeted them. "Still no sign of anybody, sirs," he said. "I don't think they're coming back today, but I'll keep looking."

"Stay here until twelve thirty, Evans," Bernard said. "We need you home for work, and then I want you back here at closing time. What time is that?"

"Eight p.m.," Abigail said.

"I don't guess I could get a nap?" Kyle asked. "I was up all night, sirs."

"Work today," Bernard said. "We'll send someone else to replace you tonight. Is that alright?"

"Yes, sir. That's fine." He looked at Abigail. "I don't guess you have coffee here, ma'am?"

"I'll get it for you. How do you take it?"

"Black is fine, ma'am."

"Be back." Abigail disappeared through the rear door, leaving the three men out front.

"Who are we sending to replace him?" Roger asked. "Jackie? Chris?"

"Chris is busy with his recruits," Bernard said. "Jackie's packing our deliveries for today. She'll be exhausted. I see only one option for now."

"You don't mean one of us?" Roger asked.

"Me, specifically." Bernard poked himself in his chest. "With Crystal here, she needs you at home."

"If we're heading into war, we need you at base." Roger spoke in a hushed voice. "You're not serious? Why not use the recruits Chris is using as a test? We could gauge their endurance. Station Chris inside as a last line of defense. It'd give him some rest and double as a test. More bodies would send a greater message too."

"Good idea, but it interferes with one thing."

"What's that?" Roger asked.

"She's cute." Kyle said. "You like her, boss?"

Bernard slapped Kyle on the shoulder hard. "In so many words."

"Don't think with your dick," Roger said. He glanced at the door she'd entered through. "Delegating is what we need. We should send Chris and the boys to guard it tonight."

"Agreed," Kyle said.

"Butt out, Evans," Bernard said. "Still, you're probably right."

"It's settled." Roger pulled out a phone and called Molly. "Molly, I have new orders."

"Hey, boss," the tech wizard said. "Who and what?"

"Chris and his recruits. Send them to the dispensary tonight for security detail. Old man Chris can rest inside while his recruits do whatever he deems necessary. Tell him to be respectful. We don't want our goodwill ruined by his shameless flirting. Make that clear, would you?"

"I'll relay the message. Is that all?"

"Everything going alright over there?"

"Jackie's pitching a fit since she's the only one packing. Besides that, Crystal and I are having a blast."

"You aren't just playing video games and smoking, are you?"

"I answered the phone, didn't I? I'm prioritizing work first. I'll get it done right after this."

"You'd better."

"Have a little faith, boss."

"I have faith in you, but my sister's sense of duty? Not so much. Prove my trust correct, Ms. Turner. That is all. Good-bye." He hung up in time for Abigail's return with a mug of steaming coffee.

She handed it over to Kyle. "Here you are, Mr. Evans. Hope you enjoy."

"Thank you, Ms. Gomez." Kyle accepted the drink and took a sip.

"Enjoy it, and then get back to work, Mr. Evans," Bernard said. "After work today you can sleep in tomorrow. You're a vital cog. Don't forget it."

"Yes, sir."

"I wrote the number for Mr. Bailey while I was back there waiting for the coffee." She dug a piece of paper out of her jeans and gave it to Bernard. "Here."

Bernard took the parchment and unfolded it. "Thank you. With this, we'll take our leave. We'll talk to him and get this sorted. We decided to send more manpower over tonight. You'll have at least five men guarding the place."

"That's a relief."

"They're good men, led by a veteran I trust with my life," Roger said. "Just ignore him if he's annoying. He's a great fighter, but he never knows when to quit. Apologies if he offends you."

Bernard crossed his arms. "The old goat never knows when to shut up."

"I'm used to the type." Abigail waved off their concern. "I'm more worried about Bailey's men."

"Chris is a combat veteran. You'll be safe. Now we need to go," Bernard said. "Business waits for no man. You know how it is."

"I appreciate the support, gentlemen. Most would just pay lip service and then do nothing. You footed the window repair bill and sent manpower. I can't thank you enough."

"Don't thank us yet." Bernard walked with Roger to the door and spoke over his shoulder. "It's not over."

7

"How many of these are there?" Kyle loaded another heavy package into the back of the van.

"We've received orders for over twenty packages," Jackie said, hefting another inside.

"Unbelievable. In a day?"

"A night, to be precise," Jackie said. "Molly set it up last night. It's no wonder with gun control being expanded. Folks want to defend themselves."

"We're just regular freedom fighters." Kyle's sarcasm was obvious. "Why do we have to drive eighty miles to ship them? There are drop off boxes here."

"If the postal service tracks it, we don't want them getting near us, simpleton." Jackie and Kyle loaded the last of the packages. "If we drive to different towns miles away, it's harder for them to track us. Make sense yet?"

"Perfect," Kyle said. "Maybe you should teach Crystal while she's here."

"Don't be a smart ass."

"I wasn't."

"Oh, sorry. I'm used to Chris and the boys." Jackie

climbed into the passenger seat up front while Kyle got into the driver's seat. "They love pushing buttons."

"You got that right." Kyle started the engine and pulled out onto the road. "I like them, but they're stubborn and juvenile."

"What's your story, Evans?" Jackie asked. "We never spoke much. I don't think I've ever seen you socialize much."

"Would it shock you if I told you I'm shy?" He adjusted the mirror hanging above for a better view.

Jackie couldn't hold back a genuine laugh. "Sorry, that's rare in this line of work. You're serious?"

"Yes. I don't mind socializing, but I just don't initiate. I joined the Syndicate for what some would call an idiotic reason. Money wasn't a problem. I didn't need it for a sick relative or anything practical before you think I'm smart."

"Why then?" Jackie asked.

Kyle gave a sidelong glance before answering. "I was in the marines."

"Really? I should've figured with your skill with a weapon."

"They dishonorably discharged me for smuggling opium back home from Afghanistan. I'm lucky to be a free man, but some important people downplayed it."

"They were in on it."

"Bingo," Kyle said. "It was a sweet gig, if I'm honest. There was plenty of cash, and it was easy. What they didn't tell me was that brass would confiscate all my earnings. I didn't want to be homeless. A guy I knew introduced me, and I did some research on the old Morris family. I wasn't aware his daughter was in charge when I joined, but it didn't matter. She's a forceful leader."

"You wanted to serve under Daniel Morris?"

"Who wouldn't? The man's famous or infamous

depending on your point of view. I wanted to meet him at least once. Now I'm serving under his nephew and grand-child, and that's good enough for me."

"You also saved his son-in-law. Don't forget that."

Kyle blushed and kept his focus on the road. "That was luck is all."

"You're too modest. We'll break you of that soon enough. How old are you anyway?"

"Aren't you curious?" Kyle asked. Despite his embarrass-ment, he had a smile on. "I'm twenty-five. You?"

"Haven't you ever learned not to ask a lady that?"

"Forgive me. You just look like you're as young as me is all."

"You have a silver tongue when you decide to use it, don't you?" Jackie asked. "I wish I was your age, young man. Let's leave it at that."

"You could have fooled me. You take care of yourself obviously."

"It's a must in this life."

"I'd have guessed twenty-seven at the oldest, if I'm honest."

"Thirty-six," Jackie said. "I joined when I was eighteen."

"What about you?" Kyle asked. "Why'd you join?"

"Me? Money, why else? I'd love to say I had some elabo-rate reason, but it's only cash. Chris recruited me. Talk about a night on the town gone bad."

"I see."

"I'm not proud of that night, but we live with our decisions."

"You mean? Oh, okay then."

"Leave it at that. You don't want the answer to that question."

Two hours later...

"You see that?" Kyle asked. He climbed inside the van after dropping off another package. "Check out the white car behind us."

"They've been following us," Jackie said. She looked into the rear-view mirror to her right.

"You think they're Bailey or Powell's men?" Kyle asked, getting the van moving again. "Are this van's windows reinforced?"

"Yes, why?"

"Just wondering. I think they're going to make their move soon. I'm taking us out in the country. No witnesses there, nor do I want one getting winged in a crossfire."

"Good thinking." Jackie pulled out her piece and made sure it was ready for action. "Less attention's always smart. How did they find us though?"

"No clue." Kyle cruised out of the small village in a hurry.

"I knew it'd come to this. I just didn't expect it so soon."

"Men with power grab hold and grip tight. That applies to arms and drug dealers in Nashville, the same as anywhere else. We're a threat, and they know it." They were out of the town now, albeit barely. Kyle surveyed their surroundings. "We'll look for a deserted stretch of land and deal with these guys. If they won't make the first move, we will."

"Damned right," Jackie said. "It's a compact car. I only see two."

"Even odds are in our favor. When I stop, we get out and find cover. They'll think we're stashing the goods and come to ambush us."

"Walking right into one themselves," Jackie said. "Smart thinking, Evans. We'll need to dispose of them afterward."

"Don't want law enforcement getting suspicious. We have gasoline and I have matches."

"We're not here to ignite a forest fire."

"You'd rather leave the bodies rotting? We don't have shovels here. We could use their car to contain it."

"Bad idea, but better than nothing."

Kyle pulled off the main road onto a dirt path and sped up once on it. "This isn't a campground or near one. There shouldn't be people here. When we stop, we take cover along this path. We shoot them before they even get out of the car. I don't want a firefight. I want a rolling execution."

"Agreed," Jackie said.

He pulled to the side, off the path and onto some grass. "Let's go."

Both leaped out and hiked through the tree line. Jackie struggled to keep up with Kyle, but managed. She saw him stop behind a nearby tree, so she did the same. The sound of an engine grew louder. Tires rolled over gravel and the sound of birds nearby blended with the scent of nature around them.

"Ten seconds," Kyle said.

"On my mark," Jackie said. She gripped the weapon tightly.

The pair waited, listening to the rumble of the engine slowly approaching along the dirt path.

"Now."

Both sidestepped out of cover and started blasting. The gunshots frightened a flock of birds that flew away from the danger lightning quick.

Their pursuer's driver was hit and fell forward, his head landing on the steering wheel. Their horn blared through the otherwise serene surroundings as the vehicle sped up. The passenger bailed out, throwing the door open and diving out.

The pair emerged from their hiding spot after they passed and shot the man scrambling to his feet. He succeeded momentarily, but fell soon after a last shot.

The car continued unabated, however. It gained speed and slammed into a tree past their vehicle.

They ran toward the man lying on the ground. Once they got close, they could hear groans and saw he was writhing on the ground in pain.

Jackie quickly reloaded and fired one more shot, putting him to rest. She turned to Kyle. "Let's drag his ass over to the car then, Smokey."

"Smokey?" Kyle asked, grabbing his arms.

"This is a forest fire waiting to happen."

They dragged the carcass to the burning car and stuffed him inside.

"Smell that?" Kyle sniffed. "It's gas. Move back." He and Jackie stepped back as he pulled out a box of matches. Striking one, he tossed it into the cabin. It quickly spread to the dead men's clothing and engulfed them.

"Let's split and finish the deliveries," Jackie said. "We can't be here when someone notices."

"I'm with you," Kyle said, following her. He absentmindedly reloaded his weapon as they walked and got back to work...

That evening...

"The deliveries go alright?" Crystal asked.

"Define alright," Jackie said. "We completed them, if that's what you're asking, but it wasn't clean."

"Elaborate," Bernard said. "What happened?"

"We were followed. My guess is they were with Bailey or Powell. It's thanks to Kyle it wasn't worse. He led them on a goose chase into the country, where we ambushed them. They were well armed and weren't on a peace mission, if you catch my drift."

"It's probably Powell's men." Bernard said.

"If they followed you, it means they're watching the place," Roger said. "They've done their homework. How about we turn the tables?"

"Hold your horses, boys," Jackie said. "I'm not finished. They're dead, but I saw the fire we started on tv earlier."

"That forest fire was you?" Molly asked, clearly surprised.

"Disposing of bodies is paramount we figured," Jackie said. "It was that or dig a grave barehanded. We still had guns to ship, so we were in a hurry. So, we used their car as an oven. We lit it on fire and had them inside."

"Quick thinking," Bernard said, pointing at Jackie. "Bailey attacked our dispensary. Now Powell is going after our guns trade."

"We don't know that." Roger leaned back in his chair. "It could have been Bailey taking more shots."

"It's street logic. Arms dealers kill competition or work it out. He's chosen kill, but let's try to be courteous and ask him."

"We only know Bailey's number."

"Odds are they're in cahoots," Bernard said. "Think about it. A partnership would benefit both parties. They can pool their money and use their clout to help the other. One controls the guns, the other, drugs. It's a perfect scheme while remaining autonomous."

"You'll love my idea," Roger said. "We need loyalty tests.

We're at war. Time to delegate the less desirable jobs to the new talent. We get to guard Ms. Gomez tonight ourselves. Molly, come with us. We'll need sleep shifts and electronic surveillance."

"Going to leave me here by myself?" Crystal asked her brother from the couch.

Roger spared Crystal a glance. "Mom would kill me if you came along too."

"You need two competent computer techs if we follow sleep schedules. I volunteer my services."

"You were right. I like your idea." Bernard snapped his fingers. "Brilliant. We follow suit as Powell and Bailey did. Send the grunts."

"Job tonight?" Jackie asked. "I'm ready for payback after today."

"Where is Kyle anyway?" Crystal asked. "He's been absent since you returned."

"Asleep probably," Jackie said. "We ran the kid ragged. He's full of youth, so he'll recover, but keep that in mind. Not all your personnel have such energy reserves."

"Noted. We need a location. Suggestions?" Bernard asked.

"Local area's message boards are a bust," Molly said. "People know of him, but no location. You said you have a phone number. Can I see it?"

"Here."

"Let's see what we find." Molly took the paper and ran upstairs. A door closed and then silence. Loud cursing followed. "Damn it!"

"So professional." Jackie shook her head. "It's probably a cell number. I doubt she'll get anything off it."

"No harm in trying," Bernard said. "What do you suggest?"

"Damn! I wish we'd let one live long enough to question." Jackie bit her lip. "We killed before we had a chance."

"Better to be cautious. You're not to blame."

"I got it!" Molly ran down the stairs with a notepad in her hand.

"What'd you find?" Roger asked.

"A location, funny enough. Turns out it's a landline. They're old school like Mrs. Morris, which made tracking easier."

"Harder to bug a landline," Jackie said. "Physical presence is needed."

"It's also possible to track if you know how," Molly said. "We have a location. Might be a base or storehouse. No way to know. Will this help?" She handed the notepad over to Roger.

He showed it to Bernard. "Where is this?"

Bernard leaned toward Roger and studied the address. "It's outside of the city."

Molly further explained her find. "The property is enormous. It has its own greenhouse and other buildings, according to the online map. I'm guessing it's a processing center for preparing shipments. They might grow grass, but his empire's not built on weed alone. There's no way it'd earn enough. He's into meth, heroin, crack, cocaine, along with God knows what else. I made a copy for safety."

"We have an address," Roger said. He handed the paper to Jackie.

"What's the mission then, bosses?" Jackie asked. "Are we torching the place?"

"It's a little early to go scorched earth," Bernard said. "We need more information. You know what that means."

"Old school questioning?" Jackie asked.

"You're damned right."

"Speaking of old school," Roger said, looking at his sister. "Mom's going to be pissed when I call tonight. She wants you back in Ohio." His phone rang as if on cue. "Hello?"

"Where is she?" Rachel's calm sounding voice asked.

"Mother, nice to hear from you again." He wiped his brow.

"Cut the bull. You said you'd talk to her. Now give her the phone. It's my turn since you apparently failed."

"Not quite true. We're busy with business today. We got hit by rival groups."

"All the more reason to send her ass back home. Hand her the phone now. That's an order."

"Yes, ma'am." Roger walked over to Crystal and handed her the phone. "She wants to talk to you personally." He mouthed the next words. "She's pissed."

Crystal took the phone and noticed everyone watching her with amused faces. "Mom?"

"Young lady, tomorrow morning you'd better get in that new car and drive back here. Your brother needs space right now. It sounds like he's heading into a war, and I don't want you there. He's not experienced enough to keep you safe. Do I make myself clear?"

"Crystal clear. There's just one problem."

"No, there's not. There's an excuse, and I don't want to hear it."

"They're following cars from this property and attacking them, as evidenced by today. You want me to risk it or stay here and be safe?"

"Quick thinking," Jackie mumbled.

"I'll send an envoy to escort you back. Is that all?"

"You send an envoy, and you make Mr. Powell and Bailey think we have more numbers down here. Then you're involved in this war. They'd take it out on Roger here. Where if you don't, they could underestimate him and give him the advantage."

"You have an answer to everything, huh? I'm not going to say just stay there the entire war. You realize that. You're playing for time, it's obvious."

"Send reinforcements down here, and I'll leave."

"This is not a negotiation," Rachel said, clearly angry now, judging by her elevated tone.

"You want something, like I do. Seems like one to me." Crystal wore an amused expression.

"I forgot how infuriating eighteen-year-olds are - how is beyond me. I dealt with this shit weeks ago." She paused for a solid minute. "Put your brother back on the line."

Crystal handed it back to Roger.

"Yeah?"

"She gave you the same attitude?"

"Yes," Roger said. "She's adamant. Want me to force the issue?"

Crystal glared at him for even suggesting it.

"No," Rachel sighed over the call. "She'd just sneak out again. She'd be alone out there. At least with you, she's relatively safe, even if you're going into a war. Who were the names you're beefing with?"

"Mr. Powell and Mr. Bailey."

"I know of Powell. Bailey's a wild card." Rachel cleared her throat. "Powell's ruthless, but his operation is small potatoes in the grand scheme. He doesn't have tons of manpower, but he's armed and dangerous. How's personnel recruiting going?"

"Mr. Bristol has at least seven ready to initiate. We're sending recruits out on a mission tonight now that we have a location. Bailey's hit our cover business, so we're juggling a lot of plates."

"I know the feeling too well, Son. That's what I warned you about. You're in the ringer. Push on. I have faith in you. I'm sending some manpower. It's all I can afford, about five people, but they're good, solid personnel. You don't have objections?"

"Not at all." Roger gave everyone a silent thumbs up. "We also made our first sales today, which was hit as well."

"Yeah, sounds like Powell. Any casualties?"

"None, Evans and Jackie got through unscathed, thankfully."

"Just those two? You didn't send more?"

"It's a unique sales system we've worked out. They had authority on how many they needed, and they chose two for subtlety's sake."

"Understood."

"Anything else?"

"No, get planning and win this war," Rachel said. "Powell and Bailey should be an adequate challenge of your abilities. Don't let me down, and stay safe."

"You too, Mom. Love you." He let her reciprocate and hung up to find everyone waiting with bated breath. "We're getting reinforcements - only five bodies, but they should arrive tomorrow."

"Extra guns are always welcome," Jackie said.

"Seriously?" Crystal asked. "So, she expects me home soon then?"

"She said nothing after she informed me. I expected she would after your negotiation, but no."

"I'm free and clear?"

"Not quite," Roger said. "Maybe until the war's over. I

think she was worried about them following people leaving this place."

"At least I can help win the war then," Crystal said. "I even brought my best drone and attachments, just in case."

"Ooh, can I see it?" Molly asked.

"You may even operate it under my supervision."

"Jackie, I want you and Chris to take recruits to this location and kidnap one of their men," Bernard said.

"Preferably someone who'd know something," Roger added. "If not, grunts hear things. This is an intel gathering operation, not a massacre. Understood? We'll hit hard and fast after we know our enemy. No sense rushing it when we're in the proverbial and literal dark."

"I agree," Jackie said. "I assume we'll all head out together then?"

Bernard nodded. "It'd be safest. We'll replace Chris and the boys at Abigail's dispensary, and you two can head out."

"Come to our room quick," Molly said. "I've got the map upstairs that you'll want to formulate a plan."

"Right." Jackie followed Molly up the stairs.

"With us, Molly, and Crystal, we'll be fine securing the dispensary," Bernard said. "I doubt they'll do it two nights running."

"You never know, but we'll soon see..."

At the dispensary soon after...

"Mr. Morris?" Chris asked, seeing his bosses arriving from out the business's front window, along with Molly and Crystal. "Girls? What's going on?"

"Mr. Bristol," Bernard said as the pair entered the building. "We've had a change of plans. We've found some targets for you."

"On the hunt again. I was wondering when it'd come."

"Take two of your best candidates and secure their allegiance. It's not a kill mission, but it'll stick them to us. If lethal force is required to escape, you're cleared; but no frivolous bloodshed. Am I clear?"

"Crystal, sir. I know just the two prospects." He grabbed the device on his belt and spoke into it with the press of a button. "Mr. King and Mr. Lionel, report inside at once. Everyone else, stay here and secure the outside with the same schedule."

"Two candidates for two veterans," Bernard said. "That will work. I pray they're as good as you think."

"What's the skinny?" Chris asked.

"Kidnapping mission. I'll let Jackie fill you in further. She's in your car outside, waiting."

"Yes, sir." He saluted the two young men. "Anything further before I start the mission?"

"Be careful, old man," Roger said. "These bastards attacked Jackie and Kyle earlier. We don't want another incident."

"I will. That goes for you two as well. Take this." Chris handed the boys the communication device. "Keep them working hard for me."

The nearby front door opened. Lyle and Wallace stepped through.

"Good. Follow me," Chris said, pushing past them. "We have a job tonight. Don't disappoint the bosses now. It's straight from them."

"Yes, sir!" both men yelled.

Bernard and Roger watched the men hurriedly leave in the car. They walked to the room's interior door and knocked. "Hello? It's Roger and Bernard Morris."

The door opened to reveal Abigail was in pajamas. "Oh,

sorry." She looked down at her clothes. "I wasn't expecting you two here. Oh, who is this?" She looked at Crystal and Molly.

"My sister Crystal," Roger said. "Crystal, meet Abigail Gomez. The other bundle of sunshine is Molly, who you've already met."

"Hello, Ms. Gomez," Crystal said. She shook Abigail's hand.

"What's up?" Molly asked. "We meet again."

"We had a shift change," Bernard said. "Do you mind if we set up shop in your main living area?"

"Sure, I have a small bedroom. It won't bother me. Come in, please."

The group entered the rear of the shop.

"The kitchen's there." She pointed to the fridge and oven on a nearby wall. "Bathroom's there." She pointed to a different door. "Questions?"

"Wi-Fi password?" Molly asked.

"On a note on the fridge. Knock yourself out. The internet package I got is unlimited so go nuts. There's no data plan."

"Wicked," Molly said. "I'll get set up here then." She moved to the lone coffee table by the sofa and placed the laptop down.

"Let's get the sleeping bags moved in before we get ahead of ourselves." Bernard raised the device to his mouth. "Bring in the sleeping bags from the vehicle out front. That's an order."

"You're not Mr. Bristol. Who's this?" a recruit asked.

"Your boss. Now do it, damn you."

"Right away, Mr. Morris." The voice was shaken. "Sorry, sir."

"I don't want apologies. I want results."

"You run a tight ship," Abigail said. "Don't be too hard on them. They're doing a fine job. Ignore me. It's not my business."

"It's fine," Bernard said. "I just don't want to keep you awake any longer."

"Considerate of you. I'm just a weaker boss. When we inevitably hire bud tenders, I'll be a softer boss. It's a weakness of mine. I don't like confrontation."

"Few do. That's not a weakness. It means you're a kind person. Never lose that trait. There are too few already."

"Reporting as ordered, sir," a voice said from behind the door. Bernard opened it to see three men holding two sleeping bags each under their arms.

"Set them down inside here," Bernard said. He stepped to the side and let them pass. "That is all. Resume your patrol. Back to it, boys."

The grunts exited soon after they delivered the payload and shut the door behind them. "Try to ignore us as best you can, Ms. Gomez. We'll try not to make noise out here."

"Thank you. Help yourselves to anything in the fridge. Good night."

"Good night," everyone said to Abigail as she left for her bedroom.

"I got the feeds up and running," Molly said. "If anyone shows up, we're ready."

The nearby landline rang. Abigail quickly opened the door and rushed to answer. "If it's not one thing, it's another. Yes, hello?" She paused, listening to the speaker on the other end. "Uh, yes. Alright." She pointed at Roger and Bernard. She covered one end of the phone. "It's for you."

"Me?" Roger stepped forward and took it. "Who is this?"

"Some call me Mr. Bailey. Did you boys enjoy my

welcoming party last night? Hopefully Ms. Gomez wasn't hurt. It'd be a shame if something happened to her."

Bernard moved toward Molly. "Can you trace this?"

"One moment and I can." Molly got up and ran toward the land line. She placed an index finger over her lips as she fiddled with the phone beside Roger.

"Ms. Gomez is not intimidated by you, and neither are we."

"Then you're a fool, child. We've estimated your combat strength and find you lacking. Lesson number one in this life, kid. Never overestimate your ability. It leads to a premature death. We're giving you one chance to rectify this. Leave Ms. Gomez's failed business venture to its rightful demise and stop buying guns from Mr. Hudson, or this war's on."

"I don't do well with ultimatums, Mr. Bailey. If you were as savvy as you act, you'd know that never works. What are you, an amateur? I should've realized by judging your accolades. What are those anyway, intimidating unarmed innocents?"

"You'll regret those words, boy."

"Have you thought this through?" Roger asked. "War's bad for business for everyone involved. Why not live and let live? Or is this about your pride? Pride's another luxury we can't afford in this life. My mother taught me that at a heavy price. Seems no one did for you. I'll teach you that lesson soon enough, old man."

"Petulant whelp." Bailey's voice became one of fury.

Molly finished after inserting the electronic device. She rushed back to the laptop.

"You know what I think? I believe you're scared of the toll this war will take. You called to learn if the new kids on the block would fold. It'd save you the trouble. It's smart, in a cowardly way, I admit. You want my associate and I gone?

You're going to have to remove us. Make no mistake, we're willing to brawl to the last man. Are you?"

"You intend to keep guards at that dispensary at all times?"

"Why not? You've shown you're not above harming an innocent woman for your own gain. Someone has to stand up with her. The community's tired of your asinine monopoly. They've heard that competition's good and drives down prices. Now I ask once more, would you like to respectfully withdraw from this stupidity? Or are you dead set on this war?"

"Consider this a formal declaration of war, you infantile moron." The line went dead.

"Shit," Molly said. "I couldn't track the location."

Roger turned after ending the call to wide eyes. "Sorry, I was trying to keep him on the line."

"On the contrary. I'm proud," Bernard said. "I take it they finally declared war formally?"

"Correct."

"So it begins..."

8

"Alright, gentlemen," Chris said. "This is your loyalty test tonight." He looked over his shoulder. "Don't disappoint me."

"What are we doing?" Lyle asked. "You just stuffed us in here and gave no explanation. I prefer to know what felonies I'm about to commit."

"Curiosity's not a smart trait to have," Jackie said from the driver's seat. "Curb that to survive longer."

"It's a fair concern," Chris said. "Our job is to secure personnel from Mr. Powell's place of work."

"Kidnapping," Wallace said.

"Correct. You're not joining the boy scouts here. We're the Syndicate. If you thought this day wouldn't come, you're a fool."

"No objections here. So long as my pay increases."

"Your pay issues are noted, Mr. King. How about earning that paycheck before bitching about it? Remember, there is a heavy price for failure."

"What's that mean?" Lyle asked.

"You've passed the point of no return," Chris said. "I

picked you two since you showed promise for tonight. You either complete the mission and I'm satisfied, or you aren't returning home. Savvy?"

"Do it, or we die. Got it," Lyle said.

"You're the smart one, Mr. Lionel, but Wallace is foolhardy, so it evens out."

"You say that like it's a positive," Jackie said.

"It is. Now we're stopping a half mile away from the address to plan this out before we commit. Planning keeps people alive. Improvisation kills. Understand? Jackie is our tactician, so know you're in excellent hands. I trust her with my life, and you will as well. Once we're inside, we protect each other. We're family, so act like it. You'd stop a man from murdering your brother, so protect each other like your blood kin. We all bleed together. We're all we've got."

"Does that make you grandpa or uncle?" Jackie couldn't hide the snicker at the jab.

Chris stifled Lyle and Wallace's laughter by slapping each of them. They went silent at the physical reprimand.

Chris faced forward again. "You will show respect unless you are of similar rank. Is that understood? Jackie's earned that right. You pukes have not. Shape up!"

"Yes, sir!"

"Let's pull over here." Jackie pulled over and shut off the engine. Trees surrounded them, and there were no lights on the country road. "I have a floor plan. You two, pay attention. Your lives depend on your memory." She pulled out the map and handed it over her shoulder. "Lyle, you're marked with an L. Wallace, you're marked with a W. Simple enough, right? When we get there, Lyle goes with me. Wallace, you're with your teacher here."

"We're scouting it out before we make a move," Chris said. "That's why that bag of binoculars is at your feet. Make sure you each take one. We're going to plan out the patrol routes first. After that, we pick out the most vulnerable and secure them. Two to each team ensures both teams can quickly haul the victim here."

"Just a simple extraction?" Wallace asked.

"Nothing simple about it," Jackie said. "Playing by ear is required this time. I'll concoct an extraction plan once we see more."

Chris grabbed the plan and looked for his position. "Wallace, you're with me. Lyle, you're with Jackie. Aim to impress. Your life depends on it, gentlemen. Jackie, where are we leaving this?"

"I figure I'll park here." She pointed to the north of the property. "Just near the road here."

"Got it. Get us in position. If you pray, now's a good time, boys."

Jackie restarted the engine and moved toward the spot she designated.

"I don't believe in superstitions," Wallace said.

Lyle didn't verbally answer. He had his eyes closed, and he mouthed some words as he traced the signs of the cross over his chest.

"Don't tell me you're one of those people," Wallace sneered.

"Mind your fucking business," Lyle said after he finished his prayers.

"Elaborate, Mr. King," Jackie said.

"Believing in a deity in the sky makes us feel better, but realistically we're more likely living in a simulation. With all respect, I have my reasons for not believing."

"There are no atheists in foxholes. You'll believe soon enough." Jackie pulled over and parked. "Make no mistake, we're walking into a potential battlefield. You'll know what I mean once you've got firefights under your belt."

"Thank you, preacher," Chris laughed, but stopped when Jackie punched his knee. "Son of a gun," Chris hissed in pain, covering his knee. "Watch the knees."

"I don't enjoy trashing people's beliefs because your ass doesn't agree is all. Live and let live, except these bastards."

"Amen to that," Chris said, rubbing his still aching knee.

Jackie took out her pistol and checked if it was ready.

"Do we get weapons for this, sir?" Lyle asked. "Bringing my fists to a gunfight doesn't seem smart. From the talk, these people are dangerous."

"You're proficient in their handling?" Chris asked. "You deserve one since you're acting members until you prove otherwise, but killing yourself is not ideal."

"We're American, sir," Lyle said. "I'm familiar with weapons and their intricacies."

"Ditto," Wallace said. "The only reason I'm unarmed is you told us to leave our pieces at home when you found us."

"Fine, you savages." Chris climbed out of the car and went to the trunk.

Jackie popped the trunk and exited along with Lyle and Wallace. "Don't fire unless strictly necessary. You fire, it's because you fear for your life. Our cover is blown, and we're outnumbered once you do."

"We understand," Lyle said.

Chris reached into the trunk and retrieved a weapon for each man. "Take a few magazines each. Best to have them just in case."

Both took a handgun and extra magazines.

Chris slammed the trunk closed. "Wallace, you're with me. We're heading this way." He grabbed Wallace's arm and dragged him away once he'd safely stowed the weapon away. "Hope you enjoy hiking, kid."

"Not really." Wallace stepped over a fallen tree and kept pace. "How can you see in this dark? I nearly took a header there."

"Years of experience," Chris said. He reached up to his ear. "Communication check."

"I'm here," Jackie said. "Give us five minutes and we're good."

"Same here." Chris led Wallace through the dark forest interior at a brisk pace until some light emerged from the trees in front. He slowed down and reached an open palm back toward Wallace.

Wallace followed the unspoken command and slowed his pace. His voice was low. "Is that the place, sir?"

Chris took cover behind a tree and reached into his jacket to retrieve a pair of binoculars. "It is. Get behind a tree, Wallace. That's an order."

Wallace took the command to heart and rushed to hide. He took the optical device they gave him and looked through it toward the buildings. He saw patrols moving around the property one at a time. "Seems simple."

"It means they're either lazy or understaffed," Chris said. "Empires are toppled by slothfulness. Mr. Bailey is going to understand that soon. He's in there - I feel it."

"You fancy yourself a psychic, sir?"

"Molly traced his call here, simpleton. Logic follows he is or was inside. Now focus on the patterns of the different patrols. We don't want one to see us while we make our move." He tapped his ear. "You in position?"

"Just arrived," Jackie said. "Do my eyes deceive me? One patrol per route?"

"It's like Christmas morning." Chris never stopped watching. "How long are we surveying before we move?"

"At least ten minutes," Jackie said. "That should give us a clear image of their patterns. Preferably longer, but it's biting cold out here. I don't want frostbite."

"I don't relish rushing forward," Chris said.

"Fine, fifteen minutes."

"Understood, fifteen minutes. Then we'll finalize the plan and move."

Fifteen minutes later...

Jackie lowered the binoculars. "I have a plan."

"Glad to hear it," Chris said over the call. "Lay it on me."

"A little whelp comes dangerously close to the tree line on my side. He'll return soon. I'm thinking that's our best option."

"Seems to be a pattern with them. A big fucker comes dangerously close over here. You thinking what I am?"

"A two for one?" Jackie asked.

"Think of the fun interrogation techniques we could try with two specimens," Chris said. "Play them off each other, see which turns first to save themselves."

Jackie let the binoculars hang below her neck. "You think you can manage over there, old timer?"

Chris leaned against the tree, still staring at the compound. "I'm young enough to show you a thing or two, pretty lady. Seriously, yes, we can. It's perfect. We can test each man this way. Simple snatch and run?"

"If you call carrying a grown ass man that far without him alerting everyone simple."

"You've got duct tape and zip ties on you, same as me.

Use it to cover their mouth and cuff their hands. The reward here is double the intel, something we desperately need."

"We'll try. Make your move when you deem necessary. I'll do the same. We meet back at the van."

"Good luck out there."

"You too." Jackie turned to Lyle. "It's showtime, kid. Next time that little bastard comes near, we're waiting until he passes and then taking him. You tackle him to the ground, control his arms, and I'll tie him up and cover his mouth. Got it?"

"What if he turns and shoots?"

"Shoot first."

The pair stayed behind the trees, watching and waiting. They weren't waiting long before their target came into view again. Jackie got behind the tree and pointed in their target's direction, making sure Lyle knew.

He nodded, and the pair waited in the shadows. The only sign someone was there was their breath appearing from the cold.

The crunch of grass nearby signaled their prey was close. Lyle watched Jackie closely. He waited for the signal to try this daring act.

Jackie pointed at Lyle and reached into her jacket with her other hand. She nodded.

That was all Lyle needed. He heard the target stomping closer to their position. The sound was only five to ten feet away, so he ran at full speed once he was out of his cover.

"Huh?" their target asked before Lyle slammed into him at full speed. His shoulder dug into the shorter man's stomach and knocked the wind out of him before lifting him off the ground and slamming him to the soil below.

Lyle covered the man's mouth and held his right hand to the ground.

Jackie appeared in a flash beside him and tore off a piece of duct tape. She covered the man's mouth. "Get him up."

Lyle lifted the man up, keeping a firm grip on his arms. Jackie secured his arms behind him with surgical precision. "He's ready."

Lyle hefted the poor victim over his shoulder like a sack of potatoes and turned to the trees.

A shot rang out. Lyle didn't feel pain, but the sound caused a surge of adrenaline. This caused a burst of speed. He found himself back in the relative safety of the forest with a warm, wet sensation on his back, but he paid it no heed.

"Christ," Jackie said behind him. "Get him to the van. We need to tend to that."

"Am I hit?"

"Not quite, big man," Jackie said. "Our prisoner caught that bullet for you. God loved you tonight it seems."

Wallace's voice entered their ears. "It's called luck."

More shots rang out and a nearby tree splintered near Lyle's head. He ducked instinctively and kept moving.

"Keep telling yourself that." She tapped her ear as the pair ran. "Was that you?"

"Not us," Chris yelled over the continued gun shots. "I think they saw you two. We got out clean. They were focused on you."

"Understood. We're on our way back."

"We'll be there."

After a few minutes the pair could hear dogs barking behind them, along with the distant chatter of their pursuers.

"Better hurry," Jackie said.

They emerged out of the tree line. Safety was within

reach; the van was there. Its rear doors were already open with a smiling Chris gesturing inside.

Lyle dumped the bleeding body into the back.

"Get us moving," Jackie said. "We'll patch his ass up on the move. They sicced dogs on us."

"On it." Chris didn't wait to slam the doors shut and hopped into the driver's seat.

Lyle got in, slammed the side door shut, and they were already moving.

Jackie climbed into the back over the seats and inspected their hostages. "This could be bad."

"Is he bleeding out back there?" Chris asked over his shoulder.

"Not quite. I'll use tape. It's all we have, but it should slow the bleeding." She tore off a huge piece of tape and slammed it against the wound, eliciting a groan of pain from the muffled criminal. "It hit him in the shoulder. Too bad for you, your partners aimed center mass, little man."

"Eventful first night, eh?" Chris asked.

"Do you always get shot at?" Wallace asked.

"You want the answer?" Chris asked. "Only on the important missions. Congratulations, boys. You've passed your test. Know that if you try to run, Jackie and I were recording all this."

"Blackmail?" Lyle asked.

"Leverage. It's how organized crime's worked since time immemorial. You're with us for good now. That means you'll draw a paycheck. The bad news is you're on the lowest rung, but good news. I was the lowest rank twenty years ago, now I'm in good with the bosses. There's room for upward mobility in this syndicate. Work hard and show respect."

"Might be difficult for him," Jackie said. "The don't be an ass part, I mean."

"Let's be honest, me too." Chris laughed.

"I can't believe they fucking shot at me without warning," Lyle said. He was staring at the back of the seat in front of him, unblinking.

"That feeling will pass," Chris said. "You're feeling surreal, yes? You get used to it."

"Doesn't seem like something I want to acclimate to," Lyle said.

"You will. The good news is, even if they'd missed and hit your other side, you'd have been fine. You'd have had a bruise, but you have your vest on, yes? I told you to equip it before we left."

"Yes, sir," he numbly said.

"You should try to relax. Sitting there questioning your life choices is a moot point now. Best to make your peace. You're one of our brothers now."

"Why shoot first?" Lyle asked. "You'd think they'd be afraid of hitting their own man, like they did."

"We and they are the type to shoot first, ask questions later." Jackie climbed into the back seat, pushing the new Syndicate members to the side. Crimson blood tinged her hands. She looked at Lyle. "You going to keep that shirt?"

Lyle shook his head.

Jackie grabbed the bloodstained shirt and wiped her hands on a remaining white space, removing some of the blood before it dried on her skin. "I'll replace it for you. Don't worry."

"Do you think our stuck pig will survive the ride back?" Chris asked, not looking back at them.

"He'll live." Jackie peeked over the seat at the prisoner from between the two new members. "He'll be woozy, but he'll survive."

Chris reached up to the dash and removed a packaged

candy bar. He tossed it over his shoulder. "Feed that to him. It should help."

"You dumbass." Jackie couldn't control the laughter as the two recruits at her side stared.

They weren't in a joking mood and couldn't comprehend the two veterans' behavior. They stayed silent the rest of the ride home, contemplating how they got to this point in their life before eventually accepting it.

9

———

Bernard stood beside Abigail behind the counter. They watched a recent customer leave with their order.

"Seems like a racket, charging that much for a smelly plant," Bernard said. "I can't believe it."

"You've never tried it, have you?" Abigail asked. She looked down at the glass case. "We need more girl scout cookies out here."

"Excuse me?"

"It's a strain. Let me fetch more before our next customer."

"I got it, don't worry. Girl scout cookies, you said?" Bernard asked. He moved to the door.

"That's right. Just grab a couple of jars out of the labeled box. It's near the back door. You saw it last night I assume?"

"Affirmative." Bernard left the front shop area and got to work.

Abigail exhaled a long breath. "At least customers are still plentiful. I was worried with the glass incident." She was broken from her reverie as a bell rang along with the front door opening. "Hello, and welcome to Heavenly Medicine." She bowed as a sign of respect for her newest visitor.

"Nice place you have," the man said. He was dressed well and had an air of superiority about him. "To be honest, I've no clue about this. My wife said I could use some for my anxiety."

"No worries, sir," Abigail said. "Anxiety is best treated with an indica variety. We have a plethora to choose from, each with a unique flavor. If you prefer not to smoke or vape your medicine, we also have a variety of edibles. It's healthier, but I'd warn to start small with them."

The man wandered over to a nearby rack of candy bars. "You mean these? I didn't know it came in candy bar form."

"We also have brownies, hard candy, suckers, taffy, or Crispy treats. There's something for everyone. Almost all of our edibles are indica, so browse at your leisure, there's no rush."

"I appreciate the patience." The middle-aged man inspected the food products while the door behind the counter opened, and Bernard emerged holding jars.

"Thank you." Abigail opened the glass case and placed the containers inside before closing it. "You're a big help."

"Nonsense," Bernard said. "It's just grabbing some jars. Oh, hello there." He finally noticed the customer.

The customer looked up. "Do I know you?"

"I don't believe so," Bernard said.

"Ah, sorry, you looked familiar." He picked a package of brownies and brought it to the register. "I'll have this, thanks."

"This should ease the anxiety. Now this is important, so please pay attention. You should only eat one half of a piece at first. Have you ever tried cannabis before?"

"No, ma'am."

"Then take a half piece. Wait a few hours before you even consider eating more. It takes a while to kick in. Do not operate motor vehicles or heavy machinery after consuming. I'm sorry to bore you, but it's important safety information."

"I appreciate that." The man pulled out his wallet and paid the total.

Abigail rang him up and threw the taffy in a bag. "Here you are, sir. We hope to see you again. If you have questions, feel free to call and ask. We're always happy to help our customers."

The man said his farewells and left.

"Did you memorize that safety speech?" Bernard asked.

"Call it common sense warnings," Abigail said with a wink. "You don't want your customer to green out the first time and call an ambulance because they weren't aware of its strength."

"Green out?"

"Taking too much. You take too much and it's not pleasant if you're a cannabis virgin. The world spins, and it can cause nausea and increased anxiety. Some even call emergency services because they think they're dying. It's silly to think about, but to them they think it's a real possibility."

Bernard stared into Abigail's eyes. "You've a passion for this. It's evident in your eyes. I envy it."

"That's a long story," Abigail said. "I don't want to bore you."

"No need to worry. It's difficult to be bored when you're with enjoyable company. You know how rare that is in my line of work?"

"Tell me, Mr. Morris," Abigail said. She looked away. "Has someone you were close to died? I have a brother named Alfonso." She wiped her eye. "He was bound for a career in medicine, went to college, worked himself through school, and took care of me in his spare time. Looking back, he burned the candle from both ends. He's six years older than me and developed pancreatic cancer. Isn't that a bitch? When he finally went to the doctor for the abdominal pain and yellowing skin, they started him on radiation and chemotherapy."

Bernard leaned on the glass counter. "Sorry to hear."

"I've seen sick people, Mr. Morris, and cleaned up after them. I'd never seen someone whittle away from a once powerful young man into a powerless husk before. He didn't get out of bed often. When he did, it was painful to watch. Nausea had a constant grip on him, and he was miserable. It was hellish." She took a deep breath, trying to collect herself and regain her composure. "I informed my friend of my problem, and she said something that would change the course of my life forever. She informed me that weed helped nausea."

"You didn't know?"

"I didn't grow up a stoner, if that's what you're asking." Abigail moved next to Bernard. "I was sheltered from drugs and alcohol. Some call it a normal upbringing, but that's wrong. I'd heard of cannabis but had no experience. So, I made it my mission to get some and offer it to Alfonso. I saved up any cash I scrounged and found a dealer. From there, I fell down the rabbit hole. Never underestimate how much learning you can accomplish with a drive and the proper internet browsing skills."

"I'm technologically challenged." Bernard scratched his cheek and didn't meet her gaze. "People always make fun of my ineptitude with machines, computers in particular."

"Really?"

"What?"

"People like that still exist? It's shocking is all. Nowadays everybody's glued to their phones or their computers. It's rare to find someone who prefers analogue. Nothing wrong with it, but you're missing out on a fantastic resource of learning."

"I take it your research paid off?"

"I scored some mid quality bud through a friend's acquaintance. Alfonso wasn't eating much and constantly had nausea. Now, it wasn't a miracle wonder drug to be clear. What it did was give him his appetite back via the munchies and suppressed his nausea. It made his quality of life higher than before. That sealed it in my mind. I wanted to help others with cannabis like my brother. It's a silly story, isn't it? To date, he's still alive since his cancer went into remission, but that wasn't the bud's doing. It did, however, make him feel better and allowed him a normal life again."

"It's a beautiful reason, if you ask me. Maybe naïve, but heartwarming nonetheless. I have a greater respect for you now. It's more selfless than my reason for this life I've found myself in."

"You never told me the nature of your work," Abigail said. Something outside caught her attention from through the recently replaced window. "Oh, no."

Roger burst through the nearby door. "You see that?" He pointed toward the window. He didn't waste more time and started toward the contest of wills outside.

Bernard turned to see whatever it was. He saw a huge fight happening outside involving some of Chris's men he'd left here and another band of troublemakers. "Excuse me. I'll see to this. One moment." He snaked around the counter and rushed outside.

"What in the hell?" Bernard got outside and was already

in the melee. He moved his head to the side, dodging an incoming punch from his attacker. He retaliated with a punch to the face that caused his aggressor to stumble backward. Pressing his advantage, he pursued him. Another punch downed the belligerent man. He assisted the remaining security until all the attackers were downed or ran away. Catching sight of his friend again, he finally calmed down. "Everyone alright out here?"

Roger turned and nursed his cheek. "Don't worry about me. I just caught a fist trying to help this dude." He reached down and helped a hopeful recruit off the ground.

"Sorry, Mr. Morris. I didn't mean for you to endanger yourself on my account."

"You showed your bravery and skill," Bernard said. "Don't blame yourself for my partner's reckless decisions." He looked at Roger. "That was stupid to come out, brother. You're too important to lose in a street brawl."

"You're out here. Besides, I can't ask my men to fight if I'm unwilling. That's poor leadership, according to father." Roger counted the remaining guards. "Where are the rest?"

"They ran as soon as the chaos started," the injured one Roger saved said. "I couldn't believe they'd abandon us like that."

"Some aren't worthy," Bernard said. "Come on, boss. Get back inside. I'll deal with this."

"Just a minute." Roger helped the remaining men up and even dusted them off. "Anyone else?"

"No, sir." They had their heads bowed, looking at the sidewalk below.

"Alright. Know that I respect every man that's staying and am taking note of your bravery. I suppose I'll head inside before my friend here has himself a conniption. Exercise caution in continuing to defend these premises. Is that understood?"

"Yes, sir!"

Roger backed off from the group. He turned, facing Bernard now. "They need medical supplies for those cuts. Make it happen."

"Right away," Bernard said. He waited until Roger was back inside before continuing. "I'll be right back with some ointment, ice, and other supplies. Good job. Keep up the outstanding work. Bailey's men didn't know what hit them. We're showing them we won't back down, and I'm damned proud."

Just afterward...

"Whoa, boss. What's that shiner?" Molly looked at Roger entering the room.

"The price of getting in a brawl," Roger said. He moved to sit on the couch and nursed his soon to be black eye. "I'm fine."

"You need ice," Crystal said. She dug into her pack and found a bag. She filled it with ice from the freezer in the kitchen and wrapped it in a towel before handing it to her brother. "Here," she said. "Press this against it. That should lower the swelling."

"Thanks." Roger pressed the ice pack to the aching wound. "I'm surprised he sent soldiers here in broad daylight. They weren't armed, granted, but still."

"He's persistent," Molly said. She snuck a peek over her shoulder at her boss. "You sure you're not concussed? You took a nasty shot."

"Don't think so." Roger kept the pressure on the swelling purple spot. "I'm not dizzy."

"You should lie down." Molly returned her attention to the laptop on the coffee table in front of Roger.

"No doctor on call yet?" Crystal asked.

"Nope. We'll find one soon. I appreciate your concern, girls, but I'm fine.

"Next time don't rush to the front line," Molly said. "Have you ever played chess?"

"Rarely," Roger said. "I know the rules. Why?"

"You're the king of this Syndicate branch. It's rarely a good idea to expose the king to danger on the front lines unless you know stratagem."

"I'd no idea you'd be this worried." Roger couldn't hide a smile as he stared into Molly's back.

"What's with you two?" Crystal asked, sitting next to her brother.

"Nothing." Molly didn't turn around.

Roger couldn't help himself and teased Molly. "Ms. Turner's kinder than first impressions impart. I think she's embarrassed."

"Bullshit," Molly said. "Who'd be embarrassed by you? I'm busy, that's all. Bailey's showed he's stubborn. He'll send more jokers."

"Is that all?" Roger asked.

"Obviously."

Roger hefted himself off the couch and took a seat beside Molly a few feet away. "Guess you wouldn't mind if I sat here then if you don't get embarrassed by me."

"Go ahead. See if I care."

Crystal watched the two and felt a wave of awkwardness wash over her. She felt like the proverbial fifth wheel suddenly. "Aren't you two too cozy? People might talk."

"Nonsense," Roger said. "I'm simply overseeing her work. Nothing wrong with that."

"Is that right?" Crystal didn't believe her brother. She recognized the look in his eyes when he looked at her friend. It sparked a long-forgotten emotion in her - jealousy. She followed suit and sat beside her brother. She leaned into him and grabbed his arm.

"You were that worried?" Roger asked. "I'm alright. There weren't any weapons, just a street fight."

Molly sneaked a quick glance over at her friend's antics. "Any family member would be concerned." She noticed Roger looking at her and turned away in haste.

"Come on." Crystal tugged Roger's arm.

"I'm not hurt." Roger patted Crystal's arm, seeing as that's all he could do with it in her control. "Don't work yourself into a frenzy over nothing." He spoke to Crystal, but his focus was on Molly. "How's the perimeter look?"

"Bernard's calling for medical supplies to be delivered," Molly said. "We lost two men. They deserted us. I doubt we'll see them again. They weren't privy to confidential secrets or even knew who we are, so they're not a problem. We have two on the roof and one outside while two sleep in shifts. We should be secure unless the next attack is a bigger group. I doubt Bailey wants to incite a street brawl with sheer numbers. It'd garner too much attention to him."

"I don't think he cares about attention," Roger said. "If you send men to fist fight during business hours, you want to cause a commotion. He's trying to drive business down the old-fashioned way, by scaring the customers from entering."

"Luckily," Molly said, "stoners don't care. So long as they get their weed, they'll enter the only dispensary in the city. I think he's underestimated his own clientele base. Most folks don't trust black market dealers when there's an official one with a better product, like Ms. Gomez. We're sitting on the proverbial golden goose here, boss. He's trying to tear it apart. It's obvious."

"If he can't have it, no one will," Roger finished her train of thought. "I know the type of man. That's why we're going after him first. We already have a plan in motion on that front."

"Speaking of which," Molly clicked the touch pad of the laptop. "In all the excitement, I didn't notice an email from Jackie. Let me decrypt it and see what she said. Give me a moment."

"Hopefully it's good news from last night's operation. I could use some."

"We'll know in a moment." She referenced the notepad at her side and input the keys and passwords. "Here we are. I'll read it aloud?"

"Go ahead."

"We captured not one, but two of Bailey's men last night. His own men shot one captured soul, but we stopped the bleeding. He may develop an infection, but who cares? We're ready to question them anytime you are. Come back at your earliest convenience."

"Guess that settles what comes next," Roger said. "Send back a response that I want Evans present, and we'll be back soon."

"On it," Molly said.

"You're heading back?" Crystal asked.

"I am. The sooner we find Bailey, the sooner we chop the head off one snake."

"The sooner I'm forced back home too."

"Sorry, Sis," Roger said. He felt her head on his shoulder.

"Why do you call me that?"

"Excuse me?" The question shocked Molly. "What's that mean?"

"Nothing," Roger said in a hurry. "She's distraught is all."

She whispered in her brother's ear. "You know we're not related now. We can't ignore it forever."

Roger redirected his attention away from Molly toward his sister. "Have you told her?"

"Told me what?" Molly asked.

"Not yet."

"You're not going to," Roger said. "It's a secret."

"How juicy sounding," Molly said, still working. "Something I should know?"

"Yeah," Crystal said. "Roger here's not my-"

Roger dropped the ice pack to use his free arm to cover Crystal's mouth and muffled the revelation before it got out. "I'm not her keeper is what she was going to say. You know the phrase, I'm not my brother's keeper? She was referencing that."

Molly looked at Crystal's face. She gathered it was not her intended meaning. "You sure about that?"

Crystal removed the hand from her mouth and blurted it out. "He's not my brother."

Molly's eyes widened. "Pardon?"

"Damn it all." Roger covered his eyes. "Why reveal that now? You know what it means?"

"Not your brother?" Molly asked in a hushed voice. "Excuse my ignorance, but I'm confused about what you mean by that. You mean it literally or figuratively?"

"Literally."

"Remind me to never tell you anything sensitive in the future," Roger said. "No one needs to know that. Ms. Turner, swear that you won't tell anyone that. It's a sensitive matter that my insensitive sister cannot grasp."

"I can keep a secret, but I'm confused. If you're not her brother, then whose son are you?"

"I don't know," Roger said. "I'm not aware of my birth parents or who they were. Mom took me away from them when I was a baby, apparently, to hear her tell it. They raised me as a Morris and taught me to believe I was a Morris. Bernard's mother gave a clue, crude as it was. She said my dad was a gangster and my mother was his, and I quote, 'his baby mama'."

"Damn." Molly whistled.

"I'm adopted without the official part," Roger said. "Why did we have to explain this, dear sister? It was supposed to be private - for good reason."

"I figured if you were close, she should know. Nothing wrong with honesty in a relationship."

"We're going to talk later about this," Roger said, clearly not happy judging by the scowl. "Count on that."

"Fine by me," Crystal said. She gripped his arm tighter and looked at Molly with a smirk. "Am I leaving with you?"

Roger extricated himself from his sister's grip and got to his feet. "I'll go see what Bernard wants to do. He may wish to stay. I'll be right back." He left and entered the front room.

Crystal locked eyes with Molly. "You know why I told you, right?"

"Don't tell me you were jealous?" Molly asked. "You were raised as his sister. That's still sick, you know."

"We're not blood related."

"He doesn't see you that way." Molly turned away, avoiding Crystal's gaze. "You see that. No amount of badgering and clinging is going to change it. You're his cute little sister in his eyes. No sense trying to sabotage him. It's not going to change anything. Besides, I think he likes me."

"So, you have working eyes."

"Ears, nose, and tongue too, yes. Bet you he'd love to inspect this up close and personal too." She stuck out her pierced tongue for a moment. "Look, I'm not trying to be a bitch. I'm just telling you and being honest. Harboring these feelings won't lead anywhere fun."

"You're interested in him too?"

"Who knows?"

10

"Where are they?" Roger asked.

"In the basement." Chris opened the basement door and led his boss downstairs to a waiting Jackie and Kyle. "Where's Bernard?

Roger reached the bottom first. "Back at the dispensary with Ms. Gomez."

"Good morning, boss," Kyle said. "Did something happen at the shop?" He reached up and touched his face, mirroring where Roger's black eye formed.

"Bailey sent some goons to test us. We drove them off. I take it these two sad sacks are our guests?" He glared at the prisoners tied to the chairs. They each had headphone looking devices over their heads and ears. "What's that?"

"Noise canceling headphones playing the worst music known to mankind, elevator music. Figured a little psychological torture would grease the cogs."

"Evans, you're in charge of questioning him. Get creative, and really sell that you hate him."

"I'm up for it. Permission to use anything down here?"

"Granted. Just leave him able to speak, and only hurt him when I tell you."

"Understood."

"Chris, if you'd do the honors." Roger stood directly in front of the two chairs and stared down his nose at his captives.

Chris took their headphones off. He placed them on a nearby table before taking off the blindfolds.

Roger paced before the two prisoners, dominating their field of view. "You two know who I am. You know what we're capable of. Here's how the game's played. I'm going to ask a question, and whoever's answer I like better doesn't get punished. Simple rules, yeah? Start screaming or being nasty and you'll earn an additional demerit. Nod if you understand."

Both prisoners nodded.

"Let them talk."

Chris got rid of the gags and backed off behind the chairs.

Roger stuck his hands in his pants pockets. "Let's start simple. What are your names?" He pointed toward the injured one to his left. "Let's start with you."

"The name's Mercutio."

"Odd fucking name for this era, but your parents were creative. I like it. You?" Roger asked the other.

"You can call me Noel."

"Mercutio, Noel, I have a problem." Roger pulled a stool over and sat on it. "You help me, I aid you. Tell me, where is Mr. Bailey's primary property? I know it couldn't be where we picked you up. It's too small for his operation."

"We can't tell you that," Mercutio said.

"He'll kill us." Noel struggled against the zip ties around his hands.

"Do it."

Kyle grabbed both men's ears and yanked hard. "Answer or every punishment gets more gruesome. Make it easy on yourselves and leave it at this."

"Old school, but effective," Chris said to himself.

"Do you require more convincing, or do you prefer to answer where his primary property is?" Roger asked.

"We can't answer that."

"Mr. Evans, show your skills to these fools. If they're afraid of Mr. Bailey, we'll show them true savagery and change their minds."

Kyle unsheathed the knife at his side. "One of each?"

"I think that's fitting."

Kyle grabbed the uninjured Noel's ear again, this time with his left hand. He used his right and steadily sawed off the ear. He spoke over Noel's screaming. "Shut up. It's infuriating to listen to this banshee wailing." He ripped the last of the ear off and tossed it in Noel's lap. He moved over to Mercutio when he was halted by Roger.

"Wait." Roger stepped forward. "Mr. Mercutio, you're already shot. There's no need for disfigurement too. Why stand up for that crotchety ancient fool? He wants war. You're his sacrifice. Be more than that."

"Do it already."

Roger nodded, and Kyle got to work. Chris stopped the bleeding from Noel while this was happening and then moved to Mercutio afterward.

"You want to know what happens next time you refuse to answer?" Roger asked. "Tell them, Mr. Evans."

"They're being disrespectful guests, so I'll up the ante. How about we chop off toes? I hear it's a horrible thing relearning how to walk with fewer digits. Not my problem. I think we'd start with the big toe for extra effect. That's a real bitch to lose, since it takes a majority of our weight with each step." He kneeled in front of each prisoner and took their boots and socks off. "We'll need another tool for this," he said after removing the last shoe. He wandered over to the table containing tools of all varieties. He took a circular saw and gave it a test whirl. It roared to life as he moved into position in front of Noel.

"Where is he?" Roger asked. "Don't make me cripple you." He leaned down, trying to get to Noel's head level. "It won't end with that. You keep this silent soldier act up and we'll get creative. Cutting off a body part will seem tame compared to what we'll do. Whoever talks first keeps their toe."

"You got a map?" Noel asked.

Chris ran up the stairs without a word to retrieve a map and marker. "I got it!" he called out.

"Noel, don't." Mercutio shook his head. "They'll kill us anyway."

"Is a quick death better, or a lingering one full of mind shattering agony?" Roger asked. "Those are your choices. Now where is Mr. Bailey's home or primary location?"

Chris returned in a hurry, out of breath. He placed it on a table and waited. "So? Where is it, Noel?"

"Northeast of town, about twenty minutes. It's out in the middle of nowhere. You know where Cottontown is? Keep going northeast on Route 125 and turn off. That's my boss's place. Nobody knows Bailey's home location. I don't even know which plant Bailey considers his primary."

"Good man. Show him his prize, Mr. Evans."

"Sir?"

"He answered, he gets to keep his toe. Mr. Mercutio was

reticent. I said earlier, one gets punished, and one does not. Carry it out."

"Yes, boss."

Chris held Mercutio's right leg and kept it from kicking violently against the encroaching saw.

Kyle brought the spinning blade down on the big toe and pressed down hard. Mercutio howled in pain, bucking against his constraints. Metal sliced through flesh. The spinning blade soon ran up against bone and sinew. He kept his resolve and pressed hard, eventually severing the appendage.

"See how much nicer it is cooperating? Now where are his businesses? I want to know where his processing plants are, his grow spots, and anywhere else he operates out of."

"Where you picked us off is one," Noel said. "You know, it'd be easier if you undid my hand restraints. I could mark them."

"Nice try, but no," Chris said. He brought the map in front of Noel and placed it on the floor so he could see, careful to avoid the pooling blood from Mercutio nearby. "You ever played hot and cold as a kid? This is a high stakes version."

The two played an elongated game of hotter and colder as Chris eventually mapped out every property of Mr. Bailey that Noel knew. The entire process took over ten minutes, and they learned of three new locations.

"Anything else?" Noel asked.

"You, Noel, have been exceedingly helpful. I'll make sure Mr. Bailey knows as much. I will give Mercutio credit too."

"Hey, I didn't tell you anything." Mercutio struggled against his bonds, to no avail. "He'll kill my family! You can't do that!"

"Maybe I can be convinced to keep my mouth shut, Mercutio. Give me something I don't know. Then it'll just be you two. I'll tell him you kept your mouths shut and played the good soldier. I'm not a total bastard. Work with me for your own good."

"You want something? Here, I got something juicy for you,"

"I'm listening."

"They put me on babysitting duty sometimes."

"Explain."

Mercutio scrambled to collect his thoughts. "Mr. Bailey has a kid and wife. He doesn't like leaving them unprotected, so he has a rotating shift of personnel stationed at his house. He only chooses the veterans he knows he can trust."

"That's why you wouldn't talk. Funny how that fades away when it's your family in the crosshairs. God, I love selfishness sometimes. Where is it? Tell us everything you know about that work detail."

"It's always five men and women. He stations three outside and two on his roof. It's out in the middle of nowhere."

"Location first." Roger pointed at the map.

Chris moved the map so he could see. He had to move the map further away to avoid the blood on the floor near Mercutio.

"East of town. Further, further, there," he said. "A little north. You're warm." He watched Chris move his thumb further up the map. "You're hotter. Stop."

Chris stopped his finger's movement. "Here?"

"Right there."

Chris marked the location with a large mark.

"Continue," Roger said.

"The ones on the roof have high-powered rifles. Guards on the ground have fully automatic weapons with orders to shoot anyone besides the boss's car. Once the guards are gone, it's free real estate. His wife is a pacifist and the kindest woman you'll ever meet. Please don't hurt them. They don't deserve it."

"Says the gangster," Roger spat on the ground, away from the map. "Mr. Bailey thinks it's fair game to go after Abigail Gomez. He's going to learn turnabout's fair play. What's that old saying about war, Bristol?"

"All's fair in love and war, sir."

"Precisely," Roger said. "You have my personal thanks, gentlemen. You've exceeded my expectations. Just know if anything you told us is a lie, your families are forfeit. Now, would either of you like to amend your testimonies? Now's the time. I know men think they're slick lying to escape physical pain, but call it my insurance policy to know you're being truthful."

Neither prisoner spoke up, choosing to hang their heads.

"Alright then. Mr. Bristol. I believe you have material for two more initiations here. I expect you to dispose of them and teach our up-and-comers how to. Mother always taught me not to waste a gift."

"Yes, Mr. Morris, I have a couple of ideas for our next personnel."

"Initiates? You're killing us?" Noel asked.

"Duh," Roger said. "You thought squealing would save your life? No, it was for your personal families. Boys, you have wallets on you." He pointed to a table where they'd placed them. "We know where you live. This was never about you. It was a test to see how much you loved your family. I'm proud to say you passed. Provided this all passes muster, we'll leave them alone. As for Bailey, I can't guarantee that. You'd know if he's a monster better than I. Is he the petty type?"

"Once he puts it together that we talked, he may well kill them." Mercutio's voice was fading. He barely spoke the words audibly. "It'll be obvious since we were kidnapped last night."

"It sucks that you picked a real horse's ass to work for then. Tell you what. I'll avenge them if he does, alright? Now, Mr. Bristol, prepare your trials. Mr. Evans, you're with me."

Kyle followed Roger up the stairs and shut the door to the basement.

"How did I do?" Roger loosened his tie and exhaled.

"It was a brutal questioning. Your mother would be proud, sir," Kyle said. "You got more information than I imagined possible. Playing one prisoner against the other was genius. It created a fear of not speaking. We can cripple Bailey's operation if we play our cards right."

"It's only half the war. We still have Powell to contend with. Still, half's a damned sight better than being blind and helpless."

"We never were going to harm their families. Right, sir?"

"No, Evans," Roger said with a friendly slap of Kyle's shoulder. "Sometimes I have to play a part. It wasn't pleasant, but men value family. I know that better than most. Playing the villain served its purpose. We're not monsters. Because of that act, less overall will die in this stupid war. See?"

"Very astute, sir."

"Your night's looking busy, Kyle," Roger said. "As the resident soldier, you're leading the spearhead into enemy territory. You up for that?"

"Always. Give me my targets, and I'll knock 'em down."

"Given our manpower limitations, it'll be stealth missions. Are you qualified for that?"

"I was no marine sniper, but I can sneak around, yes. Kill missions or destroying property?"

"Destroy their fields, their greenhouses, their buildings where they process their drugs. If anyone gets in the way, kill them. We have explosives you can use in our stash. Are you familiar with their use?"

"It wouldn't be the first time I've planted plastic explosives, boss. It won't be the last."

"Alright. Tonight at eight we finalize the plans in the living room. Don't be late, and grab a nap. That's an order. You'll need all your energy for tonight."

"Yes, sir."

"Mind you, you'll be going alone, as will Jackie. You two will have two targets each. We'll cripple his economy. He wants to target our business, so we shall target his. You succeed, and the world opens up. It'll build on your legend you've got going."

"I'm not worried about fame. I'm concerned about safety. If this will end this war soon, I'm down."

"It will. Once he's out of cash, his men will desert. They won't work for free unless he's got them petrified. If we keep our business afloat, we will win the economic war. Their men may decide they'd rather work for the winner, and our numbers swell."

"Can we trust men who'd switch allegiances that easily? Forgive my disbelief, but I wouldn't trust them."

"Bristol would still instill in them loyalty or let them go if you catch my drift. We'd separate the wheat from the chaff. Bodies are bodies, and we need more of them."

"Understood."

They heard what sounded like an engine outside.

"What is that noise outside?" Roger moved to the front window and peeked out of the curtains. Bernard, Abigail, Crystal, and Molly got out of the car and walked toward the house.

"Put a do not disturb sign on the basement door before you sleep, Evans. I don't want anyone getting curious. Also, inform Mr. Bristol we have guests over."

"I'll make sure they don't intrude."

"Good man."

Fifteen minutes later...

The group stopped when Abigail did. They had paced around the estate until she stopped.

"Here," she said. "That's your ticket to a good grow. I'd need to test the soil nutrients, but as far as natural growing's concerned, this is your plot of land."

Molly had a small notepad and wrote every piece of advice Abigail gave. She flipped a page and kept writing.

"Are you sure the shop's alright?" Bernard asked. He gazed at the dying sunlight filtering through the trees, painting the entire landscape an orange hue.

"You're talking about the bud tender I left there to run the place?" Abigail asked. "He's an old friend of mine that needed work, and he knows his cannabis. It'll be fine. I showed him everything he needed to know before we left. It's refreshing to breathe in fresh air and get my hands dirty again. Inside grows are fine, but there's something natural about an outside operation."

Roger leaned over and tried to read some of Molly's notes, not paying attention to Bernard and Abigail. He whispered in her ear, causing her to jump and redden her face. "You were a bookworm in school, weren't you?"

"Don't do that," she whispered back.

"Sorry if I startled you."

"I don't suppose you all have seeds already?" Abigail asked. "If your dealer's any good, you probably don't. Ironically, the shitty dealers are the ones who give you the seeds you need to make them obsolete."

"Seed banks exist online," Molly said.

"Illegal to import to grow, but you have a collection of seeds for educational purposes?" Abigail asked.

"Maybe. What type would you recommend?"

"In this climate? Indica all the way. It's not hot enough to cultivate sativa outside. That's usually done near the equator. I'd have to see your collection to make an informed decision and recommendation."

"Please remind me, and I'll show you before you head back," Molly said.

"You learned all this from the internet?" Bernard asked. "No schooling or anything?"

"Unless you count the high school diploma I earned, yeah," Abigail said. "Who's grown anything before? We're counting produce in this."

"Lauren had us plant tomatoes for science class when we were seven, I think," Bernard said.

"Plant is right," Roger said. "We planted, and only a few grew."

"That was mine, thank you," Crystal said. "You wouldn't listen to me, and yours died. I told you to water it but no, wait for rain you said. Never mind that it was summer."

"Thankfully, Molly will be the mastermind behind this garden." Roger placed a hand on her shoulder. "She'll make sure it succeeds, I bet. She's taking notes I see."

"A good idea," Abigail said. "I never remember unless I write it down. Remember to space out the plants, water them daily, and trimming them will help. You can use the trimmings to make butter too. It's good for pain, including menstrual cramps. Don't ask me how I know. It's a phenomenal painkiller. Not as effective as opioids, but way less addictive."

"Sounds perfect for us," Molly said. "Relaxation and pain relief will work wonders."

"What about smell?" Bernard asked. "Will anyone know we're growing?"

"All the way out here? Not a chance. Besides, it's legal to cultivate nowadays." Abigail giggled. "You're quite old school. Not good with computers and stuck in the cannabis prohibition era. You got your info from your mother, I'm guessing?"

"Indeed," Bernard said. "She was against all drugs. Period."

"She filled our heads with reefer madness." Roger exaggerated his voice to sound serious, causing everyone to laugh. During his performance, he placed a palm on Molly's shoulder.

"She did it out of love, I'm sure." Abigail reached down and scooped a handful of dirt before letting it run through her fingers. "She didn't want her boy to be an addict as she saw it. She was misinformed, but I respect her devotion and love for her child." Abigail stood up and wiped her hands. "Her tall, handsome, and strong son."

That got everyone's attention, but no one called her on it.

"Thank you, Ms. Gomez. You're dazzling yourself."

"Get a room, you two," Molly said. She reached up and removed Roger's hand from her shoulder.

ALEX J. FISCHER

Crystal got between Molly and Roger, preventing further physical touches. "Don't harass the help, dear brother. Respect her boundaries."

"Obviously," Roger said in a hurry. "Forgive a guy for trying to calm someone down. When she talks about cannabis, her eyes just light up."

"You two aren't cousins, are you?" Abigail asked.

"How'd you guess?"

"Your mannerisms. She treats you more like a boss. I'm not stupid. I know you all are a crime syndicate. My family's from Mexico. I know how the crime world works. One criminal group monopolizes the industry until another comes along and shakes things up. I take it you're the young group on the scene. That's why I never mentioned the guns your men had on them. It's normal to me. What outfit do you represent?"

"Have you heard of the Morris Syndicate?" Bernard asked. "We're descendants of Bernard Morris, the group's original founder. We're setting up a new branch free of mother dearest."

"And I'm the laundering operation," Abigail said, nodding. "It's smart. I won't ask anything else, seeing as knowledge is dangerous. Just know I'm loyal and won't say a word. You've helped me achieve my dream, and I don't take it lightly."

"Your problems with Mr. Bailey will disappear soon enough. I can't say any more." Bernard gently grabbed her hand. "Just be patient, please."

"So long as I draw breath, I'll never give up. I'm a little nervous about sleeping there, if I'm honest. Even with your personnel, I have nightmares that I'll wake up to Bailey's men pointing a gun at me."

"There is another option," Bernard said.

"You're not serious?" Crystal asked. "We have no room."

"Says who? You?" Bernard asked. "How about it, brother?" He turned to Roger. "What do you think?"

"Ms. Gomez? You want to stay here until this war ends? All we'd ask is not to enter the barn or basement. We'd also request you not to record anything."

"It'd be better than sleeping where Bailey's goons attacked twice already. I won't poke my nose where it doesn't belong. I swear."

"Sleeping in a sleeping bag alright? Our rooms are full, and the sofa's taken. It's not deluxe accommodations, but we'll keep you safe."

"I don't mind," Abigail said. "What about the store at night?"

"We'll keep the men there. They sleep in shifts, so there's always someone outside. They'll keep it safe," Bernard said. "We've ordered them to repair any damages it sustains."

"Then hell yeah," she said. "I'll pack a bag before we leave tonight."

"Tonight will be an eventful evening," Roger said. He rubbed his hands together - not from the cold either.

"You have plans?" Abigail asked.

"Big plans. Plans big enough to end this. That's all we can say."

"Don't let me interrupt it then."

That night...

"Is our guest settled in?" Roger asked.

Bernard closed the barn door. He looked up at the bright lights they'd wired before. "She's in the house speaking with Crystal. Who wired this?"

Kyle raised his hand. "I did. It's hacksaw, but it'll illuminate the space for now."

"Ms. Turner," Roger said, "have you confirmed our findings?"

"Indeed." Molly's laptop sat on a nearby table. Stacks of papers were placed beside it. They were copies of the different areas satellite images and floor plans. "Take one of each. I marked them for clarity's sake."

Everyone grabbed their copy and inspected the papers.

Jackie spoke up. "You've confirmed their Bailey's properties? They could have given you any civilian's place they knew was there."

"I checked. You want me to explain how?"

"Go ahead."

Molly sighed and rubbed her temples. "Fine, let's elongate this meeting. By cross-referencing the local real estate sites and their databases, I traced the houses back to where they were sold. After that, I tracked how they paid. Follow the money isn't just a witty saying. All the properties payments originated from the same account, presumably Mr. Bailey's primary account. I also checked that too before you ask. It's his. Any more questions?"

"No, I'm satisfied." Jackie thumbed through the pages.

"Before we start with the nitty-gritty details, let's clear one topic up." Bernard turned to Chris. "Did your recruits pass your test, Mr. Bristol?"

"Indeed. It wasn't a sporting execution, but they proved their loyalty. Why? You need them for tonight?"

"That's up to you and Ms. Thomas."

"Who?" Kyle asked.

"Me," Jackie said. "I forgot you're new for a second there. How many properties do you want to hit tonight?"

"How many can we manage?" Bernard asked. "I don't

want to spread us thin, but I want to inflict palpable damage on his empire."

"The problem with attacking is the inevitable counterattack," Chris said. "Remember, they know our property. We torch their places; they'll do the same. We want that with Ms. Gomez here and our forces at her shop? All we have here are us and two newly minted members. I don't think they could repel an invasion alone."

"Two members and us," Roger said, gesturing toward Bernard. "Still, four isn't great odds."

"Don't forget Crystal's drone and gun attachment." Bernard snapped his fingers. "We use the attack to bait an attack, and we crush them on all fronts. It's genius."

"Risky as fuck," Chris said.

"Indeed," Jackie said. "It's an all-or-nothing gambit. Odds are when they see us leave, they'll either follow or gather for an attack here tonight. Who's going?"

"Mr. Evans, you, and Chris. Depending on your confidence, you can go as a group or split up. We leave that to you," Roger said. "I don't pretend to know battle tactics like you three. That's why you're here."

"We're planting explosives you said?" Chris asked.

"Affirmative," Bernard said. "It's not a massacre we're seeking, it's cutting off Bailey's money train. When his cash runs dry, he loses all manpower and is out of this war. His empire's big, and that has its advantages, but also disadvantages. With that many properties, it's hard to defend but earns more. Where we have the compact build out of necessity. We only defend one, max two properties."

"Point taken." Chris placed the papers down. "If it's a stealth mission, the fewer the better."

"I can go alone, sir," Kyle said, eyes burning with determination. "I've done this a few times before. If we split up, we cover more ground and inflict grievous damage faster. I'd like to show Mr. Bristol and Ms. Thomas how to plant the explosives before we head out, though. I gathered the stuff beforehand, and it should do the job, judging by these pictures."

"There are three targets we'd love to hit," Bernard said. "His cannabis farm, his poppy and coca fields, and whatever this property's for. We theorize it might be a storage location."

"Wouldn't they use trap houses for that?" Jackie asked.

"Not if it's for prescription drugs they bought off the dark web," Molly said. "It'd make sense."

"Three targets for three people," Roger said. "The poppy and coca fields are the hardest target it looks like. Any volunteers?"

"That's mine." Kyle raised his hand. "You want the poppy and coca field burned? What about this nearby building structure? It looks like where they process the drugs before they ship it out."

"Preferably, we destroy it, but the fields come first," Roger said. "They can't process anything if the fields are ruined."

"Next is the storehouse. It should be easier, but if we're correct, it'll be guarded still. Who wants it?"

"I got this," Jackie said. "If you're correct, I'll steal as much as I can carry after planting the explosives. It should net us some cash to boot."

"That leaves the cannabis fields for me then," Chris said. "Do you mind if I bring a recruit to help? That's a lot of real estate, and I'll need more than one or two gas cans. It'll cut the time and risk in half."

"Do it," Bernard said. "The others remain here in case of an attack."

"You'll have how many bodies?" Kyle asked.

"The two of us," Roger said. "We also can count on Crystal's drone, which I've already told her to keep ready and charged."

"I'll take Lionel tonight and leave Wallace and the two newest recruits here to defend," Chris said.

"Six to defend, including Crystal's drone, isn't ideal," Bernard said. "We'll make do. Focus on your job, not us. Besides, if they send manpower here, it's less for you."

"It's up to you," Kyle said. "Remember, don't breathe in the smoke, old man. Getting stoned won't help you or your partner."

"One perk of the job, young whippersnapper," Chris said. "I've never got high before. What's it like?"

"Oh Lord," Molly said. "Permission to overwatch for Mr. Bristol and his partner? They're going to need guidance once they're intoxicated. The last thing we want is a panicking old man and his laughing partner getting shot since they forgot what they're doing."

"Granted," Roger said. "Provided you show Ms. Gomez how to watch the cameras inside. We'll need someone watching them here with you gone and Crystal piloting her drone."

"It's easy. She'll grasp it quickly. Make sure you're all on call. Just don't count on tech wizardry."

"Obviously." Bernard hopped up and sat on the table. He kicked his dangling legs. "Jackie, Kyle, you two sure you don't want to work together?"

"If she needs assistance, I'll help," Kyle said. "I don't though."

"Screw you, young blood." Jackie planted her hands on her hips. "I've been going on missions since you were in diapers."

"Be realistic, not prideful," Bernard said. "Cut the tough guy and girl acts. Be honest, both of you."

"Planting three loads of explosives, getting to a safe distance, and pressing the button should be fine," Kyle said.

"If he can do three targets, I can manage one," Jackie said. "Don't worry about me."

"Prioritize your safety above the mission," Bernard said. "Am I understood?"

"Yes, sir!" all three answered at the top of their lungs.

"Good," Roger said. "Evans, inform these two of the explosives you'll be working with."

"With pleasure, sir," Kyle unzipped the bag he'd brought in and set it down. "I've taken the liberty of assembling the units myself. He took out a square white brick of explosive. It had a timer attached. When you want to arm it, you press this." He hovered a hand over the one button on the timer. He pulled out a hand-held device. "When you want it to detonate, you simply press the big red button. Simple, yeah? I've tested this earlier out in the forest. It works perfectly."

"Press button on explosive, then the button on the detonator. Got it," Jackie said.

"I'm just burning the fields. I won't need any, right?" Chris asked. "I feel like I should take one just in case."

"In case of what?" Jackie asked.

"In case I see a target worthy of destroying."

"We need one pack for our defense," Roger said. "How many units do we have, Evans?"

"I made the bricks large. We have six."

"Three for Kyle, and one for Jackie and Chris. That leaves one for us. Then we're fresh out of the explosives we took from mother dearest," Roger said. "Make these count."

"You're using one for defense, you said?" Kyle asked.

"Call it a distraction that could kill. It'll be pivotal if they decide to attack tonight, along with the drone. We'll win with surprise and wit, not brute firepower.

"I'm relieved to hear you say that," Kyle said. "Yeah, that'll work."

"Alright, everyone. We have our missions tonight. Let's get to it."

11

———

She saw the property from her cover. It was a lone shack with no buildings nearby. There was only one car parked outside. "No patrols," she muttered. Jackie scanned her surroundings. Trees surrounded the shack. It looked like a rundown forgotten shack that nobody would give a second thought about, at least by her measure. "I won't argue if it makes my job easier." She reached down and patted her trusty firearm in her belt line. She pulled it out, made sure it was loaded, and then put it back.

"No one's shown up for half an hour. I think it's safe to say that now's my chance. Kill one or two guys, steal the shit, and blow it up. Easy, right?" Her heart was jack hammering in her chest and a familiar cold sweat overtook her. She adjusted the backpack slung over her shoulder, feeling the familiar weight of the explosives shift inside.

Jackie walked through the tree line, approaching the property behind cover. She paced slowly, trying not to trip over any of the assorted debris in the forest. Every step was deliberate and calculated as she got closer. "Quick in and out," she told herself. "Just like any other mission."

She was close enough now to dash toward the property when she chose. She saw the shack had windows and someone walked inside. Periodically a head was visible and disappeared as quickly. She waited until the occupant passed the window and disappeared before taking off into a full sprint toward the property.

Her back touched the wooden cabin, and she gathered herself and her breath. She took off the pack and placed it down beside the nearby door. Taking out her gun, she reached for the doorknob when she paused. She could hear talking inside now.

"Why the fuck are we out here?" a male asked. "Nobody even knows about this place. This shack looks like a rural crack house. The only people who know about it are us."

"Didn't you hear?" another asked. "Two of our men got kidnapped. Rumor is it was from the Meth lab."

"Fuck, you think they gave up locations?"

"Don't know. That's why we're here."

"Why only two of us? Shouldn't we have more if we're a target?"

"You think we have unlimited manpower, you idiot? We're all he can spare to defend this outpost. The amount of pharmaceuticals here could finance our war effort for only a year. It's nothing compared to the other locations, so we get two people. End of story. Stop bitching and help me keep an eye out already."

Two of them, Jackie thought. She frowned at the revelation. *It was idealistic to hope for one. How to tackle this? Fuck it. The* simple *solution is sometimes the best.* She tried the doorknob with her left hand to find it unlocked. She gently pushed and kicked with full force, slamming the wooden door into the wall inside.

Jackie followed it up by coming in blasting. The men

inside didn't stand a chance. They barely turned around before the lead penetrated their bodies. Both crashed to the ground from the magazine emptying barrage.

Jackie ejected the magazine and reloaded. She saw one of her targets was still breathing, so she finished him with another squeeze of the trigger. "That was easier than I imagined." She moved to the door and grabbed the backpack. Unzipping it, she took out the explosive brick and placed it in the dead center of the shack.

Once she finally took a second to look at her surroundings, she noticed the boxes of prescription drugs stacked nearby. There were containers of painkillers, benzodiazepines, research chemicals, stimulants, and even a few psychedelics like acid and DMT. She stuffed as many of the boxes inside the duffel bag as she could before zipping it up.

She hurried outside to see an unwelcome sight. A car slowed to a stop beside the shack and people exited, at least three hostiles. "Shit." That was all she managed as they started lighting her up like she did a few moments ago to the poor souls inside.

She ducked and went around the shack, desperately seeking cover. Her hand exploded in pain. Once she reached the other side, she inspected the wound. Her left hand's little finger was gone, shot off clean. A bloody nub remained. She fired around the corner blindly, trying to at least wing one of her attackers, but no cries erupted.

"Fuck it." She didn't want to stick around forever, so she ran full bore into the trees behind the shack. Diving behind a large tree, she didn't wait. She pressed the detonator's big red button.

The ground shook beneath her, and her insides hurt from the shockwave. She didn't wait around to see if her assailants were still alive. She kept running toward where she parked her getaway vehicle. No gunshots followed the blast. *They must be dead*, she thought. *They'd be in pursuit otherwise. Shit, this hurts. Guess I'll need to ask the boss where she got her prosthetic. She won't be pissed, right? Focus. We need to stop the bleeding soon. It's flowing freely and I can't pass out driving back.* She ran through the forest at full speed while she contemplated. She only slowed down once she realized she was getting dizzy, but luckily the break in the trees was within sight.

Jackie could see her car and picked up speed. Yanking the door open, she climbed inside and slammed it shut. She tore off a piece of her shirt and wrapped it tightly on the gory nub. Opening the nearby glove compartment, she ate a few pieces of candy, vainly hoping to restore some of the crimson life she'd lost. She inspected the wound and saw the blood flow stopped with the tight dressing.

That was all she needed to start the car and get driving.

Meanwhile, with Chris...

"Mr. Lionel, have you ever smoked marijuana?"

"Sir? Is that important?"

"For this operation, let's say yes." Chris stopped at an intersection. "So, have you ever partaken?"

"Yes, he has," Molly said. "If he hadn't, he'd have said so."

"She's right," Lyle said. "When I was a teenager, I smoked and ate any drug I could get my grimy paws on. What are we doing again? You said little when you dragged me along. Are we getting blasted tonight?"

"More than likely," Molly said. "You're burning cannabis fields."

"Hot damn."

"Not the proper reaction, kid," Chris said. "We're burning Bailey's money-making fields. There's a good chance they'll have personnel there. Right?"

"Possibly," Molly said. "It's a greenhouse and some fields with bud growing. They might leave it alone at night. Supervision while growing is not needed, provided they did their job during the daylight. In that case, you may as well enjoy the buzz."

"Confirming if there're any enemies comes first, before the burning." Chris turned off the four-lane road onto a two-lane path. "This isn't a recreational activity. The reason I asked was so I'd know if you'll keep your head if you breathe it in."

"He'll be fine," Molly said. "You're the one I'm worried about. You said you've never experienced it. We'll be lucky if you don't forget what you're there for and start laughing like a wild hyena. That reminds me. Before we burn the fields, can we harvest some of their bounty?"

"Planning on a celebratory doobie after the operation?" Chris asked, looking into the rear-view mirror.

"Nothing wrong with celebrating a successful operation."

"Don't hold your breath."

"I got you, tech lady," Lyle said. "Just be sure to share, eh?"

"You got it."

"Shelf the juvenile babble." Chris stopped the vehicle. "It's right there. Communication check."

"Call's online and everybody's in," Molly said, looking down at the laptop. "I'll have the engine running when you get back. Odds are neither of you will be fit to drive afterward."

"Come on, Mr. Lionel. We'll scout it out, like last time. If the coast is clear, we'll retrieve the gas cans and get working."

"Roger that," Lyle said.

Both men exited the vehicle and stayed near the edge of the tree line. Lyle had a backpack slung over his shoulder as they moved closer.

"Why is it always a fucking forest after dark?" Lyle asked. "Can't these drug farms be in the city? Put it on the rooftop for once. At least then we wouldn't trip over shit." As if on cue, Lyle tripped, landing face down in the grass.

Chris turned and helped him up. "You deserve that. Quiet down. You may be one of us, but you follow my orders. In words you will understand - the Lord may own your soul, but your ass is mine."

"I had no clue you two were so close. Guess you're the top, then?" Molly couldn't or didn't want to hide the amusement in her voice. "Hey, I don't judge. Go nuts, you two. See what I did there?"

"See what you've started?" Chris asked. He turned and walked, tired of this conversation.

"Me?" He struggled to keep up. Careful not to tumble again, his pace wasn't as quick as earlier. He eventually caught up since Chris stopped behind a tree ahead. He took cover nearby. "See anyone?"

"Negative, no cars either. It might be empty from the looks of it." Chris's voice lowered. "Is this a trap? No way they'd leave it undefended in a war, right? They know we questioned their men."

"Cannabis farms don't require a lot of tending if you don't care about quality," Molly replied. "Odds are there're personnel there during the day for maintenance, watering, etc. Besides, weed's the least of their money-making products. Coke, crack, and prescription drugs would net boat loads more. Not surprising if they leave it alone at night."

"Is that your professional opinion?" Chris asked. "Like you'd know."

"Fine, don't listen to me. Waste more time out here. That just means more time away from base. Don't let me stop your mini camp-out."

"Shall I haul the gas over?" Lyle asked. "You can scout and meet back here."

"Sounds good, Mr. Lionel. Make it happen." Chris patted Lyle on the shoulder and started walking. He kept a close eye for any signs of inhabitants as he walked. There was the greenhouse he'd seen on the map, as well as an enormous plot of land set aside for different types of cannabis plants. There were no bikes, four wheelers, or any vehicle further in like he suspected. All he saw was the hard work of whoever Bailey paid to plant his cash crops. He finally reached the back of the compound and found no sign of human activity before meeting Lyle.

Lyle was already waiting for him. Two gas cans were on the forest floor in addition to the pair he carried. "Any trouble, boss?"

"Not a peep," Chris said.

"Told you so." Molly couldn't hold her silence. "What do I know, right?"

"You're lucky the boss isn't here seeing this side of your personality. His interest would wane in a hot minute."

"Get on with it already, and, Mr. Lionel, grab us some to celebrate before you set it ablaze, yeah? I've got my grinder and papers already here."

"I'm on it, Ms. Turner."

"Kissing up to tech won't get you shit, you know." Chris bent over at the waist and picked up the gas cans. A large crack halted his movement as his eyes went wide. A hushed grunt of pain escaped him.

"Sir?" Lyle asked. "Are you alright? That sounded nasty."

"It's nothing." Chris stood up straight again out of sheer determination while keeping a straight face. "My back cracks sometimes is all."

"If you're sure." Lyle stepped past the older gangster and led the pair.

"Old man broke his back." Molly sang these words like it was a lullaby. "Lionel stepped on a crack and snap it went." Her mockery ended and seemed serious again. "Damn, that sounded better in my head."

"You want the field or the greenhouse?" Lyle asked.

"Greenhouse," Chris said. "Less ground to cover means seniority gets it."

"Damn, that's probably where they keep the good shit too. Fine, I'll take the fields."

Chris noticed the backpack Lyle had over his shoulder. "How the fuck much are you taking Lionel?"

"As much as I can carry, sir. I figured maybe we could sell the rest."

"Mm." Chris stopped once they were close to the greenhouse building. "Alright. Meet back here and we'll set them alight all at once."

"Got it."

Chris and Lyle went their separate ways. The veteran ambled over to the greenhouse door and opened it without issue. He stepped inside to a musk he'd never smelled before. He'd heard it smelled skunky, but it didn't do it justice. "Good Lord, what a stench."

"The good shit, huh? Do me a favor, Bristol. Grab a few buds. The stronger the smell, the higher the pain relief."

"Pain relief?" Chris dropped a canister of gasoline and rested a hand on his lower back. "You're serious?"

"Sure, it's great for pain. You mean you'll grab some too?"

"Which one?" He walked through the greenhouses. Rows of plants were on either side of him. Some were covered in crystals, while others had orange hair and yet others shared both characteristics.

"The crystal covered ones if there are any. Those are trichomes. We could make moon rocks if we get enough of those crystals. Those are king for pain relief."

"She's right, boss," Lyle said.

"I am dubious of your claims, but sure, I'll grab some." He tore off multiple branches of the heaviest branches near him and moved back to the door to throw them outside.

He set to work dousing the inside of the glass growing zone with gasoline afterward, careful not to step in any inside the relative darkness. The glass did little to improve visibility, since the only light outside was the moon high above. "I almost feel bad about ruining all this hard work. Almost."

Chris finished the preliminary work of soaking every plant inside with the fuel. Careful to avoid stepping into any, he made his way back to the entrance. He was the first outside and left the greenhouse door open, waiting for Lyle. He scanned the area to see the young man was working hard. "Taking your time over there?"

"Being thorough," Lyle said, never stopping his work. "I'm on my second can of gas over here. You have any to spare?"

"Sure," Chris said. He reached down and stuffed the cut off cannabis plants under his arm and picked up the spare gas can he didn't use. He carried it over and handed it off. "Why do people inhale this scent willingly?"

"You'll find out soon," Lyle said.

"You think so?"

"If we're setting this alight, yeah. I'm damned sure." Lyle tossed the empty container out into the field before picking up the brand new one. He splashed the peculiar smelling liquid on every row of psychoactive plants. He eventually finished his job and joined Chris by the greenhouse, leaving a trail leading out of the fields nearby to light.

"Took long enough," Chris said in greeting. "Let's kick this off already and get home."

"Don't be a downer, old timer," Lyle said. "We should stay and breathe in our spoils before we go. It'll help that back your favoring too."

"Who said I'm favoring anything?" Chris removed his hand from his back.

"Let's light it up. You take a few deep breaths of the smoke, and then we'll talk. I bet you'll be stoned off your ass and won't remember where the car is."

"How much?"

"I'll bet a hundred."

"You're on."

Chris pulled out a box of matches and extracted one for him and another for Lyle. He struck it and tossed it into the greenhouse. He handed the box over to Lyle and watched him light it before walking over to the fields and tossing the lit match into it.

The greenhouse was soon illuminated in bright orange light from the growing inferno inside. He'd left the door opened so smoke poured out straight into his face. He backed up, waving his hand in front of his face with big coughs. "God damn," he said between hacking. "This stuff irritates your lungs."

"This is equivalent to drinking bottles of whisky your first time drinking," Molly said. "I envy what you're about to experience if I'm honest and dread it a little. Dealing with you stoned is not an activity I envy."

Chris backed off from the impromptu hotbox he'd created. He could still smell the smoke just fine and feel the irritating feeling in his chest. "I don't feel anything."

"You will in a few minutes," Lyle said as he approached again. He was visibly taking large breaths, trying to fill his lungs with the airborne narcotic's smoke. "That's some good shit. I can tell. You taste that?"

"What?"

"I asked if you could taste it?"

"Taste what?"

"He's stoned," Lyle said with a smirk.

Chris dropped the buds to the grass below. "What's stoned? Is it supposed to make my head feel kind of fuzzy? I feel great!"

"So it begins," Molly said. "Get back here before you get lost."

Lyle picked up the greenhouse buds and shoved them in his backpack. "Come on, boss. Let's get you home before the high gets more intense."

"It gets stronger?"

"Oh yeah," Lyle said. "This is the beginning. Soon you'll be hungry, giggling, and a joy to be around. You'll also forget most everything within a few seconds." He walked past Chris only to see the Syndicate recruiter still standing still, gazing at the growing flames. "Old man?"

"Huh?" Chris stood transfixed by the flickering flames. His mind zoomed a mile a minute, yet felt foggy, slowed, and he couldn't wipe the smile off his face. He turned and walked toward the burning field. The rising smoke was mesmerizing in a way he couldn't explain.

"Oh hell," Lyle said. "Sir? Aren't we leaving?"

"Leaving? Oh right, in a minute." Chris waved his arm dismissively at his side.

"No, not a minute," Molly said. "Bailey's personnel could show any moment, and you don't want a gunfight during your first time stoned. Trust me. Follow Mr. Lionel, please."

"I understand why you like this stuff so much now," Chris said. He felt Lyle grab his arm and pull him away. "Do you use moisturizer?"

"What?"

"Your hands," Chris said. "They're extraordinarily soft. You use something, I know."

"No," Lyle said. "Hey boss, are you hungry?"

"I wasn't when we started." Chris's hand fell to his stomach and stayed there. Pangs of intense hunger gnawed away at him now. "Now I'm ravenous."

"We have food in the car. Doesn't that sound wonderful?"

"We have candy bars, chips, and soda." Molly's voice was honey glazed, trying to entice the intoxicated old man. "It's all yours and Lyle's."

"Hot damn." Chris quickened his pace, along with Lyle at his side. They were nearly off the property when the sound of an engine met their ears.

"Is that you?" Lyle asked.

"Is what me?"

"Shit," Lyle said. He pulled hard on Chris's arm. "We're getting into the forest, now. I think some of Bailey's men are coming."

"No cars passed me. They must've approached from the other direction," Molly said.

The pair barely found cover behind some trees when some headlights appeared on the dirt path leading to the greenhouse.

Chris looked up into the canopy of branches above. He had his eyes closed, listening to the fire burning and the insect chorus all around. He had a serene smile the whole while, despite the potentially imminent gunfight brewing.

Lyle still had command of his senses and whispered to Chris nearby. "Stay here and remain quiet."

A car door slamming shut and rapid footsteps along with yells met their ears. "Shit. Grab the extinguisher and help me put this out."

"We can't allow them to ruin your hard work," Molly said. "Can either of you two still aim for beans?"

"Old man?" Lyle asked in a hushed voice.

"Huh? Aim at what?"

"The men over there." Lyle pointed toward the field. "I need you to help me kill them."

"Why, man?" Chris asked. "Can't we just get along?"

"Yeah, he's stoned alright," Molly's dry voice said. "Not the time for such idealistic nonsense. Put them down and get back here."

"Can you aim?" Lyle asked.

"Probably. You're sure we need to murder them, though?" Chris asked. He pulled out his weapon.

"One hundred percent," Lyle said. "We do this, and we're out. Got it?"

"We're out," Chris giggled.

"God, I can't imagine a worst first time," Molly said. "I thought my greening out was bad. Killing drug dealers tops it for sure."

"On my signal," Chris said. It was a momentary window of seriousness, but he kept a straight face. "Ready?"

"Whenever you're ready, chuckles," Lyle said. He pulled out his own weapon and got it ready.

"Now," Chris said.

Both men leaned out of their cover and emptied their entire magazines. It wasn't a sporting firefight. It was a slaughter that ended in a single volley of lead being slung downrange. Their targets were so entranced with fighting the fire, they didn't even see their death coming. They fell in said blaze, but they weren't dead yet.

"Reload and let's finish them," Lyle said.

Chris reloaded with lightning speed. "Huh, that was bad ass."

"Quite so. Now let's go finish them, Mr. Badass."

Both left cover and marched toward the struggling, burning, injured men. Without a word, they executed them once they got close and turned to leave quickly.

"Did you see that?" Chris asked. He barely kept up. "Bang," he aimed the pistol away from the pair. "It was like I'm a movie character in a film or something."

"That's what you have to say?" Molly asked. "Right, you're not a normal person. Most would bawl their eyes out at killing on their first high. Not you. This is normal for you, isn't it?"

"Not me, baby," Chris burst into uncontrollable laughter after holstering his weapon. "That was awesome. They didn't even see it coming. What dumb assholes. You'd think they'd suspect the perpetrators were near, but not them. Did you see how they flopped on the ground? It was great."

"You're sure they're dead?" Molly asked.

"Dead as a doornail." Chris's laughing spree continued.

"We turned that farm into a funeral pyre. Is that a band name? It should be."

"Hurry back before more goons show up," Molly said. "The smoke is visible from here. No doubt every civilian on this road tonight will see and smell it. Hurry, it's late."

Before long the two intoxicated men navigated their way through the dark woods and spotted their car waiting. The passenger and back door were already open and waiting for them.

"Hop in, and I'll get us out of here," Molly said. She waved from the front seat, earning a wave in return from Chris.

Before he got inside the car, Lyle quickly ripped the buds off the plants he carried inside his pocket, leaving only the green nuggets. He got inside and slammed the door shut. "Where's the grinder and papers?"

"Beside you on the back seat," Molly said without missing a beat. She started the engine and sped up in a flash.

Lyle got to work preparing the luxury he'd procured for Molly without further words.

Chris's stoned behavior was not yet over. "You ever stopped and thought about how dangerous riding in a car is? I hadn't until now," Chris said. He leaned his head against the window on his right. "We're just zooming past in metal death boxes at sixty miles an hour only a few feet from each other. It's wild. Who came up with that idea? They were crazy thinking it was a good idea."

"If that blows your mind, here's something to ponder," Lyle said. "You know about time zones?"

"Of course."

"This'll bake your noodle. If you board a plane and head west, you're traveling back in time."

Silence filled the cabin until Chris finally put the pieces together mentally. "Holy crap, you're right. Does that make the passengers time travelers?"

"No," Molly said. "It makes them jet lagged."

Lyle opened the circular grinder with a satisfying pop and stuck one of the bigger buds into it. He slammed the cover and twisted left and right with some effort. "I've never tried rolling a joint while moving, but I'm down for a challenge. Try not to hit any potholes." He grabbed a paper and filled the middle of it with the ground up narcotic before he rolled it up.

"Don't even think of puffing on that first. It's mine," Molly said.

"So stingy," Chris said.

"You both already got yours. Talk about stingy."

"True enough," Lyle said. He licked the paper and sealed it off with a final twist of the end. "Eureka, I've done it. It's serviceable, if I say so myself."

Molly kept her left hand on the wheel and held out her right to receive the freshly rolled joint. "Hand it over."

"You're sure you should smoke and drive?"

"I've been doing it since I was seventeen," Molly said. She felt the joint drop into her palm and placed it on the dash before picking it up properly. She stuck one end in her mouth and reached for the car lighter. Lighting it, the end burned bright orange. She took a deep inhale and exhaled a thick cloud of smoke. "You've got talent, Mr. Lionel. Mr. Bristol, roll down the window and be a dear."

Chris did it without argument, allowing the excess smoke to leave the cabin.

She took a deep drag. "This will pass for top shelf at Ms. Gomez's place. You got the whole backpack full?"

"Barely zipped closed thanks to old man Bristol's grabbing so much from the greenhouse," Lyle said.

"What's that?" Chris pointed ahead.

"I don't see anything," Molly said. She took another drag when a dark figure crossed the road in front of them. She didn't have time to stop. The car passed over a large bump and a foul smell erupted in the air.

Lyle looked out the back window. "Judging by the smell, skunk. I'm sure the brass will love that stench when we return. It's all over us now."

"Blame it on the weed. They've never used it," Molly said. "They'll buy it. Leave it to me..."

Same time with Kyle...

Kyle balanced on the tree branch and used the binoculars hanging around his neck. "Damn," he whispered. "This place is big and populated. Why did I volunteer to go alone? There are over twelve units patrolling in pairs." He moved his view over to the fields. "There's no one watching the coca and poppy fields. That might be my way in." Continuing his survey, he saw a barn with its doors wide open. He could see near naked men and women inside with masks on preparing and processing the raw material into powder before bagging it.

"There it is." He spotted a couple of armed guards inside, watching the workers so they didn't steal. "I'll sneak around its back and plant the payload. The problem is patrols could wander there, and once I fire a shot, I need to leave fast. I can't kill all of them unless I use the explosives to my advantage." He checked his watch. "I've wasted enough time. I'll improvise." He climbed down the tree and hopped off.

He grabbed the rifle leaning against the tree and made sure it was ready for service before he circled around toward the fields. Stepping lightly was the key, and he knew it. He kept a close watch to his side and stopped a few times when patrols approached.

He'd just gotten close to the fields when he heard a crack nearby of a twig snapping. Hitting the deck, he rolled over on his back and prepared the rifle for whoever got close enough.

A couple of guards approached near him. He could see them about ten feet over, but darkness cloaked him from their gaze. It appeared both men stopped for a bathroom break as he heard them urinate nearby. He kept the barrel of his weapon pointed toward them the entire time. He desperately controlled his breathing to remain silent as the two spoke.

"How long you figure this war will continue?" one guard asked.

"Like I'd know. Why? You don't think we'll lose to some new snot-nosed kids, right? The boss has a plan. You think that partnership with Mr. Powell's worth something? That's the question. All he's done is target one of their deliveries while we're doing all the fucking work. You believe that?"

Both zipped up their pants after they finished and continued speaking as they left.

"Powell's biding his time, but when he strikes, they'll wish they'd left. You watch. I've got a cousin who works for him, and he says they're gearing up for war tonight. He said they're launching an attack on those dumbasses."

Their voices were no longer audible as they'd gained too much distance.

Kyle raised to his feet with care not to cause much noise. Only the grass below gave away his movement. *They're hitting the compound tonight? The bosses planned for this. Let's hope they're alright. Focus up,* he thought. *Screw the fields. I can't hope to ignite these unless it's last. Some explosives will work the same. I'll drop them on the way.*

He stayed low to the ground and crawled out of the tree line until he reached a chopped tree trunk. Getting to a knee, he peeked to see the fields sprawling out before him. "Get to the center and plant it," he said under his breath. "How hard can that be? I've got cover from the crops and everything." He waited until another group passed by on their route and hurried out from cover. Once he was cloaked in the rows of plants, he kept the map of the fields fresh in his mind. It wouldn't do, planting the explosives in the corner of the fields. Thankfully his time in the armed forces had done wonders for his sense of direction. His instructors had seen to that personally.

Kyle got to his knees and crawled through what some would call a paradise on earth surrounded by pleasure inducing substances. To him, it was his cloak, his armor, his defense against being filled full of lead and meeting a premature end. Once he was satisfied with his distance into the field, he tossed the bag on the ground and unzipped it.

He pulled out two bricks of explosives he'd devised and pressed the button on them. It sprang to life as a blinking red light started. "Stay stable, baby. This much should obliterate all these fields if I'm correct." He got to his feet and made tracks away from the now doomed fields. He stayed near the edges of the coca field. The poppy pod fields didn't offer enough visual protection for his taste, being long thin rods with a bulbous pod sitting atop. At least the coca plants were nearly as tall as a man and thick with vibrant green leaves. There was just one problem.

I can't see patrols through this crap, he thought. *I'll rely on my ears and nose then.* He stopped near the edge of the coca fields, near where he estimated to be the processing barn. He couldn't be sure, seeing as his field of vision was cluttered with nothing but green leaves and thick foliage. There was only one choice to find out his precise location, and it involved risk. *Peek through or stand up. I'll take the former. Is coca loud when you move it? Damn, I should have looked it up.*

He crawled through the thick plants with precision, trying not to disturb the plants and move them. Closing on the edge, he reached out and grabbed a fistful of leaves before moving them to the right and bringing his face near. Success, he could see. *Now we wait for the right moment.*

He didn't have to wait long for his chance. He got to his feet and wasted no time. Running the short distance between the fields and the barn, he was almost there. He cut across the open land with nothing between him and nearby hostiles other than thin air. He slowed before reaching the barn and pulled out a knife. "Please, no," he muttered under his breath. "Nobody saw me."

The Spanish language met his ears, muffled as it was. The voice sounded female, and he didn't understand what was said. He gathered it was routine since she sounded bored.

Sure enough, a male voice replied in perfect Spanish. The voice then raised, yelling in English. "New guy, go bring more raw materials. We're almost out in here!"

A faint male voice answered. "Right away, sir."

Kyle side stepped toward the edge of the building and peeked around. He saw a man in dirty, ragged clothes running toward the fields he'd just exited. What's worse was that he headed toward where he planted the explosives. "Fuck," he said under his breath. Raising the rifle, he aimed through the scope. "Improvisation time." He fired, and the man went down before he reached the field.

Screams of mortal terror erupted from the other side of the wall, along with female screeches of fear. He turned the corner leading toward the open barn door. The guards ran out first. He trained his aim and fired before his victim even noticed him. Chunks of his head flew off and landed in a pile. The next guard was smarter and dove back inside the structure after seeing his partner die.

Instead of being a sitting duck, Kyle took off running around the barn. "Vamanos!" he yelled. He stressed his blunt Spanish with a kick of the barn.

Kyle heard a veritable stampede of footsteps run away from his voice out the open barn doors. He quickly retrieved the last brick of explosives and pressed the button. Dropping it, he ran. It didn't matter where, so long as it wasn't near here. A siren blared now, the alarm proverbially and literally ringing. They knew he was here now.

He reached for one detonator he'd stashed on his belt line and pressed the red button, careful to grab the correct one. A distant explosion and screams showed he'd picked the right one and not committed suicide. "That ought to get their attention." He slung the rifle over his shoulder and ran away from the barn as more yelling behind him met his ears. He heard gun shots halfway to the cover of trees. Pulling out his pistol, he turned while running and fired a few shots. Success. His attacker wasn't hit, but they retreated around the barn seeking cover, earning him more time to make his escape.

He burst into the tree line. His distraction only earned him a few seconds though, as he was soon dodging bullets again. He could hear the leaves ripping around him along with the cracks of the guns firing. As he ran, he tried to maintain a tree between him and his attackers, but it was a guessing game since he didn't have eyes in the back of his head. Footsteps echoed in his mind along with the bullets aiming to end his life. Time ran short. Slowing was not an option. Every step was an opportunity to fall and lose precious time. Absentmindedly, he reached down and pressed the final detonator. Another explosion rocked the land and more screams faded away behind him.

A body slammed into his and interrupted his frantic escape. He ended up on his back, but his instinct forced him to punch his attacker without skipping a beat. Taking advantage, he rolled over so now he was on top. This had a cost, however. He felt a sharp pain in his right shoulder and felt cold steel embedded in him.

Kyle responded in kind by quickly unsheathing his own blade and stabbing it into his opponent's neck. He used his free hand to grip the foreign steel in his shoulder and kept his attacker from regaining the knife. Fighting to keep the blade in him, he used his knife to drag along his victim's neck. Spurts of blood rewarded his effort and within ten seconds he was too weak to fight back, so Kyle got back to his feet, knife still stuck in his shoulder.

He didn't let a little thing like a knife stop him. He could almost smell his car from here. Kyle had almost lost track of time since he started this operation, but it seemed to happen in a flash. He replayed the previous ten minutes in his mind, searching for the mistake he'd made. A pleasant interruption shocked him back to reality as he broke through the forest finally and spotted his vehicle.

He hurried over and never started the engine quicker in his life. He hit the gas, and he heard the tires squeal underneath as the car jolted forward, away from his handiwork.

Back at the farmhouse...

"Why am I doing this?" Abigail's voice asked. "I'm watching cameras, why?"

Bernard looked over to the van parked nearby. "It's a precaution is all. You're upstairs, right?"

"I am," she said.

"If war kicks off, head to the bathroom and jump in the bathtub, please."

"You do this every night?"

"No," Roger said "Tonight's special. I'm in position near the house."

Bernard looked right into the trees where he knew Roger was posted. To his left laid the barn while his forces occupied the tree line beside the driveway. "Only when we attack Bailey or Powell. As you see, we don't have tons of manpower yet. We just got set up here. As a result, when we attack, we're short on defense. All you'll do is report where you see enemies. We've installed cameras all around the manor. You're our eyes and ears here. Roger and I are watching the woods behind the house, and Crystal is our backup."

"How are you doing over there, Wallace?" Bernard asked. He looked across the property at the opposite tree line near the driveway, serving as the front line.

"It's quiet over here, sir. We're keeping an ear out. With this crossfire, they'll be fucked should they try a frontal assault."

"It's that or they trudge through miles of forest at night," Abigail said.

"Don't put that past them," Roger said. "We would and have done that. Don't get tunnel visioned out here. Keep an eye on your backs."

"Frontal assault is likely if you ask me," Wallace said. "They'll want their cars for cover and it's the only approach that allows it."

"I hope you're right," Bernard said. "Crystal, how're you holding up?"

"I hope I don't have to provide my services. I had my fill of this before."

"Quiet down," Roger said. "Cars are coming. Look."

Bernard turned his attention to the road in front of the property, and indeed, Roger was correct. A line of cars approached along the two-lane road. They turned onto their gargantuan driveway and stopped at the bottom of the hill.

"What are they doing?" Wallace asked. "Permission to light them up?"

"I'd imagine they have reinforced windows," Bernard said. "Negative. It'd give away our locations. Hold your fire until the order. Stay hidden, and be ready." He moved behind the van and climbed in the open back doors. Reaching over the seat, he grasped the parking brake. He stared out the front windshield at the cars below. "Almost there," he said to himself. He watched the procession start again and approach slowly. "That's it." He released the parking brake and hurried out the back and into cover.

The van rolled forward and down the hill, headed directly toward the procession. It gained speed in a hurry, as gravity did the work for him. He watched as men filed out of the car upon spotting the van moving toward them. They started firing at the delivery vehicle with automatic rifles, trying desperately to halt its incoming momentum, to no avail.

Eventually they gave up and scattered like roaches when the light comes on.

"Too late," Bernard said. He pressed the button on the

detonator and the vehicle, loaded with the brick of explosives, detonated. Those lucky not to be disintegrated by their proximity to the explosive blast flew a surprising distance. The unlucky ones turned into a fine red mist, hovering over the battlefield. Screams of pain rang out from the survivors. A few had their insides on their outsides, desperately trying to hold them inside. Others had limbs blown clean off, effectively crippled.

"They're coming from the woods!" Abigail's panicked voice screamed in everybody's ear. "Oh God, they're behind the house."

"Keep calm," Bernard said. "I'll check it out. Rog, you alright over here?"

"For now," he said. "Hurry back. I don't fancy being here by myself."

"Be back in a flash, old friend. Wallace, keep your partners there. You're approaching the back of the house with me."

"Understood."

Bernard ran through the trees, keeping his right side to the farmhouse and chaos. He stopped in his tracks once close enough to see behind the house. Sure enough, he spotted Powell's forces stalking toward the property, visibly armed. They were exposed and vulnerable, however. "Light them up." He took aim at them with the rifle in his arms and squeezed the trigger. He could see the muzzle flash across the clearing as Wallace followed his orders.

Their aggressors died swiftly, being in the no-man's-land between the house and the trees. One reached to his belt before rearing back, but he fell. An explosion rocked the battlefield where he landed. Bernard covered his eyes and looked back. A vast crater was all that remained of the garden area. "Must have been a grenade."

"Enemies are everywhere out there. They're behind the barn and running up the front hill. They're literally coming out of the woodwork."

"I'm fucked over here. Their sheer numbers are staggering. They're approaching my front and rear." Roger said. "It's fine covering my rear for now, but I need help soon!"

"I'm headed back there, buddy," Bernard turned and sprinted back to his original position. "Crystal, get the drone ready to deploy. We'll need it momentarily if I'm right."

"Already on it. Orders?"

"Shit!" a male voice said. "We need backup here. They're storming our position. You copy?"

"Crystal, send the drone over to them," Roger said. Gunshots were audible over the call when he spoke. "Damn it. They need help or else their side will be overrun."

"Do it," Bernard said.

Crystal didn't verbally respond to the orders.

The next thing Bernard saw was said drone flying high above, angled down. "Interesting firing position," he said. He saw the barrel spin up and lead started flying. Men rushing the tree lines near the exploded van fell like rain, giving needed relief to the team across from the house.

"Grenade!" a male voice yelled.

The explosion kicked up an enormous dust cloud and sent splinters of bark and wood in a thousand different directions across the field from Bernard's position.

"Men, you alright over there?"

No answer ever came apart from more gunshots and indistinct yelling.

Without order, the drone turned. It fired at the men charging up the hill toward Roger's position. More bodies fell, staining the grass below. Until one got wise. He turned and fired at the drone, scoring several successive hits. Sparks flew and black smoke wafted up from the engines at its sides. It lost altitude and eventually fell out of the air with a dull thud as it impacted on the grassy hill and rolled down toward the mass of wreckage.

"I'm out of commission," Crystal said.

"Fuck," Bernard said to himself. He slammed his back into a nearby tree and started firing at the men still approaching Roger's position. He took aim and, with the combined firepower of Roger and himself, all of them fell. A few brave souls got within a few feet of the tree cover but never reached their goal.

Wallace spoke up. "The ones over here are retreating, sir. I think we've driven them off with all this."

Bernard turned and saw Wallace was correct. Across the field, they ran away from the farmhouse toward the road. They turned and disappeared out of sight. "I want a perimeter check. Nobody's sleeping until I know Bailey's men have left. Is that understood? In addition, we need to clear those wrecks off the property. People will get curious. Wallace, I want you to meet us in the middle. It could be a ploy to circle around, and I don't want you caught in their kill zone."

"Understood, I'm moving now."

"Rog, we're circling around to meet him around the back near the barn. If they're out there, we stand a better chance with three guns."

"I'm on it," Roger said.

Bernard and Roger met up and quietly stalked around the property. They never heard another gunshot or man. A twig snapped in front. "King, is that you?" Bernard asked. "Don't shoot."

"Boss?" Wallace peeked around a tree and saw Roger and Bernard approaching. "I have seen nobody out here."

"Come along with us. We'll check the side where the grenade exploded and work on moving the trash littering the lawn afterward. Are we clear?"

"Crystal clear."

The three men's hike was uneventful, not finding any hostiles.

"They're not here," Bernard said. "They ran. Alright, everybody. King, we're going to need your truck for this. We're dumping these. Nobody should link the van to us since it was clean to begin with. If the police link their cars to them, that's their fault.

"Towing? Sir, they don't have wheels. I can't tow or sparks would be everywhere."

"You aren't taking it on vacation. You're going into the middle of nowhere after midnight on a country road. Nobody will notice or care. If a civilian sees it, they'll mind their business. We don't have a choice. We can't leave them here or the police will take notice and that's attention we don't need. Got it? Besides, we're using our cars to tow as well. You're not the only one risking shit tonight."

"Understood. Guess we're getting started then if we want to get some sleep."

"Our work is eternal, Mr. King," Roger said, patting the man on the shoulder.

12

"Why the field though?" Chris shoveled another shovel full of soil into the shallow crater that was their future garden. "Looks like a grenade's work."

Bernard was shirtless and working nearby. "From my vantage point, it looked like he was killed after pulling the pin. They nearly reached the house, but we held them off. Besides, why do you care about this garden?" He wiped sweat off his brow under the sun.

"Bad for morale when the tech lady's depressed."

"Is that all?"

Chris pulled out a rolled up smokeable. He stuck one end in his mouth and retrieved a match from his pocket.

"What's that?" Bernard walked over and sniffed. "Seriously?"

"Molly said it'd give us energy. That's what sativa means, she claims. We need energy, so it seems obvious."

"You had fun last night." Bernard shook his head and shoveled more dirt into the slowly filling crater. "Is that why you're chomping at the bit to smoke it again?"

"Fun's a strong word."

"Am I wrong?"

"No."

"You'd best share that." Bernard looked over with a quick grin. "It's only proper to share with superiors."

The house's back door opened and slammed shut. They looked over to see Molly coming out with two water bottles. "Catch." She tossed them underhanded.

Both caught the refreshments before opening and taking a drink.

"How's the barn looking?" Bernard asked.

"I was just there. There are some large holes, but Roger's on top of it. They're painting boards of wood red to match the barn before nailing them to preserve the look to civilians driving by. We're lucky they didn't take it out."

"They needed the cover," Chris said. "Tree cover is fine, but if you want to advance, you don't destroy your own cover. That's why they left it standing. I'm more worried about the windows and bullet holes in the house. We can't call professionals, or they'll ask questions."

"I have a working relationship with a glass repair shop. We've convinced them not to ask questions. Money talks, my friend. As far as the damage, any ideas? It needs more than spackle to seal."

"Talk to your window repairman friend," Molly said. "Even money says he has a fixer upper friend who won't ask questions. If not, I'll find one. It might be colder until it's fixed, but portable heaters will make it livable. Also, boss, regarding our reinforcements from Mrs. Morris that should've arrived last night - I received a message from them this morning informing us of their arrival today. Can you get them settled in? Mr. Hudson wants Roger for the meeting tonight."

"I can manage." He rubbed his eyes. "Evans, Rog, and I

were up all night burying the dead." Bernard looked at the trees where they buried the departed. "Wallace and Lionel got rid of the wreckage. We hit them harder though. We hampered Bailey's money, and Powell lost tons of men, assuming those jokers in the mass grave were his. From your testimonies, Bailey had guards everywhere. I sincerely doubt he sent those soldiers at us. Drug pushers keep enough muscle to run security and push the dirty work onto the junkies."

Chris struck a match and ignited the joint before taking a puff. Thick smoke billowed out, followed by a coughing fit.

"Easy, old timer." Bernard walked over and slapped Chris's back. "Molly, why don't you go see how Roger's doing? We'll fix this crater."

"That works. I have news for him specifically." Molly said her farewells and ambled over to the barn. She peeked inside and watched the two work for a minute before entering.

"This is the best we can manage?" Roger asked. "It's the wrong shade of red."

"It's what we possess, sir," Kyle said. "At least to the outside we don't own a shot up barn. It'll look old and decrepit. That's better than full of holes."

Molly knocked on wood as she stood in the open gate. "I received a message, boss."

"From whom?" Roger asked. He continued to paint the wooden boards on the table.

"From Mr. Hudson. He wants a meeting tonight to set up the specifics for our gun deal. He requested a meeting with the head kahuna, meaning you. I have ideas for the meeting I'd love to run by you."

"Go ahead." Roger looked over at Kyle, who had a large

bandage visible on his shoulder. He was painting with his uninjured arm, slower than his boss.

"Mr. Evans, head to the garden area and get Chris to share," Molly said. "We can handle a little painting by ourselves."

"Share? Whatever, fine." Kyle stepped past Molly and disappeared around the corner.

"What needed privacy?" Roger asked.

"I'm concerned that Mr. Hudson could be compromised, Rog."

"Rog?"

"Oh, sorry. It just slipped out. Mr. Morris."

"No." Roger smiled. "Rog is fine. You think because we're locked in war, Powell got to him and is using this as a trap to assassinate me? Is that it?"

"In so many words," Molly said. "Why request a meeting with Ms. Morris's son? You think negotiations on a gun deal require that? Why not deal with Bernard or whoever we sent with your authority? It stinks of a setup."

"What do you propose?" Roger asked. He dipped the paintbrush into the bright red paint. "Where's he want to meet, anyway?"

"He wanted to meet in his comedy club again, claiming security is adequate there."

"They had armed bouncers. There are worse places."

"I suggest I tag along, sir," Molly said. "I can infiltrate his phone without his noticing and see who he's been talking to. If he's compromised, we'll know before we sit down back there in case it's a trap."

"Spying on our own ally?" Roger asked with a flinch. "He'd be pissed if he found out."

"He wouldn't find out. There's another reason I volunteered. He sent two tickets to his show this evening."

"Are you asking me out on a date, Ms. Turner?"

"What? Who said that? I'm just helping my boss with his job and proposing we enjoy the circumstances. Don't get confused."

"Whatever you say," Roger said. "Yeah, I don't mind you coming along. I'd still prefer having my security there as bodyguards, especially if you're coming along. I can't risk you getting hurt. Did you hear if Jackie went to the doctor? I don't want her catching an infection from that wound."

"I believe so. She told them it was a power tool incident."

"We'll take her and Mr. Lionel. We'll give Mr. Evans a break. He deserves it since he got injured on that mission. I still can't believe he pulled it off. I was worried if I'm honest. Don't tell anyone that."

"You? Worried?"

"Obviously. I care for everyone under my command. I don't get the luxury of showing it. It doesn't mean I don't have feelings. Even if I am hotheaded sometimes, I try to remain stoic." Roger placed the paintbrush on the wooden board. "I'm only human. We're taking risks, Ms. Turner. We don't do it lightly. It's out of necessity to end this war in a hurry. Besides, he volunteered vehemently to go solo. He wanted to make a name for himself, and boy did he."

"He already had a name. He wanted to earn it," Molly said. "I bet he didn't feel he earned it since he shot Mikhail in the back after all."

"You may be right, but it's immaterial. He's proven himself to us in every way. Regarding the meeting, consider it a date, Ms. Turner."

"Date? Who said it's a date?"

"Two young people going to a comedy club and enjoying themselves sounds like one to me and anyone honest. Now let's not quibble over details and enjoy tonight."

"Can I ask a personal question?" Molly asked. "It's been bugging me ever since I met you."

"You can ask, but I can't guarantee an answer."

"How did you convince your mother to give you this post? I remember the night we met, and I got the impression we lied to acquire the guns and vans. I didn't say anything at the time since you're the boss's kid, and I followed orders. Am I in the ballpark?"

"Aren't you curious? Maybe when we're a little closer, I can reveal why. It's personal and sensitive in nature."

"Anything to do with what Crystal mentioned earlier about your mother?"

"A little."

Speak of the devil and she showed up. Crystal showed up in the barn's open gate. "I'm going too, right?"

"Huh?" Molly turned to face the blonde.

"Eavesdropping is a bad habit," Roger said. "I know mother taught you that, same as me. Remember when she grounded us for two weeks for overhearing the initiation talks with Warren?"

"You aren't mom and I figured you'd let your sister off with a warning. Don't be a killjoy. Let me get out of the farmhouse. The internet's nothing compared to a live show with a dinner. You know I never get to leave the house. Don't be like mom and dad."

"She's going to kill me if she finds out. Not a word to her, either of you."

"Fine by me," Crystal said.

"You'll stay near Jackie and Mr. Lionel. Is that clear? I want you safe. Besides, when the hell are the reinforcements from mother arriving? Did anyone hear from them?"

"They had a complication," Molly said.

"Define complication, and why wasn't I informed earlier?"

"I wanted to secure the arms deal first. They didn't elaborate. They said they'll be here tonight and offered their most sincere apologies."

"How cryptic. Could it have been a fake email?"

"I don't believe so. Last night the squad sent the encrypted email. I just decrypted it last night. They're delayed and couldn't arrive yesterday. It didn't say why. The last message I received from them said they were driving. They estimate their time of arrival at seven tonight, which lines up with the meeting. We're to be at the club by seven."

"Then Bernard and Chris will be their welcoming party. At least we held out long enough for reinforcements to arrive. It's only five bodies, but we lost two. I still feel bad for them." He turned his attention to Crystal at his side. "How about you? You alright?"

"I don't enjoy killing; but I thought you'd die, so I didn't mind."

"I thought I was going to," Roger said. He wrapped an arm around her shoulder and pulled her into an embrace. "I was surrounded. I figured the enemies in the forest were higher priority, but you and Bernard had my back. You kept them from climbing the hill and completely flanking me. I owe you and him my life."

"Then thank me by taking me along and buying my dinner." Crystal nestled into his side with a contented smile.

Molly watched the display with mild annoyance, judging by her scowl. She erased the negative emotion from her face and tried to replace it with indifference. "Your sister's correct." She couldn't hide the tiny smile at the look of anger crossing Crystal's face at the label. "Being stuck isolated in that house is grating."

"Just do everything Jackie says. That's my stipulation."

"Deal." Crystal squeezed a last time before backing off.

"Can you two send Evans back in? I'll finish this and work on the field with the rest. Inform Jackie of her assignment too, and be a dear."

"We're on it." Molly said, grabbing Crystal's hand to drag her away.

They exited the barn, and Crystal yanked her hand free. "Thanks for the help." She rubbed her wrist.

"I know what being cooped up's like," Molly said as they walked. "Wouldn't wish it on anyone, especially a friend."

"I considered us more rivals now, if I'm honest." Crystal waved to Bernard, Chris, and Kyle as they approached.

"Not a rivalry when you're not even considered," Molly said.

This comment earned her a momentary glare before returning to a smiling face as they got closer to the group.

"He's ready for you in the barn, Mr. Evans," Molly said, pointing over her shoulder with her thumb. "Anyone heard from Jackie?"

Kyle handed the joint back to Bernard.

"I think she's in her room." Bernard pointed toward the house. "Why?" He took a puff and passed it to Chris.

"She's on security detail tonight at the meeting, along with Mr. Lionel. He wanted you and Mr. Bristol here to acclimate our new arrivals while we're out securing our pipeline of guns."

"Should be easy enough," Chris said. He took an elongated inhale from the joint, downsizing it visibly.

Bernard snatched the joint out of Chris's lips. "You'll need a clear head, old timer. I have plans already. You'll handle the recruits, seeing as it's your assignment. Rog won't mind." He handed it over to Kyle. "Here kid, try a little more. It'll help with the pain."

Kyle took a drag from it before handing it back. "I'm good. If you'll excuse me." He brushed past the girls and bee-lined toward the open barn doors.

"We'll go tell Jackie then. Have fun out here," Crystal said.

The pair of women walked to the house and stopped just inside the lobby.

"Ms. Morris, I'm not trying to be adversarial with this Roger thing. I value our friendship. You know that."

"I know, but it feels like we're drifting apart recently," Crystal admitted. "He's always busy."

"I see. You should know, I believe he likes me romantically."

"You think so?" Crystal asked, sarcasm evident. "It's plain as day. I realize it. That's why I'm not pushing it. Like you said, I value our friendship and won't ruin it over trying to seize something I had no right to."

"What do I even wear tonight?" Molly looked down at her black attire. "I don't think my unique fashion sense will fit right with that clientele."

"Some guys dig the goth look. Apparently, my brother does. Dress like you normally would."

"You think so?"

"Don't put on an act if you're trying to woo my brother. He deserves to know the real you. It's not fair otherwise. He deserves a woman who'll respect and cherish him. If it crumbles, I'll swoop in and get him on the rebound."

Molly reached over and pushed Crystal on the shoulder. "Fuck off."

13

"Thank you, everybody." The comedian waved to the ground and placed the microphone on the stand. "Ya'll are fantastic and kind. We'll have a short intermission before the next comedian. Please enjoy your evening, and I hope to see you soon."

Every patron in the club clapped as the performer stepped off the stage.

A waitress stopped by Roger and Molly's table as relaxing piano music filled the newfound silence. She sat two drinks on the table. "Mr. Hudson regrets to inform you he'll be with you in a few minutes. He's busy, so please enjoy these on the house."

"Thank you." Roger picked up the beverage.

Molly grabbed Roger's hand once the waitress left and muttered. "You're sure you're old enough for that, boss? You're not twenty-one."

Roger drank some. "It's water. I'm touched by your concern for my health, Ms. Turner. One could interpret that you care if you're not careful."

Molly drank her glass with a wince. "That is not water."

"It's champagne I believe, judging by the bubbles," Roger said, eying her drink.

"What do you know about champagne?" Molly's words were adversarial, but her tone betrayed her amusement. She watched waitresses and waiters frantically moving table to table taking orders in the packed club. "Feels like we're at a Hollywood premier, almost. Did you see the line outside?"

"No ticket, no show," Roger said. "It's nice to have connections. I believe there are famous country music stars in attendance too. We're rubbing elbows with some famous performers. You think Bernard and Chris are doing alright with the new roster?"

"Bernard said he's handing that off to Chris and that he had plans."

"Probably with Abigail if I know him," Roger said. He leaned back in the chair.

"You think he's taking her on a date in the middle of a war?"

Roger used his hand to gesture to the surrounding club. "No, that'd be crazy. Who'd do that?" His wide, toothy smile gave away his meaning.

"You're such an ass sometimes," Molly laughed. "There's Mr. Hudson." She watched as Hudson went from table to table. He shook hands, laughed, spoke, and paid special attention to every patron. "That explains his success. People love that personal touch and to feel special, especially when they pay this much for a ticket."

"You like personal touches too, huh?"

"Mr. Morris," Molly placed a hand on her chest, feigning indignation. "Who do you take me for, a common harlot?"

"Far from it," Roger responded just as fast. "I was projecting my desires onto you."

"So, you're the harlot?" Molly and Roger shared a laugh

over their drinks, ignoring the world around them for a brief evening of respite.

Roger glanced over at the next table with Jackie, Lyle, and Crystal. "At least she's having a good time."

"Who? Crystal?"

"Yeah," Roger said. "She's going through a lot. Technically I'm not her brother, but she'll always be my little sister. I don't enjoy keeping her locked away like mom and dad did to us. I just hate exposing her to more danger. You know?"

"Complicated, huh? She's as stubborn as her brother, unfortunately."

"Who says I'm stubborn?"

Molly simply stared at him blankly.

"Maybe I'm a little headstrong."

"Speaking of headstrong, I don't think I've ever told you about myself, have I?" Molly asked.

"I didn't want to pry. Mother always told us it was rude to ask about an employee's past once we initiated them. I didn't mean to offend."

"People say I'm an ass or short-tempered," she said. "I'm rude and a loner. I'm aware of my reputation around the group. It's not lost on me that I'm called the ice queen of tech."

"You asked me about my family earlier. You mind if I ask a personal question in return?"

Molly was near the bottom of the glass now. "Shoot."

"What's your story?"

"You digging to hear my tragic backstory that led to my life of crime?" She swirled the remains of the alcohol in her glass before upending it. "Would it surprise you if I simply said I was a rebel? I used my skills in various illegal ways to secure a living. I attracted the attention of Lee during this period, and the rest is history."

"Being a rebel? That's the entire story?"

"Shit loads of cash sweetened the deal. Being paid to rebel against the system was all I needed.

"Not anymore though?"

"I have different goals now, more than simple rebellion. I want to prove myself. My whole life everybody's seen me as spoiled rotten because of my upbringing. I've had members tell me as much. None of them respected me, and for good reason. I'd never earned my way once. Mom and dad financed my living accommodations until I joined. That's why I'm hung up on leading this branch."

"Most coming of age stories don't involve our business model, you know," Roger said.

She accidentally brushed his leg across the table with hers. She didn't verbally acknowledge the contact, but her reddening cheeks showed she was aware of the physical intimacy. "You're a radical maverick in every aspect of life, aren't you?"

"Maverick? I'm not sure about that assessment, but I envy those digital skills of yours. I have a rudimentary understanding, but what you do?" He looked at the approaching waitress. "It's over my head."

The waitress stopped with a beaming smile. "Mr. Hudson can see you now. If you'd accompany me, I'll escort you back."

"Lead the way, ma'am." Roger reached into his suit's pocket and handed her a twenty-dollar bill before he and Molly got up. "Here, for the outstanding service."

"Thank you, Mr. Morris. It's appreciated." She extended an arm and led the pair. They passed dozens of patrons. Most talked and laughed amongst themselves. They approached a pair of security guards. "Mr. Morris is here for his meeting with Mr. Hudson."

"Head inside." The guards parted ways and opened the door behind them. "Your security will wait out here."

Roger looked over his shoulder to see Lyle and Jackie already there.

"It's boss's orders," the guard said.

"I'm heading outside around the back," Jackie said. "Lyle, you stay here with these two. Boss, you remember what I told you before."

The words of Jackie before they exited the car rang in his mind. *You text me if anything goes wrong in there. Keep your gun close just in case Molly's correct.* "Your terms are agreeable." Roger took Molly by the hand and led her inside.

"I trust you remember the way?" the guard asked.

"We'll be fine."

"Good." The guard shut the door behind them.

"It's this way." Roger pointed, using his free hand, and led her down the familiar hallway. He grabbed her hand and took point.

Molly was quiet, her focus on their hands intertwining together between them. She didn't dare let Roger catch her looking, choosing to look away at the slightest hint of being observed. It was over too soon for her liking when she felt a gentle tug. She found herself in a room with Mr. Hudson and a stranger.

"Mr. Hudson," Roger said. He extended his hand to the older gentleman, who took it.

"Mr. Morris. Please, call me Percy." The old man gestured toward the younger. "This is my son, Jonathon Hudson."

Jonathon's hair was slicked back. Combined with his formal suit, he mirrored his father's fashion sense. His full head of brown hair provided a mirror into the past, showing what the elder likely looked like at his age.

"A pleasure to meet you," Jonathon said, extending a hand. "Begging your pardon, but who is this beautiful young lady you have with you? Is it your date?"

"She works for me," Roger said.

"Mixing business with pleasure, Mr. Morris?" Jonathon asked. "It's a complicated business."

"Business relationships have worked for my mother. Ask my father the next time you speak."

"It's wonderful to meet both of you," Molly said.

Everybody sat down, and Percy cleared his throat, breaking the silence. "Getting down to brass tacks, I didn't call you here just for the negotiations. I understand you're at war with Mr. Powell and Mr. Bailey. Mr. Powell is targeting me. He said as much today. That's why security's tight out there."

"He let you know?" Roger asked. "I would have imagined he'd keep that secret."

"It's hardly a secret," Jonathon said. "It's a predictable outcome given his bloodthirsty way of doing business."

"My son's correct," Percy said. "We're aware you're in a kinetic war with Mr. Bailey and Mr. Powell. In fact, we understand you've come under attack at your home."

Roger shifted in his seat, clearly uncomfortable. "I'm more concerned that you heard about it. We've done our best to keep that secret from the public. That's right. Quick thinking and ingenuity saved us since our roster wasn't deep. You think Powell is just getting started?"

"I imagine most of your attackers were debtors of Mr. Bailey being supplied weapons from Mr. Powell," Percy said. He placed his palms flat against his desk. "That's usually their first line of defense in the past. Their MO, if you will. Once they realize that won't work, it'll kick off. On the bright side, Mr. Powell's organization isn't extensive either. He relies on others doing his dirty work. His security or soldiers are in short supply, as are yours and mine."

"Thank heaven for small miracles," Roger said. "We looted their weapons, and we plan on selling them. No sense tossing away a blessing."

"Quite so," Jonathon said. He grabbed a nearby bottle and glass from a shelf. "Hear me. This will grow worse before it gets better. Would you care for a drink?" He poured one glass and waited for an answer.

"Thank you, but no. If you're asking for protection, we're already spread thin," Roger said. "We're guarding a dispensary, our home, and our personnel. We don't have the numbers yet to make it a reality."

"That's not it." Percy shook his head and clasped his hands laying on his desk. "We're simply warning you. You learn a few lessons when you've been in the game for decades. I have bodyguards and security taken care of. I'd hate to see the partners I've hitched my wagon to die. Then I'd be target number one for betraying their trust."

"Selflessness through selfishness. I like it," Molly said. She returned her attention to her lap where her phone laid. Her gaze didn't linger on it, decorum stated she couldn't. She was forced to rush her intrusion into their phones.

"That's the crude way of putting it," Percy said. "Realize the attacks from Mr. Powell will grow frequent and without warning or pause. Now that we've waded through the unpleasant reality, let's talk guns. I have your order ready to deliver. All that stands in our way is setting up the next deal, and we're ready. Would you prefer your personnel pick it up?"

"I would," Roger said. "It'd be less risk for you. Can't have our supplier putting himself at risk. That's not a good business model."

"I appreciate the concern," Percy said. "It would have cost more had you desired delivery, so you are wise."

"Flattery will get you nowhere, Mr. Hudson." Roger wore a slick smile as he spoke. "Future shipments need to be hashed out, I assume."

"That depends if you want a reorder of this shipment or if you'd prefer different merchandise to sample. If it's the same, we can repeat the order without a problem. If new products are desired, it will take slightly longer."

"We could send a document with all we want at a later date you want," Molly said. "No sense rushing things."

"That's a possibility. Most prefer to gauge our weaponry first, so I understand the reticence to rush another shipment before you've inspected your new weaponry."

"It's not that I doubt the quality," Roger said. "It's that things are in flux. Doing business during war is always tricky, as you no doubt know."

"You misunderstand. I am not angry, quite the opposite," Percy said. "I'm relieved you showed up, and the payment cleared. Words cannot overstate how many clients I've had in the past that reneged on their side of the deal because of similar circumstances."

"I know the type," Roger said. "Remember the Russian Mafia we were in a war with recently? That war was over them deciding they didn't want to pay our price. A price they'd paid for years. One day, Oleg decided he wanted to shake up the system, and he paid the price in blood. I respect an honest businessman. Just don't surprise us like that, and we'll get along fine, Mr. Hudson."

"I'd never dream of it. I'm going to focus on survival, and I encourage you all to copy me. Until you take care of Powell, we're all in danger."

"You don't know where he's located, do you?" Roger asked.

"I wish I did, but he's a private man who's guarded his anonymity fiercely. The only personnel that'd know are high-ranking guards, and good luck finding those psychos. Your best bet would be to investigate his legitimate business."

"Which is?" Molly asked, clearly interested.

"The legal gun shop in town called Powell's Kinetics Emporium." Percy hid a laugh. "The irony is not lost on me that an arms dealer has a legal gun shop. He paid out the ass for the permits and paperwork. That's the only official shop everyone knows he has. I doubt it'll lead you anywhere, but if your tech division is as good as the rumors say, maybe it will. Likely, all you'll find are intermediaries and dummy accounts by tracing that rabbit hole."

"I appreciate the lead," Roger said. "If nothing else, it may be a clue."

Percy tore off a page from a nearby notepad and pushed it across the table. "Here is the location to pick up your order. Pick it up whenever it's convenient."

Roger picked up the paper and read the address printed. He filed it away in his jacket pocket. "Thank you. Any advice on this war before we part ways?"

"Kill them with all haste," Jonathon answered instead of his father. "They will not delay, I promise you. If they already know where you live, you're in their crosshairs. The best defense against him is a swift offense. You get me?"

"Understood."

Percy pushed away from the desk and stood, prompting everyone else to stand. He shook hands with Roger one final time. "Be careful on your way home tonight, Mr. Morris.

Any time spent away from safety's a risk. Your security is top-notch I pray, for all our sakes."

"I trust them with my life. I've known them since I was a child and am certain they're up to the task."

"We bid you farewell, and be safe." Jonathon shook Roger's hand firmly.

"Farewell, gentlemen." Roger and Molly exited the back room. He pulled out his phone and texted a quick message once they were in the hallway. "Now let's head into the club while Jackie prepares our exit."

"Sounds like a plan to me."

The pair exited out into the bustling club between the two guards.

They moved back to their table and sat down at the neighboring one with only his sister. "Hey," Roger said. "Sorry it took so long. Enjoy yourself out here?"

"Intermission was about to end, I think," Crystal said. "How'd the negotiations go?"

"Satisfactory," Roger said. "As soon as Jackie and Lyle return, we're heading home."

"So soon?" Crystal whined.

"You knew before we left the stipulation," Molly said. "Much as I empathize with you, he's right. We should limit public appearances."

"At least everyone's safe at home as we speak."

"Yeah, about that," Molly looked away.

"About what?" Roger grabbed Molly's hand. "What are you not telling me?"

"Bernard's picking up Abigail, I believe. He said he had plans, and Chris would take care of the tardy recruits."

"Damn." Roger chewed on his bottom lip. He subconsciously squeezed Molly's hand tighter.

"He knows what he's doing," Crystal said.

"If he was just picking her up, he'd leave at eight, since that's when the dispensary closes. He left at seven. That means he wants to spend more time with her. Probably taking her out on a date afterward."

"Maybe he was jealous when he heard you having your date at one of the prime spots in Nashville and didn't want to be outdone," Crystal said. "He's the competitive type."

"Or he wants to show her a fun time," Molly said. "Both can be true. No sense worrying now." She rested her other hand on his, covering it. "Try to relax. You'll need to speak to the new members when we return. Use that concern and this time to plan your speech. It'll keep your mind off Bernard's impulsiveness."

"I'll try."

"There you are," Jackie's voice said over his shoulder. "Time to head out, boss."

"Lead the way, Ms. Thomas. We'll inform you how it went on the way home."

Jackie took the front while Lyle brought up the rear of the group as they exited the club. They made it to the car without incident, and Jackie started the engine.

Lyle slammed his door shut, and they were in motion.

Roger cleared his throat. "Molly, how'd Mr. Hudson's and his son's phones look?"

"Their phones were clean. There were no unknown numbers or unusual calls." Molly reached down to the seat near their feet for her laptop. She brushed against his leg and instinctively looked up at Roger from below before realizing what she was doing. She sat up and plopped the laptop on her legs. "I also had the contents of his computer download onto this hard drive so we could peek. He struck me as a digital guy, so I figured this would illuminate things clearly. Give me a moment to analyze what we received."

"Spying on our own business partners rubs me the wrong way," Lyle said.

"Partners don't always stay partners, kid," Jackie gave a sidelong glance at Lyle in the passenger seat. "Our war with the Russians showed that."

"If he finds out, it might spark another."

"That's a risk we measured to be acceptable," Roger said. "Our payment's cleared, and the guns are available to pick up." He patted his pocket where the address lay tucked away. "I figure we'll send the new meat to secure them. Who should we send to supervise, Ms. Thomas?"

"I'll oversee it," Jackie said. "I need to keep my mind occupied. Besides, I want to gauge them."

"Do you doubt their courage?"

"Not courage exactly, but something caused their delay. I aim to discover what and why. If it's a stupid ass reason, I aim to punish them. It nearly caused your death last night, sir. I'm imagining it wasn't anything excusable, if I'm being honest. If they're arriving tonight, they didn't leave until this morning when they were ordered to the day before. I aim to see if they were fucking around while we fought and died."

"A worthy goal," Roger said. "Talk to Chris when we arrive home. He should have found out the reason."

"Acknowledged."

"Here we go," Molly said, interrupting the exchange. "The only thing I can access is a text file. This dude takes digital security seriously."

"What's it say?" Lyle asked.

"It's an income and expenses document for his comedy club. Unless I have the key, I cannot decrypt everything else, and it'd take me months to crack."

"Forget it," Roger said. "If he turned, we wouldn't have walked out of the club. His muscle would have taken us and handed us off. We needed to know, and now we're certain. Now we focus on Mr. Powell. We learned of his legitimate business. In a display of ignorance, he owns a legitimate gun shop. Who'd have seen that coming?"

"The dude probably paid off anyone who could trouble him," Molly said. "Why should he care if people suspect foul play if nobody official cares? The only break is maybe he got sloppy in setting it up. I'll make that a priority with your permission, Rog."

"Rog?" Jackie asked.

"I mean boss."

"Permission granted. We need to find this joker and show him the same lesson we taught Mr. Bailey, his business partner. I'd also like to end Mr. Bailey permanently in case he gets any ideas about supplying more bodies for Powell. Hudson informed us it's standard practice for Bailey's debtor junkies to be soldiers in their little war. Keeps them distanced from the blowback."

"That would explain why they were easy targets," Lyle said. "They ran like lemmings at our lines and fell in droves. They weren't trained. I knew that for damned sure."

"I'm not complaining," Roger said. "If they'd been organized, I'd have died in that tree line. I barely covered my ass while Crystal here and Bernard watched my back."

"That van play was poetry in motion," Lyle said.

"Van?" Jackie asked.

"They put some explosives in it and rolled it down the hill into their vehicles. It blew up and kicked the battle off. It panicked them from the start."

"Smart thinking, but now we don't have any delivery or pickup vehicles, boss," Jackie said. "What do you propose we pick up the guns with? Our normal cars?"

"We have one van in reserve, remember?" Roger asked. "We took two from mother as parting gifts. We're good."

"For now, but we need a spare."

"Fair enough."

Crystal noticed her brother's pensive expression. "Worried about Bernard?"

"Me, worried? No." His shaking hand undercut his words. She was going to grab it only to find Molly beat her to the punch.

The rest of the ride was uneventful.

14

―――――――

"Get over here!" Chris yelled at the group exiting the van. "Hurry, people."

The five Syndicate members rushed to follow the order, some almost tripping in their haste. They lined up in front of Chris and Kyle and stood up straight with their hands at their sides. Each had sunglasses hiding their eyes. They all wore the Syndicate's dress code - formal suits, dress pants, and immaculate shoes.

"I am Chris Bristol, head of recruitment and roster management here. What took so long to arrive?" Chris demanded. "You said you were delayed. I expect an adequate answer. Are you aware of last night's events? We were counting on you, and you let us down."

The one in the middle answered. "Sir, I can explain everything."

"You'd damned well better." Chris marched over and stopped in front of him. "We fought over two dozen men with only a handful of personnel. Now why weren't the odds more even, hm? Enlighten us."

The visibly nervous man glanced over at Kyle with his

injured shoulder before returning to Chris. "Promise not to tell Mrs. Morris?"

"You're not in a position to make demands. Explain before I lose my patience."

The lone female in the squad spoke. "This dumbass got us lost, sir."

Chris's attention snapped to her, and he marched over. "Lost? For your sake, I hope you're yanking my chain. How the devil do you get lost when you have the address?"

"We couldn't take a GPS locator, sir. You know that. We're all from Ohio. We don't know the terrain here. The back roads were confusing."

"Getting lost on back roads?" Kyle shook his head. "Jesus, you are morons. You couldn't take the highways? No. That'd be simple and intelligent. It would have saved you time, and you wouldn't get caught anyway. It was pointless."

"Quite so, Mr. Evans."

The group's eyes widened at hearing his name.

"Oh, you recognize his name, but not mine?" Chris asked. "He proved himself again last night in our war, something you chuckle heads can only hope to do. What shall I tell the bosses when they arrive? Shall I tell them you got lost or gloss over it?"

"Tell them," Kyle said, "unless they vow to prove themselves."

"We'll do whatever you need, sir," the one in the middle said.

"What's your names?" Chris asked the man.

The one in the middle answered first. "I'm Ian Klein. These are my partners, Isabella, Robert, Mitchell, and Greg, from left to right." Ian's tall physique towered over his partners as he stood unflinching.

Mitchell was the shortest in the group, shorter than even

Isabella. He was the only soul daring enough to stare Chris and Kyle in the eye.

Robert was the shy one, evidenced by his focus on the ground.

Greg pushed the glasses further up his nose, not wishing them to linger lower, a habit he'd had all his life. Otherwise, he appeared unphased by the verbal lashing.

Isabella was the lone female of the group with her short, black hair. Her dress shirt wasn't fully buttoned, which allowed a generous view of her bosom, but this did little to dissuade Chris.

"You all are nothing until I say different," Chris said. "You would have arrived with respect, but your dumbasses lost that already." He paced in front of the group. "You will head inside that barn." He pointed toward the damaged barn. "You will study the defense plan posted on the wall, and you will figure out who's doing what. Until the bosses get home, our job is to secure this property. That's precisely what we'll do. Is that clear?"

All five answered. "Yes, sir!"

"Good. Follow Mr. Evans. He has specifics. I'm going to resume working. I've wasted enough time with you bums." Chris walked off muttering under his breath. The only words audible were. "Can't believe these idiots got lost. Jesus."

Kyle cleared his throat, diverting their attention from Chris. "You heard him. Get over here." He turned and led the group into the barn. "We lost two men defending this property last night - new recruits." He passed through the massive open doorway. The smell of old hay, gunpowder, and paint filled their nostrils. "Before you complain that this place looks run down, realize the onslaught we endured last night took its toll." He pointed with his good arm to the nearby paper taped to the wall. "There're your assignments. Be prepared to have your orders change at a moment's notice. There're no guarantees here, boys and girls. We're in a war, make no mistake. We pissed them off royally last night."

Isabella raised her hand. "I volunteer for any operations striking at our opponents."

"That's cute," Kyle said. "You don't get a say, but I'll note that you're fearless, Ms. Isabella. You want to know how this happened?" He reached up and poked the bandaging. "I blew up coca fields, poppy pod fields, and their processing center all by myself. I caught a knife for my trouble. That was while Mr. Bristol and Ms. Thomas struck different sites. You will prove yourselves, or die trying. I sincerely hope it's the former. We don't have the luxury of a deep roster like in Toledo. We're on our own, boys and girls. Act like it, and practice caution."

"Understood, sir," Isabella said with a straight face.

"Odds are you'll be busy tonight. I'd recommend preparing yourself mentally for that eventuality," Kyle said. "How many weapons and equipment did you bring?"

"Personal only," Ian said. "A few grenades, flash, incendiary, fragmentation, a few rifles, and handguns."

"Good, our reserves are running low until we resupply from Mr. Hudson."

"Sir," Ian said. "I have a question."

"Go ahead."

"Where are we going to sleep?"

Kyle shook his head and laughed. He walked out of the entrance. "Who knows? Sleep here in the barn for all I care." He turned the corner, leaving the group alone.

"Who knows?" Isabella asked. "Is he serious?"

"He was," Robert said.

Mitchell and Greg studied the paper, not paying attention to the distressing answer from Kyle.

"Don't you two care? We may end up sleeping in this barn with the bugs." Isabella asked.

"Worrying won't change anything," Greg said. "At least it has electricity. We could get an electric heater and it'll be cozy."

"Yeah," Mitchell said. "Besides, I don't want to piss these guys off more. We should show our dedication so they're not pissed at our tardiness. We can't let Mrs. Morris hear we let her down. Stop bitching and get your assignments figured out."

"Yeah," Greg said, stepping away from the plans taped to the wall. "Come on, buddy. We won't be accused of being lazy. Let them argue."

"Right on."

The pair left, leaving Isabella, Ian, and Robert standing in the barn.

"Fuck," Isabella said. "We can't let them make us look bad. She jogged to the paper and found her assignment.

"Move." Robert rushed over to find his assignment along with Ian.

Once all three learned their patrol routes, they left the barn to see Kyle standing around the corner. "About time, you slackers. That was a test. A test Mitchell and Greg scored higher on. Pick up the pace, ladies." He kicked off the barn and headed for home.

15

"Shouldn't you have bodyguards with you?" Abigail asked, climbing into the car. "You are one boss, right?"

"What do you think those idiots are?" Bernard pointed toward the personnel they'd assigned to her property. "Seriously? I know you haven't eaten yet. I have a perfect plan."

"Dinner sounds wondrous." Abigail lowered a hand to her stomach as an audible growl punctuated her sentence. "What's your idea?"

"Aren't you curious? Because of our unique circumstances, we're eating out."

"Eating out?"

"Not what you're imagining, trust me."

Abigail watched where they were going, trying to guess their destination. It wasn't until she saw homemade signs on the road's side that she put it together. "Chili cook-off?"

"They tell me it's a first for Nashville to have this," Bernard said. "Folks said it'll be like a street fair environment. Nobody's going to screw with us on the public street, surrounded by civilians. Right? It'd be suicide. I think off-duty police are being hired as security for the event. Homemade meals, good company, and a good reason to walk."

"I haven't had homemade chili in years. How did I not realize this was happening today?"

"You've been working yourself to the bone. You need relaxation, and old Bernard won't let you work yourself to death. What kind of business partner would allow his valued manager to work herself to death?"

"Aren't you just a regular virtuous Samaritan?" Abigail joked. "I appreciate the concern. Maybe I have been ignoring my body's needs. With everything happening, it's easy to get caught up and forget to eat."

"Lady, now you're talking my language. I've learned over the past couple weeks how a hearty meal is imperative to survival. Not to mention your mental health. I've heard that folks around here make a mean chili. I'm not one for cooking, if I'm honest. It's not a skill I've nurtured, so making you dinner was out of the question. I'm working within my limits here."

"I used to cook for my brother last year, but I'm not a chef myself," Abigail said. "Would you believe I've been living off Ramen and TV dinners for the last few months?"

"We'll change that. I know we eat entirely too many pizzas, turkey sandwiches, and simple stuff, but once we're settled, how about you teach me how to cook?"

"Cook? First you all want me to teach you how to grow cannabis, and now you want me to teach cooking?" Her tone inferred she was fed up, but she turned to him with a smile. "Obviously, I'll try my best, you bum."

"Bum?" Bernard parked in a nearby packed parking lot. The nearby street was packed with crowds of people, all excited to try local chili for a modest fee for entry. "I'll ignore that jab, Ms. Gomez. Only because of the delectable food we're about to eat."

"Aren't you sweet?" she asked as they got out.

They walked side by side toward the gathering of humanity lining up. There were two booths to expedite dispensing tickets. Both moved quite fast, and, while making small talk, they were at the front purchasing their tickets before they knew it.

Once they were inside, Bernard grabbed her hand. "I'd hate to get separated in here."

Masses of humanity surrounded every side. Getting bumped was commonplace with so many bodies constantly moving and jostling for position. There were tables and chairs set aside in a common area for the patrons to sit while eating if they preferred, though many walked as they ate from the small disposable bowls.

Every stand was packed with people leaving as quickly as they arrived near the front of the line.

They got in line in the shortest queue they could spot. Bernard spoke up first. "I've never been to an event like this, if I'm honest."

"Really?" Abigail leaned into him as someone behind her wasn't careful with their movement. "Festivals were commonplace where I grew up."

Bernard helped steady her. "Yeah," he said, looking down at her. "It might surprise you, but my mother always kept me home. It's a price of the life I lead. This is my first date, too."

"Aren't you daring? You assume this is a date now?"

"Is that inappropriate?" Bernard asked as they moved forward in the line. "How dare I be so optimistic. Here I thought I'd shoot my shot and maybe succeed."

"I am a lady, Mr. Morris," Abigail said with a giggle. "You

will treat me like one. You'll ask me before the next one and not just take me. Is that understood?"

"Yes, ma'am." Bernard's serious demeanor was undercut by Abigail's failure to hold a straight face and the two devolved into laughter midline. They were interrupted by the stand owner clearing his throat while he handed them two miniature bowls. They took a plastic spoon from the nearby receptacle and went to sit. Barely finding a seat, they sat at what seemed like the last open table.

"It might surprise you, but it's my first date too," Abigail said.

"There's no way. You?"

"Why is that difficult to believe?"

"You're beautiful and smart, for one," Bernard said. "You're telling me that no one was interested before?"

"Maybe, but nobody ever asked me out. I figured they wanted someone who wasn't a nerd. You're aware I was the nerdy type in high school, right?"

"At least you went to high school," Bernard said. "My mother kept me cooped up in the house until I was eighteen. Same goes for Roger with his caretaker."

"Caretaker?"

"I was going to say mother..." Bernard looked at the nearby mass of humanity. "Never mind. It's not my place to say. The life of ours comes with costs. Our mothers were overprotective. They never let us out to go to school, date, or shop. Everything was online. I never had a normal childhood. That's why I'm weird by most standards."

"Some girls like weird. It's odd hearing you say you were held at home for eighteen years. I can't even imagine. I'd go stir crazy if I was cooped up."

"Rog and I got into a lot of mischief," Bernard said. "We'd prank Lauren, our homeschool teacher, almost every single day without fail. We had to amuse ourselves. None of them harmed her, of course. They were stupid, but annoying. We'd even drag Crystal into the schemes sometimes when she got nosy."

"You mind if I ask the story between you two?" Abigail asked. "I gather you and Roger are friends, but there's more than that - I can tell."

"We grew up together since we were babies," Bernard said. "Mother told me we were inseparable as toddlers. We'd look out for each other. We remained ignorant of our family's money-making methods until we were teens. That's when our first differences showed up. My mother wanted me to rise through the ranks. His wanted him to go to college."

"I gather he didn't go to college like his mom wanted."

"No," Bernard said. "I goaded him into going on a job with me when we turned eighteen." He looked around the table, making sure nobody was eavesdropping. "We were dealing with business partners we'd had for close to two decades, so I thought it was safe. Turns out, nothing ever is. Rog, Crystal, and I all were forced to watch as men and women we knew our whole lives were gunned down. He wanted revenge, and the rest is history. Anyway, enough of that. He's my best friend, and that will never change."

"He's the boss, though?" Abigail asked.

"Technically. His mom's the big boss, and mine was only an advisor who used to be boss. It's complicated. He'd be within his rights to treat me like hired help, but he never has. He always involves me with decision making, asks for my opinion, and gives me autonomy to do what I like. Tonight is an example. I was supposed to welcome new recruits, but I handed it off to someone with more experience. It's never felt like I was his underling. I'm his partner. I consider myself lucky to serve with him rather than some of the power-hungry morons I could have got stuck with. He'd risk his life to save mine."

"I did not expect that story," Abigail said. "I thought all you types were power hungry and obsessed with hierarchy."

"Many are in this lifestyle. That's why we formed our branch - to do it correctly."

"Two teenagers are going to show the old folks how it's done, huh? It's a tale as old as time itself. We kids always think we know better."

"Sometimes we do."

"Often we don't," Abigail said.

"Don't be that way, Ms. Gomez." Bernard finished his bowl. "We're doing our best. Your shop's still up and running. My men tell me they've had to snuff out a fire. Seems Bailey wanted to burn your place down. Without my security, it'd be up in smoke, not in the fun way."

"They have?" Her eyes went wide.

"There's a reason we have them patrolling the outside. It's not just for security invasions. We're facing nasty men who'll do anything for money, including arson. You know that."

"The groups in America aren't as brutal as the ones from my homeland."

"That you know of," Bernard said. "I guarantee they are. Personal experience taught me that."

"I'm familiar with the personality type. You and Roger surprise me. You don't quite fit the mold. Or is that because I'm your asset?"

"You're not just an asset," Bernard said with a straight face.

"Really?"

"As much as your assets are beautiful, I see you as a business owner who is dazzlingly enchanting and witty." Bernard let his eyes wander lower than was considered socially acceptable before raising it to her eyes.

"Sweet talking is not your strong suit, Mr. Morris. You're supposed to be subtle and not hit me over the head."

"I'm not a subtle man. I say it like I see it. It has its own merits I've found. I prefer being blunt to lying and dancing around. It solves nothing and wastes time. We mustn't waste time because we have limited years on this earth."

"How deep and philosophical. Are all members like you?"

"I'm one of a kind. Now, let's get more food, eh? This little sampler bowl just made me hungrier."

"I'm with you on that."

The pair threw their disposable bowls in a nearby trash can and moved to a different stall. Automatic weapon fire halted their approach dead in its tracks.

Bernard grabbed Abigail, dragged her behind the nearest booth, and pulled her to the ground. He laid on top of her, trying to shield her body with his.

Bullets ripped through many civilians nearby. Blood-curdling screams filled the air until their attacker was forced to reload.

"Put the weapon on the ground, or I'll fire!" a male voice said.

The attacker didn't respond. This culminated in three rapid shots and more groaning.

Bernard peeked over the stall and saw a police officer approaching a man on the ground. He saw pools of blood under rows of bodies. Some moaned in pain, clutching their wounds, others wailed at the top of their lungs. A few were limp and didn't move, their lives having ended from the senseless and unexpected violence.

Bernard looked down and saw Abigail stunned in shock. "Come on," he whispered. "Let's get out of here."

She didn't argue and allowed him to help her up. She followed him through the crowds of people. Some tried to help others. Unfortunate civilians were catatonic, in shock and shaking. Yet others were on their phones calling emergency services. A few ghoulish guests were filming videos to upload online. The wails of the injured overshadowed everything else. Bernard stopped her from falling after stumbling.

That moment would stick in Abigail's mind until her death. She looked down at a fatally wounded victim of circumstance, a middle-aged male with a bushy beard. He raised himself enough so a grade school child, around five, could crawl out from under. Just in time too, as his muscles gave way and his sputtering breath slowed along with his coughing.

The pair watched the ensuing scene. The child grabbed his father's arm, tears streaming down his face. "Dad?" He shook his father's bleeding body fiercer this time. "Dad? Wake up!"

Bernard placed a finger under her chin and made her look at him. "We need to leave. Now!" He helped her around the grieving son and, without further incident, made it back to Bernard's car.

Once they were inside, things were quiet as Bernard hurried to leave.

"Why?" Abigail asked. There was no emotion filling her voice, only exhaustion. "Why do that? It was senseless, all those lives altered forever. What kind of animal does that?"

Bernard looked over momentarily before continuing to drive. "We both know who ordered that tragedy."

"Bailey?"

"I doubt Bailey would. He'd supply the junkie with an option to pay back their debt. We're the target. The dumbass must have followed us from your dispensary. I should have noticed the tail." He looked into the rear-view mirror, checking for any trailing cars. "Underestimating those two is a fatal mistake. They have no morals, values, or decency."

"It's our fault that baby lost his father," Abigail said, her voice wavering. "If we'd gone home, none of this would have occurred." She lost it with those words. Bursting into tears, she covered her eyes and let loose.

"We didn't force him to shoot innocents. He chose his path, despicable as it is, not us. You can't blame yourself for others' actions."

"You said it yourself; he was there for us." Her voice was muffled.

"He could have waited until we left. He made his choices. Leave it be. Nothing productive comes from blaming ourselves."

The rest of the car ride home was tense and silent the whole way. Only one more thing was said.

"That poor kid…"

Back at the farmhouse…

"Where the hell were you?" Roger hopped down the steps toward the arriving vehicle.

Bernard got out and opened Abigail's door, momentarily ignoring his friend.

"Did you hear me?" Roger asked. "What happened?"

Molly was the next to exit the building. "We worried you had been caught in the shooting downtown. You two unharmed?"

Abigail pushed past Roger and Bernard, leaving the friends outside without a word.

"We were at the chili cook-off in town," Bernard said. "I'm assuming it's all over the television. Some lunatic tried to off us while we were walking."

"They're calling it a mass shooting. Christ!" Roger paced left and right. "This'll get all the law enforcement agencies running. Were you hurt?"

"Negative," Bernard said. "The guy was a shit shot. Instead of mass shooting, I'd call it a massacre. You know why we survived?"

"Why?"

"We were in a massive crowd. The idiot couldn't wait. He spotted us and opened fire. I think if we'd been alone, we'd be corpses. Those innocent people died to keep us alive. When we left, we tripped over a father who gave his life to save his son. It rattled Abigail to her core, dude. She's scared, and I don't blame her. This can't go on."

"It had to be Powell." Roger shook his head and growled. "That piece of shit will burn. If only we knew his locations. We only know his public shop."

"Then why wait? Get your girlfriend here to do her digital wizardry. Then we'll plan our ending of this war. Their targets are Abigail, Hudson, and us, right? We can't wait. We'll take the fight to them."

"I'll get her on it," Roger said.

"Now if you'll excuse me, I'm going to check Abigail. She's broken up."

"Alright. Our new team arrived earlier," Roger called out. "You'll love why they were late!"

Bernard didn't respond to the promise and headed inside. He entered the living room and spotted Crystal. "Where's Abigail?"

ALEX J. FISCHER

"She headed upstairs," Crystal said. "What happened to you two? She looked hurt and scared."

"It's a long story. Can you help Molly work? She has lots of projects and could use your expertise."

"Sure. I was on break since staring at the screen gives me headaches."

"Try to get any information on Powell you can. I'd recommend trying to trace from there."

"Where were you? Bub was worried sick."

"Ask your brother when he comes in. I'm in a hurry." He wasted no time and climbed the stairs, heading to his room. He leaned over and listened. Abigail was crying inside - he could hear as much. He knocked and entered the room in one swift motion.

Abigail sat on the bed nearest the window. "Sorry for barging into your room. I just needed privacy."

"You mind if I sit with you?"

She nodded, and Bernard took a seat a few feet away and leaned back, resting his palms on the bed. "I apologize for tonight. I heard about the contest and my first thoughts raced to you. How you hadn't eaten, and it'd be a fun idea to escape the whirlwind of my life. Look at what my selfishness created. If we'd gone home, they'd be alive. You were correct earlier."

"Please, not now. I hope to forget tonight's events, if only for a moment before tomorrow morning."

"Alright." Bernard and Abigail sat in silence for a few moments. "Sorry, I'm not great with moments like this. At least that's what Crystal told me growing up. She said I was an insensitive jerk who couldn't comfort someone if my life depended on it. How about we climb onto the roof? No danger of Roger coming in to sleep if we lose track of time."

"The roof?" Abigail looked up. "Is that safe?"

"I've climbed up there before. See the balcony there?" He pointed toward the double glass doors nearby. "Just grab my hand and I'll pull you up. Getting down's easy."

"If you're sure. I'd love a chance to watch the night sky and empty my head of that hellish memory."

Bernard got up to open the balcony doors. He used a chair outside to climb and jump. He grabbed hold of the roof and pulled himself up. Reaching down, he offered his hand to the shaken woman after she shut the sliding door.

She climbed and reached up to grab his outstretched hand.

He helped her up to the roof. They climbed a few feet further and came to the middle roof. It offered a suitable place to sit and look out over the dark forest and clear, star filled sky above. Insects serenaded them while the smell of nature surrounded them.

Abigail leaned her neck back and lost herself in the stars above. "How do you manage? I mean, the violent lifestyle we're caught in."

"It's all I've ever known. I've seen men and women all my life fight and die. I never learned of death growing up, but Syndicate members told me friends left and weren't ever coming back. As I grew older, I knew what they meant. It's like joining a gang you've hung out with all your life. You want to fit in, earn respect, and eventually rise in the ranks. It sounds juvenile, but I still want to earn my name. It's a prestigious one, but I've not earned it. In my haste to, I've endangered many people, including you. Truly, I'm ashamed for involving you."

"I'm a big girl and make my own decisions, Mr. Morris. Don't assume responsibility for my actions. I don't regret using your aid to open my dispensary, not at all. My medicine will help hundreds or thousands of patients over the coming years. I'll never forget the opening month."

"You ever star gaze much?" Bernard asked, changing the topic. He pointed at the stars above. "Crystal went through a stargazing phase and made us accompany her. I admit, I don't remember many of the constellations, but I remember the north star."

"No, but I find myself gazing skyward whenever things get rough. That's why I agreed to climb up here in that dangerous fashion. You need to install a ladder."

"Noted," Bernard said.

"You mind if I invade your personal space?" Abigail asked. "Just a little."

"Feel free," Bernard said.

Abigail shocked him when she didn't simply lean into him. She fully laid her head on his lap, staring at the sky. "My father used to comfort me doing this. If he noticed me outside, he'd come outside right away. We'd stare at the sky and talk it out. It's silly now that I recall, but it's been years since I've indulged."

Bernard tried to calm his racing heart rate, to no avail. He gave in to instinct and found his hands running through her hair. "Hope I'm half as relaxing as your father. This is out of my specialty. I'm running blind."

She held her silence, so he looked down to see her eyes closed.

Bernard saw patrols circling the house. One especially observant one noticed the pair above and waved. He returned the gesture before returning his attention to Abigail. "You're not falling asleep up here, are you?"

"No, just remembering memories of my father and brother. Thinking about what they'd say after tonight. Would they say I was a fool for entering this arrangement?

Would they comfort me like you're trying to? Or would they disown me? Would I deserve it? I say yes. I've entered bed with a proverbial devil."

"Am I the hot and sexy type of devil at least?"

The immature attempt at levity hit home, apparently. That earned him a momentary smile. "Maybe."

"Sometimes it takes a devil to fight another." Bernard's other hand gently traced patterns over her face with his fingertips. "Like I'd know. I've never known good. I was surrounded by outlaws throughout my entire existence. What do I know of morality, honestly?"

"Even the evilest upbringing can sprout kindness it seems." She raised a hand and gripped his, stopping his fingertips. "An evil or dishonorable man would never concern himself with my wellbeing or emotional state. He'd simply have left me alone and tried to convince me not to leave. He'd be concerned over money more."

"There are plenty that fit that bill in the Syndicate, undoubtedly. I'd love to think I'm different, but I'm not sure."

"You are." She sat up and faced Bernard. "Don't doubt yourself. Your men depend on you for strength and conviction. You and Roger have a burden hanging on your shoulders. You volunteered for it. Now prove you deserve their trust. Doubting yourself will only lead to disappointment. You kept me safe at the cook-off. You threw your body over mine, shielding me with your life. I won't forget that. It's not the action of a selfish gangster concerned with self-preservation. It was selfless. I never thought I'd find a partner - someone willing to endanger themselves for my wellbeing. Little did I know my business partner would turn out like you. I'll have to thank Mr. Keller for introducing us."

"That makes two of us," Bernard said.

Both leaned in without realizing. It didn't take long before they shared their first kiss as lips met. It was a chaste kiss, not lewd or overly passionate. More an expression, a need for fondness between two young adults who'd survived a tribulation and found comfort in momentary bliss.

Abigail leaned back, her eyes still closed. She brought a finger to her lips. "You know what we need to relax?"

"Hm?" Bernard was still on cloud nine, having received his first kiss.

She reached into her pocket and pulled out two hard candies. "Take one," she said. "No more. Each contains twenty milligrams of THC and some CBD. I figure it's early enough to take one."

Bernard unwrapped the candy and ate it. "Is it meant to taste weird?"

"It has a unique aftertaste," she said, eating hers. She leaned toward him before planting another kiss. "Did that help?"

"Don't know, let's try again."

"You're incorrigible."

"Tell me something I don't know."

———————

16

Roger knocked on Molly and Jackie's door.

"What?" Molly asked through the door.

"Can I come in?"

"Jackie's already up. It's fine. Excuse the mess."

Roger opened the door to see Crystal and Molly working on their respective laptops on her bed. "Hard at work I gather. Did you get any sleep last night?"

"No time," Molly said. "Been awake all night finding this bastard Powell. I think we're close."

"We checked every local school's roster for children with the last name of Powell," Crystal said. "There're ten names. We checked the names with social media pages to get addresses. I think we may have a lead."

"Good to hear." Roger moved closer. He sat between the girls and peeked over Molly's shoulder. "Ten names is a lot. Any way to narrow it down?"

"That's what we're doing, hotshot." Molly's screen had a map of the local area, along with ten addresses written in a notepad document to the side. "We're trying to find every address and extrapolate the likely properties."

"Of course, this could all be a wild goose chase," Crystal said. "His name may not be Powell. Naming his business Powell's Emporium doesn't guarantee his name."

"True enough," Roger said. "You all check his website?"

"The web host is outsourced. We tried to infiltrate it and find who commissioned it, but it was a bust. He paid with the prepaid cards they offer. No way of tracking money either."

"The dude has dummy corporations under different names and thus different accounts for every damned thing," Crystal said.

"He's careful compared to Bailey, who's sloppy operational security screwed him. That means he's wiser and prepared. This was my last ditch effort, Rog. If this fails, I've got nothing."

"I trust your decision making, both of you. How many candidates are we looking at?"

"Depends on who you ask," Crystal said. "I'd say five are likely. Your girlfriend thinks only three fit the bill."

"Because a single name owns all three," Molly said. "I'm betting one's for storing weapons, another for living, and the last is a vacation home. If he's rich, dollars to donuts he's flaunting it under the guise of his successful gun shop. Nobody would question it, including any family he likely has."

"Did Bernard ever calm down Abigail?" Crystal asked.

"Huh?" Roger was obviously surprised.

"She came running inside last night. She was crying, and he rushed off to find her. I assume something happened, and I never found you last night."

"He was at the shooting in town," Roger said. "He brushed me off too."

"Damn," Molly said. "That's rough. No doubt she saw

civilians hit. They're lucky they were unharmed. Police said the perp had an automatic machine pistol. We're talking real top of the line hardware."

"The last I saw," Roger said, "they were both in our room."

"Your room?" Crystal dropped what she was doing and turned around. "Ew, you had to listen and watch?"

"No, you goofball," Roger said. "They didn't fuck in front of me. That'd be nasty and wrong. Ian said they climbed on the roof last night to unwind. He claimed they were relaxed. It must have worked, whatever it was."

"How nice for them." Molly kept working as she spoke. "Sometimes I wonder why I picked tech division. We're tasked to perform miracles on little sleep daily."

"Because you didn't wish to be shot," Roger said. "Besides, you relaxed last night."

"If I'd known I was staying up all night, I'd have ordered two coffees at the club, not soda."

"You live and learn."

"Here," Crystal said, interrupting the pair. "It'll take some boots on the ground, but I think we're done."

"Yeah." Molly leaned back, inadvertently leaning into Roger's chest. "Confirming their identity will require us checking on them with surveillance. Digital surveillance, to be specific. Meaning I or Crystal will have to accompany someone to do it. Which means more work before sleep. It needs to be when they're awake and active. We're looking for them running his gun shop from home or guards patrolling. Shouldn't take more than a day to pinpoint their location, supposing we're persistent."

"Can you print this info out? You can take a nap afterward while I brief everyone on the strategy."

"Easy as pie," Molly said before a nearby printer sitting on the table sprang to life.

Roger grabbed the documents and moved to the room's door. "Get some rest. In a couple of hours we'll assemble the surveillance teams. Got it?"

"Wake me up, would you?" Molly asked. "I'm dead tired and won't wake up on my own."

"Sure thing," Roger said. "Crystal, dear, you get sleep too. Sleep in my room. Abigail and Bernard left early this morning. You don't have to worry about them."

"I'll take you up on that."

Roger bid them good night before exiting the room and hurrying down the stairs. He caught Chris walking toward the front door. "Hey, old man, gather everyone in the barn quick. We've got a lead on Powell's location, and I aim to end this war."

"With pleasure, sir," Chris said. He retrieved the device on his belt and spoke into it. "Personnel meeting in the barn on the double. Security's exempted."

"Roger that," Jackie said.

"Hope this ends soon, boss," Chris said, accompanying Roger outside. "We need to catch our breath and establish an equilibrium."

"In due time." Roger entered the barn to find Jackie and Kyle already inside. "Good and fast. I love seeing it."

"Tell me we found a mugshot and location," Jackie said. "Is it true Powell had the local cook-off shot up?"

"There's no hard evidence. Street logic checks out given the news showed the shooter's toothless mug. It's not like he can squeal since he's dead. It's sick how they operate. Anyway," Roger said, placing the papers on a table nearby. "Molly and Crystal were up all night digging into Powell, using our only lead - his gun emporium store. The financial tracking was a dead end. He's smart and careful, unlike Bailey. Too many dummy corporations and accounts. However, they got creative and searched local schools for any children named Powell."

"He has children?" Kyle asked.

"Probably." Jackie leaned over the table, studying the printout. "Rich men always want an heir and rarely have issue finding a mother."

"The point is, they found ten addresses that they believe our arms dealer could be stationed at. Molly believes the three under the same name in the boonies is our culprit. I'm inclined to believe her, seeing as he's bound to be wealthy. One's on the lake. I imagine it's their vacation home. One other property is a storage property, and the last is their home. Now, we need confirmation. I'm not sending hit squads to a possible civilian house. We're not those animals. We don't kill innocents knowingly." He gave a pointed glare at Jackie. "Are we clear?"

"Why are you looking at me? Still mad about that kid in the Russian club?"

"It's history. Focus. After they get a nap, we're assembling to escort Crystal and Molly to each of these addresses. There, we'll digitally surveil the occupants and determine if that's our man. We're looking for a guy who's running his gun business from home, his illegitimate one, anyway. If not, watch for any security. Run of the mill homeowners do not have dedicated security forces. That's our plan until we have concrete evidence. Questions?"

"Sending the new guys?" Kyle asked, pointing out of the barn.

"You need to rest," Roger said. "Jackie probably too, if we're honest. How are the injuries, you two?"

"It was my little finger." Jackie held up her hand, showcasing the nub of a little finger. "It won't affect shooting or keeping us safe."

"I'm fine to work, sir," Kyle said.

"Lift your arm for me," Chris said. "Above your head. Come on. Do it."

Kyle tried to lift his injured side's arm only for it to stop, and a hiss of pain escaped. "Damn it."

"He's not combat ready," Chris said, shaking his head. "Unless he can fire left-handed accurately."

"You're on rest leave until you're recovered, Evans," Roger said. "Your enthusiasm for work is noted."

"Understood."

"Now, who's escorting the girls to these locations?" Roger asked. "Any ideas?"

"Use the new fuck ups," Chris said. "You heard why they were late, boss?"

"I had things on my mind. Why exactly were they late, Mr. Bristol? A mere delay shouldn't have taken a whole extra day."

"They were scared shitless when they finally arrived last night." Chris recounted the tale with exaggerated body movements. "They were shaking in their boots, lining up. You should have seen it. They said they'd taken the back roads from Toledo and they got lost."

Roger blinked and kept a straight face. "While Bernard, the men, and I fought, they were arguing about taking a wrong damned turn? Are you kidding?" His voice escalated, shocking everyone. "Where are they?"

"On security detail, sir." Chris cleared his throat and knew better than to keep joking. "I scared them shitless. They were deathly afraid of Mrs. Morris finding out and having them killed. I promised we'd put them to work at our discretion."

"Gather them once we're finished here. That's an order."

"Yes, sir."

"Now," Roger said. "Why should we send those morons to get lost on Tennessee's back roads? They're apparently not the sharpest knives in the drawer."

"About that." Chris scratched his head. "They're one of the best combat squads in the syndicate. They're notoriously simple minded in their relentless pursuit, but they've proven themselves in operations. Most groups splinter when the shit hits the fan; however, these five always survived. I'd recommend reprimanding them and providing a map before they leave."

"You're telling me those buffoons are good at combat, but can't navigate?"

"Ian's a leading sniper," Jackie said. "Before he joined, he competed in competitions worldwide. He only lost to three other men. Isabella is a magician with explosives and grenades. She worked as a demolitionist while Greg, Robert, and Mitchell are the front line. Green Beret, Navy Seal, and Army Ranger in that order. Don't let their getting lost fool you, they're crack shots. Infuriating as it is, they're valuable and respected amongst their peers. You'd do well to remember that."

"Noted." Roger sighed. "If you two vouch, send them. I want one of you present in a separate car, keeping guard. Is that clear? Our two valuable techies are in the field, and they are off limits."

"Your sister's safe with us, sir," Jackie said.

"I'll guard Ms. Turner with my life." Chris bowed his head in respect.

"Maintain a defense here. With any luck, this war ends soon. I'll address the lost nimrods. Dismissed."

Everyone except Chris and Roger exited the building,

eager to move away from the impending spectacle. He reached for the device on his belt and called the five here. They arrived within a couple of minutes and lined up.

"This isn't how I expected to meet the backup dear mother sent. I expected them to fight in battle, not to drive all over creation leaving us high and dry. Now you've spoken to Mr. Bristol here. He's informed me you're reticent about my mother finding out about your delay. I don't blame you. She'd be irate. You've been told you'll work, and she'll never know. It's true. Provided you're competent and complete the mission, you've earned my silence on your buffoonery. You have a mission tonight if all goes well today. Prepare for it, drink some coffee, just be ready by midnight tonight. Come armed, armored, and prepared. Is that understood?"

"Yes, sir," all five answered.

"Your target is unavailable. That's why we're waiting. We're finding it as we speak. I won't lie. There's a good chance you're running into an enemy stronghold out in the country. Probably filled with guards, and I'm not talking about the junkies we've been fighting. I'm talking about real security forces. The bright spot being they won't have numbers. Be cautious tonight. I don't want more fucking up. Am I understood?"

All five barked their affirmatives.

"You'll receive a briefing containing the location of your target later today. I advise you to plan right afterward. Kick some ass, and we'll forget the tardy idiocy. I may even request your transfer. You'd have more freedom here and, if we win, we'll be the top dog on the block. Now get back to patrol. Dismissed."

All five Syndicate members promptly followed the order, leaving the two senior officers.

"You and Jackie better be correct about those jokers." Roger watched the last disappear.

17

"According to these plans," Greg said, studying the report, "this is likely Powell's weapon storage. They spotted armed guards during their surveillance, both inside and out."

"How many?" Ian asked.

"According to this, they found six."

Isabella shrugged. "He said they're not a deep roster. It seems the boss was right."

"He also said they'd be fierce opponents," Mitchell said.

Ian spoke up from the front seat of the van. "Quiet. Look on the south side near us. See that hill? I'll post up there. I want you all to head along the east wall. Isabella, you rig the buildings to blow, and you three watch her back. I'll watch your backs. Maintain minimum distance from each other. We won't be screwed by a single explosive, got it?"

"We're killing everyone, right?" Robert asked. "Why not start blasting and cut their manpower into a fraction?"

"Would you rather fight five aware, trained guards or get the drop closer to them? I'll cover your south side. Just watch the north, and don't let them circle around. Got it? If anything goes wrong, start firing - but try to hold off. We're better off if we kill three before they notice than only one."

"There's no way I'm getting close enough to that mansion without being seen," Isabella said. "Permission to use the launcher?"

"Granted. Shit," Ian said, "use a damned mortar if you think it'll help."

"That's not precise enough. This should help demolish the place from a distance and incapacitate any guards inside, if not outright kill."

"It'll attract attention fast," Greg said. "We'll need to leave quickly if we're blowing shit up."

"It'll also invite investigation if explosions occur," Robert said.

Isabella loaded the grenade launcher attachment for her rifle and grabbed a few to reload. "On Powell, not us. Besides, he won't call the police. There's no one around for miles. Stop worrying. That's why they pick spots like this, you anxious fool."

Robert shook his head. "It's not anxiety when we're dealing with the FBI or other federal agencies. Explosives bring them around."

"We weren't given limitations." Ian raised his voice, quieting the argument. "Our orders were to kill everyone here and destroy the guns - or steal them if possible. We're not picky. Try to find the storage building or room and destroy it. If we're lucky, we won't even be shot at."

"Like that's going to happen." Isabella rolled her eyes.

"Now, is everyone clear on our plan? I'll head out first and take my position. I'll guide you all to avoid the patrols. Comms check."

"Here," every member said in succession, confirming they were within reach verbally.

"Good luck, boys and girls. Go on my signal." Ian wasted no time and exited the vehicle. He opened the back of the van and removed the large rectangular case containing his scoped rifle, then slammed it shut, leaving the other four in silence.

"Why do we always get the shit jobs?" Mitchell asked.

"Because Ian's pissed off the powers that be," Isabella said. She kept the barrel of the rifle pointed at the ceiling, now satisfied with the explosives cache she had on her person and her rifle. "That detour and back roads shit screwed us. Now we're stuck doing this to earn our way back in their good graces. We were lucky they survived. If they hadn't, we'd be fucked even worse."

"Yeah, the boss's kid dying would seal our death certificates if it came out why we missed the battle her kid died in," Robert said.

"We got transferred to Evan's unit. This is progress." Mitchell climbed into the now vacant front seat. "If that kid can earn respect, it should be simple for us. He shot the Ghost of Moscow in the back after Mr. Adams carried the lion's share."

"Not according to the official story," Isabella said. "Greg, you're quiet. What do you think?"

"I think we'd better focus on this job and quit thinking about politics within the Syndicate. If we fail, we die, and the boss is pissed. Can't have him running to mother dearest complaining."

"True," Isabella said. "The kid may be spoiled rotten, but he's the boss."

"If you all are done gossiping like high schoolers, I'm in position and ready," Ian said over their earpieces.

They didn't need more encouragement. They left the van in a flash. Following the plan, they stayed together and stayed near the east side's tree line. Isabella led the group, with Greg bringing up the rear.

"Number of enemies on the outer perimeter?" Isabella asked as they trudged slowly through the underbrush and branches.

"From here, I've spotted three. All are solo. I can't see inside. Assume there are more behind every corner."

"I'm not sure how you expect us to find the storage location. You want my advice? I should start firing these grenades and level the entire property. That'll do it."

"You have enough explosive grenades?"

"Not quite."

"Get to solid cover and unleash hell when you're ready. Remember to spread out. Set up crossfires. They'll mobilize quickly. It'll be a shooting gallery for me here if you're in position. There's little cover there. I'm betting they'll hunker down, and that's when you can blow them to hell."

The group was now within a hundred feet of the mansion. Isabella stopped behind a suitably large tree. "Here should be good. Everyone fan out and prepare."

Mitchell, Greg, and Robert scurried and set up twenty feet away from each other.

"Everyone good?" Isabella asked.

"Good's a strong word," Greg said. "I'd prefer a plan other than a firefight relying on Ian's ass as overwatch. God knows he can't aim to save our lives."

"Shut your dumbass up," Ian said, his voice tinted with sarcasm. "You want to start this little shindig? I'd rather keep my element of surprise. They're more likely to circle around if there's no sharpshooter. I'll hit them when they least expect it. Wait until at least two are within range. I don't want to waste our element of surprise, whether it takes ten minutes or ten seconds."

"Agreed. Knocking out multiple to start is ideal," Greg said.

"Did you hear something?" Mitchell asked.

"You're paranoid." Isabella waited and listened. "There's nobody outside besides us and any animals dumb enough to stick around."

"Hold up," Greg said. "There are two patrols there. Is two enough to kick this off?"

"Combine it with a blast, Izzie," Ian said.

"With pleasure." She leaned out from cover and angled her weapon up to arc the grenade to her target. "Fire when ready. I'll blow out the east side's first floor. You should open your sightlines back there, Ian."

"You always knew how to please."

"Greg, you've got the right guard. Mitchel, you and I take the left. On three we fire, understood?"

"Fine by me."

The only words now were numbers as Robert counted. "One, two, three!"

Automatic weapons fire erupted from their barrels. Muzzle flashes were muffled by their suppressors but were still visible in the night's darkness. Their targets fell with little trouble. This was accompanied by the first floor behind exploding, with fragments flying skyward.

Yelling erupted from the mansion as the initial salvo died down.

"That kicked the hornets' nest," Ian said. "They're staying inside. Izzie, show them the error of their ways. I can't get a shot from here if they don't run outside to approach you."

"I love this part." She readied another explosive and took aim. She adjusted her aim closer to Ian's position, before firing. The entire wall that impeded his view was destroyed, leaving almost half the first floor open to the night air.

A sniper rifle's shot went off immediately after.

"That's three down," Ian said. "Where are the rest? Cowering inside, you think?"

"Shit!" Mitchell's voice called out. He never got the chance to elaborate further as automatic gunfire erupted near the group, cutting him off.

"Mitch?" Isabella heard the nearby fire. She turned her attention toward the interior of the forest. "They're in here with us." Another round of fire went off nearby. More screaming and gunfire ensued. "Watch our flanks."

"They were expecting this?" Ian asked. "Mitchell, status update. You alright over there?"

Mitchell never responded.

"Damn it," Ian said. "Regroup over there and find Mitchell."

The gunfire and ringing inside the group's collective ears made it difficult to hear the orders. Isabella knew where her partners had posted up and was careful not to enter their firing lines. "Watch the mansion. I have an idea."

"Got your back," Ian said.

Isabella slithered through the tree line and moved to Mitchell's last known location. She kept her rifle loaded and ready to fire. She glanced down at the forest floor to see Mitchell. He was still alive, but bleeding badly. They had shot him in the shoulder. He was currently trying to stop the bleeding with his hand. "Mitchell's down and hurt."

"I got one!" Greg said after another burst of rounds.

The gunfire seemed never ending in the dark, hard to see environment. Screaming and orders were being screamed by their opponents. Their voices sounded close, maybe within fifty feet. She saw a figure running to her left and turned to fire. She didn't leave it to chance and squeezed the trigger. Knowing her team wasn't near here enabled such quick thinking without worry of friendly fire.

"Anybody dead?" Ian asked.

"Maybe later," Mitchell said with a grunt.

"Greg, Robert?" Isabella asked.

More gunfire only enhanced the creepy atmosphere from nearby. "They're all over me!" Robert cried out. "I count at least three." He requested assistance, repeating his request, but his call for help was drowned out by more gunfire. He never finished his sentence.

"I got the bastards," Greg said. "I think that's all of them. Watch for reinforcements."

"Understood," Isabella said. She kneeled and dressed Mitchell's wounds. No more gunfire met her ears as she worked. "Greg, look for Robert and exercise caution. We already have one wounded."

It didn't take long for Greg to report he'd found him. "He's dead, Izzie. Shot through the head. The bastard I put down flanked him."

"Damn," Isabella said. "Come back to my position. Mitch's bleeding heavily. I need help."

"Roger that."

Two gunshots rang out in rapid succession, along with a scream of pain. "Damn it," Greg said. "He ambushed me. Fucker was lying on the grass. He's dead though."

"Were you hit?" Ian asked. "Hold on, got one heading your way."

A high-powered rifle fired in the night sky.

"He's down now, Izzie. I'm heading over to help the wounded. Once I'm there, you're planting the required explosives to blow this place to kingdom come."

"Need help over here," Greg said. "I can't move."

"Can't move?" Ian asked, sounding out of breath.

"He got me good."

Isabella kept a paranoid watch behind every tree, knowing another could be lying in wait. "Stay here, Mitch. I'll return soon." This *must be what Vietnam vets felt, watching each damned tree and bush,* she thought. After what felt like an eternity, she finally located Greg. He was on the ground, clutching at his stomach. She got to work bandaging him up and trying to stop the bleeding.

"Found Mitchell," Ian said. "Come on, buddy. Stay with me. You're not dying, not after all we've been through."

Isabella looked down at Greg's injured body. "Let's hope you're able to walk."

"I can't feel my legs," Greg said.

"Well, shit."

"No. Damn you," Ian's voice said. "Up we go, Mitch. Don't complain."

"Need you over here. Greg's stable, I think. Help me get him back before we load the boys into the back."

"I'll take them back. You plant the explosives around the place. There's no one left, or they'd have made the move already. Still, be careful. Two injured is too many."

"Understood." She grabbed Greg's hand. "Ian will be here shortly. Keep breathing and stay calm, okay? We're not leaving you here."

"Hurry already," Greg said with a sarcastic edge.

"You always were an ass." She got to her feet and hurried toward the mansion. She ignored the east side and circled around the house, planting packages of explosives she'd brought from Toledo until she wired the whole place to blow. No guards interrupted her. It seemed Ian was correct. The ambush had succeeded and failed simultaneously. "This was a trap."

"No shit," Ian said. His voice sounded strained. "They baited us with a few guards while they had forces in the forest. No doubt they spotted us when we left the van and crept up behind where they saw us enter the forest. We won in the end, though at too heavy a price."

"Damned right," Isabella finished her job and moved back to Greg to find him still sucking air. "You got Mitch and Robert?"

"Got Mitch already. I'm still looking for Robert's body."

"It's near here," Isabella said, looking over and spotting the dead body of her friend. "Let's get Greg first. He's injured and can't feel his legs."

"Ah hell. On my way."

The pair of uninjured squad mates helped Greg back to the car before finally retrieving Robert's dead body, or what was left of his mutilated carcass. His head wasn't in one piece after all.

Isabella turned to the property that claimed her friend's lives and pressed the detonator. It exploded, destroying any weapons within. With that, the mission was complete, but their somber stares betrayed their lack of jubilation or joy.

"We're leaving," Ian climbed inside. "Call the boss. Inform him of the outcome and that we'll need a doctor."

"On it," Isabella said from the back beside Greg. "Yeah, it was a success. Yes, understood. I'll dispose of this phone. We have a complication; we require a doctor. What? Oh hell. Understood. We're heading out. Got it." She opened the van door and fired off a round, breaking the phone instantly.

"Bad news?" Greg asked through the pain.

"They're going to find a doctor." Isabella slammed the door shut and buckled up. "They hadn't paid one off nearby yet. Boss said he's on it. You believe he's trying?"

Starting the car, Ian said, "He may be spoiled, but I don't

think he'd let Greg here die without a fight. He'll use his connections like the brat he is and get help, buddy. Don't you worry."

"Better to use your connections to help than to act a brat," Greg said. "I still can't feel my legs, guys. I think it may have hit my spinal cord. It hit dead center and feels like it traveled through."

"At least my wounds don't sound as grievous," Mitchel said from the van's rear compartment with Robert's body. "Why'd you stick me with Robert?"

"Shut up, Mitch. Your wound isn't bad. Greg, don't talk like that," Isabella said. "You're not crippled for life yet."

"Yet being the operative word."

"Shut the hell up."

"Right. I am tired. Guess I'll take you up on the offer of silence."

"Don't sleep either," Isabella barked. "Stay awake, and don't give in. We're right here."

"At least it happened on the job. Here I was afraid I'd die alone in bed as an old man." Greg moaned in pain as the van hit a pothole.

"Watch the damned road, you idiot!" Isabella kicked the back of Ian's seat.

"Country back roads are a treat in the dark," Ian said. "Sorry about that."

"Just get us home."

18

"Hudson's kid called us here?" Jackie exited first and slammed the car door shut. "Did he say why?"

"He requested our presence here. He said it was an emergency and to hurry." Roger walked past Jackie and adjusted his holster on his hip. "Be on alert."

"Security, move forward and secure the building's outside." Jackie ordered Isabella and Ian, who trailed behind.

"I'm more of a marksman, Ms. Thomas."

"You have a complaint?" Jackie asked. She stepped toward him, voice casual. "You can use a rifle, then I presume you're proficient with that sidearm."

"Yes, ma'am." Jackie chased the two forward ahead of Roger, who stood watching the spectacle. He heard footsteps behind him.

"They're worried about their colleague," Bernard said. He fiddled with his tie, shoulder to shoulder with Roger. "The best course of action is to keep their minds occupied. Now, let's see what Jonathon Hudson called for."

The pair walked forward. They watched their security

detail meet with one of Jonathon's guards and exchange words. Jackie gave further orders. "We're standing watch here. They have the rear. Isabella, I want you there." She pointed toward the south. "Ian, you're assigned the other side. I'll watch the door." She opened it after she saw Roger and Bernard approaching. "Place is secured, boss."

"Good. Keep it that way." Roger took point and entered the multi-story home and soon found his host.

"Good." Jonathon greeted them. He had dark bags around his eyes and a cigarette in his mouth, half smoked. "Finally, you're here." He gestured them into the nearby tiled kitchen.

"You look tired," Roger said, entering the main dining room with their host. A large table dominated the room with intricately detailed seats. Pages littered the table, some detailed property floor plans. Others were satellite images. It was obvious Jonathon had put considerable effort into collecting these.

"Doesn't matter. They took my father last night."

"Taken?" Bernard asked. "You mean kidnapped? I thought your security was top-notch. What happened?"

"They were riding home last night from the club. I was on the phone with him when I heard gunshots and screaming. I believe a car rode up beside them and rammed them to boot. Now, I know he survived the crash, since I heard him moaning in pain afterward. The last thing I heard was someone dragging him off to God knows where."

"That explains the wreck we passed on the way here," Roger said.

"I know his location." Jonathon was quick and succinct.

"Where?" Bernard asked. He moved closer to Jonathon, trying to peek at the maps.

"Here," Jonathon pointed at the sprawling analogue map on the table.

"That's not one of the locations we received from our investigation," Bernard said. "Rog, come look for yourself."

Roger rubbed his chin as he thought. "How do you know?"

"His phone," Jonathon said. "Those morons didn't destroy the GPS tracker in it. The phone is there, without doubt. I want to mount a rescue mission. I'm aware you've been fighting Powell. We've watched and gauged you're faring well, given how angry I hear he's become."

"We've had our share of casualties," Roger said. "You think we're able to mount a rescue with our lack of manpower?"

"You've enough to station multiple men at a dispensary. Rescuing your supplier seems high on the priority list compared to that. Let's sweeten the pot. You let me tag along and observe, and you get the next shipment free and double the product. Not a terrible deal, huh?"

Roger and Bernard exchanged a quick glance.

"Deal," Bernard said, reaching to shake Jonathon's hand.

Jonathon snatched the hand in a flash and shook vigorously. "You won't regret this."

"It'll require a little scouting," Roger said. "We won't send our people in without due diligence. Traps and misdirection are common with Powell's forces. Their shrewd tactics cost us three more soldiers yesterday."

"Don't delay," Jonathon said. "There's no knowing how long they'll keep my father alive. Odds are they're questioning him for intel on you two. He won't talk. That's why I'm worried."

"The sooner he talks, the sooner they kill him," Roger said. "We'll send our best personnel and find him. If you wish to ride along, we'll escort you, and you can supervise the preparation."

"You misunderstand me," Jonathon said. "I'm escorting them on the operation. That's the deal. I'll supervise from the field. You want something done right? Do it yourself. That's what my father taught me."

"If there're dozens of enemies there, you realize the plan will change. We won't force a suicide mission. That's our stipulation. We won't sacrifice our employees senselessly, even for guns."

"I don't blame you. Agreed. I've a sneaking suspicion they're housing him there. I've found it's Powell's lieutenant's personal home." He pressed his finger on the satellite imagery. The dwarfed building behind the home looked comparatively like a shack. "Come, we've no time to waste."

A few hours later...

"Daytime operations always spook me," Jackie said. "I realize he's your father, but it's true. How many in there?"

Molly gazed at the monitor. "Two in the home. No electronic equipment in the shed. No clue."

They'd taken two cars and were forced to park farther away than usual. Molly and Chis rode in one car, while Jackie, Jonathan, Lyle, and Wallace packed into the other.

"You're clear to go. Watch the windows, and you're good," Molly said.

"Recommend taking Powell's men down first," Chris said. "Shots through the window will suffice. Then move to the shed for extraction, Hudson."

"Roger that," Jackie said. "Jonathon, you're leading Wallace and Lyle. On your signal it starts."

"We're going now," Jonathon said. "Get moving, Wallace

and Lyle. We're hiking toward the back of the property. We'll eliminate the vermin holding my father hostage and then free him. Clear on the plan?"

"Yes sir, Mr. Jonathon."

"Good. Follow me."

Molly and Chris watched them file out of the van and disappear into the nearby woods. Chris reached up and muted his microphone. "Let's hope Jonathon's as calm a leader as his father. On the bright side, they shouldn't expect a daytime raid. We're flipping the script here."

Jonathon led the trio of armed personnel in silence through the mercifully bright surroundings. Beams of light shone through the canopy above. They marched through the rural setting for over twenty minutes before they saw something besides more trees, twigs, and logs.

Jonathon stopped and held a fist up, indicating to stop. "Found the property," he whispered. "Where are the hostiles inside, Ms. Turner?"

"I see one in the kitchen, and the other's heading outside as we speak via the backdoor. Looks like he's checking on pops in the shed."

The group's position was around a hundred feet from the property. There was no cover between their goal and their position.

Jonathon looked over his shoulder. "Mr. Wallace, once he's in the shed, you'll approach and kill the shed visitor. Mr. Lionel, you're with me. We're keeping his back-up occupied. Take no chances. Shoot first, and fire accurately."

A man exited the backdoor and strolled toward the shed behind the house.

"Hold, Mr. Wallace," Jonathon said. "Only after he's inside do you move. It wouldn't do for him to turn and spot us. On my mark, we move - all of us."

"Understood," Wallace and Lyle said.

Every man had a rifle in their arms, ready to kill from a distance or up close and personal. Wallace's wasn't of the automatic variety, instead choosing a shotgun. It was something he requested before they departed.

"Now," Jonathon said. "God speed, gentlemen. Once the hostiles are down, we meet at the shed. Move up."

Wallace split off from the pair and ran through the open field toward the shed, while his partners flanked him to his left. He didn't have the luxury of watching them as he kept his shotgun pointed toward the shed's door. He wasn't trying to get caught off guard, not after recent events. Finally making it to the shed, he circled around it to check for a rear entrance. Finding none, he moved to the front and waited, with the barrel of his shotgun pointed toward the exit.

A series of gunshots to his left startled him, but didn't break his focus. The door burst open with a string of curse words best left unmentioned. His finger squeezed the trigger and the boom stick roared to life. His target flew away from Wallace from the mass of buckshot impacting his chest. The sheer impact sent him flying backwards.

Wallace wasted no time rushing forward and kicking the handgun away from his victim. He stood over his victim's chest, who now laid on his back facing his executioner. Wallace aimed higher, seeing no penetration from his center mass shot. "Sucks to be you." He squeezed again, and the man's head was no longer in one piece. Brain matter was visible on the grass beside the door to the shed. He cautiously kicked the door open, not knowing if any more hostiles were inside. An awful stench met his nostrils, but he ignored it.

A gunshot and wood splintered to his right. Shrapnel embedded into his body, but he was quick enough to turn and fire blindly in that direction. A wailing scream met his efforts. He angled his aim down and fired again, silencing the ambusher. He swung the barrel of the weapon left, checking the other corner, but found no extra enemies lying in wait. Inspecting the wound on his arm, he spoke. "Shed's clear, barely. Son of a bitch. That hurts."

"You're hit?" Lionel asked.

"Not by a bullet or shell, no." Wallace picked an especially large wooden piece of shrapnel out of his arm with his left. "Disgusting."

"House is clear," Molly said. "Don't leave us in suspense, King. Is the VIP there?"

Wallace looked up from his wound at the confined space. There was a seat sitting in the middle with a light above. Unfortunately, there was a barrel behind it where a blood trail led. "I think so, but I'm guessing it's bad news."

"What the hell's that mean?" Jonathon asked over the call, obviously out of breath.

Wallace looked behind to see Jonathon already there, having ran over. Lyle wasn't far behind.

"What is that smell?" Lyle asked, covering his nose.

"Like I said," Wallace pointed at the barrel. "Look there."

Jonathon hurried over and opened the barrel. It had an acidic smell comprising untold amounts of chemicals. It was a slurry of chemicals, meat, and teeth. The meat was only partially disintegrated as some stubbornly clung to the bones of his father. The skull stared up toward him, muscle and skin melting off it as it stared into his soul. He stared into it before moving his head to the side and promptly unloading the contents of his stomach onto the floor.

"We'll need to burn it now," Chris said, "if that was vomiting I heard. We can't leave DNA."

Lyle spotted a wallet placed on the few cabinets

nearby. He opened it and dug out an identification card. Sure enough, the picture showed Mr. Hudson. "Mr. Hudson, you should see this." He handed over the wallet to the son.

Jonathon rifled through the wallet. "It's him alright. Damn. We were too late."

"We should leave - like now," Lyle said. He trailed the sign of the cross over his chest. "God rest his soul. Someone may have heard these shots."

"True, there are neighbors within a mile. Get out now," Jackie said.

"Acknowledged," Jonathon said quietly. "Goodbye, Father."

"Good thing this is wooden." Wallace pulled out a box of matches and struck one. He tossed it to the floor as his partners vacated the room. "It's sizzling, boss. We're leaving asap."

"Understood."

"Use your phones to track me. I moved nearer to the property to expedite us leaving. It should take a couple minutes walking to arrive," Jackie said.

The group was already in the tree line as the fire spiraled into an inferno enveloping the shed they'd left. Lyle had his phone out on the tracking app he'd installed and followed the signal, leading the three to their exit.

"That's fucked up how they did your father," Wallace said. "My condolences, Mr. Hudson."

"They'll get theirs," Jonathon said. "If they wanted to anger the Hudson family, they've succeeded. The Morris syndicate will receive all the hardware they can manage to facilitate that. On my father's grave, I swear it."

"For what it's worth," Lyle said, "I pray for your father's immortal soul that he may find peace."

"I was never a religious man, Mr. Lionel, but my father was. It's appreciated."

"There you all are. Get in."

Lyle looked and saw they were near the forest's edge by the road. "There's our ride."

"Chris and Molly already left. Get your asses in here."

Everyone got inside and left, but Jonathon's blank stare didn't abate the entire ride home.

19

The entire entourage consisting of Roger, Bernard, Isabella, Molly, and Ian got out of the car before heading inside the dispensary. It was just before eight o'clock, closing time. They saw Abigail tending to three customers who were trying to beat closing time.

"What are you trying to pull?" Abigail asked. She glanced over at Bernard and company. "You need to pay."

"Trouble?" Bernard took a confident, swaggering step forward. Isabella and Ian flanked him while Roger trailed behind.

"I'd recognize that voice anywhere," the ringleader of the trio turned. "Ah, we meet again, Mr. Morris."

"Do I know you?" Bernard asked the older gentleman.

"The younger generation is rude. You don't remember me? We've already met. You should know the man you're trying to ruin."

"Sorry, I don't remember nobodies."

"Nobody?" This struck a chord with the seventy plus year old customer. "Kids have no respect for their elders or their superiors. You're the same as your snot-nosed boss. You don't recognize me?"

Roger moved to the side, finally seeing the confrontation unobstructed. "That voice," he said. Gears in his head proverbially turned, trying desperately to connect the voice he'd swear he'd heard before. "I know you."

"Ironic that the one who'd simply spoke remembers, but the one who met me cannot. No wonder mother dearest placed you in charge. This simpleton cannot even remember his betters. I assume you're the moron who was on the phone before and ran your mouth."

"Made it simple to gain access to your locations. You fell for it hook, line, and sinker. I know your type, old timer. Show a little disrespect and you turn fussy. Made it easy for us to track that landline. Why are you here, Mr. Bailey?"

Bernard's eyes widened, finally putting it together. Flashes of their previous meeting finally raced through his head. He remembered the meeting, followed by the brawl just outside afterward. "You sent those men to brawl with us."

"The dullard finally puts it together." Mr. Bailey smirked. "Aren't you supposed to be the blood relative of grave digger Morris? I suppose he was never the brightest, but he was street smart. You, you're neither. You're both spoiled little brats trading in on your forefather's achievements. Standing on the shoulders of giants." Mr. Bailey cleared his throat. "Meet my security, Rufus and Randy. They've been dying to meet both of you."

Both men at his sides audibly growled.

"I forgot my purse. Silly me." Molly was visibly shaken and backed off and out the glass doors.

Isabella pulled Bernard back behind her and Ian. "You want to dance, big boy? I doubt you could handle me."

Rufus took a step forward, only for Bailey to stop him. "Hold, Rufus. There are cameras in here. Can't allow it to catch us causing an incident for the police to see, can we?"

"Yeah, run and hide. It's what you're best at," Bernard said. "Or is that causing mass shootings with your little junkies? He failed, obviously. The dude killed quite a few civilians though. Rumor is they're investigating the dregs, aka your clientele. It's only a matter of time before they connect the dots, and you have a full scale investigation from the FBI. You realize that, yes? You'd do better to run and hide and leave Nashville for the competent."

"Attempts to infuriate me into starting an incident will be unsuccessful, whelp. The gloves are off now. You wanted war, you got it."

Roger looked outside at the cars and saw Molly leaning against Bailey's vehicle while trying to look nonchalant. She jumped when the window rolled down to reveal an angry man with sunglasses. "You're out of men and you know it," Roger said, giving his attention to Bailey. "You've been throwing your meth addled freaks at us. They've died one and all. How many do you have left? A dozen? They're not trained like Rufus and Randy. You only have enough trained personnel to keep the junkie dealers honest. We're not stupid. We know the business model you practice. Now Powell, he's the actual challenge."

"Mr. Powell's had enough of you upstarts."

"Why stand up for a partner who's afraid to show his ugly mug?" Bernard asked. "You're at least brave and stupid enough to meet face to face. You think he'd offer you the same luxury? No. He's leaving you out to dry. Think about it. All this shit comes back to you, while he remains anonymous. He's smarter than you, old timer, and you've convinced yourself you're best buddies because you ran a monopoly on this hick town for a while. It's a proverbial marriage of convenience. That's all."

"What do you know of business? You're not even old enough to drink legally. Children shouldn't try lecturing their elders on matters they know nothing of. It only proves their naivete."

"Let's ask Rufus and Randy here," Bernard said. "You see this war ending well?"

Neither bodyguard answered verbally, responding only with a heated glare toward Isabella and Ian.

"Anytime you want to tango," Ian said. "I'm ready. Don't be shy."

"Leave the dance related zingers to me." Isabella glared at Ian.

"What a merry bunch," Mr. Bailey said with a smug look. "This ends in the next days. Trust that, boys. I don't care who your mother is."

"Something tells me thinking isn't your strong suit," Roger said. "Let's say you win, hypothetically speaking. You kill us. What happens next? Did you even think of the future? You think Rachel Morris will give up and say 'Golly, guess I'll leave it be.'? Get real. If you think we're bad, you're as ignorant as your personnel."

"Tell me, how are Hudson's captors?" Bernard asked.

Rufus stepped forward, past Bailey's arm, disobeying his employer.

"Aw," Bernard looked up at Rufus. "Were his guards your little friends? I say were since they're past tense. All you managed with that act of pettiness was to secure us a partnership. Neither of you can manage a single thing correctly, other than murdering innocents in the street. We can't forget that, now can we, boss? If I were you," Bernard said, pushing Ian to the side, coming face to face with a growling

Rufus, "I'd run away and pray the authorities don't find you. At least then you'll live. If you choose to stay and fight, we'll finish this war."

"Best obey your master, lapdog," Roger said. He stood beside his best friend, locking eyes with Rufus.

Rufus grabbed Roger by his collar and yanked him away from his formation.

"Sir!" Abigail called from behind the counter, pointing at the cameras above in the corners of the shop. "You should know the cameras up there record. There's no sound, but visual's crystal clear."

"Mere threats from your little business partner won't save you," Rufus said.

Isabella approached Rufus without words, closing the distance before he could react. She reached into her coat's pocket and pulled out a device that looked like a small metal device. It had putty on one side. She attached the device to the rear of Rufus's head with a brutal slap. She pulled out a device. "See this?"

Rufus reached up with his free hand and touched the foreign device attached to his head. "What is this?"

"That, my stupid body building friend, is an explosive device. Not enough explosives to cause harm to bystanders or this building, but adequate to blow your skull clean off. My boss may get singed a little, but that's a risk I'm willing to take. He's turning red. Let him go. Don't lose your head, big fella. One push of this and you're ten pounds lighter. You reach for your weapons, you go boom as well."

Meanwhile, Ian and Randy clutched their holstered pistols. Both had eyes locked on the other.

"Drop him, and I consider letting you live." Isabella's thumb hovered over the red button. "Or fuck around and find out. Am I bluffing or not?"

"Enough!" Mr. Bailey slapped Rufus's hand, causing Roger to regain his breath amidst a coughing fit as he lowered to planet Earth again beside Bernard. "We're leaving. Remember, we have witnesses."

"Your security needs to learn their manners." Roger finally regained some composure, enough to talk anyway. "You're lucky we control the camera."

"Is that right?" Bailey asked. "Two bodyguards is not all I'm packing, whelp. I have marksmen around the area."

"Then they're already spotted," Roger said.

"You're referring to your quaint guards, correct?" Bailey asked. "They'll do nothing to stop a rifle bullet."

Isabella tried an encore performance, except this time with Bailey. Randy gripped her hand, not content with having his paycheck signer's head blown off.

Ian's solution to this wasn't as elegant as Isabella's, but it was undoubtedly effective. A swift kick to Randy's groin caused him to groan, but his grip on Isabella's hand remained iron-tight.

"Enough," Bernard said. "Release her, and we allow you to leave alive, at least for one more night. That's the deal. Or we could end it here. It's up to you, but I don't favor your odds. How much do you trust your sharpshooters? Maybe you underestimated our guards? Are you one hundred percent willing to bet your lives on it?"

"We're leaving," Bailey said, clearly displeased at how this turned out. "Remove the explosive from my guard at once."

Isabella didn't move to comply. She simply looked over at Bernard and Roger quizzically.

"I believe I said we'd allow you to leave alive. I said nothing about removing explosives. Remove it yourself if you dare. What's the worst that could happen? You get brain matter on you and some singed facial hair?"

"Petulant child!" Bailey pushed his guards and followed them, fuming all the way. They exited, Rufus still clawing at the explosive device.

Every remaining soul looked at Isabella.

"What?" Isabella asked. "We needed a trump card. I gave us one. Shall the weasel go pop, boss?" She held the detonator up, watching the group enter their car out front. "Range is only about a hundred fifty feet. Decision time."

"It won't hit Bailey though?" Roger said.

"That's right. Just enough to pop his guard's head and stain that pretty limousine of his. Wouldn't that be a shame?"

"Do it." Roger rubbed his throat and looked at the departing limousine.

"With pleasure," Isabella said. She watched as the car took off. She pressed the button with a feral grin and watched the back window turn a deep crimson red as the car swerved. "That'll keep them busy cleaning that shit."

Bernard had already moved to the front counter. "You need to delete that footage on the double to be safe."

"Already on it," she said. She disappeared into the store's rear for a few minutes and returned. "It's done and recording again."

"Good, let's get out of here."

The door opened to an annoyed Molly. "Damn it. You think they'll go home after that spectacle?"

"Why do we care?" Isabella asked.

"I planted a tracker, dumbass. If they ditch that car, we won't find their location."

"That won't happen," Isabella said. "He'll get his minions to clean it out. A car like that costs too much. Especially with his business shot to hell. He'll opt to clean it, mark my words."

"We'll see in fifteen minutes if it disappears in flames or if it delivers us to the promised lands. Who gave the order anyway?"

"That may have been me," Roger said. "What?" He shrugged. "He grabbed me by the neck. The ancient codger needed to be knocked down a peg."

"Let's pray Ms. Know-It-All is right."

"Let me delete this footage too, for safety's sake." Abigail sighed and went to delete the footage a second time...

20

"Heard you and Bub ran into Bailey earlier," Crystal said. She laid on the couch while Molly had one of the recliners. The flat screen television droned in the background, long forgotten by the two occupants. "How'd that go?"

"We met Bailey. That was interesting. I attached a tracker to his car before your brother let his desire for petty vengeance screw up my plan."

"Did you inform him beforehand? What does that mean anyway?"

"No, and Isabella attached an explosive to one of Bailey's bodyguard's head. He set it off while they made their escape. I'm trying to find whether they dumped the car or are cleaning it out. I thought this would be our chance to finally get Bailey's home location to end him."

"You can't blame him if you didn't inform him," Crystal said. "Nice to hear that ass received a wake-up call."

"His bodyguard did anyway. I just wish he'd kept his cool instead of firing back on the whim of the new guard,

Isabella I think was her name. Granted, that ass throttled Rog."

"How about it? Where's it located?"

Molly watched the dot move on the map. "It's out in the country at some address. I'm assuming it's his address. No confirmation though."

"Then we've found both Bailey and Powell's location, yeah? This war may be over soon."

"Assaulting their home base will be deadly, more than any other operation so far. Don't get excited. More will die before this war ends. Let's hope it's none of us - no more anyway."

"It's a mystery to me why Roger insisted on this career," Crystal said. She sat up and leaned on the end of the couch. "It's the least appreciated, dangerous, hell of an occupation I can imagine."

"Yet here you are," Molly said.

"What's that supposed to mean?"

"Why disobey mother dearest to visit your brother entrenched in this job if it's so dangerous? You have another reason?"

"Making sure he's safe, obviously. To help with my skill set and to escape the prison of that mansion. At least here I'm allowed to leave occasionally and explore the city."

"Is that why?"

"Obviously."

"I'll remember that for later." Molly gazed at the screen, a little smile painting her features. "Guess Bailey's cheap, as Isabella claimed. That limo's still alive and well."

"Fantastic," Crystal said sarcastically. "That means I'll be under house arrest soon enough when mother demands I'm sent back."

"She may not," Molly said.

"You're delusional if you believe that. You don't remember the phone call where she demanded I return? No, I'll pack my bags soon and be shipped off like cattle."

"Whatever. At least you won't sleep on a couch back home. That's worth something."

"I'll be learning from Lee again. He's such a crap teacher. He's one of those teachers that always seems distracted. We end up copying chapters down to memorize information more than any lecture. He barely takes questions. I'm supposed to understand the course from that?"

"He's not teacher material. He's barely a networking specialist compared to me. Rumor is your grandfather was tech illiterate, yeah?"

"As far as I know. Why? He supposedly asked Lee to infiltrate the FBI database as his initiation, and he was impressed. That's how he got the job."

"He has some skill, granted," Molly said. "That test was the most nervous he'd ever been, guaranteed. The FBI is no joke. They'll track you and send men in suits to scare the piss out of you. He must have covered his tracks. Maybe he was driven in the past. Who knows?"

"The point is, it's torture being locked in solitary confinement with your only human contact being with Lee and the other members' kids. I love guiding and helping the kids and all, but I'm seventeen. I yearn to explore the world and experience life, not be locked away by my mother in her impenetrable fortress. Even this is better compared."

"Someone complaining about my accommodations in here?" Roger entered the room. "Sofa not to your liking, Sister?"

"She's bitching about how she'll be sent back home after the war."

Crystal glared at Molly for a moment before turning to her brother.

"It's only for a year longer," Roger said. "Then you'll be off to college and making something of yourself. You won't be near any of this bloodshed, which'll be a load off my psyche."

"College?"

"Sure," Roger said. He took a seat beside Crystal. "You could study to be anything you desire. Hell, go to a trade school. The entire world's open to you. Don't follow in my and mother's footsteps."

"It's odd you wouldn't recommend it after taking that road," Molly said.

"I have my reasons. I'd prefer my baby sister to become a banker, accountant, electrician, or actress. Something, anything other than this. It's lucrative, but we both know this life isn't for everyone."

"How do you all manage your emotions after killing so many?" Crystal asked.

"I can't speak for others, but I ignore it," Roger said with a shrug. "I'm sure psychologists would say that's dangerous, but it works. Sitting and dwelling on your own sins may come naturally, but its benefits are few. You've already saved my ass twice. I wish that burden was never loaded on you."

"I tried to view it as a war since I've read stories that soldiers rationalized killing by telling themselves they were protecting their brothers in arms. In my case, it was my actual brother and his friends." Crystal leaned her head back and stared at the ceiling, illuminated by the artificial light from the television. "It doesn't help all that much, if I'm honest."

"College should be a fresh start for you. Go to a distant college and live there among fresh faces where nobody knows you," Roger said. "You can experience life without all this to distract you and drag you down. You'll make friends, find a boyfriend, and get a degree. Hell, become a lawyer if you want to flip the bird to fate. God knows mother would fund the tuition. She'd be tickled pink."

"I'll think about it." Crystal flopped down, laying down again. This time her head rested in her brother's lap, looking skyward. "What about you? You're making a life here outside Nashville after this war?"

"That was the plan," Roger said.

"Any colleges near here?"

"You have difficulties grasping what distant college means, don't you?" Molly asked, earning a chuckle from Roger.

"Staying all alone in an unfamiliar place does not interest me. It'd be a nightmare trying to sleep at night. I get homesick easily unless family's nearby."

"You could float the idea to mother. I doubt she'd be angry. Truthfully, she'd probably prefer you go to Ohio State, but it's your life, so you choose the college."

"Sure, go to Memphis's College. It's renowned for something I'm sure," Molly said. "Best bet for electronics is going out west though."

"Are you nuts? I'm not going to California. Those people are fucking weird. I hear tale there's sewage in the streets along with hypodermic needles. Screw that."

"I don't think we're normal, Sis," Roger said. "Whatever you decide, I'll support your decision and vouch for you to Mother."

"Thanks."

"Rog, you should know the limousine is still in one piece, I believe," Molly said. She got up, bringing the laptop over. She placed it on the nearby edge of the sofa so he could see. Resting a hand on his upper back, she steadied the laptop with her other. "See here?"

"You think this is his home property?" Roger asked, a twinkle in his eyes.

"That's my guess."

"Then we know our opponent's homes. We'll show them how it's done. It's scary to think if their onslaught of junkies had succeeded, none of this would have occurred. If a stray bullet had struck me or Bernard, we'd be in a totally different circumstance."

"Cut the head off the snakes, and they die," Crystal said. "New leaders will seize their spots. You realize that? Someone in the organization will seize power after that power vacuum appears."

"Hopefully they'll be willing to work with us," Roger said. "Establishing trade relations would be optimal for everybody's checkbook and health."

"They'll beg for peace, I bet anything," Molly said. "Are we planning this out tonight or tomorrow?"

"Tomorrow morning, and then tomorrow night we'll end this war. I just pray we have enough bodies to strike both locations at once. We still don't know which location Powell's at."

"What about the families?" Crystal asked. "You know Powell has a kid and probably a wife living there. We're not harming them, are we?"

"Not if we can help it," Roger said.

"Good. Soldiers are one thing, innocents are another."

"Can I speak to you in private, boss?" Molly asked.

"Yeah, go with your girlfriend. It'll allow me to focus on getting some shuteye and catch up on my beauty sleep after the pizza finishes and the boys outside are fed." Crystal punctuated her sentence with a massive yawn. She sat up, allowing Roger to stand before claiming the entire couch again.

Roger accompanied Molly, laptop and all, to her room. Jackie wasn't in the spacious two bedroom.

"Jackie shouldn't come until eleven. It's when she normally turns in for the night," Molly said. She checked the clock on her laptop to see it was only nine p.m. "We have a couple hours of privacy here."

"What's on your mind?" Roger asked.

"Your sister."

"What'd she do now?"

"Nothing," Molly said. "Look, first promise me this is private. She must never know I told you."

"I promise it's between us. You're worrying me. What's wrong?"

"She doesn't quite love you like a sister."

"Uh huh."

"What kind of response is that?"

"You think I'm thick? It wasn't hard to figure out," Roger said. "We find out we're not related, and she continues her clingy behavior. I was hoping it was just since she's a touchy-feely person, but I suspected as much. I'm not dumb, despite my best efforts to appear otherwise. What brother wants that conversation? I've been avoiding it."

"Oh. Why didn't you at least let me know? You know how stressed I was? Dating the boss's son is already ballsy, but I didn't want to cross the daughter too."

"Dating the boss's son, huh? Sorry, babe," Roger said. "Nothing's ever simple in the Morris family. You know that. Besides, she's already given her blessing, you idiot."

"Excuse me?"

"She wouldn't call you my girlfriend with that smile if

she disapproved. You didn't notice her facial expression earlier?"

"I figured she was simply stoned off my stash."

"You let her smoke?"

"Let her is a powerful expression. More like she stole some and smoked it."

"That's the official story?" Roger asked.

"Yes."

"Right, well regardless, don't worry. Jealousy doesn't suit you,"

"Who said I was jealous?" she asked, looking away. "Not me, that's for sure."

"The whole denying act is cute and all, but sometimes us guys like to know we're wanted. Honesty is okay sometimes, you know."

"It wasn't jealousy, idiot. It was worry that I'd piss off the daughter of the boss. Even you wouldn't be able to shelter me if she got a stick up her ass and squealed to your mother. She'd relocate me if she knew of us."

"She'd try," Roger said. "Besides, she can't talk. She married her own bodyguard."

"Your mother's not immune to hypocrisy."

"Don't you find it thrilling doing this under her nose, just a little?" Roger leaned over close.

She could feel his hot breath dancing against her skin and lost her focus. "Huh? Who would?"

"Forget the politics of it and lose yourself in the moment. Doesn't that sound fun?" Roger scooted closer to her on the bed. "If you want me to stop or slow, speak. Do you want me to back off? Tell me what you want."

Molly's face was completely red, though it was impossible to spot in the darkness. The only source of light pouring in came from the window nearby, along with faint artificial light radiating from the laptop, long forgotten.

She finally gained the wherewithal to answer him. "I want you to..." she trailed off.

"Want me to do what?" Roger asked. "I'm at your service in every way."

"I want you to focus on ending this war." Molly backed off. "After that, we can explore this further."

Roger backed off, true to his word. "Aw, what a shame. Here I hoped you were going to ask for a kiss."

"In your dreams, boss."

"That's another thing," Roger said. "If you truly don't want this relationship, you know you can inform me. I realize it's unprofessional of me, but I won't pressure you into anything. I'm not the type of guy to force a relationship. We'll stay working acquaintances until you decide."

"We're not having this conversation right now. That's a postwar discussion. Sorry, Mr. Morris, but I'm not that kind of girl. I've only known you for a few weeks. I'd be down to see where this relationship goes, however."

"Not even a goodnight kiss?"

"If you count sharing a joint as a kiss, sure." She reached over to her night table to a collection of pre rolled joints in a jar. "Agreed?"

"I'll take what I can get."

Simultaneously, in the barn...

"We should construct another building once this war's finished and place a pool table in it," Chris said.

"Hand me the screwdriver, old man." Kyle was elevated on a ladder working on the wiring. "This isn't a vacation home. Why a billiards table?"

"Recreation is vital," Chris said. "What do you two think?" He turned to Lyle and Wallace, both on temporary break while others patrolled outside. "Anything's better than this barn, right?"

"You want my opinion?" Wallace asked. "I don't care two damns about the facilities here. I have my home nearby. All I care about is making money and ending this damned war so I can take care of my family."

This caught Jackie's attention as she climbed out of the tunnel door in the corner. "Family? You're married?"

"Not that kind," Wallace said. "I take care of my parents. They're in their seventies. They think I work as a bodyguard to a wealthy entrepreneur. My mother worries herself sick, but I'd love more time to spend with them."

"I never pictured you for a family type," Lyle said, glancing up from his phone.

"Give me that." Wallace swiped Lyle's phone. "Who's this?"

"Never mind her name." Lyle tried to take it back, but found it out of reach as Wallace held it above his head. "Give it."

"It's a girl." Wallace whistled. "She's cute. She your girl-friend? Waiting for things to calm down before getting married? Is that it?"

"You've got it all wrong." Lyle desperately attempted to take the device back, to no avail. "We're not together."

"Let me see." Chris reached up and grabbed the device. "Sister?"

"No. Why do you guys care?"

"You had the picture available for viewing," Kyle said. He finished attaching the box to the wall, hiding the tangle of wires. "Just elaborate. It'll end quicker, trust me."

"It's the girl I like, alright?" Lyle knew it was coming, but the oncoming laughter and jeers still embarrassed him. "Fuck off. What's wrong with that?"

"Nothing," Jackie said. She walked over and peeked over Chris's shoulder. She couldn't help herself and moved to pinch Lyle's cheek. "Our little guy's all grown up." She released the grip and moved back. "Was that your first date?"

"Not quite." Lyle tried his luck with Chris but had no luck.

Jackie elbowed Chris in the gut, forcing him to bend over before she stole the phone and handed it to Lyle. "Nothing to be ashamed of. Denying our feelings is more destructive than pretending they don't exist. Never take these men's advice on love unless you're ready for catastrophic failure. You see any of them married?"

"Are you?" Chris got out.

"No, but I'm a romantic type."

Lyle pocketed the infernal device. "I was thinking of asking her out after we get into a routine."

"Go for it, kid," Jackie said. "Or else you'll wonder what might have been. Trust me when I say that's the worst-case scenario, not her saying no. At least then you know where you stand."

"What about you, you tough old bird?" Chris asked.

"Who you calling an old bird, grandpa?" Jackie asked.

"What's your long-term plan?"

"None of your business." Jackie planted both hands on her hips.

"I know I'll be working." Chris said. "More recruits don't find and test themselves. Maybe if you're not busy, you can help fill in. A member can only test so many souls alone. After all, you're the only other person I trust for the job."

"More than likely I'll be a bodyguard for the bosses,"

Jackie said. She looked up the ladder to Kyle. "You, Mr. Evans. Don't think you'll escape this conversation by acting busy."

"Who's acting?" Kyle climbed down and flicked the nearby light switch. The lights above turned on. "See? Perfectly functional and improved. My brother was an electrician. He taught me a few tricks. You all thought I'd burn the place down." He glared at Chris. "Shows what the old goat knows."

"I didn't say you'd burn the place down, young buck. I said you'd shock the piss out of yourself, which you did."

"Whatever."

"Should you even be working?" Lyle asked. "With all due respect, that wound looks nasty."

"I will not be an invalid as I recover, Mr. Lionel. My father instilled a strong work ethic in me, and I don't intend on disappointing him. He never took a sick day and hardly vacationed with us growing up."

"That explains the Marine's choice," Chris said.

"You have something to say, Bristol?"

"Take it easy, kid," Chris said. "You're talking to a fellow veteran. People don't join the armed forces unless they're in a few camps. They're either going for the free college, they're true naïve patriots, or they're kids from broken homes who figure leaving at any cost is worth it. Normally the last type excels."

"Nothing was broken about my home."

"Group two then?"

"Closest to your three imaginary groups I guess. I learned the truth once I was inside. The whole thing's a scam to score some criminal politicians some extra cash. I figured I deserved some of that scratch, and they didn't like that. Dishonorable discharge was right on all counts."

"You have plans after this war?"

"Yeah, it's called work. Maybe finding you some fresh blood, since you're getting up there in age, grandpa. I would angle for Ms. Thomas's job, but I don't fancy a feud with her." Kyle left it at that. He exited the barn, apparently tired of this conversation.

"The kid has sense anyway," Chris said with a shrug. "Nobody wants a beef with Ms. Thomas here."

"Damned right you don't."

Ten minutes later in the barn's loft...

"What was that racket about earlier?" Greg asked.

"Who knows?" Mitchell responded. "Sounded like an argument. How you doing over there?" He planted his elbows on the dirty wood planks and propped up to see Greg across the way. "I can't believe they dumped us here. They couldn't even arrange us a room."

"The bedrooms were taken I suppose," Greg said. He laid atop a sleeping bag and had a thick blanket sprawled over him to keep warm. "I'm more concerned with my future in the syndicate, if I'm honest, Mitch. We both know wheelchair bound men aren't what they want. I still can't feel my feet, and I don't figure I ever will again. I'm lucky to be alive at all. Old man Bristol said the exit wound was near my spine, so I suppose it nicked something important on its exit."

"At least you get Ms. Thomas changing your dressing. I get Bristol himself. I'd love to get tender loving care from her." Mitchell rubbed his injured shoulder with a grimace.

"You always were the thirsty bastard of the group. Do you think Izzie and Ian are doing alright?" Greg raised an arm, reaching for the barn's roof, testing his arm's ability.

"Ian said they'd visit tonight on break. It's about that time. Until then, you're stuck with me."

"Heaven help me. You're enough to drive a man insane."

"I'm trying to entertain us," Mitchell said. "It's not my fault you don't appreciate the fine literature I picked out to read for us."

"You picked a joke book that was written by a ten-year-old, I believe. How does your phone have charge left?"

"Evans wired up an outlet over here. Look." Mitchel rolled onto his side and pointed at the nearby outlet with a phone charger plugged in. "Were you asleep or something?"

"Probably. It's my only respite from your ass."

"I know you love me like family. You're just cold and withholding."

"What are you, my ex?" Greg asked.

Both men shared a laugh at the friendly jab at the fairer sex.

"You lazy bums still awake up there?" Ian called out.

"Unfortunately," Greg called out. "Hurry and relieve me of dealing with this idiot."

Both men turned and saw Isabella and Ian climbing the nearby ladder. Ian took a seat near Mitchell while Isabella sat near Greg.

"Izzie's ignoring me again today?" Mitchell asked. "Damn my luck."

"I know if I didn't, you'd cop a feel of my ass."

"Damn, you didn't need to call a dude out."

"How's business going today, Izzie?" Greg asked. "Blow any dumb bastard up?"

"As a matter of fact, I did."

"Pardon?"

"She stuck explosives on the back of Bailey's bodyguard's

head. When they left, she asked the boss permission to explode it."

"He actually said yes?" Mitchell asked.

"Damned skippy he did," Isabella said. She had a wistful look. "It was beautiful and invigorating. I'm surprised Mr. Morris even said yes."

"He got a talking to from Ms. Turner, if you'll recall," Ian said.

"It required balls to say yes," Isabella said. "Maybe not brains, but I guess my initial fear of them being spoiled rich pussies was proven wrong. Now my next concern is their impulsivity."

"That should fit right in with you, Izzie," Greg said.

"You're lucky I don't hit injured people, Mr. Comedian. Any progress today?"

Greg's face fell. "I still can't feel my feet or toes. I don't imagine I'll ever walk again, especially seeing as I can't go to the hospital. Back-alley doctors are limited by their lack of x-rays and MRIs, among other equipment. Not that anything'd help other than possibly spinal surgery, which isn't possible. I wonder if I can receive training helping with the computer side of things. It's about the only duty I'm fit for now."

"You want me to ask the boss to request Ms. Turner to train you?" Isabella asked. She took a tissue from her pocket and wiped the side of Greg's head free of sweat.

"I could watch your back from the car. It's the only course ahead if I stay. We don't get disability or hazard pay. Other branches would have cut me loose by now. Say what you want about the boys, but they value their personnel as best they can manage. That means something, as you all know."

"You're serious?" Mitchell asked. "If they cared, they wouldn't have sent us into that trap."

"War requires sacrifices," Greg said. "We usually avoid that role, but not this time. Sorry I missed Robert's funeral. He is buried, I trust?"

"The very night we returned; Bernard insisted we give him a proper burial." Ian splayed out on the floor, trying to get comfortable. "He personally helped dig the hole. I asked about Roger, you know."

"What did you say?" Greg asked.

"I asked him about the rumors."

"You didn't," Mitchell said. "Tell me you're joking. He's best friends with the man. I can't imagine he enjoyed hearing the rumors."

"He didn't," Ian said. "The boss explained how Roger fought alongside the grunts and him the other night. I gather they're close friends. He talked Roger Morris up and explained how he's hot-headed but genuine. He hates those rumors and advised we keep those to ourselves and to never mention them in front of Roger."

"Pissing off a hot-tempered boss is not on my priority list," Isabella said. She helped Greg elevate his head and grabbed the nearby water bottle. "Here, drink some. You need fluids to recover. This thing looks half full. You haven't been drinking?"

"It's hard to drink lying down. You expect that horse's ass across from me to help? He's injured too."

"Yeah, don't forget that," Mitchell said. "Don't blame me."

"I'll blame whoever I please," Isabella said.

"What did Mr. Bristol say about your wounds?" Greg asked.

"Bristol?" Isabella asked. "He's treating your wounds?"

"He's changing my dressing and remarked how lucky I was. I don't feel lucky, being stuffed in this barn with Mr. Monotone over there. I thought I'd die of boredom before you all came in here."

"We should lobby for a laptop in here to distract ourselves," Greg chuckled. "At least then I could ignore Mitchell's inane rambling."

"I'll see what I can do," Isabella said. "I'm no miracle worker, and the training comes first. We'll make sure you're taken care of, Greg. You received this injury on their behalf. They should be thrilled you're willing to work."

"She works on the training and you, Ian, should ask about the laptops. Seriously, we've even got a charging outlet over there."

"We'll see. I swear you're like a ten-year-old when you're idle."

"You've no idea," Greg said. "This guy started rating all the Syndicate ladies on a scale of one to ten earlier."

"It's not my fault I appreciate the female form." Mitchel stuck his tongue out toward Greg.

"You two are insane," Isabella said. "I'd be boiling up here in a rage. You aren't pissed off this happened?"

"Of course I'm angry," Greg said, as calm as ever. "You think throwing a tantrum would help my case? I don't. In my experience, those that kick up a fuss don't receive benefits. Those agreeable and amenable, however, tend to receive preferential treatment. It's all a political game, and I've had nothing but time to calculate the odds. The odds are furthered if Isabella gets on the boss's good side."

"I kept their asses alive today."

"And caused a spectacle at their place of business," Ian said over his shoulder.

"In my defense, that was Bailey and his men that

caused it. I just finished it. It's not my fault Rufus lost his head. Okay, maybe it was. His mama should've taught him not to put his hands on other people's property."

"So the boss is your property now, huh?" Mitchell asked. "I'll inform him of that."

"Shut the fuck up, you moron."

Everybody found the exchange amusing and shared in a laugh at Mitchell's expense.

Mitchell's tone turned unusually somber. "For real though, I miss Rob. It's hard to believe he's never coming back."

"Yeah," Ian said.

The four shared a moment of tranquil peace as they remembered their fallen brother in arms.

"Sorry," Mitchell said. "I've had tons of time to let my mind wander."

"Go find it because you've lost your mind."

Mitchell exaggerated a fake laugh. "You're hilarious. Maybe you should perform at Mr. Hudson's club tonight."

"You all think we're winning this war?" Greg asked out of nowhere.

"Supposedly," Ian said. "We've discovered Bailey and Powell's home locations. All that's left is assassinating them, and we've won. Nashville would be ours then."

"Who do you think they'll send?" Greg asked. "I doubt the bosses will expose themselves to danger."

"I don't know," Isabella said. "They're growing on me. I know we'll be called again, Ian, but if I know anything of Morris' history, the patriarchs of the family love the field. I'm betting they'll follow tradition and handle it themselves."

"Don't get too fond of them, Izzie," Mitchell said.

"Rumor is Ms. Turner's trying for Roger and Bernard's chasing Abigail Gomez, the dispensary owner."

"Admiration doesn't automatically equal romantic love, you damned fool. Contrary to your sexist beliefs, men and women can be friends only."

"Friends, she says. You're an employee, not his friend. A coworker who got verbally dressed down, I might add."

"We were a late show," Isabella said. "We deserved it, to be fair. Because your ass, Mitchell, can't read a fucking map. Remember?"

"You're blaming me? It's not my fault Greg took a wrong turn."

"Oh no you don't," Greg said, more animated than he'd been the entire time. He propped himself up on his elbows and used his other hand to point at Mitch. "You're the one who gave bad directions."

"My directions were immaculate. Reading a map isn't rocket science."

"Yet you screwed it up anyway." Ian tried to keep a straight face as he spoke, but failed. "Have you two eaten anything since lunch?" Ian asked.

"Not yet."

"I'll go fetch you something," Isabella said.

"What about me?" Mitchell asked.

"Maybe if I feel like it."

Mitchell watched Isabella get up before descending the ladder. "Come on, Izzie. Grant a guy a favor."

"You know she loves teasing you. You're too easy," Ian said, standing up. He wiped his pants clear of the dust. "This war ends soon, boys. After it's settled, if we're staying, I'll find us housing. This barn isn't fit for human habitation."

"You think they'd want to keep us down here after our reception?" Greg asked.

"Don't know. We'll see. I'll go inquire about the laptop. Don't get excited. The odds are bad."

"Seriously? You're asking Ms. Turner?"

"Her, or the boss's sister. She's a techie I hear. She's always a sweetie I've gathered from our interactions."

Isabella's voice returned from below. "Miss Morris? You're too kind, delivering this here yourself. Hope you boys like pizza. Ms. Morris made these for you bums, so you better eat it all!"

"Ms. Isabella, it's alright if they don't," Crystal said as she walked in with Isabella at her side. Her voice got louder as they climbed the ladder. Isabella held the pizza in one hand as she climbed. "I'm sorry it took so long. I lost track of time."

Isabella reached the top first and brought a box full of pizza over. She divided the pizza and allocated both an equal share while the others spoke.

"No worries, Ms. Morris," Greg said.

"You made this?" Mitchell asked.

"I did. Hopefully it's not terrible. I'm no chef." Crystal bit her lip as both men took tentative bites. "For what it's worth, I'm sorry for what happened to you both. I pray you don't blame my brother or Bernard. If they'd known, they'd never have sent you."

"Forget it, Ms. Morris," Isabella said. "We appreciate you taking the time. Do you know where a heater is? We'd like to place one upstairs in the loft."

"I'm not sure, but I'll search. I'll set it up before I head to bed. Sound alright?"

"Thank you, Ms. Morris," Greg said.

"I'll be back." Crystal descended the ladder and disappeared outside.

"Time for us to leave," Ian said, standing up. "We'll be

back tomorrow morning if we're not working."

"Don't worry about us." Greg pointed over at Mitchell. "His bitching keeping me awake is my concern."

"Be sure to thank Ms. Morris." Isabella glared at Mitchell before she stepped onto the ladder.

"I got it."

"Don't hit on her either."

"Uh huh."

Soon the injured men settled into silence after the crowd left.

"Mitch?"

"Yeah?"

"You think I'll ever walk again?"

"I don't know."

"Me either," Greg said. "That terrifies me."

"You'll survive, thrive, and adapt. You always did."

"I can only pray Ms. Turner will teach me, and they need another techie. What conceivable use is there for a crippled member in this Syndicate? I'll be released, alive if I'm lucky. My life will be collecting welfare, battling bed sores, and sitting in front of the television."

"To my understanding, the only techs are Ms. Turner and Ms. Morris. She's heading home afterward, leaving the spot open. Odds are good, I'd say."

"Of course you'd say that. I resent that others are deciding my life, and now I'm dependent on them.

"You feel helpless. Shit, I do too. I can only imagine your headspace currently. Whatever happens, we'll be here."

The men halted their conversation when footsteps came from below. "Found it. You won't sleep cold tonight, gentlemen." Crystal climbed the ladder and plopped the portable heater down beside the outlet before plugging it in. "Sorry to say I overheard that last bit. You want a teacher for tech stuff?"

"Ms. Morris, don't concern yourself," Greg said. "It's not my intention to steal your job."

"You want a marketable skill in the Syndicate. I understand perfectly. A small tip. I can convince my brother of almost anything. You guard him with your skills, and I'll make it a reality. Hell, I can teach you myself, though Molly's better."

"I'd be in your debt." Greg locked eyes with her, one of the few actions he could muster.

"I'll leave you boys to finish eating and rest. Try not to exert yourselves." She reached into her pocket and placed two devices on the floor. She tossed one to Mitchell and took the other to Greg. "Press if there's an emergency. I'll know from the house and run over."

"We'll try not to rely on your kindness."

"Good night, boys." Crystal climbed down the ladder.

Both injured gangsters called out. "Good night, Ms. Morris."

21

It was bright and early. Roger, Bernard, Molly, Kyle, Chris, Jackie, Lyle, Wallace, Isabella, and Ian gathered. Bernard cleared his throat as everyone got comfortable, either sitting or leaning on something. "This war ends tonight, regardless. We've gathered you this morning to plan our move.

"We'd love to hit Powell and Bailey in one swift stroke," Roger said. "Odds are this will be ugly. They won't give up without a fight. That won't dissuade our plans. Ms. Turner, if you'd please elaborate on the situation."

Molly cleared her throat. "We've narrowed down Powell's location to two addresses. We've destroyed his weapon storage. Now we're guessing which location is his primary home and which is the vacation home. We've seen him on camera here." She poked a finger on the map laying on the coffee table. "We're supposing that's his home. There's a problem, however. We know he has a family - a wife and at least one kid. Possibly he has older relatives living with him. We overheard him speaking to his sister.

She claimed she'd be visiting this week, and this fits the timeline."

"Civilians?" Kyle asked.

"Possibly."

"Don't tell me the famed Kyle Evans is afraid of bloodshed," Isabella said. "It wouldn't be the first time we've eliminated civilians sticking their noses where they don't belong."

"Don't put words in my mouth." Kyle gave a pointed glare toward Isabella. "Innocent blood attracts authorities."

"Simply saying, send Ian and me if you're concerned about squeamishness." Isabella gloated over her perceived win by smirking at Kyle.

"We'll take that under advisement," Roger said. "Please continue, Ms. Turner."

"Now this property is enormous. It has five bedrooms, three floors, an attic above it all, and a huge in-ground swimming pool outside. With proper tactical support, it shouldn't be difficult to find Powell's quarters, but be aware if you head inside not to get lost. God knows the number of guards inside. There could be ten, twenty, or more."

"With family there," Chris said, "security would cluster outside, unless his family knows his business model. He'd want them nearly invisible, so he doesn't receive questions to dodge. Odds are they'd be in the woods."

"A repeat of the weapons storage?" Ian asked.

"That's my bet."

"We can't afford to lose any more personnel," Roger said. "Suggestions to counter such an ambush?"

"It's a short list," Jackie said. "The most effective but time-consuming method is to eliminate all security. The downside would be it'd be noisy and everyone would know you're coming, unless you're special forces trained. Even with suppressors, those inside the mansion would hear, unless you used a knife or something quiet. It's not feasible."

"You said the most effective. What's the other option?" Bernard asked.

"Overwhelming force and speed," Jackie said. "It's riskier, but if it works, it's safer. If it fails, you'd have operators out in no-man's-land surrounded by lead. You'd plant explosives near where Powell is. This banks on remaining unseen and disappearing quickly after the blast."

"I don't feel comfortable asking Isabella to go on a suicide mission," Roger said.

"That's touching, boss, but I'm not afraid. I want vengeance for what they did to Greg, Mitch, and Robert. Besides, I see a third option, if I may?"

"Go ahead," Jackie said. "More options are better."

"I suggest we bombard them from a distance," Isabella said. She moved to the coffee table and knelt. She pointed toward a tree cover farthest from the house. "We may be forced to dispatch a few guards if they're stationed there. Even if Powell heard and ran, it wouldn't matter. We brought five rifles with grenade launcher attachments along with proper ordinance. We've three spares for any personnel tagging along. Let's eliminate the guards and then rain down hell."

"Must every plan you devise involve raining down hell and destruction?" Ian asked. "Wait, it's you. Of course it does."

"It presents the least risk," Isabella said.

"Obliterates the civilians inside, however," Molly clearly wasn't thrilled with the plan. "They'd die with the rest."

"Don't lie in bed with dogs if you don't want fleas," was Isabella's response. "If he never told his family, their deaths are on him. If they're aware, then they're knowingly profiting off death and misery, and they deserve it. Either way, not our fault. Don't worry your little head, Ms. Turner."

"Evaluation of said plan?" Bernard asked.

"Effective if ruthless," Chris said. "With enough fire-power, we'd reduce it to ashes. The only downside I foresee is the rest of the security stationed in the woods would immediately start searching once the onslaught started. If they're quick, he may survive, and then you're caught between running and fighting to the last man."

"With five launchers aiming at different locations of the home, he wouldn't survive," Isabella said. "The amount of shrapnel would get him if the blasts didn't."

"It'll still kill his child," Molly said. "Regardless of whether his father is a murderer, he isn't. We know he has a high school aged child. It's how we found him."

"Unless we infiltrate that home and endanger ourselves, this is the only realistic way I see of achieving our goal," Isabella said. "Powell knows he's in danger. If he's hiding with his family, again, it's half his fault for endangering them."

"It seems the first stipulation we need clearing up is civilian loss of life," Kyle said, crossing his arms. "Acceptable or not, boss? Personally, I say fuck them. Why endanger ourselves more for a false sense of moral superiority? We're gangsters at the end of the day. Why concern ourselves with moral imperatives of right and wrong?"

Everyone turned to Roger and Bernard, awaiting an answer.

Roger and Bernard turned and whispered to each other, trying to gain a consensus. This lasted over a minute before they reached a decision.

"We've decided that we prioritize our personnel over the target's family," Bernard said.

"Unanimous decision?" Chris asked.

"Based on pragmatism," Roger said.

"Way to go, boss," Isabella said. "Ignore Ms. Turner's adorable concern for civilians for our safety." She directed her words to either of the Morris boys, but her gaze was locked on Roger specifically. She licked her lips, untold scenarios playing through her mind best left unsaid.

"I don't like it," Molly said.

"Noted," Bernard said. "Think of it, Ms. Turner. Ending this war will end further loss of life. If a wife and kid's the price, then so be it. We can't afford to lose more lives chasing after foolish ideals."

"Rog?" Molly looked up at him, imploring him to say something.

Roger looked away. "I don't like it. However, we have a duty to protect our own members above strangers. You know that."

"Fine then," Molly frowned and looked at the photos and map atop the coffee table.

"If civilian casualties are off the radar," Jackie asked, "then are we bombarding them with explosives? That kind of assault could lead to the FBI being called. Explosives are fed territory."

"We've already crossed that bridge," Ian said. "We blew up the weapon storage property. The genie's already out of the bottle. May as well use it."

"Not to mention Bailey's drug fields. All that's left is destroying anyone who can testify," Chris said. "Which means I'm in favor of leveling the place. What about the security forces hiding in waiting?"

"I've a plan for that too," Isabella said. "If I may?"

"Go ahead," Bernard said.

"Incendiary grenades lobbed into the woods

surrounding the place before we use the high explosive grenades should send them running. Bonus points since the thermite grenades aren't loud. Only the personnel nearest would hear the sizzling as it ignites. By the time they realized, they'd bolt to get out of the inferno. Only suicidal idiots would stay and hunt us."

"Range on the rifle's grenade launcher?" Roger asked.

"A hundred and fifty yards. It should be enough to turn the surrounding woods into an inferno easily. Range isn't the problem."

"Sounds like a plan. What do you think, sirs?" Chris asked.

Roger and Bernard conferred, this time not turning around.

"Unless anyone has further objections, that's the plan," Bernard said afterward. "Now for roster assignments. Mr. Klein will lead the team headed to Powell's. I assume Isabella here will accompany him."

"This one's different," Roger said. "I'll be accompanying you as well."

"Fine by me," Isabella said. "We'd need two more for a full set to bombard with."

"Volunteers?" Bernard asked, looking around the room.

"I'll go," Wallace said.

"That leaves one spot open," Roger said. "Bernard's accompanying the Bailey team, so he's out. What about you, Kyle? Your shoulder well enough for duty?"

"I'm perfectly able," Kyle said. "I'll go."

"That settles roster assignments then. That leaves Ms. Thomas, Bernard, Mr. Lionel, and Mr. Bristol for Bailey. Ms. Turner, what's the word on Bailey's property?"

"Straightforward," Molly said. "His underling claimed he has family, is married, and has guards stationed inside.

Who knows if he lied? There are guards, although I wager only a handful. We should find it easier than Powell's. Don't get reckless. They're still armed to the teeth."

"Recommendations?" Bernard asked.

"We should approach from different angles," Chris said. "We'd disable guards faster and sow chaos. A pincer approach is viable given the natural cover we have access to."

"We've also seen he has a guard on his roof," Molly said. "Someone should kill him before heading into the open."

"They're going to know they're under attack as soon as the first shot sounds," Jackie said. "He should be top priority. They lose the high ground sharpshooter, they're in the dark."

"Most sharpshooters have a spotter," Chris said. "You didn't see one?"

"Not from the angle we viewed," Molly said. "There are no electronic devices up there. He may well have a partner, but he wasn't visible."

"I'll bring a rifle," Chris said. "With the element of surprise, they're dead."

"Make that two," Jackie said. "Long ranger weaponry will be key. Our team will all carry rifles with scopes and suppressors for muzzle flash suppression. Taking them out simultaneously is safer."

"Then we either explode the house or barge in like we own the joint," Chris said.

"All our explosives will be tied up at Powell's," Bernard said. "We'll need to make do with kinetic force and flashbangs. Any questions about either operation?"

"The techies going to join us?" Kyle asked.

"They could be useful turning off their cameras or

causing a distraction," Bernard said. "Molly, do you prefer going with Bailey's team?"

"Why? You think I'm too squeamish?"

"The thought crossed our mind," Isabella said.

"Hold on!" Crystal rushed down the stairs. "I'm watching Roger's back, and that's final."

"I guess you're on Bailey's team after all," Isabella said. "Don't worry. I'll watch Mr. Morris's back for you, Ms. Turner."

"Gee, thanks," Molly's tone conveyed no actual appreciation, only apathy.

"We're razing Powell's place to the ground while we obliterate Bailey." Bernard held his chin up, showing no fear. "Tonight the war will end with a bang. I want everyone to grab a nap today. Take rotating shifts napping. We'll need our energy for tonight."

"Roger that," Ian said.

"We've got ourselves a barbecue tonight," Isabella said. "Should be a fun party. They won't know what hit them when we're done."

"I'm heading to my room to sleep." Molly stood without further words and left the group. She headed upstairs, and everyone heard a door slam.

"She's mad about the civilian casualties," Roger said. It wasn't a question, but a statement.

"She'll get over it," Bernard said. "Or she won't. Either way, it's happening. Don't stress it. Focus on tonight."

"Yeah. Mr. Klein," Roger said, "I'm going to need familiarization with the armaments we're using tonight."

Ian gesture to Isabella. "Izzie here would be a better teacher. How about it, Izzie?"

Isabella smirked. "I'd be delighted to help familiarize Mr. Morris. We'll need everyone accustomed to their operation. It's not complicated. You'll grasp it quickly with your intellect."

"No one likes a kiss ass, Izzie." Ian found an elbow embedded in his side after the words escaped his mouth. "She's right." His words were strained.

"I usually am."

"You mind showing me now?" Roger asked. "I'd like to practice using dummy rounds throughout the day."

"Always ready to help someone eager to learn. Mr. Evans, you said the range is out back, correct?"

"That's right. Mr. Morris knows the way. Have fun, you two." He smiled as he left the room. He gave a lingering look to the stairs Molly traversed earlier before continuing his duties.

"Bub, can I talk to you in private before your practice?" Crystal grabbed Roger's arm and dragged him outside. Once the door slammed shut, she started in. "What's wrong with you?"

"Huh?"

"Molly's pissed."

"She'll get over it. I won't send more personnel to die for a gangster's family. Mind you, he tried to kill both of us. He didn't give a damn if we had family. Why should we? It's only handicapping ourselves."

"So we lower ourselves to his level? How does that make us any better?"

"It doesn't, but it keeps us alive. That's my concern. Keeping as many of us breathing as we can. This isn't some idealistic position. We make decisions that endanger lives. It's a calculated gamble, and I estimated it's better to keep mine alive over Powell's."

"This isn't you. Is this what happens when you gain power? I want no part of it." She backed off while shaking her head. "You think this is why mother acts cold? There's more to life than winning. You used to know that lesson, but you've changed."

"What would you have me do?" Roger asked, clearly annoyed by this conversation. "Endanger the soldiers who depend on us? It'd be a betrayal of the trust they've placed in us. Don't you understand?"

"Heavy is the head that holds the crown, as mother told us growing up. Now I suppose you understand. You need to speak to Molly. I don't know if she'll forgive this, but you should try - unless you want to try your luck with Isabella, your newest mentor. She seemed into you. Lock yourself into the same cycle mother and father did, why don't you? You've been hell bent on it. I've come to realize you're serious, and I'm finished trying to talk sense into you." She threw the door open and left Roger to his thoughts with a slam.

He sat down on a nearby rocking chair and leaned forward, placing both elbows on his knees and cradling his head. Thoughts raced through his head. *Maybe she's right. I sound like mother; I've given the order to kill innocents. Is it truly worth the stain on my soul?*

He heard a door closing and light footsteps.

"Boss?" Isabella asked. "You alright?"

Roger quickly perked up, trying to hide any turmoil in front of his employee. He dusted himself off before speaking. "It'll take more than an argument to rattle me. Pardon me, I've never caught your full name. It's rude to not know my impromptu bodyguard who got that ape off me."

"Name's Isabella Moreno, boss. Apologies for the late arrival. Blame Mitchell for that. He read the map. Besides, don't even mention it. Rufus is nothing but a memory because he tried to manhandle you."

"I'd say eliminate the tried." He rubbed his throat, reliving yesterday in his mind. "It was a rookie move of me getting that close. Anyway, you're not here to listen to my gripes. No doubt you'd like to show off your toys. You strike me as the type."

"The type to what, Mr. Morris?" Isabella asked.

"To maintain your equipment and be proud to show off your tools of the trade. It wouldn't surprise me if you named your hardware. Please, let's make tracks. We have enough to prepare for tonight without forcing you to waste time."

"They're over here." Isabella led Roger outside toward the van they drove. She opened the back and climbed inside as Roger stood outside. She leaned over and picked up a case.

Roger inadvertently glanced at the wrong time and received a view of Isabella bending over. He averted his eyes in time for her to turn around.

"Here we are." She handed the case over. "Let's get to the range."

"It's barebones, but we built it recently. Don't get your hopes up. Follow me." He slammed the door shut after she hopped out and led her into the woods behind the farm-house. "I'm proficient in rifles, but never used attachments before."

"Life's full of new experiences. Happy to guide you through this one."

Roger tried to not focus on the unspoken innuendo and kept pace. "How many rounds are we working with?"

Isabella raised a hand to her mouth to stifle a giggle. "They're not rounds, boss. They're miniature grenades. It's easy to load and fire after trying a few times. It takes some practice aiming the arc for the distance, but lucky for us, I have dummy grenades for practice. Well, flash bang rounds.

Don't worry, the others have plenty. It'll prime you for how to load and aim accurately."

Roger stared down at the dirt path they walked. "I'm truly sorry for what occurred before."

"Huh?"

"With your group at the weapon storage."

"That is not a word I often hear from the boss," Isabella said.

"I may be spoiled rotten, but I know common decency, Ms. Moreno. I imagine a strong woman like yourself feels trapped under the inept guidance of a boss younger than yourself purely for nepotism's sake. Doubly so since it unfortunately claimed the life of one partner and injured another badly. Don't deny it, please. That's the other reason I wanted lessons. To finally express my sympathies. Rest assured, we will nurse Greg and Mitchell back to health. I've also ordered Ms. Turner to train Greg, as per my sister's wishes." He looked away at the mention of his sister.

"I admit, when I first arrived, I thought you were spoiled."

"Don't even try to say you've changed your mind. I don't appreciate liars, Ms. Moreno. I realize I've yet to earn respect from my employees. My hope is my actions will demonstrate my ability." He emerged into a small clearing. Hay bales lined the tree line across the field with paper humanoid targets affixed to them. A basic table sat a dozen feet ahead in the morning shade.

"Damn, boss. Let a girl finish her thought."

"Sorry," Roger said. He placed the case on the table and opened it. Numerous pieces of a rifle laid inside on velvety material. He got to work assembling the weapon as they spoke. "I guess I've yet to prove myself to the Syndicate."

"You fought in that firefight, yeah?" Isabella asked, monitoring his progress. "I hear tale you were surrounded in the trees."

"That's right. I was a damned fool trying to play soldier and got in a pickle."

"What did you do?" Isabella asked.

"Huh?"

"Exactly what I asked, boss," Isabella said. "Did you keep fighting? Did you panic, run, or buckle down and pray?"

"I didn't run. Hell, even if I wanted to, I'd have been shot. I hunkered down low and focused on my rear. Bernard and Crystal watched my back. Powell's forces got lost, I believe. I think they split into two groups, one on each side of the property. One was behind me, and the other across from my position. That's how Bernard could move freely. At least that's if my battle assessment's worth a damn. Who knows if it was. I'm relatively new to combat, Ms. Moreno."

"That sounds like you, boss." Isabella wore a smile. "You didn't back down in the dispensary despite the menacing atmosphere. You pissed off Bailey, and you're honest."

"Whatever you say." Roger finished attaching the last piece and tested the slide with a satisfying click. "Presenting for inspection." He held the weapon out for her to grab.

She inspected his handiwork with a meticulous eye. "Immaculate work. It's simple to load. Watch me."

Roger watched as she slid the flashbang projectile into the attachment. She directed the muzzle downrange. "Easy as that. Watch your ears and eyes."

Roger covered his ears and watched her hands. He heard the projectile leave the chamber. A few seconds later, a blinding blast caused him to close his eyes. The blast was muffled thanks to his hands covering his ears. He looked down range and saw her handiwork. "Nice accuracy."

"Adjust the launch angle to compensate for distance." She handed the weapon over. "Let's see you in action."

He grabbed the remaining flashbang and loaded it, using the same method she used, before taking aim and firing. After the blast, he noticed his aim wasn't nearly as accurate.

"Good job. Accuracy will get better with practice. It's good enough for tonight at any rate, boss. May I?"

"Go ahead."

Isabella moved behind him and wrapped her arms around him. Her hands grasped the weapon, pressing her chest into his back. "Hold it like so." She adjusted his posture and form. "It's easier to aim this way. See?"

"Noted." Roger tried to play it cool, but his heart rate betrayed him. "I'll remember that for tonight."

"You'd better. We're going to blast Powell off the face of the Earth tonight."

"Not to mention starting another fire for the fire department to combat. I'm sure they'll love that."

She shrugged. "It's what they're paid for. They should thank us for giving them a reason to exist." She paused a few minutes as Roger disassembled the rifle and packed it away. "Boss, are you concerned with Ms. Turner's tantrum?"

"She's entitled to her opinion, Ms. Moreno. I agree with her moral stance but not at the cost of your lives. She and my sister think us heartless, but my duty is to protect my soldiers, not play the good Samaritan."

"I appreciate that. Too many leaders in power are concerned with politics and optics. It's refreshing to see a leader who's beholden to his personnel. Especially one willing to stand side by side with us."

"Don't put me on a pedestal yet." Roger finished packing the weapon and shut the case. "I understand you've requisitioned a laptop for the recovering Mitchell and Greg in the barn? They can use Mr. Bristol's. He won't mind. The old goat was happy to volunteer to have an excuse to avoid paperwork. It's not enough for both at once, but until we're settled, it's the best we can manage."

"Laptops?"

"My sister sent me an email last night, after talking to you all. Figured boredom would kill them if I denied it. I feel bad enough housing them in the barn, anyway. I'm informed Evans has provided them an outlet to charge it as well."

"Yes, boss. Thank you."

Roger hefted the case upward and faced the direction they came from. "Shall we head back, Ms. Moreno? We both need our rest before tonight's operation."

"Lead the way, boss." Isabella walked a bit closer to his side than before, brushing against him occasionally.

22

Bernard, Chris, Jackie, and Lyle traipsed through the thick forest canopy. Darkness surrounded them, along with insects droning in the background. Their only illumination was the flashlight in Bernard's grasp. He kept it angled down, trying not to give away their position by having it shine too far ahead. "See anything different inside, Ms. Turner?"

He didn't receive an answer.

"Ms. Turner?" Bernard asked, this time forcefully. "You with us?"

"Sorry. I only see what's inside. He's watching television as we speak. I see three guards inside. There are no cameras outside, so you're on your own."

"Thank you. Now pay attention. We can't have our overwatch zoning out on an operation like that. Don't focus on Powell's family. We need you here and now."

"Right."

"She's in a fine mood," Lyle said in a hushed voice.

"No doubt angry at Roger and I for our decision, but

she'll get over it." Bernard had a rifle in his arm, barrel pointed down.

"He didn't even try talking to her afterward," Jackie said.

"Why should he?" Chris asked. "He's the authority. The world doesn't revolve around Ms. Turner's feelings. Better to keep our forces alive than some gangster and his family."

"Cut the chatter," Bernard said. "We're nearing the location, judging by the break in the trees ahead." He pointed ahead. "Let's see what we're working with before getting closer." He raised the rifle and used the scope as a makeshift binocular. "I see one on the roof."

"Smart money says there's a second," Chris said.

"They could be stupid and not use a spotter," Lyle said. "Or is that wishful thinking?"

"If these are his personal guards, the smart bet is they're craftier than we're giving them credit for. There's another up there." Chris looked through the scope, trying to find the spotter for their sharpshooter. "He may be nearby, not necessarily beside the shooter."

"There are only so many suitable locations where he'd post up inside," Jackie said, scanning the property. "Found him."

"Where?" Bernard asked.

"Look on the balcony below. He's hard to see because he's laying down, but he's there alright."

"Why take the lower ground?" Chris asked. "That makes no sense."

"It's not as obvious - meaning they're expecting company," Jackie said.

Lyle shivered. "You think it's a trap?"

"Easy, kid," Chris said. He placed a hand on Lyle's forearm for a second, trying to calm the religious man. "Just say a prayer. That always calms you believers down. Right?"

"Spotter or marksman first?" Lyle asked.

"Shooter," Bernard said.

"We should kill both in one stroke," Chris said. "Spotters are accomplished marksmen themselves, often swapping roles. Odds are he has a rifle there. I'd bet my left nut."

"I count a dozen guards wandering around outside the home's perimeter," Bernard said, looking through the scope at the ground level. They'll be alerted as soon as we do.

"Better than the sharpshooters hunting for us and having target practice," Chris said. "They either fire from there or charge us. There's no cover between us, so it's our advantage."

"The place is a dump," Lyle said. "We're sure this is his place?"

"According to the tracker, yes," Molly said in their ears. "The limousine he took is there, and I can see him watching his shows."

"Any cell phones in the nearby forest?" Bernard asked.

"Let me run a scan of the nearby area. Give me a few minutes."

"You think there's an ambush waiting for us to attack?" Jackie asked. "That'd be ballsy for him, using himself as bait."

"Desperate men do drastic things, Ms. Thomas," Bernard said. "No doubt he feels backed into a corner. I won't rush headlong until I know if it's a trap."

"I'm seeing three signals in the woods. One to each side of your location and one dangerously close. I'd guess within fifty feet of your location."

"Hunting time. Split up," Bernard whispered. "You're with me, kid." He grabbed Lyle's arm and went in a different direction from Chris and Jackie. "You watch left, I've got right."

The pair stalked through the dark woods until Lyle felt something brush his left foot. He stopped, suspecting it was his enemy lying in wait. Time stood still. Countless permutations of this situation raced through his mind. Should he swing his barrel toward the threat and open fire immediately? Maybe the knife would be better? Maybe if he lets on his suspicions, that's when they fire.

Lyle settled on kicking whatever it was after pausing for a good ten seconds. He felt his boot impact with something solid and heard the clack of a gun landing nearby. He looked down and confirmed his suspicions. "Sir, here!" He angled the rifle toward the still lying enemy, now disarmed. "Stay right there, and stay quiet. You move, I blow your damned head off."

"What have we here?" Bernard asked. He flashed the light over the prone man. "Why didn't you fire, little man?"

"I was hoping you'd pass by. I didn't figure I could kill four by my lonesome."

"That was your last mistake." Bernard reached down to his belt line and unsheathed his knife. "What happens next will shape your life forever. Where are the others out here? You don't talk, I slit your throat and leave you. You talk, and maybe you leave alive." He reached down and frisked the laying man. Bernard found a knife on his person, but his own blade pressing against his victim's throat kept him from trying anything. "Now, answer me. Are there more lurking outside?"

"There're two others in the forest. Over a dozen inside. Can I leave now? All are trained marksmen."

A burst of static drew Bernard's attention. A male voice followed. "Status report."

Two other male voices reported all clear.

Bernard spotted a walkie-talkie on his belt line and

snatched it up. He pressed it to the man's face. "You do this, you walk away. You try something cute, you're dead. Now tell them everything's peaceful over here." He pressed the button, enabling transmission.

"All good on the south side."

"Roger that."

Bernard stopped transmitting and tossed the device away. "Good boy. Now get to your feet slowly." He watched his captive follow the order. "Now run. You're done working for Bailey. He's dying tonight. Get it?"

"Don't guess you're hiring?"

"Not hiring someone who'll give up and betray his employer like this, no. Don't press your luck. In fact, let me reconsider. You know what? I've changed my mind."

"You have?"

"Sure, kid." Bernard's bright demeanor was undercut by his hand thrusting upward. The knife plunged into the guard's throat before he yanked it hard to the side. He kicked him, causing his victim to tumble backward, desperately trying to staunch the flow of blood quickly leaving his body with every heartbeat. His panic was his own demise, as he was quickly unconscious from the blood loss and died right there on the forest floor.

"That was gnarly," Lyle said, still watching the bleeding body.

Bernard reached up to his ear and pressed a button. "Nearby signal is dead. They just had a status check, so we've got another fifteen or twenty minutes before they grow suspicious. We're heading back. Meet us, and we'll kick this party off properly."

"Roger that."

They left the body and backtracked. Eventually they met up with Jackie and Chris again.

"I suggest we split into two again," Bernard said. "The dude said there are two bodies in these woods."

"We should deal with them first," Jackie said. "Walking in the open before that is suicide."

"We're hunting more of those psychos lying in the grass?" Lyle asked. He pointed out into the darkness. "We were lucky before. It's suicidal to waltz through blind. Maybe my leg doesn't graze them next time."

"Then use the proper scope, dumbass." Chris tapped the low light scope attached to his weapon. "You brought it, right?"

Lyle avoided everyone's expecting gaze. "No."

"Then he's coming with me," Jackie said. She stomped over and grabbed his wrist before pulling it. "Chris, you accompany the boss. I'll watch the rookie."

"Understood. Be careful."

"Worry about yourselves first," Jackie said. She pulled Lyle away toward their target. "Get your forgetful ass over here. I told you to be prepared, and you pull this stunt?"

The verbal lashing faded as Bernard and Chris moved in the other direction.

"Bet you hoped you'd never be a part of this shit again when you were promoted to roster management," Bernard said.

"Once we have more bodies, I can retire from combat; this old body has one more mission to complete. Now be quiet, sir. Let me take point." Chris sped up, overtaking Bernard.

"Covering our six," Bernard whispered. He focused on watching their flanks and checking behind every new tree, not wanting any more surprises tonight. He checked through his scope, careful to look for any humanlike shapes lurking in the looming darkness.

"Hold," Chris whispered. "I heard something."

Bernard heard the rustling of grass and the wind blowing through his hair. He turned toward the noise, but it was too late. He saw someone peeking around a nearby tree with a weapon pointed at Chris. Quick to react, he fired off a round just after their attacker squeezed the trigger.

His shot missed. A chunk of bark splintered off where Bernard's shot landed.

Chris screamed and charged toward the offending tree. "Shoot at me, will you?"

Bernard fired another shot toward the other side of the tree, clear of Chris. His efforts were rewarded with a groan and a spatter of blood on the grass below.

Chris made it to the tree unpunctured by any projectiles. Dropping his rifle, he secured his aggressor's weapon arm and raised it to the sky. His other hand grasped the wounded man's left arm and pinned him to the tree. "Stupid bastard." He grunted, trying to push the weapon's barrel back and eventually succeeding. The guard's gun barrel pressed against his chin now. Chris's left reached over and tried to squeeze the trigger, but the guard had the where-withal to block it with his own finger.

"Old man?" Bernard called out as he approached. The sound of the scuffle and the grunting of the combatants filled the night air.

Chris abandoned this plan in favor of a simpler one. He pulled his left hand from the trigger and down to his waistline. He quickly unholstered the weapon with practiced ease before shoving it against the man's temple and squeezing the trigger.

The body fell, and more blood and gore decorated the foliage below. "If you aim at the best, don't miss, chuckles." Chris looked down at his bloodstained suit. "Damn it."

"You hit?" Bernard asked.

"Negative." Chris patted himself down, checking for any leaks. "Not sure how. The guy was a terrible marksman. We were within spitting distance, and he choked. Talk about luck."

Another gunshot was heard in the distance, drawing both men's attention.

"Got ours, no thanks to Mr. Lionel," Jackie said in their ear. "You both alright? We heard gunshots."

Bernard answered. "We found ours. He nearly killed Chris, but we're whole."

"Acknowledged. You two see our sharpshooter? He's no doubt shitting bricks with those gunshots nearby. Don't present a target. No doubt he's jumpy."

"I would be," Chris said. He placed the handgun away and bent over to get his scoped rifle. He grabbed Bernard and dragged him behind the cover. "Stay here, boss. I got this. Cover your ears."

"Can you see a second shooter from your position?" Jackie asked.

"Checking now." Chris pressed the butt of the rifle against his shoulder and looked through the scope with one eye. He saw the lookout, currently looking in Jackie's direction. "No eyes on our second marksman, but hold on." He saw puffs of white smoke coming from beside their target. "There is a second, but he's prone. He's smoking, I believe. The fool gave away his position."

"I see it too," Jackie said.

The lookout fired.

"Shit!" Jackie cried out.

Chris didn't hesitate. He fired, and the shot punctured his target's back. He fell forward off the roof. Their mysterious spotter hopped up, already armed with his own rifle.

He tried to hop off the roof and was successful. He crashed down to the grass below and scrambled to his feet, trying to get inside.

Chris was about to squeeze the trigger when he was beaten to the punch. The spotter died before he reached the back door. He looked to his side to see Bernard already aiming.

"Got him. Jackie, Lyle, you alright over there?"

"There are more!" Lyle's shaken voice cried. Soon more shots rang out.

"That means there's more," Chris said. "Damn."

Meanwhile, across the property...

"Move your ass!" Jackie yelled over the bullets she and Lyle dodged. She reached down and pulled out a grenade. "Get clear and behind cover!"

Lyle dove behind a nearby tree. Tracer rounds replaced where he stood previously as she threw the explosive device where they'd just retreated. "Jesus help us." Jackie could not hear him over the chaos erupting all over. He hunkered down behind the thick tree until an earth-shattering explosion shook the ground beneath his feet. "Christ!" He peeked around and fired off a few rounds.

Another scream signaled his success. He ejected the spent magazine while hearing the whiz of a bullet passing by mere inches from his left ear. "How many more are there?" His raised voice barely pierced the cacophony of the battle.

Lyle felt a warm drip on his forearm, along with a fetid fecal smell. He looked up to see intestines hanging from the branches above. He fought a wave of nausea caused from looking at the viscera of human remains dangling above.

Locking in the new magazine and pulling back the slide, he sidestepped out of cover and spotted a couple of aggressors charging. Without thinking he fired, knocking the front attacker to the soil. He wasn't done yet. His aim shifted in one swift motion to the second, and he fired center mass.

"There can't be many still breathing." Jackie was behind a nearby log, laying down for cover. "Cover me while I move."

"On it."

Jackie waited for Lyle to fire and jumped to her feet. She moved back another ten feet and ducked behind another suitable tree. The number of bullets whizzing by had dropped precipitously since the blast and Lyle's shots. A few bullets zoomed by every few seconds, but it sounded like their opposition had dwindled. The shots were not coming from a static position, however, and this concerned her. She was hesitant to peek her head out from cover for fear of catching a bullet. "See anything, kid?"

"Negative."

"Move back. I'll cover."

"On my way." Lyle took a deep breath and sprinted toward Jackie.

She peeked around the corner and covered his retreat. A figure poked out of cover behind him. "Down!" She raised the weapon and fired after Lyle hit the deck. The shot hit its mark and put him down. "Got him."

Lyle scrambled to his feet and moved to a nearby tree. "I hear nothing."

"Could be everyone, or they're smarter than the rest." Jackie looked around. No grass crunched, and no twigs snapped. The only sound was the wind and the occasional distant gunshot. She raised a finger to her ear. "Moving to the target. How are you two doing?"

"Finishing up the remnants. They winged me with a flesh wound, but it's minor. After we finish here, we'll be ready to move."

"Roger that. It'll be best if we wait and pincer attack. He'll arm himself if he's desperate." She looked and saw Lyle shaking. She approached him and spoke in a soft voice. "You alright?"

"Fine." He tried to stop his shaking by gripping his other hand, but the effort was unsuccessful. "Damn it."

"Stay strong. We're almost finished. Come on, kid." She led him through the forest back toward the target's home until they were near the tree line leading into the open field around the home.

"Right." Lyle soldiered on and never complained. "Thanks for saving me twice back there."

"You nailed your share. We'd both be dead alone."

A last gunshot accompanied another message from Chris. "We're finished over here, I believe. Moving to position for the assault. Give us a couple minutes, and then we'll charge."

"Anyone called the cops?" Jackie asked.

"Negative," Molly said. "There are no neighbors for miles. No one inside has called for the authorities. Bailey's scared to call the boys in blue. I don't blame him, since his drug fields and warehouses have been seized by them. He's probably praying no positive identifications come back linking him to them."

"Acknowledged. Hey, Lionel," Jackie said. "Tell me something. That girl you're sweet on. What's she like?"

"Girl I was sweet on is more like it," Lyle said. He kept his gaze locked on the home. "I found out today she got engaged to some police officer."

"You called and asked her?"

"Not quite. I keep in touch with friends via the phone. They texted me, knowing damned well I had a crush. Probably to keep me from embarrassing myself and making it awkward. I'm fine, Ms. Thomas. I'm a big boy and would never allow my personal matters to affect my professional ability, as you saw earlier."

"Damn, sorry to hear. You'll find someone. Focus on the job. It'll dull the pain."

"That was my thinking."

Another transmission interrupted the conversation. "We're ready over here."

"He could be perched by the windows," Bernard said. "Do we have a plan for that?"

"Keep watch on the windows as we approach," Jackie said. "There are no other options except to run fast and try to stay low."

"Got it. Good luck, everyone. Are we ready?"

Everybody reported their readiness.

Jackie muted her mic before looking at Lyle. "You'll do fine. You watch the left side windows. I'll watch the right. Use the pistol. You won't be able to fire the rifle accurately on the run."

"Understood." Lyle slung the rifle over his shoulder and unholstered the 9mm on his hip. He made sure it was ready for action and pulled the slide back.

"We go on three," Bernard said. "One, two, three!"

Both Jackie and Lyle sprinted as fast as they could. They kept their guns pointed at their assigned windows as they moved, but saw no unfamiliar shapes. Jackie tripped and fell mid- stride.

Lyle turned and went back for her. He extended a hand to help her up when another shot rang out along with glass shattering nearby. He fell to the side on the ground, wheezing.

Jackie took aim at the figure in the window from the ground and fired. The window now completely shattered and the figure inside went down. She scurried over to Lyle. "Please, God. No." She ran her hand over his back to find a bullet lodged in the vest. "Thank God. Come on, kid. There'll be a bruise, but you're lucky." She pulled the still coughing young man to his feet, and they continued their perilous trek. "Watch the windows. We had one wiseass." The pair eventually reached their goal and stayed away from the windows. They took a knee outside. "We're here."

"Same," Bernard said. "Move to your assigned door, and let's give this man a proper send off from his mortal coil."

Jackie and Lyle hugged the wall until they reached the side door. Jackie checked and found the door locked. "It's locked on this side. Give me a minute."

"Same over here. At least they have common sense," Chris said. "Lock-picking contest?"

"Grow up, old man," Jackie said. "We both know I'd win anyway. I always did."

"Those are fighting words."

"You know how to lock pick?" Lyle asked.

"You don't?" Jackie asked. "I'll teach you later." She reached into her back pocket for her trusty tools. She got busy with the delicate work. Within a few minutes she placed them in her pocket. "Done on this side."

"Damn," Bernard said. "You beat Chris."

"We're ready over here," Chris said, all bravado gone from his voice. "You win this round."

"Let's all win this war, children," Bernard said. "Focus up. This is for all the marbles. Watch your corners and watch each other's backs. I'm betting he's upstairs shitting himself right about now. He will shoot, make no mistake."

"You're really selling us on this, boss," Lyle said with sarcasm in his voice.

"You know the drill. On three we breach. Make sure you're loaded. We can't afford anyone getting hurt over something foolish."

Lyle and Jackie both ejected the current magazines and loaded a fresh one to make sure their weapons were loaded.

"We're ready," Jackie said. She stood shoulder to shoulder with Lyle in front of the door.

"Ready," Chris said.

"One," Bernard said, "two, three!"

Jackie threw open the door and took point. Lyle trailed close behind.

He watched her back and walked sideways, keeping watch on her flank. He saw movement, knowing it couldn't be the other team from the location alone. Lyle fired and was rewarded with a scream and a thud. "Hostile on first floor!"

"Kitchen's clear," Jackie said.

"Living room's clear," Chris said.

"Man cave's clear," Bernard rattled off.

"The dude's still alive and armed in there," Lyle said. He hadn't taken his aim off the hostile who was still breathing. He heard deep breaths from his adversary on the other side of the thin hallway wall.

"Keep him distracted," Chris said.

"Hey, jackass," Lyle said. He knocked on the nearby wall and moved a few feet to the left. It's a good thing he did, as bullets ripped through the wall where he knocked. "Is that any way to treat guests? Bailey always was rude and stupid to hire an ape like you to defend him."

More gunshots met his taunting words, but this time they didn't pierce through the wall.

"Hostile down," Chris said. "Nice work, kid. You immobilized him and kept him occupied for me to flank. Damn nice."

"Don't celebrate just yet," Bernard said. "Now we face the hardest obstacle, climbing to the second floor."

"Stairs not your thing, boss?" Lyle attempted to lighten the situation, but it didn't work.

"Stairs are a natural kill funnel," Jackie said.

"Meet in the living room. I have an idea," Bernard said.

Jackie and Lyle met up with Bernard and Chris. Jackie kept a trained eye on the top of the stairs nearby, watching for any ambush as they spoke.

"What's the plan, boss?" Chris asked.

"Anybody have their grenade still?" Bernard asked. "We could toss one upstairs and follow the blast up. There will be a cloud of dust, but it's our best bet unless someone finds a ladder to climb up from outside."

"Awfully ghetto way of getting upstairs, isn't it?" Chris snuck a peek at Jackie.

"I'd smack you if I wasn't busy, old ass. I used mine earlier, boss."

Lyle plucked the one grenade off his belt line. "Here. Who wants to make the throw?"

"I got this," Chris took it. "That means you're running point, Lionel."

"I am?"

"I'm throwing it. You run point. That's the deal."

"Fuck it. Then I'll throw it."

"Children, please," Bernard snatched the ordinance. "I'll throw it, and you'll both lead the pack. Deal with it."

"I'll watch right, you cover left," Chris said. "You'd better not miss, kid, or I'll haunt you with my eternal soul if Bailey ends me."

"Move, Jackie. Everyone take cover." Bernard repositioned himself near the stairs. He pulled the pin and waited a few seconds before throwing it hard up the stairs, bouncing it off the wall and into the upstairs hallway.

"You realize that was a flashbang," Lyle said.

A deafening boom and a flash of light erupted upstairs. Lyle and Chris didn't wait. They rushed upstairs and came to an empty hallway. It housed four different doors, all closed.

"Clear up here so far. Looks like we're playing what's behind door number one through four. My favorite game of all," he said.

"Everybody gets a door," Bernard said, arriving upstairs with Jackie. "God speed, everyone. Pick a door and happy hunting."

"Any more flashbangs?" Lyle asked.

"No, kid," Chris said. "Old fashioned room to room combat to finish the evening awaits. Aim quick and true is my advice." He quickly took one of the remaining doors not already claimed by Bernard and Jackie, leaving one for Lyle.

Lyle's heart jack-hammered in his chest, and his hands shook. He knew this maneuver could spell his end, but there was no choice. He reached and grabbed the knob with his left hand, keeping his pistol trained on the door.

"We all go at once," Bernard said. "No more warnings for them. On three. One, two, three!"

Lyle pushed the door. Time appeared to slow as the door swung open. He saw their target across the room, holding a scantily clad woman in front of him as a human shield and leveling his own gun toward him. Hesitating was not an option, and he knew it. He fired the entire magazine.

Numerous shots punctured Bailey's poor wife, but a lucky shot found its mark in Bailey's skull before he could fire too many rounds.

"Jesus." Jackie rushed over. She inspected the wall behind Lyle and noticed three bullet holes that came from Bailey. She peeked into the room and noticed the dead bodies slumped together. "Sick fuck used his whore as a human shield." She looked at Lyle and noticed him staring with dead eyes at the woman. "Hey, it's alright. You did good."

Chris approached the pair and looked inside with a whistle. "Damn nice shooting, kid. You've got the luck of God," he said, turning to face the bullet holes behind the trembling Lyle. "Lucky as hell."

"I believe the term would be blessed," Bernard said. He patted Lyle on the shoulder. "Nice work. Let's torch the place and vamoose. We earned some rest after tonight. Don't relax until we're in the car. Am I clear?"

"Yes, sir," everyone said, though Lyle's was not as enthusiastic.

The trip back to the vehicle was uneventful, thankfully. Everyone climbed inside. Bernard and Chris took the front seats while Jackie, Lyle, and Molly crammed into the backseat.

"You alright?" Chris asked, looking back at Lyle. "You seem kind of off."

"I'm fine," Lyle said, his voice distant, along with his eyes. "Just shaken after that last encounter. I'd never killed an innocent before and wish I hadn't."

"I wouldn't call her innocent," Chris said. "An unarmed bystander is more like it."

"Whatever."

Jackie didn't take her eyes off Lyle's thousand-yard stare while the van's engine started.

"Come here," Jackie said. She reached over and rested a hand on the back of Lyle's neck. She gently coaxed him to place his head on her shoulder. "You did good."

Chris watched the touching scene before turning around with a shake of his head. He muttered under his breath. "Seriously?"

She rested a hand on Lyle's shaking arm and traced her fingertips over his skin. "You're fine. She knew the risks of the profession. Don't blame yourself for her death."

"Little hard to not when I literally shot her."

"In fear of your own life," Jackie said, her voice soft, almost motherly. "No one can fault you for that. We'd have done the same."

Molly gave a sidelong glance, not able to contain her inherent curiosity. She'd never seen this side of Jackie before, nor even heard about it.

"That doesn't matter. She was an innocent." Lyle raised a hand to cover his eyes. He didn't wheeze or give an audible clue to his crying, but the tears fell nonetheless. Everyone in the vehicle understood, but had enough sense to not prod the traumatized young Mr. Lionel.

Jackie glared in Chris's direction, silently warning him not to joke at Lyle's expense.

Chris, for all his faults, understood the feelings being hidden in the back seat. He'd experienced it once and understood to keep quiet.

Bernard, however, was a different story. "Let's hope the other team succeeds like us. That's half the war machine gone. Nice work."

Jackie could feel some tears that escaped Lyle's hand rolling down her shoulder. She wasn't versed in tender moments, so she did what came naturally. She kept trying to soothe the young hero of the Morris family. Her ministrations didn't seem to help as far as she could tell, but she'd be damned if she'd stop.

Chris reached into his pocket and pulled out a joint and a disposable lighter. A flick later and the cabin soon filled with the smell of burning narcotic plant-based bliss. "Here, kid. Try this." He took it out of his mouth and handed it back.

Jackie tried to deny it, but Lyle beat her to the punch and snatched it. He took a deep drag and inhaled before passing it to Molly. "Thanks."

"You know," Molly said, lowering the window, "for someone experiencing an emotional break, you know stoner etiquette. It's supposed to be two puffs before you pass, but I'll chalk that up to the trauma."

"I am fine." Lyle tried to raise his head from Jackie's shoulder, only to find her hand snake around the back of his head and hold it firmly.

"Just don't get addicted," Chris said. "That should help with the emotional baggage. It did for me."

"That means you have an addictive personality," Jackie said. "Don't push it on Mr. Lionel."

"Geez, I was simply trying to help." Chris took the rolled-up cannabis smokeable back, and the cabin fell into silence.

23

"Make sure you're carrying as many incendiary and fragmentation grenades as you can, boys and girls," Isabella said. "You still remember my lessons earlier today, Mr. King?"

Wallace secured his weapons and munitions. "I remember."

"Good," Kyle said. "Just wait, boss. We'll end this tonight."

"Your shoulder alright, Evans?" Roger asked.

"Good as new." Kyle flexed his shoulder.

"Yeah. This should be a regular turkey shoot," Ian said. "They'll be running scared after our first volley when their security cooks alive. Then it's explosives time, and we're heading home."

"Comparing humans to turkeys?" Crystal asked over the call? "Why not? You're already planning a massacre."

"We're not going to identify the dead before we leave?" Wallace asked. "Aren't we worried about him surviving?"

"We'll light it on fire before we demolish it," Isabella said. "It depends on how many volleys of incendiary we needed before. I made sure we'd have plenty to work with before we departed. Even mixed a few with my recipe for fun."

"You brought your kit with you? Why am I asking? Obviously you would," Ian said.

"I prefer creating our rounds myself," Isabella said. "It can cause a variable yield, depending on the mix. These we're firing tonight are the maximum area of affect. This'll be a regular inferno."

"There aren't campgrounds near here, right?" Roger asked.

"Not to my knowledge," Wallace said.

Crystal spoke up after a minute. "There's one a few miles away. I'd hope the flames don't reach that far."

"Good. Everybody ready?" Roger asked.

Isabella reached into the car's trunk and pulled out a set of goggles. She tossed it to Ian, then pulled out another. She strapped them to her head and let them rest atop her short black hair. "Got pairs for you three as well. I don't figure Robert would mind, nor Greg. Here." She handed Wallace, Kyle, and Roger their own visual aiding goggles.

"Here, boss," Isabella said, rushing over. "Please allow me." She aided him in preparing the equipment while Wallace struggled mere feet away. "See?" She secured the device with a final tug of the thread. "Simply flick the hardware over your eyes and hit the switch on the side." She grabbed Roger's hand and guided it to the small button. She moved the goggles over his eyes. "Press it and see what you think."

Roger pushed the button with a quiet click and the world turned shades of green and darker green. "Looks odd, like a low budget paranormal movie." He turned them off and flicked it up, regaining his normal vision.

"You get used to it." Isabella released Roger's hand after a delay.

Kyle, meanwhile, was no stranger to the gear and was already finished. He moved to help Wallace after seeing Ian wasn't chomping at the bit. "Loop it here and tie. Easy, right?"

"Thanks."

"Now that we're armed to the gills and armored, let's complete this operation." Roger slammed the car door shut, but still unlocked. "We're moving out."

"Happy hunting," Kyle said, following Roger and the rest into the wilderness.

They'd parked on a trail leading off the main road. It wasn't large, nor well-traveled. There were no signs it was frequented, which made it the perfect parking spot while they worked.

"Keep alert," Roger said. "There could be patrols nearby."

Nobody verbally acknowledged the command, fearful any enemies might hear. Everyone kept their heads on a proverbial swivel. Once the light level fell too low, some lowered their low light goggles and turned them on, including Roger, Isabella, Ian, and Kyle. Only Wallace didn't.

Kyle tapped Wallace's shoulder and pointed toward the goggles.

Wallace followed the unspoken request, and soon everyone could see in the low light environment.

With every step, grass crunched beneath their feet as legions of insects droned on.

"Keep your eyes on the ground," Kyle said. "It wouldn't surprise me if they're lying in wait." He brought up the rear of the group, keeping watch of the foliage below while others were preoccupied watching behind every tree and bush.

Roger led the group for over ten minutes through the underbrush in silence. His heart pounded the entire time. Memories of the previous firefight in the woods near their place weighed heavily on his mind. He fought hard to keep focused on the here and now. It took everything he had to suppress his thoughts deep down and keep soldiering on.

They reached their target destination without incident. Roger stopped and surveyed the nearby area for any sign of human life. "What do you think, Ms. Moreno? You think these launchers will hit the tree line over yonder?"

Isabella came up shoulder to shoulder with Roger and gazed across the clearing. A long driveway cut through the middle, leading to a road. A large greenhouse sat in the backyard, no doubt growing something illegal. "It should. We'll need the proper angle there. I suggest we start over there and work our way around. No sense setting ourselves on fire by starting too close. We'll know if there's security from the screams, anyway."

"Agreed," Kyle said, already loading an incendiary charge. "We'll need to leave in a hurry. It won't take long for someone to notice the fire."

"No doubt." Ian looked through his scope at the property, not content with his naked eye's view of the place. Maybe it had to do with his sharpshooting affinity, but it afforded him an in-depth analysis. "No visible guards."

"There may not be any," Wallace said. "Is he aware his home address is compromised?"

"He's not stupid," Roger said. "Powell knows his weapon storage was attacked. He'd panic and lock his home down, especially with family. Do not underestimate this man."

"We did before," Ian said.

"Look what happened to Robert, Greg, and Mitch," Isabella said with a sour expression.

"Ms. Moreno, I leave the firing plan in your capable hands. Who do you want firing where?"

"Since Ian and I are the most experienced, we'll handle across the way. Boss," she said, pointing further to the side, "you'll fire there. Mr. Evans, you're further to the right, and so on. Once our first volleys are finished, we'll reassess if we need any more, or if we're moving on to the main event. It won't take long. They'll make it obvious. I figure we'll all launch an explosive round into the house to be safe before switching to the incendiary variety. Load up and prepare to fire. Let's flush out these rats from their nests. Line up. Give yourself plenty of clearance from the branches above. We don't want one affecting the trajectory."

Everyone stood by Roger and Isabella's sides and formed a perfect line. Those that hadn't loaded their round did so.

"Everyone loaded?" Isabella asked, angling her barrel toward the sky.

They gave their affirmatives.

"On your order, boss."

"Please don't do this," Crystal pleaded with her brother over his earpiece. No one else heard her voice. This was a private plea.

Roger adjusted the angle of his shot, taking his time before speaking. "Take aim."

The others all set their sights on their target, and it's a good thing they insisted on this time-honored tradition.

"King, you're firing further to the right." Kyle used a hand to guide his aim to the correct area. "There."

"Awfully close to our position, isn't it?"

"Fifty yards isn't that close, kid. Besides, you'll love it if you hear screaming afterward. Put them on the defensive."

"Everyone got their target?" Roger asked.

"We do now," Kyle said. "Hopefully no one's asthmatic here."

"Oh, shit," Wallace said. He quickly reached down into his pocket and retrieved an inhaler before taking a puff.

"Too late now," Roger said. "Ready arms."

"Bub, please no. Don't massacre innocents to win this war quicker. Do it the right way, I beg you."

They took aim and waited for Roger's command.

Crystal's words echoed in Roger's mind. It took everything in his being to speak up. "Fire."

The sound of numerous rounds sliding out of the barrels was satisfying. It took only a few seconds before the fireworks began in earnest. Across the way, the entire tree line ignited, going up in flames. Black smoke rose to the heavens above within only a few seconds. The entire tree line to its side was soon engulfed in the hellish heat of the growing flames. Only their slice of trees was safe from the inferno. They could smell smoke since only a few dozen yards away the trees were burning.

"Good Lord," Crystal said over the call. "I can smell it from here."

"Hurry and reload," Roger said. "I can already smell the smoke."

Screams soon made themselves heard over the audible sound of the fire burning. Some barked out orders, others were filled with panic. It wasn't long before they ran out of the tree lines and into their field of view.

"Ballistics," Roger said. "Kill them all. It's a shooting gallery, boys and girls. Show them we mean business."

"The highest score gets a prize?" Kyle asked, already aiming.

"You know it," Isabella said.

They opened fire on the poor souls out in the open who were trying to escape burning to death. Bodies fell with impunity. Some were even on fire as they fell, their magazines eventually catching fire and discharging once the flames met the munitions.

It wasn't just a few personnel running, either. It was dozens of souls making a sprint toward the house or the main road. All five moved from target to target between squeezes of the triggers. The sound of fire, screams, and gunshots filled the air. The smell of both smoke and the sickly sweet scent of burning flesh filled their nostrils as they ended more lives by the second.

They put down the last of the unfortunate souls trying to make their escape through the open ground and finally reloaded their attachments.

"Next volley's on the home," Roger said. He took aim after reloading his grenade launcher attachment with explosive canisters and waited for everyone to do the same. "Take aim. Fire!"

The five canisters of death seemed to float toward the home in a majestic arc until they fell and graced the home with its payload of explosive material. The home withered from the onslaught, crashing to a single story.

"Reload with incendiary." Roger barked the order, ignoring the icy feeling in the pit of his stomach telling him he was committing a horrific sin. His sister's earlier pleading piled on to the growing feeling. Still, he stayed the course and led by example, regardless of his personal turmoil. "Fire!"

Before they could fire, three figures rushed out of the burning home. The volley launched coated the home behind their rapidly fleeing targets in an inferno.

"Two men and a woman," Ian said. "The old man's our target. He's looking this way, and the teen's armed."

Powell pointed in their direction and his teenaged son leveled the automatic rifle their way.

Isabella took a shot, preventing the teenager from defending his mother and father preemptively with a single burst of bullets.

Instead of kneeling in front of his dead son, Powell did something truly desperate. He grabbed his wife by the throat and held her in front of him as a human shield.

"The piece of shit's hiding behind his wife," Roger said, aiming through his scope. "Put him down, and let's leave." He turned his head and noticed the flames growing, inching closer by the minute.

"I got this, boss," Ian said. He took aim and squeezed the trigger a single time.

Roger watched through his scope as the bullet hit its mark, a testament to his accuracy with his weapon of choice. Powell's arm holding his wife was hit, allowing the woman freedom to leave. She, however, didn't leave her husband, instead rushing over to him.

"Loyal to the end, huh lady? Fine by me," Ian said.

"End him." Roger's voice was full of steel. He fired, aiming at Powell, but his wife knew where she knelt made it difficult.

Bullets ripped through her lithe frame under the barrage of lead flung their way. She fell on top of him and neither moved.

"Let's be doubly sure," Isabella loaded another explosive with practiced quickness and fired. The three's bodies were obliterated by the excessive force. Once the dirt cleared, there were no more bodies left, merely a large crater and a burning piece of rubble once resembling a home.

"Let's move." Roger lowered his rifle and turned around. "This war's over." The feeling of icy fear for his soul growing in his stomach did not abate, only grew stronger, but he never let it show to his partners. "Leave this for the emergency services to deal with." He turned and led the group back toward Crystal and their car.

"Yes, sir," everyone said, following behind.

"You're going to rue this night and regret your actions, Brother," Crystal said.

"Maybe."

"Maybe, sir?" Isabella asked at his side.

"Talking to my sister."

"No maybes about it," Crystal said. "You ordered the murder of an innocent teenager who was simply defending his mother and father. That could have been you. You grew up in the same circumstances - a crime family."

"I'd have deserved it too, Sis," Roger said. "I've accepted what I am - a monster. One who keeps his forces alive at all costs. There are worse fates as a leader."

Isabella didn't dare interrupt this seemingly serious conversation, judging by the dour look on Roger's face.

"On second thought," Crystal said, "don't bother trying to make amends with Molly. She deserves better."

Roger didn't fire back, knowing deep down she was correct in her assessment. He knew Molly never approved of this, for excellent reason. He trudged on, looking down at the ground all the while, avoiding everyone's gaze and silently mauling over what he'd just done.

"Don't be sad, boss," Kyle said. He came up on Roger's side and looped an arm over Roger's neck, pulling him close. "It's a successful mission with no hitches for once. I, for one, am ecstatic. The last job I caught a blade. This time, we're alive and healthy."

"At what cost, Mr. Evans?" Roger asked. "At what cost?"

"Don't think acting melancholy erases tonight," Crystal said over the private call. "I still love you, but you fucked up tonight in a monumental way. You excelled as a gangster, yet failed as a human. I can't believe my brother ordered such heinous actions and justified it by keeping other murderers alive and well."

"Enough!" Roger said, startling the surrounding group. "Sorry, private conversation got testy. I'm happy we're all uninjured."

"Don't depress the boss so much, little lady," Kyle said. "You should be proud of his work tonight."

"Proud?" Crystal asked over the public call. "That's a far cry from a proper response. Appalled is more like it. The wife and child were innocent. I don't give a fuck about the guards. They were dirty, but the civilians? This should leave a foul taste in all your mouths."

"I figured that was the smoke," Wallace said.

"Laugh it up." Crystal's voice was full of righteous anger. "You're the ones who just massacred dozens. Guess laughter will help you sleep, so go ahead, chuckles."

"Enough!" Roger said. "Your disapproval is noted. Give it a rest already."

"Fine." That was the last Crystal spoke as she exited the call, leaving the five gangsters in privacy as they retreated.

"She'll be a proper treat to ride home with," Isabella said. "Ignore her, boss. You led by example and kept you and yours safe. If she's too idealistic to understand that, it's her problem, not yours."

"She's not wrong," Roger said. "It doesn't feel right. From a numbers standpoint, it was. I know that. Ending this war will prevent further unnecessary loss of life."

"There's an old war time quote from the civil war from

General Tecumseh Sherman that fits here, boss," Ian said. "You might as well appeal against a thunderstorm as against these terrible hardships of war. War is cruelty. There is no use trying to reform it; the crueler it is, the sooner it will be over."

"Wasn't that the guy who marched through the south, pillaging farms and civilian families as they went?" Wallace asked.

"He marched to the sea, Mr. King," Ian said. "It was thanks to him and his men that the Civil War ended as soon as it did and prevented further loss of life. The south was demoralized and deserted to protect their families. Depending on where you live, you either revere him or revile him for his actions."

"The point is, drastic measures are taken by powerful men, not cowards too fearful." Isabella was still checking their sides, awaiting any poor soul fleeing in this direction. She fired off a round before they heard a scream. "Keep watch. We aren't home free yet."

"Dumb bastards," Kyle said, firing a round from where they came, earning another body on his conscience. Silence filled the air again following the death rattle of his latest victim. "The money's cut off."

"Loyalty," Ian said.

"Stow it and keep moving," Roger said. He kept watch as they moved in a group, covering each other's flanks and backs. Occasionally Roger would call out a larger tree trunk so the rear wouldn't trip as they walked backwards.

No more attacks came, and they reached the vehicle without further incident.

Everyone climbed in - Roger in the front, while Isabella drove. Everyone else surrounded Crystal in the back.

Isabella wasted no time and got them away from the growing wildfire they'd set alight.

"Can I say it now?" Ian asked.

"If you must," Isabella said, driving down the dirt road. She pulled onto the paved asphalt again, heading home.

"Mission accomplished," Ian said.

"Yeah, hurrah. Let's party." Crystal's voice was full of sarcasm.

"Give it a rest," Roger said. "The war's over. That's worth celebrating."

Crystal didn't fire back. She simply kept typing on her laptop, ignoring the commendations happening.

Kyle and Ian bumped knuckles in the back while Roger was more reserved, keeping to himself.

Isabella noticed her boss's reclusive body language. "I'm impressed, boss."

"Thank you, Ms. Moreno."

"You can call me Izzie if you want."

"Say what?" Ian asked. He leaned forward between the front seats. "Are you serious?"

"What business is it of yours?" Isabella asked. "He's proven himself worthy of using my nickname."

"I'm honored." There was a flippant edge to Roger's tone.

"Big whoop," Crystal said.

"There's a lot of power in a name, Ms. Morris," Isabella said. "Any word from Bernard, Bristol, and the others?"

"I can't tell. We're without a network since you blew up the house of the nearest wireless router."

"We'll learn soon," Roger said. "No sense worrying, or so I tell myself. Let's revel in this win to occupy our minds."

24

The group sat around the television. Multiple pizza boxes sat on the table, one long forgotten and full. The group crammed on the sofa, as well as the extra seats brought downstairs. They were forced to bring in foldable chairs to accommodate everyone sitting and chatting. Soft music played as the television droned. It showed a wildfire showing their exploits last night. A ticker ran across the bottom claiming two campers suffocated in the smoke and died.

"Would you look?" Crystal asked, pointing at the screen and the unfortunate news. "Seems bad karma has far-reaching consequences."

"What's that mean?" Abigail asked, looking at Bernard beside her on the couch.

"Nothing. Ignore her. She's in a bad mood the past few days."

"Oh," Abigail said. "I see."

"It's not what you're thinking," Crystal said. She stood and moved to the connecting lobby. She stopped at the foot

303

of the stairs. "I'll be back." Without further word, she stomped upstairs.

"We won't let her douse our spirits though," Chris said, raising a can of beer.

Roger wasn't drinking, nor smoking the joint being passed around, choosing instead to pass it.

"Something on your mind, boss?" Isabella asked, sitting next to him. "Problems with the family?"

"Nothing you need concern yourself with, Ms. Moreno, though the gesture is appreciated. My sister has always pouted. That won't change now. Besides, she's right." He pointed at the television. "Two innocent campers died as a result."

"It was impossible to predict."

"Maybe, but it still doesn't feel alright," Roger said. "Still, we received the calls for surrender today through Jonathon Hudson. The war is officially over, so we deserve some rest and relaxation. Securing housing for personnel is also high on the priority list you'll be happy to learn."

"Thank God. I was tired of sleeping in the barn."

"Apologies," Roger said. "We're packed to the brim in here."

"I'm a girl familiar with getting dirty, sir. However, a house or apartment would be a massive improvement."

Roger leaned forward and grabbed one of the few untouched boxes of pizza and stood. "Would you accompany me, Ms. Moreno? Let's visit your friends and guarantee they aren't left out of the festivities."

"I'd love to." She stood and followed her boss out of the bustling room.

"Party on, boys!" Roger opened the rear door and held it open for Isabella behind. "Hopefully they like these toppings."

"They won't complain. Mitch will be ecstatic to receive any. Greg's a little down recently."

"Who wouldn't be?" Roger asked. "On the bright side, he'll receive a helper forthwith. It'll be something all the new recruits take turns in, being his servant."

"Really?"

"Of course. He's a respected member. He did his duty and deserves everything accompanying that, especially from new hopefuls."

"I don't know that he'd accept that. He's prideful."

"Then he can have them do chores - whatever he wants," Roger said. "The point is, Molly's starting his tech training soon, and we'll all get settled. Those who choose to stay here can, but it's not required." He stopped in front of the barn's open doors and listened. He lowered his voice to a whisper. "Hold up."

Isabella accidentally bumped into Roger's broad back and lingered a few moments too long before backing up. "What's up?"

"Hear that?" Roger pointed up into the barn's loft.

Isabella cupped a hand around an ear to amplify her hearing. She heard keys clacking and a few words.

"Can you believe they're partying without us, man?" Mitch asked.

"Not my concern," Greg said.

"I have an idea." Isabella took the pizza from Roger and headed inside. "Follow me."

Roger trailed behind and watched Isabella climb the ladder one handed before following.

"How'd I know we'd hear you complain?" Isabella reached the top. "Almost like I've known you for years."

"Izzie? You brought us pizza? I knew you loved us."

Roger reached the top. "Gentlemen."

"Wasn't my idea." Isabella gestured toward Roger. "It was the boss."

"Mr. Morris?" Greg looked away from the laptop's screen upon hearing the news. His eyes were wide in surprise.

"Didn't want you boys to feel forgotten. You both gave it your all to help win this war. You deserve to be honored the same. I know my mother would never deign to deliver pizza herself, but I'm not her. I like to think I keep my ear to the ground and relate with my workers."

"Thank you," Mitch said.

"Here," Isabella placed the box down beside Mitch. Paper plates were already on top. "Take a few slices and we'll get Greg settled next."

"Enjoying the hardware?" Roger asked Greg. "We'll get you a better model soon. It's all we had in storage. I realize it's crap as far as laptops go."

"No worries, sir. It relieves boredom. Having internet access changes the ball game out here. Ms. Turner sent me a list of websites to study, and I've been throwing myself into that. May as well make myself useful even when injured."

"So long as you don't feel compelled to. Me personally? My first stop would have been a movie streaming service."

"You should have seen Mitchell's first stop." Greg shook his head at the traumatic memory.

"What was it?" Isabella took a seat near Roger and placed the pizza so Greg could help himself with the remaining plate. "Let me guess, a porn site?"

"Why do you always assume the worst of me?" Mitchell asked, his mouth full of pizza.

"Because she's right." Greg placed two slices on the remaining plate with a shake of his head. "At least wait for that until you have private quarters."

"I can't help if I'm a young, virile specimen of a man," Mitchell said, puffing out his chest.

"I'm sorry for him," Isabella said, "just in general." She turned to Mitchell. "The boss doesn't want to hear about fictitious matters of that variety. Have some common sense for once."

"It's alright," Roger said. "He has a knack for distracting not only himself, but everyone, doesn't he? I can see why you kept him on the team."

"Charming at base, dangerous in the field," Greg said.

"What's up, boss? You seem down," Mitchell asked.

"Mitchell!" Isabella barked.

"Easy," Roger said, his voice soothing. "He's right. I don't feel much like celebrating, if I'm honest. A distraction is welcome."

"Don't tell him that," Greg said. "You'll never get him to stop now. He's like a child at heart, sir. You give him permission to slack off or be a class clown, and that's all you'll get."

"If I didn't know you two loved me, I'd be offended," Mitchell said, taking another bite of his meal. "Ignore them, boss. You can trust me to behave myself on duty."

"How are you two doing health-wise?" Roger asked. "I'm aware of Greg's difficulties, but I never heard about you, Mitchell. You lost a lot of blood before?"

"I was weak the next day, but I'm growing stronger every day. I'll be out working again as soon as Izzie gives me the green light."

"You're just lucky none of the bullets lodged in you, either of you."

"I don't feel lucky," Greg said.

"You're still alive," Mitchell said. "That's something."

"As a cripple," Greg said. "Don't get me wrong. I appreciate the aid in helping me train, sir, and I don't mean to sound ungrateful. I'm coming to terms with my life now."

"Did you not hear our conversation as we approached?" Roger asked.

"No, I was busy tuning out this idiot across from me," Greg said, glaring at Mitchell. "What's up?"

"How would you feel about having a personal attendant? I was thinking Bristol could pick out the most promising aspirants and assign them to you. You name it, they'd do it. Call it an underwhelming perk because of your tragic injury."

"A personal attendant? Sir, I'm not used to being waited on."

"Something tells me you're going to become familiarized with many new concepts soon out of necessity. Why make it harder on yourself? It's not mandatory, but it was my idea of a gift for your service. We honor our hard workers, and that's you."

"Take the deal, Greg," Isabella said. "It'd make the boss feel better, and you deserve it."

Greg thought about it for a good ten seconds before answering. "Alright. While I'm acclimating to my new life, a little help would be appreciated."

"It's settled," Roger said. "Soon enough you'll both be outside this barn acclimating to a new town. Sorry again for housing you all inside here." He sat beside Greg, and Isabella took a seat beside him.

"Necessity breeds innovation, or, in this case, housing," Greg said. "Can you relay my thanks to your sister, sir? She hasn't visited tonight."

"I can try, but she's in one of her moods now," Roger said. He leaned his head back on the wooden boards. "Because of me, no doubt. She's too pure for this profession.

I knew that beforehand. I'll make my best effort to relay those thanks. She'll appreciate it, I'm sure."

"What's she mad about anyway?" Mitchell asked. "We won the war. She should be joyous her brother proved himself hugely."

Isabella tried to silence Mitchell with nonverbal communication, but it was futile.

"She's an idealistic young woman, Mitchell," Roger said, closing his eyes. "She and Ms. Turner are upset about the civilian casualties in last night's operation to end Mr. Powell. They're right too. Powell's wife, child, and two innocent campers died because of my plan."

"I believe it was my plan, boss," Isabella said.

"I approved it. That makes it my responsibility, Ms. Moreno."

"The kid was armed and pointing a rifle at us. I'd hardly call that innocent."

"Your attempts to cheer me up are noted, Izzie," Roger said. "If it weren't for us, he wouldn't have been armed. Crystal's correct - leave it at that. Trust me. I've learned that, frustratingly enough, she usually is."

"Aren't women always?" Mitchell asked.

"No." Greg's answer was short and concise. "That kind of thinking's dangerous. No one's ideas are always correct, despite who they are."

"Greg's right, but that's why I said usually, not always. I've accepted my fault last night, but I do not regret my decision. If we'd tried to infiltrate the home, we'd have been dead. Even if we'd tried to hunt all the security waiting in the woods, odds are we'd have missed someone and gotten shot in the back. To keep us alive, it was the only solution. I don't have the luxury of principles when lives depend on me. A lesson my mother no doubt never wanted me to learn."

"What's that mean?" Mitchell asked.

"Must you pry into the boss's private business?" Greg asked.

"I'm not at liberty to discuss intricate details, but she never wanted me to get involved in the Syndicate business. Let's leave it at that." He got to his feet. "You boys need anything else?"

"No, sir," Greg said. "Thanks for checking on us."

"I wish I could do more," Roger said. "Then I'll take my leave and leave you to it. Don't study too hard now. Rest is important to refresh the mind. Don't forget that, Greg. Can I call you Greg?"

"Of course, sir."

Roger got on the ladder. "Then I bid you all good night." He descended the ladder, then heard rushed footsteps climbing down the ladder. He turned to see Isabella rushing to catch up. "Ms. Moreno, you didn't have to cut your visit short on my account."

"It's almost time for their bunk time anyway," she said. She rushed to catch up and walked towards the house with him, nearly brushing arms. "You know, boss, it means a lot to me, you looking out for them."

"Nonsense," Roger waved the compliment off. "I'm doing what's right. Besides, it helps my conscience. So, it's not entirely altruistic."

"Still, few leaders would personally visit the wounded and sick. Your mother only ever visited your father, I heard. Nobody else. That ranks you above Mrs. Morris in being a leader of the people."

"Leader of the people's a fancy term," Roger said. He stopped midway between the barn and the farmhouse. He looked up at the clear, star-filled night sky. "I'm simply trying my best to lead."

"Ignore the detractors, sir," Isabella said. "The rank and file notice your dedication and respect for their lives. I notice too."

That caught Roger's attention, bringing his focus down from the heavens.

"Can I ask you a personal question, sir?" Isabella looked up at Roger.

"Depending on the question, I cannot guarantee an answer, but ask away."

"Are you and Ms. Turner an item?"

"I don't believe so. She wanted to wait on that decision."

"Then she's a fool," Isabella said.

"Who's a fool now?" The nearby rear house door opened, and Molly stepped into the backyard.

"Ms. Turner," Isabella said, clearly not enthused about the newest guest. "How nice of you to join us."

"Yes, Ms. Turner?" Roger asked. "Is something the matter?"

"I was wondering where you both disappeared to. Crystal said she wishes to leave soon."

"Did she now?" Roger asked. He looked away, trying to hide the hurt those words caused him. "When?"

"She didn't specify. You should speak with her."

"Funny, she echoed those exact words about you," Roger said.

"Yet I had to chase you down."

"Mr. Morris is not obligated to chase down a tech specialist," Isabella said, still at Roger's side. "Your personal objections are immaterial outside of the tech realm. Leave the tactics to us combat types."

"Who are you supposed to be? Ms. Soldier lady?" Molly

asked. "I'm surprised you didn't get lost out there. That's your group's specialty, right?"

"We specialize in accomplishing the mission at any cost. My friend gave his life to end this war. Mr. Morris was simply making sure none of my other partners did the same. He doesn't need you second guessing his judgement."

"What did you say?" Molly stomped forward.

"I wouldn't do that, Ms. Turner," Roger said.

"You be quiet. Now, Ms. Moreno was it? You helped end this war. Hurrah. That doesn't give you the right to insert yourself into my business with Rog."

"Rog?" Izzie asked. "I didn't realize you two were so close, what with you avoiding him and all."

"What business is it of yours?" Molly fired back. "People have disagreements. It happens. I guess not if you're a kiss ass. I see why the concept confuses you."

"Ladies, please," Roger moved between the two. "Can we cool it, please? I'm in no mood for a catfight on the lawn."

"Wouldn't be much of a fight," Isabella scoffed. "Waifs like you should stick to online arguments where you're best suited."

"Ms. Moreno, that means you too."

"Yes, sir."

Molly smirked at Isabella getting disciplined verbally.

The rear door opened again to reveal Crystal stepping outside...

Just earlier...

Bernard and Abigail escaped from the party just after Roger and Isabella did. They, however, didn't sneak outside. They snuck upstairs to their room. Bernard locked the door behind him to see Abigail already sitting on his bed.

"Hopefully you remember to unlock that, or Mr. Morris will be pissed at sitting outside all night," she said. She made herself comfortable lying on his bed.

"It's early," Bernard said, moving over. "He won't come knocking."

"Come here." She grabbed his arm and pulled him. They laid together face to face. "I wasn't going to say anything, but this bender resembles a high school party rather than an organized outfit's." She giggled.

"You'd be surprised how often the two overlap." Bernard rested his hand on her thigh. It wandered no further, content to rest. "Sorry about the scene earlier."

"With Crystal? I wasn't going to ask since I figured it was business."

"She disagreed with our methods. She's leaving for Toledo soon, I believe. It's best for her. She's like a little sister."

Abigail's hand traced over his chest. "So, you want her gone?"

"I didn't mean it like that. We both understand this is a dangerous business. I figure maybe that's why Roger isn't kicking up more of a fuss about sending her home. She ran away from her mother, the boss, you know. I doubt she'll stay longer than a day or two more."

"She's worried about him," Abigail said. "Perhaps not physically, but I read the television ticker myself. Two innocents died, right? I assume it's related to Mr. Powell's or Mr. Bailey's unfortunate demise."

"You're quick. I'd be concerned if I wasn't sure of your allegiances."

"Loose lips sink ships, my father's associates used to say. Did I tell you what he did?"

"I don't believe so."

Abigail traced her finger across Bernard's lips as she explained. "I mentioned he had associates. They were a local Mexican cartel branch. My father was a police officer. A good man, if not exactly legal. He'd receive payments for looking the other way. He figured it wasn't a big deal, and the extra cash would help with payments around the house."

"Nothing wrong with some extra cash to sit on your butt," Bernard said.

"Shush." Abigail placed her finger across his lips, effectively silencing him. "You know what happened to him?"

"He's still alive?"

"Goober, if he was alive, why would I be opening the store by my lonesome? He'd have been there with a camera, causing a scene because of his precious princess opening a business. No, he'd have put forth every cent to help. He died over a decade ago."

"Sorry."

"He was eventually asked to take part in an operation against his ethics. He refused. As you're aware, men in this profession don't take a negative answer lightly."

Bernard grabbed her hand tenderly and moved it. "Must have been egregious to deny."

"The night he received the request, he ran home. We gathered our belongings and paperwork. We crossed the border that same night, legally, mind you. Survival was rough for a few months. We eked out a living just north of the border. Eventually we'd saved enough to move, and we moved here over a decade ago. I only lived here with him for a year before they found us. It didn't matter to them if he'd left it behind. They hadn't let his refusal and disrespect go."

"Nor his knowledge of their operation, I imagine," Bernard said. "They feared he would talk."

"Probably."

"Then why sign on with us?"

"Why does a troubled son with an alcoholic father take up drinking in adulthood? Why does the daughter with an abusive father love bad boys? I don't know. Maybe I wanted to spread the painkiller that's made my brother's life tolerable. God knows I didn't have the finances myself. Then a big strong Syndicate member comes by offering to invest and make it a reality."

"I won't let any harm happen to you or your dispensary."

"I'd love to believe that. "

"You don't?"

"I know karma's real. Remember the chili cookoff shooting? Those dead bodies weigh on our karma, and it will deliver payback. Call it karmic justice or divine retribution. I'm sure of it. That's what I'm scared of. Am I afraid of you?" She leaned forward and kissed his lips. "No. Am I afraid of the comeuppance our actions cause? Deathly so. Or what about those campers? I don't need nor desire to know specifics, but you don't believe in some form of karma? Those were innocents ended before their time."

"You're a unique gal," Bernard said. "Who thinks of such existential concepts at a party after sneaking off?"

"Someone cross faded."

"Cross what?"

"Drunk and stoned." She laughed, clearly intoxicated. "You've never partied much, have you?"

"I've been around when parties erupted because wars were won, but never hosted them. Rog and I didn't hang out with soldiers. They kept away from us, no doubt on his mother's orders. We hung around together and made our own fun. I never even smoked before I met you, never mind drinking."

"Oh right, you're not even twenty-one years old. Didn't you drink downstairs?"

"You think that's the law I'm going to obey? Don't be silly." He grabbed her wrists and rolled until he was on top.

She squealed at the sudden movement and laughed. "Aren't you forceful? You know anyone could hear." She looked at the door. Raucous male laughter sounded like it was near.

"Who's going to bust into the boss's quarters? Nobody'd be dumb enough when it's locked."

The door busted open, nearly flying off its hinges.

Wallace and Chris stumbled inside, clearly intoxicated beyond belief. "Hey," Chris slurred. "This isn't my room. Oh, hi, boss. Is that Ms. Gomez?" he asked with a wave. "Hi, Ms. Gomez."

Bernard glared at the pair. "Get out."

Wallace moved forward to Chris's side. "Come on, brother. I think we interrupted."

"Interrupted? Sorry, boss. Maybe you'll last longer now that we distracted you. Maybe you should thank us."

Bernard climbed off Abigail and the bed, still relatively sober. He'd only had a couple of beers, as opposed to these two drunks. "Didn't you hear me?"

"Huh? Don't worry. We were about to leave, boss. We'll leave you to your business with Ms. Gomez." Chris backed away, apparently realizing the hornets' nest his drunk ass had kicked with Mr. King through the haze of the booze clouding his brain.

Bernard pushed the pair backward out of the room without warning. Both of his drunk cohorts staggered from the force applied but remained on their feet.

"Good luck, boss," Chris called out before Bernard slammed the door.

This, however, didn't work as he planned since they'd busted down the door. The door didn't slam as much as flew into the hallway and instead slammed into the wall before creaking back toward its original closed position.

"Sorry about breaking the door." Chris scratched his face. "I thought it was my room."

Bernard was still in full view as the door inched its way back toward him on the return trip from his tantrum.

"We're still getting a joint from your room, right?" Wallace asked Chris beside him.

"You're damned right we are." The two drunken fools finally turned and continued down the hallway.

Abigail got up and inspected the door. "Yep, it's broken. It won't close until it's fixed. Guess that derails our plans since I'm not into exhibitionism. Is that why you don't let them drink often?"

"Apparently that's why no drug use is usually a tenant in crime families."

"No sense going all puritan. Just no booze allowed would work fine."

"Always advertising the product, huh?"

"It's what you invested in me for, right?"

Bernard turned and pecked her on the cheek. "One of the many reasons, sure."

In Rachel and Molly's room earlier...

"Heard you caused a scene," Molly said, still on her laptop.

"Heard or saw?"

"Both. I've planted cameras all over the place to keep tabs on everybody."

"Not in our personal rooms, I trust?"

"You think I want to see that shit?" Molly asked with a disgusted grimace. "Let them masturbate or fuck all they like. That's not my business. No, I meant the common rooms and the barn. Pick your moments, it works better."

"Like it worked for you?"

"I expressed my thoughts in a planning meeting. You did at a party that was meant to lift spirits. Big difference - time and place, my friend. Makes you look like a major downer and complainer."

"Whatever," Crystal said. She rolled over on the bed and faced the wall while crossing her arms. "Why aren't you still pissed? He disregarded your wishes."

"I am not his mother, nor his keeper. He's a grown ass man, and my boss to boot," Molly said. "I can disapprove all I like. That just means I can give him the cold shoulder."

"Yeah? You must love Isabella's flirting with him then. She's not subtle."

"People who blow things up for a living rarely exhibit moderation," Molly said.

"That doesn't bother you?"

"He asked me if I wanted to make it official. I turned him down. It was too quick for my tastes. I can hardly complain if he shops around."

"You're not a damned car," Crystal said. "He's young, Molly. What do you think's going to result when a hot, slightly older femme fatale shows interest and doesn't need to wait? They aren't going to stay platonic friends for much longer with the stares she gives him."

"We're not together, so it's not my business. We had one date."

Crystal got off the bed and marched over, keeping her voice hushed. She sat beside Molly. "Stop with the cold and distant act for one moment. You enjoyed yourself that night at the comedy club, right?"

"What if I did?"

"Then fight for him. Don't concede and roll over like a beaten dog."

"I would have imagined you'd have preferred it if I did, considering he pissed you off the same as me."

"Just because he's heading down the wrong road doesn't mean I want him to suffer. He's my brother for God's sake. You think him sleeping with the explosives expert will bring happiness? She's a little minx using him for leverage. It's clear as day. Ever since she sunk her claws into him, what's happened? He's bent over backwards for her and her friends. She's using him."

"His life, his business."

Crystal made an audible noise of utter frustration as she frazzled her hair in annoyance. "You're impossible. Fine." She moved back to Molly's bed and laid down. "On your head be it. I'm done trying to talk sense into either of you."

Molly spoke up after a few minutes of silence in the dim bedroom. "Rog and Isabella are heading to the barn."

"Like I said, twisting him around her little finger. She'll kiss ass and garner favors. You think she cares about his well-being? She suggested killing the family to make her job easier. She's selfish."

"Seems like a normal conversation, though. Besides, it seems he's feeling bad enough."

"You're listening in on them?" Crystal jumped up and sat beside her. She leaned over, trying to hear.

"Aren't you nosy?" Molly asked. "Roger's trying to play it off as the unflappable boss, but ultimately he's let his guard down."

"He doesn't know the first thing about leading personnel

or battles. He's been making it up." Crystal grabbed a nearby headset and plugged it in before putting them on. "Is it any wonder he's trying to ingratiate himself?"

"I don't feel much like celebrating, if I'm honest. A distraction is welcome." Roger's voice said over the headsets.

"She'll seize this opportunity and exploit this. You watch."

Molly gave Crystal a sidelong glance. "Aren't you a little too interested? Why worry so much about dear brother's romantic life?"

"He may not be my blood brother, but I still want him to live happily."

"Sure, I believe that." Molly never took her eyes off the camera feed from high in the barn's loft. It showed Greg and Mitchell both laying on their sleeping bags. Roger and Isabella sat beside Greg, Isabella leaning a bit too into Roger's side for Molly's liking. She narrowed her eyes, watching it unfold. On the surface, it didn't seem Roger realized the close contact. That didn't stop this unpleasant feeling bubbling in her chest from growing or intensifying.

"Can't say I disagree with making their lives easier," Crystal said. "Who do you think's been delivering food and water to them? Greg won't walk again, according to Mr. Bristol. Maybe he feels guilty."

"That's obvious," Molly said. "Here we are piling on. He didn't want another Greg, so he authorized the plan."

"His concern doesn't make it right."

"No, but we didn't consider why he was hellbent on okaying the plan. In a vacuum, we were correct."

"Don't even tell me you see his point."

"Only a fool would deny it. That doesn't mean I agree totally. It was still wrong, morally speaking. Maybe he needs support, not the cold shoulder." Molly frowned. "A role this

Isabella is filling with gusto it seems. That doesn't mean she has to be that physically close."

"You're jealous?"

"Who'd be jealous? I dislike all forms of public displays of affection."

"You didn't seem to mind at the comedy club." This comment earned Crystal a momentary glare. "What do I care, right? I'm leaving soon, hopefully."

Without warning, Molly got to her feet. "I'll be right back."

"Where are you going?" Crystal watched her friend leave without further words. She scooted over and took Molly's original position, intent on spying on her friend's intentions.

Molly, however, didn't know why she was pursuing this course of action. Something deep inside told her to get off her ass. Molly normally ignored this voice but couldn't summon the fortitude this time. She marched down the stairs and past the partygoers having a fun time. She noted Jackie and Lyle in a room by themselves. It wasn't her business, but it was the first time she'd seen Jackie being caring. She mentally noted the aberration in behavior before she opened the rear door and stepped outside. She saw Isabella and Roger nearby and heard Isabella talking as Roger stargazed at her side.

"Then she's a fool," Isabella said.

"Who's a fool now?" Molly stepped into the front yard. She felt a fire burning in her belly and couldn't stop the words from becoming more confrontational than intended.

"Ms. Turner," Isabella said, clearly not enthused about the newest guest. "How nice of you to join us."

"Yes, Ms. Turner?" Roger asked. "Is something the matter?"

"I was wondering where you both disappeared to," Molly said. "Crystal said she wishes to leave soon."

"Did she now?" Roger asked. He looked away, trying to hide the hurt those words caused him. "When?"

"She didn't specify. You should speak with her."

"Funny, she echoed those exact words about you," Roger said.

"Yet I had to chase you down."

"Mr. Morris is not obligated to chase down a tech specialist," Isabella said, still at Roger's side. "Your personal objections are immaterial outside of the tech realm. Leave the tactics to us combat types."

"Who are you supposed to be? Ms. Soldier lady?" Molly asked. "I'm surprised you didn't get lost out there. That's your group's specialty, right?"

"We specialize in accomplishing the mission at any cost. My friend gave his life to end this war. Mr. Morris was simply making sure none of my other partners did the same. He doesn't need you second guessing his judgement."

"What did you say?" Molly stomped forward.

"I wouldn't do that, Ms. Turner," Roger said.

"You be quiet. Now, Ms. Moreno was it? You helped end this war. Hurrah. That doesn't give you the right to insert yourself into my business with Rog."

"Rog?" Izzie asked. "I didn't realize you two were so close, what with you avoiding him and all."

"What business is it of yours?" Molly fired back. "People have disagreements. It happens. I guess not if you're a kiss ass. I see why the concept confuses you."

"Ladies, please," Roger moved between the two. "Can we cool it, please? I'm in no mood for a catfight on the front lawn."

"Wouldn't be much of a fight." Isabella scoffed. "Waifs

like you should stick to online arguments where you're best suited."

"Ms. Moreno, that means you too."

"Yes, sir."

Molly smirked at Isabella getting disciplined verbally.

The door she'd exited from swung open. Crystal rushed out, breathless.

"Yet another shows," Isabella said under her breath. "Ms. Morris, good evening."

"Yeah, whatever," Crystal said.

"Something wrong, Sis?" Roger asked.

"Just making certain we don't have a new rumor to fill the annals of the Syndicate's history. We don't need a catfight." She stopped beside Molly.

"I hear you wanted to leave soon," Roger said.

"That's right."

Roger nodded. "Name the time, and I'll send an escort. Mother will be thrilled to hear that."

"I'm not out here for me."

"Then why?" Roger asked. "Making sure I'm not getting into trouble?"

"That's one way of wording it," Crystal said, sneaking a glance at Isabella. She couldn't deny Isabella's physical attractiveness. The sculpted, toned, and fit body would make any man fall for her advances, especially compared to her friend's typical body type. "You never were good with women's arguments. Remember that time involving the girls in class?"

Roger looked up, trying to recall the incident in question. "I remember trying to stop it."

"You failed miserably, as you were about to again. Now, ladies, let's be civil."

"I'm perfectly calm," Isabella said. She leaned into Roger's side. "I wish no harm to anyone."

"Right."

Molly took another step forward toward Roger and Isabella. "Training starts tomorrow morning for your friend. I hope he's ready. My curriculum won't be easy."

"Greg's always been the overachiever type. You won't be disappointed. He may lack initial knowledge, but he'll acclimate soon."

"Good, because I don't enjoy wasting my time."

"Ms. Turner, I firmly believe he won't waste your precious time," Roger said.

"As for you, Mr. Morris," Molly said. "You owe us another couple of laptops. We'll need them for learning exercises and dummy hacks. Don't forget your duty to keep us stocked."

"I doubt you'd allow me to forget."

"You saying I nag?"

"You remind me when I forget. Nothing rude intended. Along with your expertise, you're invaluable."

"Buttering me up won't help," Molly said. She reached forward and grabbed Roger's hand and yanked him nearly off balance. "Come with me. I have all the business set up." She led him toward the house. "We need your sign off, and I won't let you procrastinate. Not with my department, mister."

Isabella glared at the back of Molly as she dragged Roger back inside the house, leaving her with Crystal.

"Disappointed?" Crystal asked.

"Yeah. We were arriving at the fun part when she interrupted," Isabella said. "I hope you have a pleasant evening, Ms. Morris."

"Just know I'm not as naïve as my brother is with females. I see what you're trying."

"What's that?"

"Kissing ass may get you far with him, but not me. You want my blessing? Prove your good intentions. All I've seen is you using him to provide for your friends."

"Something wrong with taking care of the injured, Ms. Morris? I wouldn't expect that from you. Mitchell and Greg sing your praises."

"Nothing wrong with the idea, but we both know your angle. Don't treat me like I'm stupid, Ms. Moreno. You're into my brother, and I don't blame you. Molly's my friend."

"I see where this is going."

"I won't forbid anything, but here's some advice. Pursue this, but if I find out you hurt my brother, I won't hold back."

"I'd never dream of harming anyone, emotionally or physically. I know you must think me a tramp or whore, but I genuinely admire your brother. He's turning into a formidable leader."

"You want in on the ground floor?"

"Nothing so materialistic. There're precious few upstanding men in this profession. No sense playing passive if winning's the goal. Ms. Morris, don't worry. I'd never harm Mr. Morris. Quite the opposite."

"That better be all…"

25

"Gentlemen." Jonathon shook hands with Roger and Bernard around their kitchen table. "It's a pleasure to congratulate you on winning the war. My father's avenged and, while it'll never fill the void, I thank you for assisting me." He took a seat across from Bernard and Roger.

"People coming after our business partners is unacceptable, and we've shown that," Bernard said. "Nobody's dumb enough to bother you now."

"There is the matter of the local street gangs," Jonathon said.

"Hood rats?" Bernard asked. "Nashville area has them?"

"There're tons of different gangs, each laying claim to their specific real estate. My father had a lucrative side business selling to all of them. He was a true neutral party. No doubt they see me as allied with newcomers. That may be an issue later, but matters are settling. All that smoke and noise stirred up a commotion. I recommend lying low for a while. Let the news crews leave the city. You know it's been all over the national news - the chili cookoff massacre, not to mention the forest fires. People are asking questions, and the hood rats are watching and waiting."

Bernard shrugged. "I never heard of gangs around here."

"They're inconsequential." Jonathon placed an elbow on the table. "They usually shoot one another. It barely makes the morning news most days. I'm surprised this is news to you gentlemen."

"Why?" Roger asked. "We arrived recently."

"You're serious?" Jonathon asked with a wide smile.

"Deadly," Bernard said. "What do you know?"

"Your business associate, Ms. Gomez was it? Her shop's near their little operation ghetto storm stomping grounds. Mind you her location is neutral. It's the only shopping area near their homes. I'd recommend keeping watch. If they find out your connection, Ms. Gomez could be targeted. I'll keep my mouth shut, obviously, but you've had men stationed there. Odds are the gangs spotted them."

"Thanks for the warning," Roger said. "How many gangs are we referring to?"

"Over eight different flavors of gangbangers await. I trust you gentlemen will survive. If they declare war, my weapons won't be available to them, obviously."

"We'll deal with them should it prove necessary," Bernard said.

"Now let's discuss future business," Jonathon said. "Your reward for assisting me with father is waiting here. It's further outside the immediate area, but it's for safety's sake. You can pick it up anytime. Pickup is here." He reached into his coat pocket and placed a paper. "Again, my thanks for the assistance in bringing those morons to justice."

"We'll send someone to secure that merchandise today," Roger said.

"Right. Before I forget," Jonathon said, "I've upgraded

both your memberships to the club. You're always welcome and will gain access to the VIP tables whenever you join us."

"Our thanks," Bernard said.

"You know protocol for placing another order. There're no changes since father's passing. Send that shopping list sooner rather than later, gentlemen. Don't allow yourselves to get caught without a stockpile to sell or use."

"We've certainly learned the use of being fully loaded," Bernard said. "We look forward to our continued business transactions together. You ever need help again, contact us like before."

"Same here," Jonathon said. "It's always a pleasure, gentlemen, but I've other affairs to tend to today. Sorry I can't stay, but business waits for nobody's desires."

"True."

Jonathon shook hands with both Roger and Bernard before they led him to the front door.

Roger opened the door for Jonathon to see their partner's bodyguards ready and waiting outside. "Be safe, Mr. Hudson."

"You too. Come on, boys," Jonathon's guards escorted him to his vehicle as Roger and Bernard stepped outside.

"One more meeting off the checklist," Bernard said.

"The worst is coming," Roger said. He stood in front of the house with Bernard and watched their guests leave.

"You still haven't called her?"

"Would you? I'll do it after Crystal leaves. At least that way I have good news to report - well, for her anyway."

"You really don't want her to leave."

"She's family. Of course I don't, but it's her wish. She's made that clear. Getting away from me is her top priority. I won't block her wishes."

"It'll be quieter soon," Bernard watched the procession

of cars leave their driveway. "Soon everyone will have cash to grab their own property near. We'll be here alone, minus security of course."

"At least then we won't have to bunk together," Roger said.

"Our own rooms would be a pleasure." Bernard's eyes glazed over imagining the luxury of their future sleeping arrangements. "Privacy would be delightful."

"They haven't moved out yet," Roger said. "Don't get too ahead of yourself."

"It won't be long." Bernard and Roger turned around and headed inside...

26

"You remembered everything?" Molly asked.

"I didn't own a ton of possessions, living on the couch," Crystal said. "Just what I hauled, wore, and collected here. The scrap of the drone is already packed. Everything else is stowed away."

"I can't believe you're willingly heading back north."

"I want free of this circus lifestyle," Crystal said, zipping up the backpack. "You knew the life, but I didn't. I wanted to keep Rog safe, and I've done that; but if I stay, I turn into a gangster. I'd rather be a prisoner locked inside my room for another year before heading off to college like Mother wanted."

"It's the wise decision," Molly said. "That's why I'm surprised."

"Screw you." There was no animus or anger cloaked in the playful verbal jab. Crystal slung the pack over her shoulder. "I wonder who my escort is."

"Better hope it's not Ms. Moreno."

"We have an understanding. She's your and Roger's problem now."

"An understanding? What's that mean?"

"Ask her if you're interested. I have a ride to catch." She approached and gave Molly a warm embrace. "Be careful, alright? I know you're tech, but stay careful. And try to keep my idiot brother safe, will you?"

"I'll try."

The front door opened, and Jackie peeked her head in. "We're ready whenever you are."

"Be right there. Let's get this tearful farewell over." She led Molly outside to see Jackie, Roger, Bernard, Chris, Ian, Kyle and even Isabella. Her vehicle was ready and waiting nearby.

"It was an honor, Ms. Morris," Chris said from the bottom of the stairs as she hopped to the grass below.

"See you, Mr. Bristol. Keep my idiot brother safe, okay?"

"Always, Ms. Morris."

Crystal and Molly walked past and stopped by Roger.

"Leaving so soon?" Roger asked.

"Studying for college doesn't happen by itself. Besides, this isn't the environment to study peacefully. It's not too late for you to join me. We could rent a room and take classes together - make something of our lives."

Roger's smile faded. "You know my answer already."

"I had to try." She gave him a brief hug. "Don't get yourself killed trying to play hero or over something stupid." She stepped backward and looked at the guards. "I don't guess any of you can talk sense into him?" No one answered her question. "Didn't think so. Who's my escort?"

"Jackie will escort you home," Roger said, gesturing toward Jackie. "She'll keep you safe. Besides, she has something to ask mother."

"I need a damned good prosthetic." She held up her four-fingered hand. "You don't think she'll mind, do you?"

"I'll make sure she doesn't," Crystal said. "You received that by keeping her son safe. She'll love you, Ms. Thomas, when I'm done."

"I'm going to miss you," Bernard said. He received a brief hug from Crystal while Jackie stood by the car. "What are you studying to be, anyway?"

"I hadn't decided yet. I was thinking about being a programmer, maybe make video games? Hell, I'd develop artificial intelligence too if given the chance. You'll know when I return to visit in a few years."

"We look forward to your visit, Ms. Morris." Isabella said, standing at attention nearby.

"Uh huh," Crystal said. "Time to make tracks, everybody. I appreciate the warm sending off party, but this is farewell. None of you better die before I come back, or I'll be pissed." She grabbed the front passenger door and pulled it open. "See you."

Roger walked to the door as Jackie climbed inside. He knocked on the window until Crystal rolled it down. His words were soft, barely audible so only she could hear. "Please don't think me a monster."

"I don't. I think you're misguided and a fool."

He stood up straight and spoke at normal volume. "That's much better." He backed up as the car engine roared to life.

"Be back soon," Jackie said from the driver side's open window. She hit the gas, and the vehicle drove down the driveway and descended the hill.

Roger watched the car leave with his only family. He felt a hand on his shoulder, looked, and found Bernard standing beside him. "I'm worried I'll never see her again, buddy."

"Nonsense," Bernard said. "She said she'd return. She wouldn't lie."

"I hope you're right." Roger stood watching the car until it eventually turned out of sight behind the trees.

Molly came up on his left. "College will treat her better than this lifestyle. We all realize that. Right? We should celebrate her chasing her dreams, not mourning her departure."

"Easier said than done, Ms. Turner," Isabella stood only a few feet away, having ambled over. "It's never easy to say farewell to family."

27

Roger leaned back on the sofa, finally enjoying the first relative peace and relaxation since they'd arrived. There was no one present to interrupt or speak. It was blissful peace. That is, until his cell phone rang in his pocket. He sighed and answered. "Yes?"

"How nice to finally speak again. It's been too long. I've heard many things have transpired since last we spoke."

"That's wording it mildly," Roger said. "Judging by your tone, you're not pleased."

"Why? Should I be delighted?"

"Let's get this over with. Why are you angry now? Disappointed your son lived through the war? Or were you hoping I'd die to solve your problems?"

"How dare you? How can you say those awful things?"

"You planned on saying nasty things to me, judging by your tone. I figured I'd learn from you and beat you to the punch. Like mother, like stepson."

"What you call a successful war, I call a full three-ring circus. You've attracted tons of attention. You think all those fires and that mass shooting will fly under the radar? No. It's bringing tons of attention."

"It's finished. It's difficult for any evidence to point at us, considering any witnesses are dead and any DNA burned away. Yeah, it's bustling here. That's why we are lying low until the heat dies down. Anything else?"

"Do not speak to me with such reckless abandon. I may be your mother, but I'm still your acting commander."

"Awfully prissy attitude for someone whose son proved his mettle to his men, won a war, and kept the peace, along with establishing Syndicate dominance. You wanted extra theft in the form of percentages off our shipments. I'm making sure you get paid. Why question the method? God knows you probably never did. At least if the stories Warren recounted were true."

"Eighteen years old and you think you know everything. I remember that age, but do not grow cocky, Son. A trifling success ousting two old fogeys from their brittle throne does not equal glory. You had trouble with those two. Now shut up and listen for once."

Roger obeyed the order, keeping his silence.

"What is this I hear about you boys selling drugs?"

"We don't, though."

"You don't have a dispensary as your business front?"

"Totally legal nowadays, Mom." Roger rolled his eyes. "This isn't the war on drugs era anymore. It's the lucrative edgy thing now, but still legal. Besides, your guy suggested the idea. Blame him."

"And the tales of members engaging in their use recreationally? You didn't think I'd hear about that?"

"The afterparty? You're concerned about party rules? Seriously? Slow news day up there in Toledo?"

"We both know it's not just the party."

"You're trying to tell me how to run my branch? Don't you have business to tend to, instead of attempting to micro-manage my group?"

"You are a representative of us," Rachel said. "I won't allow you to sully our image."

"Nowhere in the Syndicate rules your father created did it mention drug use. I suppose his hard on drugs stance stood on precedent, but not anymore. Nice to know you think I'm a failure."

"I didn't say that."

"You did, in so many words. You disapprove of every action, decision, and matter. I can't possibly think of another way to frame it."

"I'm trying to watch out for you, to protect you. People talk, and that's my concern."

"My soldiers are thrilled under my leadership, with all due respect. What works for you may not work for me. Don't you understand? New styles of leadership have their own merits. Maybe a congratulations wouldn't kill you. At least I know one thing you'll enjoy hearing."

"I doubt it. What's that?"

"Crystal's on her way back home. I sent Ms. Thomas as her escort. She'll be back soon - she left this morning. She should arrive in a couple of hours. You'll be happy to know she insisted on leaving."

"Huh?" This was the first time Roger had heard his mother react so cluelessly. "She insisted? What did you do?"

Roger heaved a deep sigh. "I learned a lesson you no doubt did at my age."

"Explain, immediately."

Roger paused, trying to think how to word it. "We'd finally found Powell and Bailey's location, but there was a problem. Powell had a wife and child, a teenage boy specifically. I asked for tactical advice from Jackie, Chris, and the new team to hear their recommendations. They know combat better than I do, so I figured I'd use their expertise. I received two options. One was to breach normally, but considering their security in the nearby woods, it was highly risky and outright dangerous to my personnel."

"The other?"

"The option I employed was carpet bombing the trees nearby with fire. It worked. The security fled for their lives. On top of that, we implemented a carpet-bombing strategy with the home."

"She was upset at the loss of innocent life." His mother's voice finally softened.

"Bingo. She and Ms. Turner disapproved of the plan for moral reasons; but tactically, it was the right move. Crystal never let it go, and she informed me I'd changed into a monster - more like you, she said specifically. Imagine my surprise when my supposed role model calls and reams me a new asshole. I truly feel the love in this family."

"Damn it," Rachel said. "That's why I never wanted you to pursue this lifestyle."

"Too late now, Mother. The good news is she's hell bent on college. One of your children is a success now. You may as well celebrate that."

"At least you learned that lesson as quickly as I did. There's no room for morals or scruples when it comes to war. You saved more lives than you ended. That doesn't change your reckless behavior."

"I did what was necessary to eradicate our enemies. That's all."

"All I know is Nashville's turned into a damned national debate since your little war started. Do not cause more trouble. You're lucky if no one's aware of your involvement. If they are, then deal with it. Silence any witnesses who prove troublesome. We cannot afford federal law enforcement getting suspicious. That'll lead them here."

"Only one person's aware, and he's Hudson's son. Old man Hudson died. Powell killed him. We aided him in recovering his father's remains. He's a staunch ally now."

"To your knowledge," Rachel said. "Keep an eye on him. If you see any law enforcement talking to him, prepare for possibly the worst. If he gets arrested, you need to run. He'll squeal if they've got dirt. Stay hidden, never resurface. Hell, come home to Toledo. I'll house you off the grid."

"Your concern is noted. Anything else?"

"Yeah, when's my squad coming back?"

"About that," Roger said. "They want to stay."

"Irrelevant," Rachel said. "They're one of my best teams. I need their services."

"Look, Mom. Robert's dead, Greg's paralyzed from the hips down, and Mitchell's laid up with an injury. Only two are healthy, and they're thrilled here. I ask you to allow them to stay here under my command. Besides, Isabella saved my life. I'd like to employ her as a possible bodyguard. She's proven her mettle."

"Isabella? You mean Ms. Moreno? Don't get involved with your bodyguard."

"Not like you and father?"

"You little shit," Rachel said. "I'm saying don't coerce her into anything. You're the boss. Your influence matters. She may feel compelled to stay. You don't want that. You say Ms. Moreno saved your life?" Rachel paused. "Fine, keep them."

"Any orders before we cut this off?"

"Yeah, lie low. Keep a watch out for trouble. Also, congratulations on the win, but don't let it inflate your ego. You saw firsthand how easy it is to die from laziness."

"Thanks, Mom. I'm going to go destroy this phone now. I suggest you do the same."

"Always do, dear. Remember what I've told you, and be careful. Love you, goodbye."

"Love you." Roger tossed the phone on the ground and stomped hard, shattering it to pieces. He glanced nearby to see Bernard heading down the stairs.

"Who was that?" Bernard asked.

"Mother. She called to complain about my leadership style. Complained about every aspect of our business, especially the marijuana industry we invested in. Apparently, someone's been telling her our employees light up occasionally. Not to mention she criticized our handling of the war, calling it a three-ring circus."

"Damn."

"It would be mighty convenient to not pay that tax on our shipments," Roger said. "Her constant criticism always frays my nerves, dude. It's like she wants to micromanage every aspect of our business from hundreds of miles away. It's infuriating."

"That's dangerous talking, buddy." Bernard leaned on the sofa Roger sat on. "Don't let anyone hear that. It could be construed as treason."

"Whatever. Let's focus on getting this empire set up. Many of our employees would like their own homes. Let's assist them in that endeavor. We'll keep a security contingent here, but I want my own room. We own enough land. Maybe we could build more homes on the property."

"You and me both, brother. We'll run this town soon, and I can't wait..."

THANK YOU FOR READING!

The Syndicate will likely return soon. If you'd like to support this work, please consider leaving an honest review on Amazon. Thank you and have a wonderful day!

ABOUT THE AUTHOR

Alex J. Fischer has written over eighteen action/adventure novels and aims to release many more over the coming years.

He lives in Ohio and enjoys his quiet life. He enjoys writing, revising, and playing video games in his spare time.

ALSO BY ALEX J. FISCHER

The Morris Crime Family:

Welcome to the Family

The Silver Lining

Any Means Necessary

The Fourth Bullet

A New Generation

Full Circle

Sons of the Syndicate

Fractured Legacy

The Order of Vengeance Motorcycle Club:

The Order of Vengeance

Vengeance Above All

Masked Justice:

The End of Innocence

Masked Justice

Blind Justice

Silent Justice

True Justice

The Collector:

The Debt Collector

Pawns on the Hunt

Queen's Gambit